# A GOOD REPUTATION

After a career in television, Shirley McLaughlin became a business and management consultant and is the author of several highly successful non-fiction books. She has dreamt of writing fiction since writing her first story, aged four, and *A Good Reputation* is her first novel. She lives in Sydney, Australia.

GW00712381

# SHIRLEY McLAUGHLIN

# *A Good Reputation*

HarperCollins*Publishers*

HarperCollins*Publishers*
77–85 Fulham Palace Road
Hammersmith, London W6 8JB

This paperback edition 1995

1 3 5 7 9 8 6 4 2

ISBN 0 00 647925 1

Set in Palatino
at The Spartan Press Ltd
Lymington, Hants

Printed in Great Britain by
HarperCollinsManufacturing Glasgow

**For everyone who loved her,
'specially Dad**

# ACKNOWLEDGEMENTS

This story is loosely based on my mother's life. Her 'Friendship Circle' on 3BA Ballarat (Victoria) in 1936, was the first country women's radio programme in Australia. Her radio name was Margery Daw.

The character of Billy Batchelor has been drawn from memory and imagination, as have some of the other family members. While I have also drawn upon historical facts as a background to this novel, all other characters are fictitious.

I am deeply indebted to Ken Moon and Geoff Wright for their impeccable advice and generosity of spirit, to the grand staff at the Australian Inland Mission, the Royal Flying Doctor Service plus others too numerous to mention in Alice Springs, and to a host of friends and acquaintances for their excellent recall of the past and their patient assistance with technical details.

# CONTENTS

## PART ONE: CHILD
### *You're Just a Girl*

## PART TWO: WOMAN
### *The Great Career of Billy Batchelor*

## PART THREE: WIFE AND MOTHER
### *The Brolga*

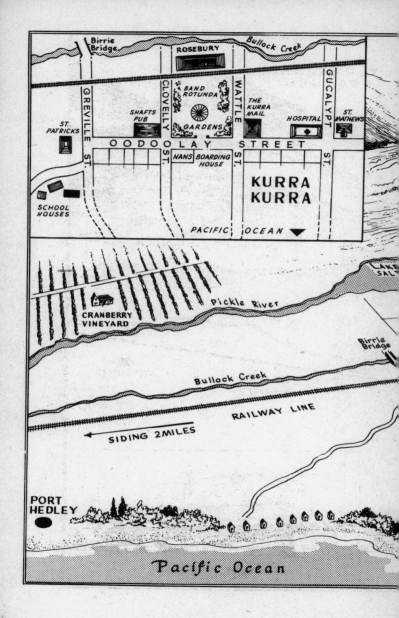

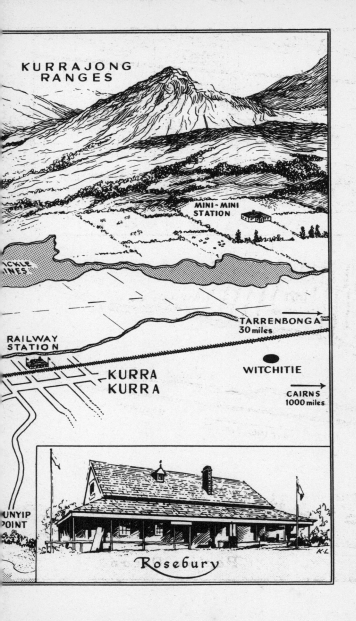

KURRAJONG
RANGES

MINI~MINI
STATION

CKLE
INES

TARRENBONGA
30 miles

RAILWAY
STATION

KURRA
KURRA

WITCHITIE

CAIRNS
1000 miles

UNYIP
POINT

Rosebury

K·L

## PART ONE: CHILD

# *You're Just a Girl*

There are few visitors any more. People get tired of sickness. Of late, those who do drop in have taken to telling me all about their lives, how much trouble they've seen, how tough the world is today, how lucky I am to be out of it!

I listen. I counsel too. Why not? I have nothing better to do. Sometimes I laugh, unkindly I suppose, watch the dream as it breaks in the widened pupils of their eyes. Wish I could catch those short glimpses, little bits of future as they dawn . . . wish I could gather them up, put them back into my eyes, my heart. But to no avail.

It's too late for me.

Yet, I had it all once. Had it all! We all did. We were such new chums in a new, fair land. We had no fear of failure, no cluttered dreams, a simpler time, the clearest roles to play. Why wasn't I satisfied with that? Why couldn't I accept my fate? Why can't I fall back on my pillows, leave the past alone? Is vanity my greatest weakness, still?

I am ugly now. Palsied face, misshapen body, hardened heart. But in my mind . . . in my mind, I am the beautiful Billy Batchelor. I command my audience without effort. They listen to me. They love me.

This is my time, my country, and the whole world applauds . . .

# ONE

# 1914...

I was born in a condemned house in Kurra Kurra on 4 July 1914.

On arrival into this world, I sneezed, and did little else, so I've been told, for the next sixty hours. All three and a half pounds of me was wrapped in a grey army blanket and placed in a chipped green enamel bath, along with five other new people, each of whom was apparently of normal weight, looks and behaviour. Much can be read into such comment, but I took it to mean that I was but a weak pittance worth, particularly ugly and totally incapable of sensible baby antics, like crying.

The Great War clouds had joined the grey mist hanging over our corrugated town and nobody had the money or the inclination to do anything about the condemned order placed on the ancient bush hospital. There were similar orders on every second building in town that year.

Our town, Kurra Kurra – Kurra for short – was nestled between an uninterrupted stretch of Forty Mile Beach of the Pacific Ocean and the awesome wall of the Kurrajong Ranges. Millions of years of erosion had cracked scales like a reptile's skin into the crevices and curves of the ranges, layer after layer casting deep shadows over our narrow town until they seemed to mesh and overlap with the waves of the sea.

The railway line and Bullock Creek ran right through our town, unmoved by the brooding dominance of these two great prehistoric giants that ruled our lives. Most of the population had only come to Kurra since the railway line went through. It was our lifeline. Papa said the trains made communication fast, helping to cement the colonies into a great nation. In any case, by the time I was born, the demand for goods could not be met by bullock wagons, and the nearest port was three hundred miles away. Experienced horn jostlers had grown too old to drive the long hauls and besides which, the Pickle River that ran inland from Port Hedley had all but dried up.

Figgy Barnawarren, who'd owned the *Kurra Mail* since 1894, 'took it personal' that the town was dying before it had hardly got started and went all the way to the top to get the politicians to support a railway line from Port Hedley in the south to Witchitie, a thousand miles to our north. Barnawarren fought a good fight to get that line to run right through the centre of our town. He was a real worker and didn't mind fifteen-hour days. The first Mrs Barnawarren hardly ever saw him. Mama said, if the truth be known it probably killed her. She died giving birth to their daughter, Saucy, just two months after I was born. Mama said that men were so stupid anyway, they only built the railway line to move the troops to all the wars they had to have. Mama had a way of bringing everything down to earth, no matter how close to the bone she got. Papa made his living out of the railways after all – when he wasn't making it at the wars, that is.

It was winter when I was born and winter in Kurra Kurra was a time for hibernation, not new life. A great grey cloud would descend over the Kurrajong Ranges and sit ominously low over our town for months. The rain would start around May, filling our tanks quickly, then it would join the sea and pass over to someplace else, leaving us with frosts and fogs that were too big, or too tired, to struggle over the top of the mountains. Our old blue-violet gums and dark emerald pines suffered as we did, losing their colour and their shine until a fragile August sun returned.

Sometimes the mist would lift with an afternoon easterly charging in from the ocean. The smell of the sea would get so strong, Mama used to say she could stop using salt in the cooking until it passed over. The sheep-farmers – and cattlemen seemed driven by it too, herding their flocks to the saleyards south of Sydney through the mud and slush of winter's sway. Only the grapevines seemed immune to the morning mists and the afternoon razor-sharp winds. The Prescotts' wines made at Cranberry Vineyard were well known in New South Wales by the time I was allowed to taste them.

The bush hospital was an old miner's cottage made of mud brick. It had long since been renovated with iron lean-tos, jutting out on three sides to accommodate the baby wing, an operating theatre and the matron's bedroom and sitting room.

On my third day of life, when it was clear that sneezing was keeping me alive, the matron, Sister MacKenzie, named me Billy. The dubious honour of giving me a title fell upon her for a couple of reasons. First, my mother was too sick to know and my father was too worried about my mother to care. Secondly, and mainly, it was because of Sister Mac.

Sister MacKenzie, Mama's closest friend, was a devout Catholic, as well as a dedicated spinster – or a devout spinster and a dedicated Catholic, as the town loved to debate. She was twenty-four when I was born and had already spent nine years of her life nursing Kurra Kurrans. Her rough hands and generous heart had seen lives come and go without so much as a tear shed, without so much as a name! In my circumstances, what with no medical reason why Mama should live through the ordeal, and only continued sneezing keeping my skeleton form alive, Sister Mac decided I just had to have a name, in case of sudden departure.

Unbeknownst to Mama and Papa, she ushered in the parish priest for total insurance. 'I've named 'er Billy, Father, after our next PM,' she said matter-of-factly. ''Er parents are only Presbyterian, but that's 'ardly good reason for 'er ta 'ave ta go ta Purgatory, now is it?'

In the midst of all this clandestine activity, my papa got called up. War was expected any day now. Besides Sister Mac, he told nobody about it for two weeks. 'It woulda killed ya mama,' she told me years later. 'An' God knows what it woulda done ta you!'

During the following two weeks, while Papa maintained his own heartbroken counsel and Sister Mac ruled everyone's lives with a pseudo-ferocity we were all glad to lean on, Mama's condition deteriorated, and I took a turn for the worse.

'Must be pneumonia, sure ain't the flu,' she proclaimed, just as the Prime Minister announced that war had been declared.

Australians gathered up their British pride, and Kurra Kurra's loved ones were farewelled from a makeshift corrugated iron and wheat stack shed at Port Hedley. Papa got measured up for his uniform and began two weeks' intensive training. All whose lives he touched were sworn to secrecy: the local tailor, his boss at the railway station, the clerk at Tarrenbonga War Centre, his commanding officer, plus Sister Mac, of course.

Ignorant of the weight on Papa's shoulders, Mama on her deathbed gathered strength to avenge the goodwill intended in the naming of her baby. 'Mackie is my dearest friend, and a God-fearing soul, no way she isn't,' she conceded, 'but she had no right to call my daughter after a man whose reputation might best be described as a tough little Aussie battler!'

Papa sat quietly. Tears streamed down his face, relief and joy unleashed. She was going to live!

'How could you, Nathan? How could you stand by and let this happen? Where were you when I was dying? For heaven's sake, Nathan, where were you?'

In a barrage of words befitting the most competent barrister of the day, she ploughed heartily into my papa. 'Billy Hughes may well make Prime Minister, *dearest*, but I see him as a Londoner, a locksmith by trade, a mutineer by nature. While I've been lying here, dying, the matron of this hospital . . . hospital? Hospital! Huh! that's a laugh . . . has taken the matter into her own hands, as if she had the right! She can burn candles all she likes, dear, but what has she ever done to change anything? Nothing. She's hadly fit to judge what old Billy Hughes is trying to change for the likes of his own trades people. Hardly, dearest, hardly indeed.'

Papa blinked, shook his head in a mystified sort of way, and gently took her hand. 'Your argument is sound, dear, but you seem to be missing your own point. Why, I overheard Mackie looking down on Billy in the bath this morning. "Ugly little one in the moth-eaten grey blanket," she cooed, "ya don't know 'ow ta cry an' ya don't wanna die. You're a real surprise to Kurra's year, ya sure are, Billy!' That's what she said, darling.'

It was a long speech for Papa. My mama fell back into her delirium after that. But not before she'd instructed my father to give me the name of Rachel. Rachel! Can you imagine it? Billy Rachel Batchelor, no less. Naturally, Sister Mac got the credit (or took it) when I upped and lived to spite them. 'Who ever 'eard of anyone with a name like Billy Rachel Batch-elor dyin' of a cold, eh? Who ever 'eard o' sich a thing! Ain't none of us 'ere gettin' away with trans-ferrin' this 'n from a chipped green bath to a wee brown box, no sirree!' Everyone in town later agreed that Sister MacKenzie had a heap of insight, espec-ially for a Mick.

Mama and I went home together three weeks later and Papa went off to the war two weeks after that.

We had no near relatives, like cousins or uncles. We didn't have grandparents either. I didn't under-stand why we didn't. We just didn't. But there were always lots of women around. There was Sister Mac, who took on the role of surrogate father with blood ownership rights equal to none. And there was Ruth, dear Ruth.

Ruth was our nurse-girl. She was dark brown, nearly black, the colour of our dog, Chocolate. Her eyebrows were thicker than any I'd ever seen and she had huge black eyes with white sparklers in the centres. Looking at her was like watching the fire-crackers in Oodoolay Street on 5 November. Some-times I stared at her so hard, she seemed to blush under the sunburnt skin and long willow tree waves of straw-like hair that fell clumsily around her wide, square face. She shone like a beacon on a dark night to me, or like a big shady tree, always there, warm and calm and magical. Ruth was eleven when she first came to our house and Mama started trying to improve her.

By the time I was at all aware of a lifestyle, it seemed perfectly natural to be surrounded by women of various shapes and colours and per-sonalities. I was also learning that I had to share most things with a horrid brother, Joey, and quickly caught on that any envelope with blue lines deliv-ered by our postie, Mugga, was cause for celebration. A letter from Papa at The Great War always put Mama in a good mood for at least a day.

On top of all these wondrous blessings, as Mama called them, we also had Chocolate. Chocolate was a big, gawky-looking mongrel who came home one day, and stayed. She barked at anything that moved, but never bit a soul. Even when she was angry, her tail wagged. On first glance, she seemed the same as the rest of the women in my family, but she wasn't.

Chocolate really understood me and loved everything I loved. She never criticized or cajoled. The first time I realized how much I treasured her was the day Wendy Barr came to our house. Wendy Barr was very beautiful, a real lady, the kind of daughter every mother would be proud to own. She became my friend the day Joey started school.

Wendy Barr liked everything I liked. Afternoon tea parties, dressing up, reading picture books, climbing trees, eating mud. And Chocolate; she just adored Chocolate. We three were inseparable, sharing our whole lives together, most especially our secret meal times of mud pies and hose water. Wendy Barr tolerated my brother, who frankly didn't believe she existed. He was allowed to be extremely rude and bad-mannered to her as I saw it, which didn't seem at all fair. 'Joey's a boy,' Mama used to say. What sense was that? Wendy Barr said it didn't matter, since she loved Ruth and thought Sister Mac was okay, in a tough kind of way. She was largely afraid of Mama, but then, we all were.

Wendy Barr stayed with me for years, but always went home each night. When I was nearly four, she didn't show up one day. I was miserable. Inconsolable. My lack of incessant chatter caused Mama to sigh greatly, constantly putting her hand on my forehead, as if that was going to bring Wendy Barr back! The next day, I had the mumps. It was the first of an unremitting stream of childhood illnesses that would afflict me.

Chocolate sat at the end of my bed for seven long days and nights, going outside only at the insistence of good housekeeping, as Mama was prone to say. Mama tendered me with unusual gentleness when I was sick and Ruth managed to sneak an hour off every afternoon to tell me stories of the Dreamtime.

Before I had memory, I knew about the Dreaming, about the field of creation. I knew that the sun is the woman, rising every morning to provide heat and sunlight for the world. At the end of each day, she travels through a long underground tunnel to reach her camp in the east, to begin yet another journey across the sky. I knew that the moon is the man, making the same journey at different times from the sun, dying for three days every month, restored to life for ever. And when it was dark, from my bedroom window I could look up to the Milky Way, to the River of the Sky, and know that the sky people were catching their food; stingrays, turtles, fish . . . Being sick, dreaming with my Ruthy, wasn't all bad.

On my first day out of bed, I found Wendy Barr waiting in the backyard. For reasons unknown to me, she was strictly a fair-weather friend.

I can't remember much about our first house, but I can still see that backyard! It was the sort of yard kids can get lost in. We had lemon trees, three of them, and an orange tree and a big gum tree, lots of blackberries that were totally overgrown (since Papa left for The Great War, Mama said), and a lot of tall, dead weeds and collapsed shrubs that were just perfect for hide and seek.

When it rained in Kurra, we had to wear gumboots every time we went outside. Joey thought gumboots were dreadful things that only Abos wore. I can't imagine why he ever thought that because I never saw a blackfella wearing gumboots, but Wendy Barr and I just loved them. Mama always bought them too big so we could get two seasons out of them. They were freedom to us, freedom to squelch everything in our way, freedom to climb trees without ruining our shoes, freedom to escape the rules and regulations of the women who ran our lives. Mostly, it was hard to get water to really gush out of the hose, so when the rains came we had mud pie picnics that were the best and slushiest in the world. On highly adventurous days, the mud would seep inside the top of our boots, leaving our stockinged feet dirty, creating great trouble when we came running back into the house across the polished floors Mama kept so well. 'Lift your feet!' she'd scream, as we rushed across the verandah and into the parlour. 'Lift your feet, ladies! Lift your feet! Your brother isn't as dirty,' her voice would echo along the passage. 'You're a girl, Billy, not a boy!' It was obvious to me that Joey was her favourite, though he didn't seem to do anything much at all.

When Mama was really mad, she'd acknowledge Wendy Barr. 'For heaven's sake, dear, what will become of you if you continue to carry on with these stupid fantasies and tomboy antics? You can tell your friend to lift her feet too!' she'd add. When we were naughty, I was Billy and it was Wendy Barr's fault. When we were good, I was Rachel and Wendy Barr didn't exist! I learnt not to protest too much. I got to thinking Mama should really have had another boy. They didn't have to be anywhere near as perfect. That she'd decided to have a girl seemed to be the only mistake she ever made.

We sensed that Ruth was only a girl after all too. She was a lot older than us, and wonderfully smart, but I didn't think much about her in those early days. She was just there, ever there, beautiful and serene.

She was our friend. She used to take us aside and sit with us in the afternoons, sipping make-believe tea out of my precious willow pattern china doll cups. All four of us together, Wendy Barr, Chocolate, Ruth and me. When we came in from the garden covered in mud and scratched and bleeding from the blackberries, she'd fuss around us. 'You girls better get cleaned up before the Missus sees you looking like good for nothing piccaninnies,' she'd laugh. Then, more seriously: 'Young ladies never sip tea 'less they've got clean hands, you know,' mimicking Mama's tone closely enough for us to obey at once. She never noticed the trail of mud we dragged in from our exploits in fairyland.

Mama said she was lazy and sly and hadn't improved a bit since she'd let Papa talk her into giving the useless girl a life away from The Orphanage. I thought The Orphanage sounded very grand, but Ruth told us it was pretty bad. We liked her all the more for that.

Sometimes, when Mama went to church on her own, Ruth would tell us the secrets of the Never Never land, how the kangaroo got his tail and why kookaburras can't do anything but laugh. Some of the stories were so incredible, they were hard to believe. But I didn't dare let on, in case she grew cross and decided to stop.

When I was four, much excitement was hatched in our house about my forthcoming change of life. Mama especially made great business of the advantages of a solid, well-rounded education and pointed out every other day how lucky I was to be born at a time in history when all children got the opportunity to go to school, even wilful, stubborn girls like me.

'You have quite a reputation to live up to, Rachel,' she'd say. 'Your brother, Joe, has, and so have you.'

I was rarely mentioned in the same breath as Joe. I listened attentively to the advice and started watching him carefully in the hope of picking up *a reputation* before I began. Nobody told me I couldn't take Wendy Barr and Chocolate to school to help me get one. It was never mentioned that the three Rs I'd heard so much about were learnt by repetition, and the ruler! And it never occurred to the women in my life to prepare me for all boys to be rude, dirty, insensitive, obnoxious and incomprehensibly superior. My world acknowledged Joe as spoilt and horrid, but totally removed from life at large. I was ill equipped for more than one boy at a time. The adventure ahead looked such fun, I determined to get an education and a reputation, whatever they were, and make Wendy Barr and Mama and Ruth and Sister Mac and Chocolate as proud of me as they were of Joe.

Added to this flurry of activity came the news that The Great War was over and Papa would be home sometime after Christmas, maybe even before I started school. It didn't mean much to me, but Mama's overwhelming preoccupation with running our lives to strict Victorian imperatives loosened instantly, her sharp features and quick tongue softened appreciably, and I was happier than I could remember being before. Sister Mac spent more time with us, helping with the myriad sewing and cleaning and rearranging chores that suddenly accrued. 'This is what good friends are about,' Mama preached, often enough. I was more excited about Santa Claus coming than Papa returning home, but even the thought of a strange man living with us could not spoil my high spirits.

I thought I was the luckiest girl in the whole world when Santa left me a brand-new blue bicycle of my very own. I vowed I would never complain about getting Joe's cast-offs again. The year before, the first Christmas I can remember, Santa brought me stupid girlie things that I was bored with by Boxing Day. Even Joe said Santa wasn't too smart to bring a Billy dolls and fairy dresses.

It certainly took me no time to learn to handle a bicycle. I escaped at every opportunity, riding off into my dreamworld, always dinking Wendy Barr, her arms wound tightly around my waist, our long black curls blowing behind us in the breeze. Chocolate ran easily at the pace I could pedal, often finishing up more black than brown. We rode across the sheep and cattle paddocks of the O'Ryans' Mini Mini station and back across the Prescotts' Cranberry Vineyard, splashing through the Lake Pickle salt mines on the way home. We cupped new birds in our hands, giving them imaginary Aboriginal names Ruth had taught us, but our very favourite game was riding out to Billadambo on the far northern tip of Mini Mini and wading into the shallow, muddy water, digging for tadpoles.

Ruth became our chief conspirator, bringing buckets of water and old towels onto the back verandah to wash us down and dry us off before we would dare enter the house. Once or twice Mama saw us and was crosser with Ruth than with me, but we learnt to be more cautious, and I was an experienced traveller by the time February dawned.

When the day arrived for me to get an education, I held back the tears as I stumbled through the school gates, holding my little brown bag (Joe's cast-off brown bag), in both hands. The primary and secondary schools were joined with one classroom for all under twelve and another for the big children over twelve. Without Wendy Barr and Chocolate, I was alone.

During playtime, I met some of the boys, all of

whom were saved lives of Sister MacKenzie; it quite shocked me to realize that Sister Mac made mistakes. How could she have saved these frightful children? In the second lesson, I stole Jock O'Ryan's red chalk. He had two pieces and I had none. He was a couple of years older than me and big for his age, a nasty, red-haired boy with huge pimples and blackheads all over his ugly red face, and a stomach as fat as any I'd ever seen. Mama always said that fat people had no pride.

'Billy Batchelor stole my red chalk!' Jock called out, while we were singing 'Onward Christian Soldiers'.

'I did not!' I lied.

'What's in your hand, Miss Batchelor?' interrogated Mr Hunt.

'It's my red chalk,' I whispered. All the Christian soldiers stopped singing.

'You're lying,' accused Jock.

Mr Hunt obviously agreed. 'Stand up!' he roared, picking up Jock's ruler, taking two hands to it. 'Now, bend over, you . . . you wicked, wicked girl.'

I did as I was told. I'd never been hit before in my life, but I knew what was coming. And in front of the whole class!

'And you the daughter of Rosey and Nathan Batchelor, no less,' he chided, verbally completing the whipping. I never got over it. I never stole anyone's red chalk again and I never got another belting in a school room.

There were twenty-three of us all told in the Kurra Kurra primary school house that year. Not one of them spoke to me at lunchtime. I got through the afternoon behind glazed eyes and took the long way home, avoiding Oodoolay Street where Reverend Moon might see me, over the railway crossing on Grevillea Street, across the Birrie Bridge and along Bullock Creek where the Aborigines lived. To make the trip last as long as possible, I zigzagged my bicycle along the dry creek bed, sure that I couldn't possibly let Mama and Sister Mac and Ruth know I was a wicked, wicked girl. I prayed very hard that Joe would not tell them of my crime.

Wendy Barr would understand though, and as I neared home, I began to pedal hard, certain she'd be there waiting for me, ready to comfort me, tell me it wasn't my fault at all. But she was nowhere to be seen. Only Mama rushed out to greet me at our gate.

'Child! Where have you been? I've been worried sick about you.' She pumped her matriarchal bosom with coconut-covered fingers, wiping the tears that immediately flowed from my eyes until little bits of coconut and chocolate stuck to my face like smallpox. 'Well? What's all this crying about?' Her stern voice held not the slightest edge of sympathy.

'I don't want to go to school any more, Mama,' I sobbed.

'You'll never get to heaven, my girl, if you don't go to school!'

'I don't want to go to heaven either,' I sobbed more adamantly.

'Where would you like to go, child?' she heaved, her generous bosom rising high, nearly touching her chin.

'I dunno,' I whimpered.

'I don't know, Billy, don't know. Not dunno.'

'Don't know, Mama,' I repeated dutifully, sniffling noisily again. And that was the end of that communication.

I escaped to the backyard, desperately needing to find Wendy Barr and Chocolate. They must be down at the beach, I decided, gathering up my bicycle, pedalling silently out the back gate.

We often played on the rocks of Bunyip Point, rocks all grooved and worn, like the wrinkles in an old, old face. Ruth taught us to fish for pennies and three-penny bits and it was such a good game to play when you were feeling poorly. 'Don't go down to the edge of the point, don't cross the Birrie Bridge,' Mama's words rang in my ears. 'Don't take gifts from strangers. Don't go deep into the fields. Don't leave your bicycle where it can be pinched. Don't be long, don't talk to people you don't know, don't tell lies, don't, don't, don't . . .' I hid my bicycle behind the last bathing box and clambered over the rocks. I was a bad, no, a truly wicked girl. What did it matter how many more rules I broke?

An old, dark-skinned man, sunburnt like Ruth, was sitting on a craggy bit of rock, his feet dangling in the sea, his fishing line limp and wasting by his side. He beckoned me over.

'Have you seen Wendy Barr or Chocolate?' I asked.

He considered me thoughtfully. 'No, I haven't,' he replied at length, 'but I've got a sixpence for you.' He produced a shiny silver sixpence from behind his ear. I was thrilled.

'Did you see that, Wendy Barr?' I turned to my friend, but she wasn't there.

'Take it,' he said, pushing it into my hand. I thanked him several times, was about to ask how he found it, when Wendy Barr spoke. 'We should go back now, Billy. Mama will be worried.'

My heart replied sharply, 'No, she won't. She only worries about us when we're being naughty.'

I sat down on the rock beside the old man. He put his hand on my hot left knee. It was a huge hand, covered in browny orange stains as if he'd been cutting down trees. He smelt awful, garlic I thought, but it was his hand that bothered me most. It was so strong, I couldn't move.

'You must be Billy Batchelor,' he said brightly. 'You're very pretty. You goes to school now with my boys and girls. I'm Mr O'Ryan.'

'Oh!' I gasped. 'Hello, Mr O'Ryan. Did you catch that sixpence in the ocean?'

He didn't answer my question but lifted the hem of my grey tunic. 'What colour are your panties?'

'White, of course!' I replied indignantly, straightening my slip and pulling down my hem. Mr O'Ryan is just as rude as his sons, I thought.

'Do you know what's inside your panties?' he said, as though he was really interested.

'I'm sorry, sir, I don't.' I shook my head, trying hard to think what he meant.

'I'll show you,' he smiled encouragingly.

At that moment, my enemy Jock came hurtling around the point in his canoe. 'Hi, Billy! What's you doin' talkin' ta my old man?' he called. I stood up quickly. So did Mr O'Ryan.

'He gave me sixpence,' I explained thoroughly.

When Jock stood up in the canoe, I thought it was going to capsize. His face changed from its normal red to a sort of pale grey. 'You go home, Billy Batchelor. Don't you know you ought not ta speak ta strange men?'

'I'll go home when I'm good and ready, Jock O'Ryan,' I shouted. 'Your father isn't a strange man anyway, stupid!'

'You go home,' he repeated angrily.

Wendy Barr had gone, but something deep in my subconscious told me I was in a kind of danger. I ambled reluctantly back to my bicycle alone, and slowly pedalled home. At our gate, I realized I'd forgotten to give back the sixpence.

I fully expected to see Jesus in the parlour when I peered nervously through our back door. But no, the women in my life had gathered, curious to know about my first day at school. I found myself being thumped on the back, my face ignominiously patted, pinched and almost slapped because I didn't answer the questions at sufficient length. I felt like the straw man in the Cranberry Vineyard when the crows heckled and pecked.

As the realization of the day's disasters settled heavily upon me, my conscience prickled my hands, tucked deep inside the pockets of my second-hand tunic – one bitterly clutching the sixpence, the other making a hole bigger. I'm a liar and a thief, I said to myself. Wendy Barr has left me because I'm not a nice girl. The war is over, but still Papa doesn't come home. He knows! And Jesus knows! I will never ever get a reputation now!

As surely as I knew I must 'rise and shine' and go to school tomorrow, I knew that the devil was laughing at me, glad I wasn't good enough to get to heaven, even if I'd wanted to go. Any child who could eat mud, steal Jock O'Ryan's red chalk and his old man's sixpence, and tell lies about a Wendy Barr who didn't exist, was just not fit for Jesus.

And Wendy Barr never came again. My dreams had flown, with the stroke of a ruler, with the horror of a small piece of silver that would never be spent. I was alone in the world; even Chocolate seemed distant and as for Ruth, well, Mama said she was a bad influence on me and sent her back to The Orphanage the following week. My Ruthy had left me! My Dreamtime, my stars, my galaxies . . . Up there, in the dark, Goolagaya, the spirit woman, haunted the night, seizing and devouring any children who were foolish enough to stray from the safety of the campfires . . .

'Without Ruth, we don't have any hope,' I told Sister Mac, like a little old lady. Ruth believed everyone, whoever they were, could have a dream, but my dreams, and Ruth, had gone. Sister Mac said Mama sent Ruth away because she didn't need her any more, now that us kids were both at school, and Papa was coming home from The Great War.

But I knew it was Goolagaya who'd done it. And God's Wrath thrown in, for good measure. Every spirit woman, and every father and son in the whole world, hated me.

The thought of my own father coming home any day now reduced me to a fresh round of tears. I was sent to bed without my supper. I would have refused to eat it anyway.

# TWO

# 1919...

Papa came home one hot Saturday on the 3.30 from Port Hedley.

From the roof of our old shed, I could see everything but nobody could see me. I could watch the trains pulling into the station and mostly make out who was arriving and who was leaving. I spent a lot of time up there, especially during my first few weeks at school.

There were two of them actually, two men in khaki uniforms and digger hats. They stepped cautiously onto the platform, loaded down with bags and cases and brown paper parcels. At the bend in the road at the top of our street, they embraced. One walked on. The other one walked up to our front door.

He stood there for a long time, the sweat pouring from his face. He tried to mop it up with a crumpled handkerchief but no sooner had he finished than he had to start again. Was it . . .? Could it be my papa? He didn't look at all like his pictures. I began to think it couldn't possibly be him. He was slightly bent, shorter and thinner, yet . . . he had the most beautiful face, my papa's face! His eyes were bluer than our mountains and they seemed to stare longingly at our rusty old door knocker, as though it were gold. Just as I dared myself to jump off the roof, rush over and fling my arms around him, his expression altered, cooled, hard and measured as he turned around and limped back towards the gate. He stopped abruptly. I could feel his heart beating in my own, but I couldn't move. Spread-eagled like the windmill, I lay there, licking salty tears from my gaping mouth.

At last, he walked back to the door. There was enormous strength in the movement that my tender years could sense, though he was old and weak and stumbling. I could not quite grasp what I was seeing, feeling. I began to pray and wish as hard as I had ever prayed and wished before that Mama would sense his presence and rush to his rescue. As if she heard me, suddenly she came. The door opened quietly and she stood there, her mouth open too, tears falling down her face, tears I had never seen before.

She fell into his arms and he held her, stopping her from falling, wiping her tears, kissing her face, everywhere. He raised her off the doorstep, his thin arms gathering her up like a doll. She wept openly. He buried his head in her huge bosoms and her whole body seemed to sob. I lay transfixed, shocked, incredulous. If this was my papa, where had the mama I used to know gone? He carried her inside, kicking the door shut with his dirty boots. I waited. I waited to hear Mama's voice screaming to him to lift his feet, but all was still.

Presently, the back door opened. Joe and Sister Mac came onto the verandah. 'Billy!' Sister Mac called. 'Billy, where are you?'

I couldn't speak. I flattened my body and head against the roof, praying they would give up quickly.

'Billy, come down off that roof,' called Joe. 'Papa's home,' he added unnecessarily.

'Ya papa is home from The Great War, child,' called Sister Mac. 'Come down at once an' say hello.' As an afterthought she added, 'An' mind ya manners.'

That was the familiar cut that did it. My stiffened legs moved slowly as I clambered down the drainpipe. 'Come on, Billy, don't loiter,' she urged.

Mama and Papa stood arm in arm at the back door. Sister Mac bustled me onto the verandah, gave me an encouraging squeeze, pushing me towards them. I fixed my gaze on Mama; it was too hard to look at Papa.

'You must be Billy,' he said stupidly, in a voice much younger than could possibly be true.

'Hello, darling,' said Mama silkily, putting out her arm that was free. She looked as though she wanted to rush towards me and gather me up in her arms, but she couldn't because she was holding Papa.

'Hello, Mama,' I croaked, standing perfectly still.

'How are you enjoying school, Billy?' the man asked.

'I hate it,' I replied shakily, spontaneously letting all the shock and fear and uncertainty flood my soul. I rushed for Mama's skirts without thought for the moment. She held me close to her body. He ran his fingers through my hair, as though he'd done so many times before.

'It's very difficult, your first few weeks at school, Billy,' he whispered confidentially. 'I cried a lot – at first.'

'Oh, sir,' I sniffled, 'did you? Did you really?'

'Of course I did,' he reassured. 'But I loved it, after a while.'

Mama wiped her eyes and straightened up. 'Rachel, this is your father, darling. He'll be home with us from now on.' Papa nodded. 'Why don't you go and find Chocolate and Wendy Barr, Billy? Tea won't be for a while yet and you'll want to tell them all about it.'

My stomach knotted. My heart started pounding again. 'Did you see Wendy Barr when you came in, Papa?' I cried, as steadily as I could manage. Papa looked at Mama, then at Sister Mac. They jerked their heads nervously and Mama's free hand rushed involuntarily to her breast, her eyes lifting upwards, invoking help from heaven. Sister Mac hiccupped.

Joe recovered smartly. He spoke in his gruffest, most grown-up voice. 'Wendy Barr went to Sydney the day Billy started school, sir. She's not coming back. But Chocolate's around, someplace. Chocolate? Chocolate! Come on, Billy. Let's go and find Chocolate.'

Papa took over his natural role as head of the household and I fell in love with him, as little girls do with quiet, calm, good-looking men. His photos told me he was a solidly built man before the war, but the newly acquired limp and fragile frame had not weakened his character, rather, increased his stature before Mama. Many of the old-timers in our town however, still viewed him as a fool.

To outsiders and casual observers, Nathan Batchelor was not a man's man. War service afforded him a certain begrudging respect, but many said it had made him even softer. That he never flinched at his wife's catty remarks and was incapable of resisting Rosey Batchelor's stupendous domination and organization over all activities in our lives was ample proof. According to most, he was a man broken by the thumb of a woman.

When Mama abused and ranted and bellowed, Papa would exit to the workshop to his second greatest love, carpentry. 'The Lord chose carpentry,' he'd say. 'It was good enough for Him.' Mama would stand in the kitchen, hands on hips in a comical position at odds with the expression on her face, and finish her verbal attacks at a closed door. When Papa returned, often hours later, Mama would say, 'Cup of tea, dear?' Papa would smile warmly, with practised surprise. 'Why thank you, Rosey. That would be very nice.'

He called her his own special Rose and seemed in awe of her marathon endeavours and martyr-like faith. He shared neither her Victorian morals nor her Irish temper, and never raised his voice to her when she challenged him to fight. The more he turned the other cheek, the angrier she became, of course, but her tantrums had to run their course. Sister Mac said he was the most intelligent man she'd ever known.

With Papa's return, a steady stream of visitors created a new world for us all. Papa had two close friends, Figgy Barnawarren and Luther Prescott, and an easy rapport with his boss, Carter Pip, the station-master. Mr Pip had been in the job for thirty years and dropped in to tell Papa he expected him at work the following Monday. He was an old tyrant, accord-ing to Mama. When he bowed deeply and told her he was visiting to pay his respects, she scoffed under her breath. As soon as he was out the door, she stormed aloud that she'd never met such a cynical blackguard.

'What respect indeed did he pay during the long years when you were facing death, Nathan, while he was waving his insidious flags?' Papa suggested that perhaps she meant incessant? Insipid? Mama was unshakable. 'Red flags are hardly insipid, Nathan.'

It took many months for us to get to know the men, though. Mama's renewed wifely status led to the sudden emergence of a dozen close women friends. She took to entertaining in such grand style, you'd have thought she'd become the stationmaster herself! Most afternoons I had detention and missed all the cakes, but as winter crept in and our school house could no longer afford wood after three in the after-noon, detentions grew less. I came home early one day to a house full of ladies. Afternoon tea was served in the parlour; Mama was using her glory box double dinner damask napkins and Royal Albert china so I knew the guests must be important and I determined to be on my best behaviour. The cream cakes looked delicious.

Curtsying, as I had been taught, I was introduced by Mama. There was Mrs O'Ryan, whose younger children went to our school. The Catholic school didn't start until grade seven, 'because, thank God, we're a Protestant town!' Mama explained. Mrs O'Ryan seemed far too nice to be married to the rude man with the stained hands who'd wanted to know what was in my panties, but I'd got over hating Jock O'Ryan since making friends with his sister Frances. There was Reverend Moon's housekeeper, Mary, 'a prim spinster if ever there was one,' Sister Mac said. Mrs Prescott, from Cranberry Vineyard, greeted me with a hug. Mama said she was so well heeled before she met Mr Prescott, it was quite beyond her to work out why she'd married at all. While I was trying to sort out who all the other ladies were, Mama handed me two cream cakes, promptly dismissing me to play. I disappeared into the kitchen, leaving the door a little ajar.

Mama was wearing her best satin dress. Every time she got up or sat down, she crackled. It was a delicious sound. I could imagine her straightening the pleats of her skirt in proper folds over the green ottoman. They were chatting about the latest goings-on of George and Mary. Mama was a true royalist. When a lull fell in the conversation, Mama told her favourite story. 'The fact that my mother was first cousin to the Earl of Rosebery, whom you'd all know is tenth in line to the throne,' she added sweetly, 'has nothing to do with my attitude to royalty. Who you are doesn't matter in this modern age! It's quality that counts.' A little gasp was audible from the parlour. Some of the ladies involuntarily straightened their jackets. It always worked.

On this afternoon, Papa entered the house to see if

the ladies needed more firewood. He stood at the doorway, a gentle smile lingering in his eyes. 'Don't forget to tell the ladies how we came by the name Batchelor, dear. You know the story . . . how we would be Jones but for Father changing his name when he crossed the border to avoid the taxes.'

He scratched his head, muttering vaguely to himself as he departed. 'Still think that's why the expression, "keeping up with the Joneses", is not one of your favourites, Rosey.'

I followed him out to the workshop, never to know quite what happened in the parlour after that. Mama didn't ever tell her blue blood story again though, and from that day on, I thought Papa was Jesus with magical powers over everyone, especially Mama and me.

Joe and I were brought up staunch Presbyterians, as staunch as Presbyterian can be, that is. Sister Mac often argued with Mama about the omission of true doctrine outside the Only Church of Rome. She said Protestants stunk to high heaven because they held chapel in churches not much bigger or better than an ordinary dining room and built for profane purposes 'with no odour of sanctity'. She spoke at length every Sunday after tea. Joe would excuse himself early and Papa would retire with his pipe to the verandah. When it suited Papa, he never smoked inside.

I'd sit quietly making myself as small as possible, afraid Mama would notice me and order me off to bed. I loved their fights, though I didn't understand the half of what they said.

'Divine services is 'eld by Reverend Moon at nine on the Sabbath an' that's called religion! Poof! The choir don't wear no surplices, worse still, there ain't no candles on the altar. No wonder the clergy got a lowly name, Rosey,' Sister Mac would argue.

Mama's back would stiffen and her bosom would rise. She'd finger her working hands through her soft brown hair in preparation to reply. Her face would flush, just slightly, enough to highlight the strong high cheekbones, the palest complexion, the piercing brown eyes. I think I loved her more when she was in full flight with Sister Mac than I did at any other time. She was powerful, but oddly feminine, vulnerable. I felt a part of it, a part of her. 'Being a Presbyterian is a most satisfying religion I can assure you, Mackie, without all that mumbo jumbo and ritualistic nonsense you lot go in for.'

Sister Mac would then remind Mama that she and little Billy may not be alive today but for the burning of candles by her own dear self. 'Utter fantasy!' Mama would ridicule, though softly enough. She could never quite rid herself of the possibility that Sister Mac's religion forced a louder, more immediate hearing from the Lord. Sometimes she'd say that God was a showman in pious clothing and the Tivoli would be a more suitable stage for His talents. Sister Mac would laugh heartily and Mama would laugh quite uncontrollably and if I was feeling really brave, I would laugh out loud too.

Papa's pipe always finished about that time. He'd wander back in, ask if he could make us all a cup of tea. Mama would smile, thank him, Sister Mac would say she had to go. Mama would say, 'It's past your bedtime, Rachel.' I would kiss everyone goodnight, go to bed and dream that Jesus was Papa and Papa was the Sentimental Bloke, dancing on the vaudeville boards of the fabulous Tivoli.

At the beginning of her marriage Mama had determined to be the best wife, mother and hostess in town. What with one thing and another – two young children, the rations, and Papa going to The Great

War and all – she'd been forced to postpone her social ambitions. But when the news came that Papa was to be awarded a Victoria Cross for bravery at Amiens, she grabbed the moment.

She had never liked Papa's boss and knew that all men had secrets. Carter Pip had secrets. He was a sleaze with no breeding. She began at the *Kurra Mail*. Figgy Barnawarren was only too pleased to oblige with her search for Mr Pip's humble beginnings. Nathan Batchelor should definitely be stationmaster! He had earned that right, fighting for his country. 'Why, it has nothing to do with friendship.' Figgy Barnawarren loved a mission. He was tough, with a strong forehead and a 'brawny character ta match'. If anybody could get to the bottom of Carter Pip's un-savoury soul, Figgy could.

But their searches unearthed nothing. Just before the Christmas of 1920, when the long wait until Carter Pip's retirement seemed inevitable, Mr Barna-warren had a letter from a Maria Vaccaro.

She had just arrived in Melbourne on a troop ship, working her passage as a nurse. Her father's brother lived in Melbourne. He last heard that her cousin Mimo was a toff, living as a respected British gent, running a railway station on the northeast coast. It unfolded that Carter Pip was none other, having been adopted by a fine English family in Manchester in 1870, six months after his birth to a young Italian girl of mixed parentage, en route from Naples to Rome. 'But the genes will out,' Mama's hubristic tongue relished repeating for years. Caught stealing in London in 1884, he'd escaped the King's Cross jail house where he was being held overnight, joined the shortest queue at Southampton docks and finished up in Australia. He was transferred to Tarrenbonga Receiving Station, one hour up the track from Kurra, using papers stolen from a young man who died of scurvy on the way over. He cleverly kept his new identity to himself until precisely the right moment, when arriving at the medical check point in Tarrenbonga.

Even without the town's usual embellishment, it was an ingenious coup. Papa never ceased to be amazed at the control of the man, on the run, calculating his moves with the understanding of a born and bred Australian. Long after he had been made stationmaster, Papa would cut Mama short when she began her *dago* story.

'My dear,' he'd begin, like a full sentence, his resonant voice demanding silence. 'Carter Pip or Mimo Vaccaro, whatever name, knew people exceedingly well. He outguessed the system. He knew the doctors were more concerned with his health than his credentials. They wouldn't look closely at his papers. He knew about trains – he'd been born on one in Italy, for goodness' sakes! And he knew that railways had just become the *crème de la crème* of Australian life. He was a smart, tough old cookie and deserved a better end,' Papa would conclude convincingly.

Mama would shake her head many times before sinking low for the last word. 'He was a convict, a liar and a cheat – and a dago!' she'd add bitterly.

'He was a free settler, and a naturalized Australian, dear,' Papa would correct.

'I don't care what you think he was, Nathan, he was a dago, through and through.'

Papa would pick up his pipe, unlit, and amble up and down the room for a minute or two before reaching for a match. His gentle pacing unsettled Mama. Sometimes you could see her mind working, ready to explode, but Papa would light his pipe very deliberately, stilling her tongue.

Mr Pip left Kurra Kurra immediately following his public sacking. Through his editorials, Figgy wouldn't let anyone forget the dethroned station-master's Italian heritage and deceitful character.

Papa wouldn't allow us to forget the man for quite different reasons. He reminded us that Mr Pip was a workaholic and a bachelor, making few friends but earning the silent respect of the local business and farming community. His trains always ran on time. Papa said he had a lot to live up to. 'Sadly, it's human nature for folk to forget the good things about a man,' he said. 'It's a lot easier for me than it ever was for Carter Pip.'

A few weeks after he'd gone, Mr Pip sent for Mary, Reverend Moon's tight-lipped spinster nursemaid for the little ones, David and Amelia. Because of his connections in high places, our Reverend managed to secure the immediate services of another white spinster nanny, a Miss Prinkett; Kurra Kurra got enough gossip and speculation out of the entire affair to mortify Mama, making her completely forget her part in the exposé in the first place. 'I've a good mind not to move to the stationmaster's residence!' she repeated often. 'Fancy, why, I can hardly bare to think about what was going on in that house, just minutes ago!'

For my part, I was scared of the move. I still missed Ruth every single day, and lived in hope she'd come back. If she did, how would she know where to find us?

But, move to the big house we did, along with Mama's fourteen chooks, two roosters, Chocolate, one nearly dead rabbit that belonged to Joe, dozens of cartons of jams, pickled and preserved fruits and an odd collection of bits and pieces of furniture. Mama was determined to have nothing but the best for our Grand New Life and had discarded much of what used to be our essentials.

To Mama, our new home was most respectable,

befitting our standing in the community. To Sister Mac, it was a longer walk from her rooms at the hospital. To Papa, it was a dream come true and he turned to the job with an enthusiasm I had not seen in him before.

The railway station was part of a small village within our town. It comprised not only the train and telegraph stations, but the post office, weather lookout, old barracks, buggy shed, stables, shoeing yard and, of course, Bluey, our blacksmith. But it was a far cry from the way life had been in 1889 when the first settlers arrived. Apart from the trains and telegraph, it had fallen into disrepair with the departure of the prospectors, and the war and all. Papa told us stories of the old days when Kurra was alive with hundreds of young men, hopeful of finding their fortunes in the shallow waters of the Pickle River and the harsh earth of the drought-ridden fields. The population swelled to 3,000 men before it became clear that the dream would never be realized. A few stayed on, those with families mainly, and took up land to farm cattle and sheep and plant grapes and wheat.

The stables and stockyards still standing on our station used to service the bustling community unchallenged, but there was no chance they would ever be reopened now. A few of the townsfolk agisted their horses with us, but the farmers had installed their own bush gallows for killing their beasts and the linesmen maintaining the telegraph and railway lines were all accommodated at Nan's Boarding House in Oodoolay Street, instead of the old barrack houses lining the northern tip of the property.

The stationmaster's residence was made of local stone. It had wide shady verandahs all round and was laid out in an oblong block, bisected by a thirty-foot passage downstairs and a full rectangular landing upstairs. It had been designed in such a way that

34

the mistress of the house had maximum protection from bushrangers and hostile Aborigines. In the downstairs central octagonal room, called the fortress, you could safely see through the windows in every direction, provided, of course, that all the doors and windows were open. It didn't seem too smart to me that everything had to be opened, right when you were scared stiff and about to be attacked. When I said as much, Mama explained that it was built to an English design for homes in India, that it was warm in the winter and cool in the summer, and that settled that.

To Joe and me, it was a palace. Ruth would find us after all – anyone who lived in such a fine mansion would not be difficult to find! As we entered the fortress, we stared in wonderment at the oak balustrade of the steep stairwell. The passage led one way to two bedrooms, a formal sitting room and a bathroom. The station kitchen took up the whole east side downstairs, with a small separate coverway alcove outside for the workers to leave their boots and coats. There were three toilets under the coverway near the back door. Three nearly inside toilets!

'I've never seen anything like it!' I shrieked.

'You're just a girl,' Joe shrugged, in his grown-up voice.

Upstairs consisted of two large, attic-style bedrooms that were to be ours; we tumbled and tripped in our haste up the stairs to inspect them. There were views of the sea from our windows, but the walls beckoned more urgently. Oak-panelled, every four panels had a handle. All the doors in the house had low knobs so that children could enter or exit quickly, in case of fire or flood, but these doors, miniature doors lining the walls, led into dark cubby-rooms between the inside ceiling and the roof – a secret world all of our very own!

'Oh Joey,' I squealed, 'do you think there's witches and spooks in here?'

'Don't be stupid,' he said. 'Might be snakes and spiders though . . .'

Not even the thought of them could stop us. We crawled along the creaking beams, exploring, slipping, shrieking, laughing, scratching and bruising ourselves mindlessly. The heat under the tin roof finally, predictably, overwhelmed me.

Joe scrambled around until he fell over me, propped my head between my legs, waited for me to come round and dragged me back into the bedroom. I'd been fainting since I was three – flat feet and a funny balance, Sister Mac said. It was nothing untoward to Joey, or me. Within a few minutes, I was dreaming about the fun Chocolate and I were going to have in our new mansion with its secret panels and mysterious rooms in the roof. Maybe I could even convince Amelia Moon and Frances O'Ryan to play with me now?

When we were properly tidied up, looking not much the worse for it, we sauntered proudly down the great, narrow staircase. Mama was at the foot of the stairs with tears in her eyes. It was such a rare sight, I started crying too.

'What's the matter, Mama?' I sobbed, realizing many strange people were in our fortress room. Men, all men, tall and short men, fat men, men with beards and men with hats in their hands. My eyes rushed to the floor, unsure and shy. At our feet was a crimson and gold tapestry square, woven in patterns of dragons and flowers. I saw a marble mantelpiece with a huge scolloped mirror above. There were gents' blue armchairs and ladies' low-pillowed chairs. Mama took my hand, patted her eyes with her lace handkerchief and walked me into the kitchen. The men all stood back, watching us closely, chuckling at some private joke.

In the centre of the room was a large oval table made of cedar, a matching sideboard, and a long cutting bench ran the length of the outside wall, broken only by the stove. Above the chimney place Mama had already placed her grandmother clock and a jug of sunflowers. I began to cry again.

Within the hour, Mama prepared a welcome meal for all of us. Apart from Papa and Joe and Sister Mac and me, there was the telegraph-post master and the weather man and a couple of linesmen, Bluey the blacksmith, Reverend Moon, Prinky (as we'd nick-named Miss Prinkett), David and Amelia, Mr and Mrs Prescott, and Nan from the boarding house. Nan was a new friend of Mama's. Sister Mac told me Mama invited her into the fold because she didn't have any family, and even fewer friends. We were more than a baker's dozen.

Usually Reverend Moon said grace when he was at our table, but because it was our first dinner at The Residence, Papa wanted to say it. 'Dear God, thank you for this new home and job and bless our colleagues and friends who share bread with us tonight. And dear God, thank you for man's greatest asset, a rare and special Rose, Amen.'

Sister Mac hiccupped, Mama wiped her eyes again, Joe sniggered and hopped straight into the potatoes and a few of the men nodded warmly at Mama.

I sat with my mouth open. 'Close your mouth, child, and eat your dinner,' Mama snapped. She didn't like too much soppiness. The adults all stared at her curiously, then at me, but I heard nothing contradictory in the instruction. I did as I was told.

My poor self-esteem of a few months earlier took a turn for the better as we settled into Rosebery. Mama had renamed the station residence, of course, after her blue-blooded cousin, the Earl. Papa didn't mind and Mama said it might make me feel less inferior, since I obviously had little going for me that could be recommended in fine company.

Mama's strident ways were not easy to like, and while I loved her, I both loved and liked Papa. He took me into his confidence in a way I had not known, chatting with me at length of The Great War, of trains and carpentry. He showed me how to build things too, no more nor less than Joe. Sometimes he held my hand or put his arm around my shoulders as if we were mates. He let me fill his pipe and pour his Madeira, much to Mama's chagrin.

He was so interested in everything I'd done before he came home, I must have driven him crazy with my tales of Wendy Barr and Chocolate, Sister Mac and Jock O'Ryan and Ruth. I now knew that Wendy Barr would not return, but I couldn't quite give up the thought of never seeing Ruth again. I began to pester him.

'Now that Mama has so much to do, with all the men and everything, Papa, why can't we get Ruth back?'

He wrinkled his brow slightly, scrunching his eyes until they were narrow and dulled. 'Your Mama doesn't want Ruth in the house again, Billy,' he answered flatly.

'But why, Papa? Why doesn't she? Ruth was so good to us and there's so many things she could do around the station. She could even learn the telegraph. They don't teach her anything at The Orphanage, you know.'

Papa opened his eyes wide. 'Ruth told you about The Orphanage?' His surprised voice pleased me, though I didn't know why.

'Of course, Papa. I'm quite grown up, for a girl!'

'And so you are,' he smiled, 'so you are.'

38

With the advent of Papa, my confidence also improved at school, though my happy childhood at Rosebery was constantly undermined by those five days a week in class. I was a sickly child too, and often absent. Every youthful illness attacked me. Joe escaped measles, mumps, chickenpox, boils, glandular fever, flu and every other virus that swept through our school. I got them all. And I always had a relapse. Sister Mac was ordered out of my sick room during the first illnesses. Mama made it clear that it was her job as a mother to nurse me back to health. She was good at it too, as she was at everything. No matter what was wrong with me, she would bring our Arnott's biscuit barrel into my bedroom immediately, along with a glass of home-made lemonade, forgetting to remove the barrel when she bustled off to tend the kitchen. The Bickford's Sal Vital Health Salts were administered twice daily and she'd sit with me in the afternoons, telling me stories, teaching me poems. She never called the doctor – didn't believe in them. Anyway, by the time Doc Halliday from Tarrenbonga could get to us, most childhood illnesses were over.

'It'll take its course, child,' she said every time. 'Rest and love is all you need,' as she poured a dessertspoon of olive oil down my throat.

The first time Sister Mac was called in followed my first day back at school after ten days off with huge red and blue boils on my legs and head. Micky O'Ryan hit me on the head with a baseball when we were playing at recess. I fell to the ground and three of the O'Ryan sisters rushed onto the field, poring over me in great distress.

'You're a bully, Micky!' accused Veronica.

'You did it on purpose,' shouted Frances.

'I can't believe you're my brother,' echoed Sarah. 'Just because you go to the Catholic school next year, don't mean you can throw your weight around here!'

Sarah was Jock's twin. She was big and strong for her age too. I didn't know the O'Ryan girls liked me until that moment. It was almost worth the pain.

Mr Hunt carried me off the field. For weeks my school mates talked of the trail of blood pouring from my head. Sister Mac arrived the next morning, when Mama was clearly at a loss to calm me. Without discussion, she rolled me over. I screamed, even before the injection went in.

'Don't be such a sook, Billy,' she chastised gently. 'You're a big girl now!' I cried myself to sleep, wondering whether Mama and Sister Mac understood what it was like to be a girl, let alone a big one.

My teeth created more problems. The school dentist said it was just a matter of time.

'What does that mean, sir?' I asked.

'Don't ask questions, dear. Just open your mouth,' he replied. He would drill and pull and drill and pull. When he pulled, I was left with dry sockets and that meant twice-daily dressings for weeks.

At school assemblies, we all put our right hand on our left breast to recite the Royal Oath. I often fainted on or just before the fourth line was finished.

> 'I love God and my country
> I will honour the flag,
> I will serve the King.
> And cheerfully obey . . .'

'Don't worry, Billy,' Papa used to say. 'They'll never conscript you into the army.'

'I'd like the army, Papa,' I'd wail.

Mr Hunt was a firm disciplinarian and insisted nobody stirred until the oath was completed. He would then walk briskly through the three rows of pupils, aged from four and a half to sixteen, gather me up and take me to sickbay, a lean-to shed we called the prison. We had a name for everything. I spent a lot of time in there, one way and another. The kids would swap pennies, for I soon came to be known as Silly Billy. 'Will she faint on the third line? Will she faint on the fourth?' Sometimes, I didn't faint at all. Fights would break out as the boys tried to figure who'd propped me up.

At the end of the day, Mr Hunt would drive me home. He and Mama struck up quite a friendship. 'Oh Billy, was there ever such a girl as you?' Mama would sigh profoundly.

'She's not the easiest pupil I've ever had,' Mr Hunt would willingly agree, accepting a cup of tea. Mama would rush around, opening cake tins and apologizing for the mess. There was never a mess in our house, but Mama always thought there was.

Papa quickly caught on that Mondays were my fainting days and always arrived in time to shake Mr Hunt's hand and thank him for bringing me home. While Mama and Mr Hunt discussed my disastrous assimilation into the education system, Papa would excuse himself on one pretext or another and quietly walk up the stairwell to my bedroom.

'How are you feeling now, Billy?' he'd begin. 'You look a little pale, dear.' I would weep and he would hug me. Then I'd clutch him quite fiercely until the sobbing eased and my shame subsided.

Sometimes Joe visited me in my room before supper on a Monday too. 'How ya doin', old girl?' he'd say, brash and coy all at the same time. He'd give me a sort of punch, right into the bedclothes near where he thought my arm would be. Now and then he got my stomach and it hurt, but I never let on.

'I'm a failure, Joey,' I'd confide helplessly. 'I'm much better at reading and writing than you, and I hate dolls and girls' games. What's the matter with me? You don't cry all the time and you don't get sick

41

and you almost never get yelled at. Why was I born a girl, Joey? I'd be much better as a boy!'

Joe would nod his head, unable to argue. 'You can't help it, Billy. It's not your fault.'

'Then whose is it?' I'd plead.

'I dunno, Billy,' he'd say.

'Don't say dunno, Joey. It's bad English.'

'Okay, Billy,' he'd say.

The worst of my sick bouts was that my imagination deserted me, leaving me in the ugly world, the real world. When, aged seven, I got rheumatic fever, I was quite sure it had gone for ever. I couldn't dream, I couldn't even sleep. Mama's stories didn't make sense any more and Sister Mac looked like a man, digging and prodding and sticking needles into me every chance she got.

They took it in turns to nurse me, wash me, change sheets, hold me when I shook, open the blinds, close the blinds, talk to me. Papa read to me at the beginning, but I got to the point where I couldn't stand Charles Dickens or Henry Lawson any more. They were too real. Where were my dreams? Where had my beloved Ruth's Dreamtime flown? My fairyland world . . . a galaxy where you can be anything you want to be, if you wish for it hard enough . . . where was it now? I couldn't tell anyone. I had no words for fantasy. I was no longer sure that Santa Claus existed. Wendy Barr was long gone, but I still wanted my dreams. Why couldn't I make them understand that there was another place, a real place that was magical?

I was desperate to explain, to tell somebody how I felt. I longed for Ruth, who would have understood . . . my Ruthy, she would have been able to help me find my dreams again.

Without Papa reading to me, I lost him too in those long, dark months. He was at The Great War, killing. He'd left me to return to The Great War. He was needed more there than here. I was just a girl. He was very brave though, brave and strong and oddly proud of his little one at home, dying of lost imagination.

For the second time in her twenty-eight years, my mother faced death. She had faced it herself, at my birth. Now she knew with all her senses that her baby's life was drifting, floating high in the clouds, reaching up to the heaven she believed in. Seven years were about to pass before her eyes, without measure or reason, without justice.

'We're not winning, Mackie,' she whispered to Sister Mac, one fine afternoon when the sun strobed the dyed pink calico curtains she had sewn by the night lamp, night after night until they were done.

'God don't want 'er, Rosey,' Sister Mac improvised wildly. 'She's a mischief maker an' a tomboy. She's so full o' dreams an' wild imaginins', 'eaven got no place for 'er yet, lovey!'

Mama laid her head on my chest but the tears were a long way off. 'What can I do?' she tortured herself. 'What can I do? I never told her I loved her, Mackie. I wasn't brought up that way, you know, don't you? You weren't either.' Her voice broke momentarily. She continued, like a small child, talking to her doll. 'I can tell her now, Mackie, but it's too late. Too late! But for Nathan, she would never have known people do speak of love.'

'She ain't dead yet, Rosey,' Sister Mac consoled.

Mama was rambling on, from habits of old, snippets of good housekeeping that were meant to hold the panic in check. 'A safety pin placed in the saucepan while boiling an egg will stop the white from leaking if the egg is cracked.'

'Will it?' I heard myself ask, unsure whether to just be pleased, or really amazed.

'When you save small bits of toilet soap . . . enclose them in pieces of foam rubber, sew around the edges, you've . . . you've got useful things that lather well and save waste,' she stumbled forward, as though emerging from a trance.

I could see her then, a shadow of her former body, the generous bulges now limp and sagging. Her eyes had narrowed and dulled, the high cheekbones sucked into her lips, thinner and more severe than I remembered.

'Mama, if you saved our old school cases, they'd be a good size for first-aid kits, wouldn't they?'

Her face opened up slowly, like a flower on the first day of spring. The sad eyes glistened in the sunlight. She looked so slim and pretty, just sitting there, holding her favourite picture recipe book.

'Tell me the recipe of a happy home, Mama,' I asked. I imagined I'd heard it all before, but she was so happy, I didn't want her to stop and go get Papa to read one of my Henry Lawson poems.

She began tentatively, as though she'd forgotten the words. They were there, in front of her, but her eyes were glazed over. 'The recipe for a happy home, Rachel dear,' she almost sang, 'is one pound of good temper, two pounds of forbearance.' She paused to blow her nose. 'Three pounds of unselfishness, one pound of patience. One pound of fun, two pounds of cheerfulness. Mix well with two quarts of human kindness.'

'What's the dose, Mama?' I asked from memory.

'One tablespoon first thing in the morning, dear. Repeat as soon as effects wear off.'

With that, she gathered me up from my pillows and hugged and kissed me, combing her big working hands through my wet, dangling hair. A storm of tears streamed down her beautiful face.

\*　　\*　　\*

Ruth came home on the 3.30 one foggy afternoon in May 1923, just as Papa had done a little over four years before.

Perhaps it was Mama's stubborn pride that kept Ruth away so long. Maybe Papa just wore Mama down in the end. We accepted her stature and social responsibilities in Kurra had expanded so dramatically, she couldn't possibly manage without our Ruthy any more.

Papa led her into the kitchen in his unassuming way, as though we'd been expecting her all along. She looked nervously at Mama. Mama looked tentatively at her. Papa's eyes sought mine, silencing me in a glance. I held my breath and clutched my heart.

'Here, I'll do that, Mrs Rosey,' Ruth said, lifting the large black pot of soup from the bench to the stove.

Mama's bosom remained so high and still, I thought she would likely burst. Instead, she smiled: 'Why, thank you, Ruth.' Papa took up his pipe from the mantel and quietly left the room.

Two small white tears dropped from Ruth's big black eyes. Mama's wet hands absently rubbed her own eyes, then she took her apron to them, muttering under her breath about onions and needing to feed the chooks. She left quickly, the back door slamming behind her.

We stood apart momentarily, precious time gone for ever, everlasting time within our grasp. Ruth opened her arms. I fell into them, hugging her with all my might, a fearful pain tugging, whispering that it was only the Dreamtime, that she would fly away like the brolga, carried away by the wicked winds, over the ranges to the Never Never land. But she hugged me back! I could feel her heart beating next to mine. It was true, it was true.

'Oh Ruthy, I missed you so much, Ruthy. Thank God you've come home.'

'Ah, my warm, wild Billy! It's real good to be back.'

'You'll never go away again, Ruth, will you? This is your home, this is where you belong.'

Her eyes misted right over then. The small drops of rain sheltering there grew large, falling heavily between us. My childish heart sensed that I had hurt her deeply – no happy tears these. But what had I said? How could my grateful heart have wounded hers so badly?

'What did I say, Ruthy? Please, Ruth, don't cry. I love you. I'm sorry. I'm sorry, Ruthy. Forgive me, please forgive me?'

'Darling Billy,' she rallied swiftly, wiping my eyes, then hers, then mine again. 'You didn't say anything wrong. I . . . I just wish you were my real family and this was . . . where I belonged. But it isn't. I have a mother too, you see.'

I opened my mouth to speak, but I couldn't think of anything to say. The idea was incredible, impossible. Ruth? A mother of her own? No, it couldn't be. She came from The Orphanage.

'You can't have,' I said at last. 'Children only go to The Orphanage when they don't have a mother, or a father,' I added unsteadily.

She was smiling slightly, an old, sad smile. 'Yes, I know that's how it should be, but it isn't. Not for us.'

'I don't understand.'

She knew me too well to hope it would pass, but how could she speak the unspeakable truth? How could she tell me what my people had done? I felt her struggle, but I just had to know.

'Is your mama in heaven, Ruthy?'

'No, no, Billy.'

'If she's not dead then, why don't you live with her?'

'I used to . . . till I was about your age; eight, maybe nine.'

'Why did she send you to The Orphanage?'

'She didn't send me. They . . . took me.'

My heart quickened. I could feel the blood rushing to my cheeks, powerless to stop it. 'They . . . who took you?'

'You must promise, Billy, that you'll keep it a secret, just between you and me, if I tell you?'

'Cross my heart,' and I did.

'My mama worked on a white station a hundred miles north of Stuart Town. The owner of the station let her stay after she had me 'cos she was a good cook and didn't make no trouble. Then the white missionaries and the Government men came. They said she couldn't keep me any more 'cos I was getting too old and had to go to school. We lived with the other black labourers by the creek, so we had a big family, with our very own little school. Some of the other kids had to go too. I don't know why they picked us. They just bussed us out one night. Some said we were being punished 'cos we had *the white blood* in us. My mama didn't cry. I think she was too sad.'

She picked up the wooden spoon and began to stir the soup. 'We ain't gonna talk of it ever again, Billy.'

'I'm never going to let anyone take you away from us, Ruth!' I caught my tongue as I said it. 'I'll never let them send you away either,' I rushed on, not knowing where to stop.

She rocked her head from side to side and wound her free arm around my waist, pulling me to her like a mother with her child.

'It's kinda funny, Billy, but I reckon you need me jist about as much as I need you, eh?'

# THREE

# 1926

I had no premonition of the explosive events that would unfold in the year of 1926, events that would change our secure, insular lives for ever; events that would set my own future in motion.

I was in my twelfth year, though the seeds of change began long before I was born. The overland telegraph line erected across thousands of miles of our rugged, unforgiving country had long since linked us in just seven hours to London. But it was the coming of the wireless that awakened Kurra Kurra, transforming our dreams.

For nearly two years, Mama valiantly resisted installing a wireless at Rosebery. With practised indifference, she was always able to divert us without protest, yet it was Mama who finally asked Papa if we could have a wireless machine. She wanted to hear Nellie Melba's farewell concert.

The wireless was installed on New Year's Eve and we sat around the kitchen table, transfixed, waiting impatiently for something to happen. Even Joey was still, heightening the mood of anticipation.

At last it began, the orchestra bursting into our lives like a crash of thunder. A man with a beautiful voice, unlike anything I had ever heard before, wished us a Happy New Year, no matter where we were listening; in the cities and the towns, on outback stations all over this great nation of Australia; the home of the pioneer, the country that had nurtured and grown the remarkable, unique talent of Miss Nellie Melba. Mama's bosom was so high, her face almost disappeared as the deep velvet voice held us in its thrall.

Nellie began, her voice, light and low, grew strong and bold, shivering and shimmering higher and higher, clear over the Kurrajong Ranges. I could hear summer rain cascading over the rocks and scrub, loitering in rings and ripples on the creek below . . . the quivering nostrils of the dingo on the scent of his prey, the trumpeting of the brolgas . . .

'She sounds like the bokkun-bokkun,' Ruth whispered.

'What's the bokkun-bokkun?'

'It's the Koorie word for the bellbird,' she smiled proudly.

'How does the voice get to us, Papa?' I asked. 'It must be magic!'

The very next day, he took us on a tour of the telegraph operations room; console-tables inlaid with dials and buttons, plugs and cords, wires protruding from behind, ear plugs and microphones everywhere, gauges, graphs and little lights flashing up and down. We sat at the big black typewriter with the shiny silver-rimmed keys and talked at the wall through a mouthpiece, like a miniature megaphone. The linesman at Port Hedley talked back!

Papa explained how the radio waves occur naturally in space, emitted by all my stars and galaxies. He told us about Mr Marconi and how he sat in his parents' attic in Italy and made a bell ring by sending a radio message across the room. So that was how it had begun! 'Then why does Mama think all Italians are fools, Papa?' I'd asked.

For the first few weeks of 1926, Mama's worst fears of installing the wireless machine were realized. We came home from school and hung around her feet, uninterested in the self-made games and amusements that had occupied our lives until then, waiting for the radio to come on. Ruth was not bothered too much – she had chores to do – but Joe and I were desperate.

'Go out and play,' Mama pleaded.

'Nothing to do,' we answered in unison. Mama shook her head and spread a large hand over her breast. Could these be the same children who but a few weeks ago had been unable to find enough hours in the day to do all the things they wanted to do?

To make matters worse, we could receive two stations most of the time. Joe wanted to listen to the cricket, I wanted to listen to the plays. We fought as we'd never fought before. In no time at all, we drove Mama to absolute distraction. With the full force of her Irish temper, she banned the wireless altogether. But it had already worked its magic on me and I would never again be free of the spell it cast.

As the year unfolded, it became perfectly obvious to me that Mama was not happy, not so much with me, since I was just a girl, but something would certainly have to be done about Joey. What had happened to his energy and interests, and the pride he felt when he made up new tests for arithmetic and biology classes? He was fifteen now, but all he seemed to want to do was play cricket. And there was his strange behaviour in the mornings.

In spite of Mama's best efforts, Joe always left for school looking like he'd been there all day. Now suddenly, I could never get into the bathroom before breakfast. He'd shut the door and stay, holding everybody up. Whatever he did in there made no difference. He still looked a mess, but he'd come out with a shiny, preening sort of look on his face. Mama was clearly worried sick.

I started to worry too. I hadn't exactly been spying on Joe, but I'd overheard him talking about girls with David Moon. The things they were saying were so disgusting, I hadn't even been able to tell Ruth.

Of course I'd known for years where babies came from, but the boys said they grew in women's stomachs and giggled and made jerking movements with their hips, pulling their ugly little carloos until their faces screwed up and I couldn't look any more. They said some of the girls at school had already had a baby because they'd seen blood on their dresses. I knew that was a bare-faced lie, but Isobella O'Ryan had been taken home one day with blood running down her legs, and I'd seen bloodied white napkins in the girls' toilets. I'd seen them at home too, but thought one of the men must have had an accident on the station. Now I wasn't so sure. I didn't seem to be sure about anything any more. If babies didn't come from storks, and blood was going to start running down my legs, I had some serious questions that had to be asked, and soon.

As preoccupied and confused as I was about what had gone wrong with Joey, and whatever was going to happen to me, I had at last made up my mind what I was going to be when I grew up. Not an opera singer or an actress as I had first thought, but finally, irrevocably, I was going to be a radio announcer, a velvet-smooth radio announcer. I was going to be the first female radio announcer in Australia. Just as Joe was deciding he wanted to take private cricket lessons from the new secondary teacher, Mr Merryweather, an ex-Olympic runner and a bowler with Victoria's XI the previous season, I decided I wanted to take elocution lessons. I was expecting a battle.

If it bemused Mama that we had set our sights on highly individual, star-struck careers, she didn't show it. I determined to find a way to secure her support and crept to my usual spot, halfway down the stairwell, hopeful of catching an up-to-the-minute summary of the situation. My Great Questions of Life were never quite fit for genteel company; with our table so highly sought after, I rarely got the chance to ask them.

Mama and Papa had moved into our formal dining room, as they often did when everyone had gone. A southeasterly was blowing in from the ocean, cooling Rosebery right through. Mama's knitting needles clicked rhythmically as she talked. I could hear Papa's pipe being prodded and tapped now and then, and picture Chocolate asleep at their feet, breathing heavily. The ocean breeze rattled the back fly wire screens, and a faint smell of salt drifted up the stairs, tickling my nostrils. I plunged my nose hard into my hanky, the thought of discovery never far from mind.

'We have a son who wants to be a sporting hero, Nathan, and no thanks to you he may even succeed, and a daughter who wants to do a man's job! What on earth are we going to do?' I was expecting to hear Papa allaying her fears, perhaps suggesting we might change our minds several times over before we had to decide. But Mama was just drawing breath. 'Joe seems to have lost interest in everything except becoming a test cricketer! How are we going to get him back on track for medicine? At this rate, he'll finish up without a job and no prospects and –'

'Rosey,' Papa interrupted, his voice pitched low and strangely depressed, 'we're not going to be able to afford to put Joe through university, dear, even if he wants to go. Frankly, I'm not sure how we're going to keep them both in school . . .' His tired voice trailed away.

The world fell still. The wind had dropped and the back door no longer flapped. Mama had put down her knitting, Papa's pipe must have been full. Chocolate's breathing was loud and irregular now. An owl hooted from our telegraph pole. I silently willed Papa to speak again since Mama had obviously cut her tongue. I could sense that she was shocked, uncertain, perhaps even disbelieving, emotions that seemed extreme for the situation. We were going through tough times, everyone said. There might even be a depression coming. Very few people could afford to send their children to university; if school was cut short, well, what harm would that do? We already knew the three Rs and would begin piano and dancing lessons this year. I would learn elocution, and all the technical knowledge I needed from Papa for my radio career and Joe would learn how to play professional cricket from Mr Merryweather. Surely there was no need for panic?

In the small, wide voice of a child sharing a secret, Mama asked Papa how this could be. Papa sounded old, just as he did when he came back from The Great War.

'We have been living beyond our means, dear,' he began apologetically. 'I should have told you earlier, I realize that now, but I kept hoping somehow that we'd get through without having to burden you. It's just that . . . well, we've spent the nest egg from my war pay, dear, and with the cost of food, even though you grow the vegetables when you can, dear, and keep the hens, it's just not enough. We should have stopped feeding everyone long ago . . . should never have refurbished Rosebery . . . new clothes for Christmas . . .' I felt his shoulders droop and imagined his fists closing tightly until the knuckles stood up like sharpened mountains.

'It has to stop, Rosey, right now. The children's shortened education is the least of our problems. I have to put off all but essential staff. I'm tempted to put off two more than I need and give the work to Joe and Billy.' A faint gasp escaped Mama's lips.

'No!' she cried. 'No.'

'I'm so sorry, my dear special Rose,' he whispered, 'I'm so sorry.'

I tiptoed to the door, peeping in, horrified. If Papa was going to put off the radio men, how could I be sure he would not send Ruth away? An idea jumped to my mind. She would make a perfect trainee, be of real help in the telegraph room. She'd be keen for the chance, would need to volunteer quickly. I saw Papa shudder, leaning over to take Mama's large, firm hands in his.

'Joe and Rachel will stay in school,' she responded presently. 'We'll manage – somehow.'

Almost instantly, it was business as usual. 'How much will I have for the housekeeping now?' she asked steadily.

'Half . . .' Papa groaned. Mama's face was a picture, but her voice was in control again and it would only be a minute or two before she had the situation under control too. I scurried back to bed. Any minute she would decide they needed a cup of tea; that meant walking through the fortress room and into the kitchen.

The very next morning, Mama advised us that since we'd both come to our senses and decided to take lessons in cricket and elocution, we needn't study piano and tap dancing if we preferred not, and we could take it in turns to listen to the wireless. She must insist however that we continue our ballroom dancing at school and Papa would be happy to show Joe the railway station and the telegraph station too, in case he decided he wanted to do something other than medicine. It was all settled with such cheer and good grace, I had to pinch myself to believe I'd heard the conversation the night before.

But when Sister Mac and Mama were talking later in the day, it was quite a different story. Out on the back verandah, ears bent to the door, Ruth and I couldn't help overhearing. I'd conveyed the conversation of the night before and urged her to ask Papa for a job immediately. Yet she still feared being sent back to The Orphanage at once.

'Why, for heaven's sake?' I railed indignantly. 'You don't eat much and you don't get a wage, do you?'

Ruth laughed, a short, shallow, piqued little laugh. 'This might be the first time since the whites arrived here that we Koories are less problem than you lot,' she smiled disquietly. 'Actually, wars too – during wars and recessions we appease the white gods, Billy, 'cos you can kill us honest like, and don't have to pray to Jesus for forgiveness. When we're this useful though, some of the Christians get all guilty and try to make amends. Trouble is, they usually make everything much worse.'

Even though we shared the secret of Ruth's past, I had never heard her talk like this. Neither had Papa, who emerged around the side of the house at that moment.

'Why, Ruth!' he reprimanded mildly. 'You've certainly picked up some fancy words since you learnt to read, haven't you? And who'd be putting such ideas into your head anyway?'

'Not ideas, sir,' she muttered, eyes cast to her feet.

'Look up, Ruth, look up please, dear.' Papa blushed slightly. He was not comfortable with self-effacing manners.

'Sir?'

'Mr Nathan, Ruth, not sir,' Papa corrected.

'Mr Nathan, I want to learn to operate the telegraph, sir. I know it's probably real ungrateful of me to ask, but I'll do it for nothing, sir. I mean, I know

55

you can't pay me, and I'll still help Mrs Rosey in the house and all, but, sir, the children are getting older and I'm getting older and, well, I won't be a house-maid for ever, Mr Batchelor, sir, I simply won't!' She finished with such a flourish, I wanted to applaud.

Papa shook his head and the corners of his gen-erous burgundy lips curled. 'Well, well, well,' he sighed, 'seems everybody wants to be somebody around here.' He paced the verandah, talking to him-self. 'Here we are, heading for a depression, and my girls are dreaming of careers while my son and his friends dream of frivolities. Joe wants to play cricket, Micky O'Ryan wants to get a licence and fly planes, foolish lad, Jimmy Barnawarren wants to be a union leader! What kind of jobs are these? What is happen-ing to the world?' He seemed to forget we were there, stepping carefully into the kitchen and right into Mama and Sister Mac's discussion about our financial ruin.

Mama had the floor. 'You know, Nathan has always held that the nation's survival depends on the railways and the roads and the telegraph. The tools for fast communication and transportation, he says, but what good's it done us? We're broke, Mackie, flat broke!' Her voice crackled, her chest heaved.

Sister Mac could not allow Mama to drown in self-pity. It was simply not acceptable. 'Rosey, look at the facts, lovey. Ellie an' Willy O'Ryan, an' Sabella an' Luther Prescott, they reckon the nation depends on the farmer an' the fertile land. The O'Ryans can't feed their snotty-nosed kids, and the Prescotts is only managin' 'cos they got no young 'uns an' 'e got the pension for his injuries. An' anyways, Sabella 'ad 'er inheritance, an' a fat one at that.' She paused, acknowledging Papa, before continuing. 'An' the Discharged Soldiers' Settlement Board Scheme is four million pounds in the flamin' red an' there's the drought, an' prices 'ave dropped an' wages keep goin' up –'

Papa suddenly spoke from the doorway, startling them both. 'The Reverend believes our country's only chance of survival is via the soul; Barnawarren's belief in the power of press communications runs close to my own heart – and as for our children, well, it seems to me we have a new generation on our hands, Rosey. We are not going to be able to make them think like us, and perhaps that's a good thing,' he nodded wryly.

Mama and Sister Mac were nonplussed. Papa's financial disaster had loosened his tongue. Mama was not at all sure she liked it.

'Our girls have role models by the dozens that should make them want to be movie stars,' he continued. 'There's Nellie, and Gladys Moncrieff, Anna Pavlova, Greta Garbo, Mary Pickford, Clara Bow! Even the Queen of Mystery, Agatha Christie! But what do they want? They want men's jobs in telegraphy and radio!'

'The role models close to home are the ones that have the most impact,' Mama interjected cynically.

My foot slipped on the edge of the back door step. 'Shush!' Ruth breathed in my ear.

'Yes, dear, though sarcasm is not your greatest weapon.' Papa scratched his head as Mama flushed. 'I think it has more to do with the social changes, dear. They're reading and hearing and seeing the outside world on the silver screen and the wireless these days. They want to be a part of it – they're not going to settle for less. Your generation slipped back into female duties after the war, made room for us men to take up where we left off. It's simpler in the country, of course, less confusion about what has to be done – whose job to do it. You made room for our egos and kept everyone's role-playing neat and tidy.

Maybe it's been easier for you this way too? But city women and today's young girls can see right through it . . . it's not what they're looking for.'

Mama fell heavily into her chair. 'Well, Nathan, I'm sure I don't know what they're going to find, what with the boys all running away from reality!'

'Ah yes,' Papa nodded. 'Joe's afraid of war – and depressions. It's not manly to admit it, but the glamorous dreams of our son and his friends help them escape the moment. They've found their role models in sporting and exploration heroes. Much safer than war heroes, maimed, injured, unemployed – dead.'

Sister Mac nodded sadly. 'We were blessed that ya come 'ome to us, Nathan. A fifth of our boys killed in action! An' for what? A Great Depression?'

'Let's hope not. I think we fought for quite a bit more than that, Mackie.'

Mama rescued the situation, only to plunge into deeper waters. 'Yes, our men go to wars to fight for freedom and when we get it, it's more than we can handle. Scarcely have our girls reached twenty these days and they've got lines on their faces that befit middle age! Smoking and drinking, working along-side men, fighting for equal pay and equal rights, out until all hours of the night, unchaperoned! And now they want weedy, willowy figures and short haircuts like men. Mark my words, we'll have an increase in consumption before the decade is out!' With that, she puffed out her ample bosom with a fierce degree of satisfaction and put on the kettle.

Thereafter, Our Financial Ruination reduced conversation and entertainment immeasurably. Tea at Rosebery became a predominantly subdued family affair. Reverend Moon still came for supper after chapel on Fridays, Sister Mac dropped in whenever she wasn't working and Papa periodically invited one or two of his friends for tea. The Prescotts turned up whenever they liked; they brought their own, plus a bottle of alcohol for sharing.

The radio informed us of what was going on in the world, often before Mr Barnawarren could run the story in the *Kurra Mail*. There was a report from the Royal Institution in London that a Mr John Logie Baird had converted a scene into a picture through electrical signals. One day every house would have its own picture theatre! Getting into radio was the smartest thing I could do, I told everyone, repeatedly.

We went to the flicks occasionally and sat in deck chairs on our Botanical Garden lawns; the band rotunda was used most Saturday nights for open-air picture shows. We were always allowed to go when Rudolph Valentino was featured (Mama was in love with him), but we went when Australian movies were showing too. Sometimes Mr Hunt played the school piano. The O'Ryan boys would carry it down Oodoolay Street and James Barnawarren and our Joey would help them carry it all the way back up. They looked like pallbearers with a musical coffin.

Joe began cricket lessons with Mr Merryweather, but there was a price to be paid; he had to knuckle down and study for his Intermediate. It would be his last year at school. At the Oval, in London, live into our kitchen in Kurra Kurra, we heard England regain the Ashes. Australia was all out for 125 runs; Papa and Joe were devastated.

'They didn't even put up a decent fight!' Joe wailed, determined to work harder at his practice. 'They need me, Pa,' he added gallantly.

I was totally engrossed in my elocution and telegraphic lessons and began to resent school again. Apart from English, it was interfering with my life. I could see no point whatever in anything else we were learning, particularly sport, since I had no talent or strength for it following my rheumatic fever.

Mama towered over all of our endeavours, implementing a rigorous schedule of instructions at home, covering every conceivable womanly occupation. Ruth was included, whenever she wasn't working at the very things Mama was intent on teaching me. Obsessed with my feminine education, my skills increased so much, I found it difficult to reconcile that girls couldn't do things boys could do. Ruth certainly could, and it seemed to me I was learning to be much more useful than Joe. I even had to become an expert cook.

It was not sufficient for a woman to be able to make a sponge rise or a pan of potatoes crisp. It was not enough to know how to set a fine table or serve a perfect meringue pie.

'Remember child, the proof of the professional homemaker is in the art of substitution!' Mama would dictate with a sort of religious fervour. 'Any good housewife knows she can substitute chopped dates or prunes for mixed fruit in cakes and puddings, Billy. But a woman of class, a woman of style, will substitute undiluted evaporated milk to save expensive cream. She'll thicken soups and stews with rolled oats, not barley or cornflour! Knowing which replacement ingredients are as nourishing and digestible is the trick, my dear!'

On the one hand, I got to thinking we must be down to our last fiver. On the other, you'd have thought we were cooking for the King of England. 'No, no, no, no, no, Billy! The glycerine is only added to the mixture if you don't have any eggs . . . that's why we keep chooks. Goodness gracious, child, what have I ever done to deserve you!'

Perhaps for balance, or just for peace, Papa had agreed that Ruth and I could have typing lessons. It was decided we would take turns to be instructed by Blondy and Clay, whoever had time, using the station's modern Underwood typewriter. We called Blondy and Clay our Wonder Boys. They had been at the station since Carter Pip's time, and kept their jobs right through the Depression because Papa just simply couldn't have managed without them. They ran the telegraph room, worked on the railway lines, exercised the horses, helped Bluey with the shoeing, and anything else that needed doing about the place. Mama never had a word to say against them. Blondy was a big, powerful man with a mop of pitch-black, unruly hair. Clay looked pretty much the same, but Papa said he got his name because he was as hard as the earth in the middle of a drought.

The rule was laid down that if one of us dropped out of our lessons, we both had to drop out. 'Dems da' breaks,' Blondy said. 'Sich conditions'll keep yous honest,' Clay confirmed.

We also continued our practical activities around the station; our favourite day was Sunday. After church, the weekly cleaning of the telegraph office was my job. I'd listen hungrily to the broadcasts and cross-conversations as I scrubbed. Ruth had the job of taking a weekly turn with the men in cleaning out the stables. When we were both finished, we were allowed to exercise the horses on the beach, a grand reward for work neither of us minded in the least.

Time for school friends was always cut short because of our work load, but I was becoming aware that my life offered considerably greater variety than my peers. Amelia and Frances learnt all the domestic and craft work I did, but they didn't have my papa, or my Ruth. Neither did they dream of conquering new worlds and forging a career. They dreamt of marriage and children, as though they really wanted to cook and clean and pick up after a man for the rest of their lives. I couldn't fathom it.

'Who are you going to marry when you grow up, Billy?' Amelia asked. 'My brother David likes you.'

'I'm not going to marry anyone!' I'd boast. 'I wouldn't marry anyone from Kurra anyway.'

'Why not? Our boys aren't good enough for Miss Stuck-Up Billy Batchelor?' Frances had the rudeness of an O'Ryan, but I liked her all the same. She was my best school friend and very straight, like Sister Mac.

'I just wouldn't marry anyone from here till I find out what boys are like from other places,' I responded confidently.

'Who's going to look after you if you don't marry?' Amelia asked, her mind caught at the beginning. She was not particularly bright, but it didn't matter. She was so pretty, so fragile, her long blonde hair framing the sweetest face I'd ever seen. I couldn't understand why she'd want a husband. All the boys I knew were far too rough and ugly for her.

'Women can look after themselves better than men, Amelia,' I asserted boldly, 'and we can earn money these days too!'

'But who wants to?' Frances whined.

Amelia looked slowly from Frannie to me. 'I think I would like to, if I possibly could,' she stuttered.

'I'm going to, and you can too!' I persisted, un-deterred.

'I always thought you were the brightest girl in the school,' Frances said.. 'Now I think you're really dumb.'

While I was arguing with Frannie and Amelia, and my world was being shaped by familial encouragement and opportunity, Joe's seemed to be reducing. I felt a bit sorry for him. He didn't know how to do anything much.

His dreams of making the Australian side were not looking good either. He simply didn't have the discipline to stay with the practice and after a few late arrivals for lessons, coupled with poor performances in the school eleven, Mr Merryweather informed Papa that Joe was wasting everybody's time.

'He doesn't have the killer instinct, Mr Batchelor,' Mr Merryweather explained unnecessarily.

'Nor the talent,' Papa echoed involuntarily.

'He's not alone, sir. I've got a yard full of them. They want to be heroe but they don't want to work for it. I guess they'll have to learn the hard way.'

It put the fear of the devil into me. The boys didn't want to work and the girls wanted to get married so they could be looked after. The more I thought about it, the more determined to succeed I became. My enthusiasm for every task asked of me was overwhelming. Joe said I'd become a real jerk, a do-gooder.

'Who're you trying to impress, Billy? Lay off, huh? You don't have to be a superwoman.'

'What's it to you?' I said. 'You don't have to be anything.'

If it was true that Mama tried to get Joe to pull his weight about the place, he was able to get around her. He had homework, or cricket practice. As often as not, he was spooning over girls. He and David Moon spent a lot of time mucking around with Saucy Barnawarren and the girls from St Pat's.

'Why doesn't Joe clean Papa's shoes, Mama? I clean yours.'

'Don't be insolent, child,' she'd reply, though she no longer added, 'You're just a girl' to explain such differences in our upbringing.

Ruth was my only chance at understanding any of it, but there was little time for chat these days. I had to wait for a diversion and it came one day, via the wireless.

Rudolph Valentino had died. His appendix ruptured but he'd died from the complications of a gastric ulcer. It sounded like a Hollywood script to me; when I said as much to Mama, she burst into uncharacteristic tears, removing herself from 'all responsibilities until tea time'. Ruth and I comforted her as best we could, insisting she lie down. She did not need much persuasion, asking as she departed if we'd get Papa to send Blondy or Clay out to the Prescotts and the O'Ryans to invite them for supper. It was like a death in the family.

Ruth and I were so excited, we could hardly contain ourselves. We rushed to the icebox, but it was disappointing. If we were to serve meat, it would have to be cottage pie – again. I thought about Mama's lessons on substitution and opened the sideboard dresser expectantly. This was exactly the crisis she'd been preparing me for! Beans. Kippers. Flour and sugar and rows of jams.

'Could we serve a Yorkshire pudding with jam?' I suggested hesitantly.

'Cottage pie,' Ruth declared pragmatically. 'Let's try and get that good-for-nothing brother of yours to pick some spring peas for us. Joey!' she bellowed out the back door.

I suddenly recalled my burning questions. I'd been waiting such a long time, trying to sort out the difference between boys and girls, the truth from the myriad stories I'd heard at school. This was surely the moment.

'Ruth, where do babies come from?' I blurted without warning.

Ruth looked aghast. 'You mean, you don't know?'

I shook my head. 'I thought I did, but I'm not sure any more.'

'Oh Lord,' she gasped. 'Sit down and peel the potatoes.'

'I need to know if Santa Claus is true as well . . .' I stumbled on, seeing her face move from horror to disbelief. 'Everyone's ribbing me at school. They say he doesn't exist, but how could Mama and Papa afford all those presents?'

Ruth seemed to be weighing up what to answer first. I began my peeling. 'Billy, babies grow in their mothers' wombs, jist like the animals. I know a real good book I'll get out of the library for you tomorrow. It'll tell you everything you want to know.'

'Will it tell me if blood's going to pour out of me all over my dress and down my legs?' She moved swiftly towards me and put her arms around my shoulders, hugging my neck. I could feel the wet of her tears as she brushed my cheek with her dark claret lips.

'Dear little one,' she sighed, 'you're a wonder girl, but you're so ignorant!' Quickly then, she set about braising the mince. 'As for Santa Claus, Billy, I'm real sad to say but your friends are right. Santa Claus is a fairytale, invented to make dreams come true for girls and boys all over the white world.'

Several large tears plopped onto the potatoes. The moment she spoke, I knew it was true, that I'd known it before. I had caught the full implication of her words far more than I realized. After a few minutes: 'If Santa Claus is white, and Jesus is white, who's black? Who do the Koorie kids believe in, Ruth?'

She smiled, as though the question was strange. '*We* have the Dreamtime. You know that! And who says Jesus was white, Billy? How do you know He was white? I think He was black,' she said convincingly.

It was my turn to be shocked. I peeled the potatoes frantically, afraid to ask any more.

Reverend Moon got word of Rosey's Great Mourning Party For Valentino, as it came to be known, and turned up uninvited, 'completing the table nicely,' Mama said later. He thought she might need ministering, I supposed.

She dressed in her new imported black satin Chanel suit with the black and white spotted Pickford blouse. The outfit had been on order for months, before Papa stopped all nonessential spending. Her white lace handkerchief, carefully plunged into the suit top pocket, was periodically and deftly lifted out to dab the eyes, then pushed neatly back into the pocket. The whole effect was stunning. She could have been one of Valentino's lovers, I thought wickedly, believing I now knew everything there was to know about such things.

Ruth and I served supper. The conversation moved beyond Mr Valentino to the collapse of the Empire and the coming of a Commonwealth of Nations. The conversation darted around, shifting from the likelihood of a Great Depression to Reverend Moon's wonderful children. David was going to become a doctor and Amelia was a lady who would marry a fine gentleman, possibly one of David's university friends.

'What are your youngsters going to do, William?' Reverend Moon asked Mr O'Ryan, chuckling to himself, not waiting for an answer. Since Danny was already working on the farm, I thought it very rude of him to ask in the first place. 'And yours, Nathan? Joey no doubt will do something, I suppose? Billy, do you think you'll be able to keep a dress clean long enough to catch yourself a husband, eh?' He chuckled some more, a triumphant, crowning smile in his green, beady eyes. I sent a little prayer up to God in advance.

'Reverend Moon, I wouldn't marry any of the boys in this town if my life depended on it! Useless, good-for-nothings, they are. Spoilt rotten by their mothers and feared by their fathers,' I said in a very grown-up manner, amazed at how fluent I was on the subject. Everyone else looked pretty amazed too. 'It's because of the war and the coming depression you know. Fathers are afraid to be tough with their sons because they know they'll have to go to war again, but it's so stupid because it's fathers who make it happen! I've heard it on the radio,' I added proudly. They seemed to have cut their tongues, so I kept on. It was fun to have the floor.

'Oh yes, by the way, Reverend, did you know that Jesus is black?'

'My God!' Mama cried, reaching for her handkerchief.

'Yes, I suppose He must be too,' I nodded sagely.

Mama buried her head in the flattened palms of her hands. The Reverend's mouth kept opening, but no sound emerged.

'Don't worry, Reverend,' I patted his hand tenderly, 'Mama's overreacting 'cos she's still in mourning for Valentino. She'll be all right tomorrow.'

I sent up another prayer to God, this time to ask for Mama's forgiveness. I tried to picture a black God, but it was very difficult. Just another thing to practise, I thought to myself. And before the year was out, the question that occupied Kurra Kurra was not whether Jesus and God were black or white, but how much they intended us all to suffer.

# FOUR

# 1927...

My outburst was the talk of the town for some weeks, but as small towns go, Kurra had its fair share of scandals and disasters. That my outrageous manners and new wave thinking did not receive elongated attention was due to the devastating bush fires that closed out 1926 for us. As Ma commented dourly later, vain and selfish attitudes are seen for what they are when a whole town rallies together for the good of the group. Kurra had suffered and survived catastrophic bush fires for as long as anyone could remember, and while they strengthened community spirit, past tragedies also united us in fear.

The start of the fire was missed at the station. As we had begun the year, so we concluded it, all gathered around our wonderful wireless machine. An earnest banging of the front door knocker was finally heard by Chocolate. She was old now, her senses dimmed, her crooked legs slow to react. She alerted us with a whimper and cowered between our feet the moment the door was opened. The hint of smoke reached our nostrils before we saw it. At once we guessed the worst. I looked at Ma's face and felt the same dread gripping my heart.

'The black bastards have lit the hills again and she's raging out of control,' Mr Hunt yelled. 'It's coming right for the town!'

We were all outside instantly, looking up to the ranges. At first glance, red cumulus clouds seemed to be dancing a wild, erotic corroboree across the sky, billowing over the high points of our mountains. As we watched, a struggling northwesterly gathered momentum and began fanning the flames down, curling and licking their way back to earth. Our first breaths consumed a piquant, aromatic drift of smoke that spread thinly over our clothes and hair; within minutes we were spluttering and coughing under the continuous veil of thick, grey, pungent ash.

The river was dry and the creek bed held barely a trickle. The fire had no choice but to come straight for us.

St Patrick's church bell, usually rung by children for Mass on Sundays, now sounded the emergency call to the town. There was no mistaking it, a constant, piercing ringing for ten minutes without pause, Kurra's bush fire brigade requiring all volunteers to assemble at the band rotunda in Oodoolay Street. All boys over twelve joined the men. All girls over twelve joined the women. 'It doesn't matter that I'm just a girl now!' I declared proudly, as Joey and I charged upstairs to shut all the windows, change our shoes and grab a coat and hat. 'I hope you won't be sorry you said that,' he quipped. I was so excited, I barely acknowledged the implied danger.

At the band rotunda, the men were heralded to one side, divided into groups and allocated a leader. One group was immediately designated to assist the women, bringing trestle tables from the church hall, carrying urns and mugs from the school house, loading the milkman's buggy with loaves of bread from the bakery and drums of water from the shops' tanks.

'Looks like we're diggin' in for a long night,' Sister Mac said stoically, instructing her group to lay out the first-aid equipment and bandages on the end table. We still did not have a local doctor, relying on Doc Halliday's weekly visits from Tarrenbonga. 'We'll manage,' she told us, while quietly informing Ma she was worried about her short supply of antiseptic creams and painkillers. Ma was well aware of the bush hospital's funding crisis. It had been in one since before Joe was born.

Pa immediately went to radio Tarrenbonga for a special train, organizing railway staff to pick up Doc Halliday, and more supplies en route to the station. By the time the doc arrived four hours later, we were watering the roofs of the stores along Oodoolay Street and our first customers were staggering back into town. The news was confusing and, in part, encouraging. Micky O'Ryan had flooded the south of Mini Mini by unplugging the cattle troughs fed by a twenty-four-metre-deep bore casing near Billadambo. The fire was contained out by the Lake Pickle salt mines on the north side of the property. Southwest, no one seemed certain. Northeast, it was anybody's guess.

The gravity of the situation came to me slowly. Reverend Moon collapsed from heat exhaustion and had to be carried into the rotunda, followed by James Barnawarren, who had first-degree burns. His face was distorted in pain and I began to worry about Joe and Pa, fighting the scorched, bloodied earth with no more than hearts full of hope and quick-drying hessian bags for protection.

As soon as each group returned, the youngest members of the town ran the bags down to the sea for a fresh soaking while we fed and bandaged the men and Sister Mac checked their blood pressures.

'They're all up,' she sighed philosophically, 'but we can't send 'em back into that inferno without lookin' like we care, can we?' As she spoke, the wind swished itself on again, soot and ash and dust converging upon us, then shooting up in crackling black and orange striped welts – back to the falling mountains, mountains close enough to touch.

'My God, the wind has changed!' Micky O'Ryan screamed, standing on blistered, half-bandaged feet.

'Sit down,' Ruth ordered, pushing him back to the ground, bandaging more quickly now.

'Isn't it good that the wind's changed?' I asked naïvely.

Micky shook his head. 'The wind's gustin', Billy, making its path unpredictable. Mum and Dad wouldn't leave the station. Danny and the little ones are with 'em. And the Prescotts only got as far as the railway siding. We could see 'em, but we couldn't get to 'em. They was headin' south, where the creek widens.'

'Oh no!' someone gasped.

'Oh my God!' Ruth cried. I looked around frantically, locating Veronica and Isobella.

'Where's Jock?' I half whispered, half screamed.

'Baggin' near Birrie Bridge, with Joe,' Micky replied. 'We need more horses. We'll take the track along the railway line. It's our only 'ope.'

The word went out, no horse too old for service now. Micky rose tentatively, then stood firmly, gritting his teeth against the pain. Sister Mac thrust a packet of Aspros in his hand and two straight into his mouth. 'You make sure Jock and Joey take some o' these,' she said firmly, 'an' your folk, when you get to 'em . . .' She coughed, smoke and fear pervading her brisk speech and tough exterior. Micky swayed, his handsome face blood red and smudged with ash and sweat. He took the painkillers without question and pressed his manly hands against his heart, as though to stop the burning.

Helplessly comprehending the smell of death – of trees and birds and roos and dogs, maybe even human flesh – I sensed our childhood passing in that desperate waiting time. Involuntarily I pressed my own hands into my chest, willing the pain to go

71

away, to let us go back, be as we were, before the fire.

At last Jock galloped up, with Mr Merryweather close behind. 'Joe will mind the bridge,' he said, 'and the rest of us will go. There's more horses coming, thank God.' Bluey the blacksmith, Blondy and Clay and our linesmen were among those close behind. Pa was with them. I couldn't hold back.

'Oh no, Pa!' I gulped, squeezing Ruth's hand with a strength I didn't know I had.

'You come with us, Doc,' Mr Hunt stepped forward, giving instructions in his cool, authoritarian manner, helping Doc Halliday onto the nearest empty stock horse. James reappeared from the rotunda, bandaged and watered down. He jumped onto the last horse as though he'd been born to it.

The posse left at full gallop, sweat rising on their flanks, muscles rippling behind flying manes. An unlikely troupe; seasoned riders with enough years in the saddle to meet any fate, Sunday riders with enough purpose and courage to make them do it. Silhouetted against the raging sky, men six feet tall on mighty stallions disappeared over the hill like sticks of coal, burning out.

I stood with the women and watched them go. I wished so desperately that I could go with them; I hated being a girl, so utterly useless when it really counted! More plates of food arrived, as is the country woman's way. Such mindless business for men who wouldn't eat, couldn't eat if they were here to eat! Chattering and folding bandages, emptying the urn and remaking the tea, buttering the bread and stacking the blankets, what use was this? How could they carry on, as though life was real and the red sky a sunset?

The wind interrupted my thoughts, curling back against us for a moment of triumph, gathering its last breath along our blackened ranges, pouring ash upon ash until its energy was spent. We could taste the grit from the cattletracks between our teeth, hear the crackling boulders and the dry gums snapping, smell the bottlebrush and the teatree cooking, like shoe leather smouldering on the hearth. Our nostrils still worked; our brains had seized.

'Have a sandwich,' someone proffered. I took one, feeling guilty in the silent bedlam of my raging head. It tasted good. I hated the fact that I was hungry and it tasted good.

'How long will we have to wait?' Ruth was nearby, willing me strength.

'It won't be long now, Billy,' she said. 'We'll know soon enough.'

We waited all night, sleeping fitfully, propped up by pillows against the walls of the stores and the posts of the multifarious verandahs that lined our main street. We looked to the ocean for solace. The sky grew lighter. We stared back at the Kurrajong Ranges, fearing the worst. Reverend Moon had recovered and started offering prayers to anyone who'd listen.

'They'll be grabbing a moment's sleep before they return,' Ma counselled unsteadily.

'Yes, they'll give thanks to God before they return,' Reverend Moon embellished piously.

'How could you thank God for this?' I exclaimed, drawing no comment for my insolence from Ma.

'God is all merciful, my child, and He moves in mysterious ways, not always understood by us.'

'Oh Lord!' Ruth muttered under her breath.

'I would expect nothing better from a heretic,' the Reverend quipped in his best Scottish voice, rarely remembered these days.

'Don't you mean Abo?' Ruth answered back, not pausing for correction by anyone who might be listening, namely Ma and Sister Mac. 'Don't forget, Reverend, that you lot taught us!'

The conversation lulled as the long vigil continued. More sandwiches were handed around and we ate them. A part of me laughed privately, hysterically. I had never eaten so many sandwiches and drunk so much tea in my life. And I had never loved life, as I loved it then. The time, the waiting time! From dusk to dawn, nature's greed, sucking away at our landscape, never content, never able to leave well alone! When there was no rain, there was drought. No drought, floods and devastating rains. No rains, there was fire, tearing everything into tiny black shreds. The sun came up, right up, staggering under the weight of the ash-laden atmosphere. And still we waited.

They rode in at a walk. A coterie of defeated heroes, more anonymous than their horses, eyes receded under flattened hats, torn shirts and trousers hanging loosely over childlike bodies. I saw Pa first, though he was two-deep back. I wouldn't have recognized him, but for the faint memory of a man returning from The Great War; there was something in his slouch, his determination to arrive, that I had seen before. He had won – and lost. I wept, aloud, unable to behave in the manner to which I had been brought up. I looked around self-consciously, desperately seeking the anonymity of the group, just like Pa riding in with the men. Others began crying too, tears streaming down their faces as they searched for their men.

I rushed to Pa, scrambling up the saddlecloth, falling back as it disintegrated beneath my grasping hands, hugging and kissing. Ma stood back, waiting.

Mr and Mrs Prescott were pulled from their horses and laid to rest on army blankets, unconscious of the miracle of their lives. Doc Halliday dismounted as Sister Mac diagnosed second-degree burns and shock, calling for stretchers and the milk cart to get them to the hospital. 'I'll go with them, Matron, you'd better stay here,' he said ominously. 'The O'Ryans are going to need you.'

All at once I was cold, an involuntary shiver ran around my shoulders, forming a lump in my chest. Nervously I turned back towards the horses being watered down and fed by some of the men. Micky and Jock had their arms wrapped around Veronica and Isobella. They were rocking together, a mess of arms and tears and sweat, lost in shock and grief and anger. My voice caught in my throat, a brief squeal of panic emerging instead of the question too terrible to ask. Sister Mac wrapped her arms around me and held me close.

'Mr and Mrs O'Ryan, Danny and the little ones didn't make it,' she said.

'Frannie? Sarah and Frannie?'

Ma and Pa moved closer to us; soon we were all entwined and rocking too.

Only Ruth was missing, wandering up and down the street with James Barnawarren. 'Where's Joey?' she shouted above our grief, her voice far away but laced with panic, with an urgency we could not ignore. Everyone started, loosening their hold on each other.

'My God, 'e must be still mindin' the bridge?' Sister Mac suggested nervously. 'We'd better go get 'im.'

Ma and Pa unlocked arms. Their eyes widened, poker heat and fear rising where cold heartache and exhaustion had been but a moment before.

'Dear God, he can't still be there?' Ma asked, her voice an octave higher than it had been all night. Her face drained white, like coal gone to ash. 'I knew he was meant to stay at the bridge,' she whispered to Pa, 'but I didn't think he had!'

Jock O'Ryan picked up the reins and mounted his horse, nudging the bleeding nag in the ribs, turning back towards the bridge. The posse answered, spitting smoke and sweat and fallen debris in their wake, young boys a day ago. Ruth and James took Veronica and Isobella inside the newspaper office. Reverend Moon went with them. I wondered what kind of help he'd be, preaching a kind and merciful God. How could such a God take Mrs O'Ryan, Sarah, Frannie? I had to admit He mightn't care too much about Mr O'Ryan and since I barely knew Danny, I couldn't comment on His opinion of him. I knew that God took all the good people early though – that's why he'd taken my Frannie. But why would he want Mr O'Ryan at all?

The women gathered strength in numbers and buttered bread, like it was life itself. Ma chattered away, keeping everyone's spirits up. Sister Mac stayed close by her side, strangely quiet.

No wait was longer than the hours it took the men to return from that trip. Pa led the procession.

As they came onto Oodoolay Street, Ma and Sister Mac and Ruth and I all knew that Joey was gone. They used the freshest beast, a light brown gelding, to bring him home ahead of all the rest, by Pa's side. The horse promenaded with a gentle, sauntering gait that told us he knew he held the prize.

Joe's body was small and crumpled.

'He climbed into a water tank,' someone said. 'The heat from the flames . . .'

'Boiled alive?' a youngster asked.

'Oh my God, dear merciful God,' Sister Mac crossed herself.

They lifted him off the horse. Unrecognizable. My Joey! My Joey!

We held a memorial service for the O'Ryans at St Patrick's the next morning, and a funeral for Joey at the band rotunda in the afternoon.

Though unconventional, it was definitely fitting in God's eyes. Ma and Pa wanted it in the church, but I fought hard that Joey was an outdoor bloke who was going to be a Test cricketer. He'd want to be out in the heat, standing tall amongst the hydrangeas, though they were dead now too. Mainly, I couldn't bare to think Joey might have to share the same ceremony as Mr O'Ryan if the Reverend and Father O'Donagan got it into their heads to join forces. It might handicap him in heaven. For once, Ma agreed. Reverend Moon surprised us all by immediately accepting the proposition; surrounded by the singed remains of Kurra's town gardens, we said goodbye to Joey.

After the service, the traditional open house for both funerals was held at Rosebery. When we opened the back door, we found Chocolate dead on the hearth. Doc Halliday said she'd had a heart attack. I wanted to cry so badly, but the tears wouldn't come. When Ma and Pa hugged me close, I couldn't even sniffle. 'You'd best watch that one,' Sister Mac warned. 'She's bottlin' it all up inside.'

With fierce, unrelenting mettle, Ma and Pa got us through, plus half the town as well. It seemed to me when people came to pay their respects for Joey, they finished up doing the crying and needing the sympathy. Ma and Pa took in Veronica and Isobella for several weeks too while Mrs O'Ryan's spinster sister, Jane, packed up and travelled overland from Perth.

Ma insisted we set about our usual daily routines but Ruth and I were released from all but essential house duties. It was Ruth's job to keep us busy and entertained. The town still talks about the three sad little girls with their sad little black nursemaid, all trying to behave like adults. Succeeding too, more or less.

Micky and Jock stayed on their station, cleaning up the debris, shooting the dying sheep and cattle. 'First time we ain't had to worry about the bloody dingo attacks on the lambs,' Micky attempted humour at our kitchen table one night. Nobody laughed. The Mini Mini homestead was completely destroyed, the charred bodies trapped inside, indistinguishable amongst the wreckage and the rubble.

''Twas jist as well,' Clay said to Blondy. Pa had released them both to dig in at Mini Mini, get the job done as quickly as possible. Ruth and I could handle most duties at the telegraph station and took turns to help Pa, giving Veronica and Isobella a new distraction.

We laughed less often and talked more circumspectly than we had done before, conversing across the tea table with exaggerated consideration for each other's feelings. The wild and raucous animation of yesterday was lost, replaced with solid opinions, backed up by facts, as best we knew them. Our depleted spirits needed time to heal. While we waited, we behaved more formally, with the decorum of our time and upbringing. Perhaps we were simply reverting to form? Ma said that at least with a good reputation early in life, we'd likely never get into too much trouble later . . .

The cause of the fire was much debated. Our Figgy Barnawarren grew more belligerent 'with every flippin' day 'e lives,' Sister Mac said. He took it upon himself, with what everyone imagined to be a homicide detective's approach, to investigate the fire, the fire that killed twelve people in all. An Aboriginal family were trapped in the creek and met the same fate as Joey. He had tried to reach them, struggling for air in the shallow creek bed, been pushed back and jumped into the nearest tank as the flames came rolling back. Some said it was Mr Barnawarren's beautiful new wife, Constance, who was driving him on, but Mama said it was his sense of justice and his temperament that demanded the trail-blazing, war-like pursuit.

Mr Hunt's continued intransigence that the Koories were to blame fuelled rumours and counter-theories until finally Pa stepped in and put a stop to all conjecture.

'The Aborigines have never been irresponsible on the land, Mr Hunt, as you, a student of history, must certainly know. They burn off to protect life, not destroy it! I must ask you also to consider my wife's feelings in this matter. It is not easy to lose your son, knowing he gave his life to help these people.'

Sometimes I wanted to scream, 'Come back, Joey! Come back!' but it would not have done. Screaming would not have brought him back for me to get to know him, play with him, laugh with him, grow up with him, cheer him at the Melbourne Cricket Ground, be a bridesmaid at his wedding to Amelia Moon . . . or Saucy Barnawarren. Ruth talked about him often, as though he were still here. I resented her intimacy and said so. 'Why don't you just stop talking about him, Ruth? He was my brother, not yours!'

Tears rose slowly in her dark eyes. Her striking, shiny brown face flushed with an equivocal pain I did not understand.

'It's better to talk about it, Billy,' she said. 'You gotta get it out. You've lost your brother and your dog and your best friend. It's an awful lot to carry.'

'But I don't miss Frannie or Chocolate, Ruthy, and I hated Joey half the time!' escaped my lips before I could stop it. Months of confusion and anguish spilt over, as though they had been lying close to the surface all along. 'I didn't realize until I saw Joey's little body on the horse how much I loved him, and now it's too late!' I sobbed uncontrollably. 'I miss him so much, Ruthy, it hurts all the time and it's getting worse. I must be a terrible girl, what's to become of me? Why don't I miss Chocolate and Frannie? I knew them better than I knew Joey.' Ruth couched me in her arms. 'Why did God have to take him? Why didn't God show me how to love him when he was alive? What's the sense in knowing now?'

Pa found us huddled together on the verandah, our last pure days of childhood washing away with our tears and the first decent rain in months. We were cold and wet, and desperately alone. I had turned thirteen the day before. Ruth had turned twenty-one. We had long since celebrated our birthdays on the same day. The difference in our ages had only lately become overtly obvious, her body and mind ahead of mine, lush and strong from the years at Rosebery.

Pa sat down slowly, stiffly, beside us on the step, his pale blue eyes ever thoughtful. His hair had thinned and greyed over recent months, the ready smile less frequent than before. I saw him as he was, as if for the very first time. I looked from him to Ruth and saw her too, the dark brown face, a face I loved, had always loved. Her eyes were black and stained like Pa's, both older, wiser than I would ever be.

'There are many different kinds of love,' Pa's soothing voice began, tugging at my injured heart with the strength of his own. 'Love can't be forced. You are too hard on yourself, Billy. Brothers and sisters take time to grow and show their love for one another. Sometimes . . . sometimes it's easier to love a girlfriend, or a dog. But Joey knew you loved him, though you never told him. He's in heaven with Frances and Chocolate now, and they don't want you to be unhappy.'

'Oh Papa,' I cried, 'I have so much to live up to, don't I?'

'You just have to be yourself, dear. You have a lot of love to give,' he added, wiping my face, then his own.

'But I miss him so, Pa,' I began anew, fresh tears to replace those gone.

'I know, my darling, but you must be brave and comfort Ruth. She's your dearest friend now – she misses him too.'

My heart quickened as I felt the softest sting. Only Pa could reach that deep dark place where ego lives, in spite of everything, intact and barely scarred. It shocked me that he could know my vanity, my life-blood, so well! I turned to Ruth and hugged her, told her I loved her, told her she was beautiful, told her I would die for her. She hugged me back, told me how much she loved me too.

Pa left us there. I heard him blow his nose, heard Ma ask if he'd like a cup of tea, heard the bellbirds in the bottlebrush and a distant brolga seeking company. Heard Ruth telling me she'd fallen head over heels in love with Micky O'Ryan.

Finally 1927 drew to a close. We were all relieved to see it go, with only New Year's Eve to get through.

To our surprise, it was nowhere near as bad as we'd expected, mainly because of our racist, dyed-in-the-wool pastor, Reverend Moon. Preaching less hellfire and damnation since the fire, he'd conspired with Father O'Donagan to hold a combined anniversary service for all the lives we had lost on Black Tuesday, as that terrible day had become known.

When Ma first heard about it, she frankly didn't believe it. 'Giles? Holding a nondenominational service? Impossible!' dismissing it out of hand as a joke, in particularly poor taste. Since Joey's death Ma's commitment to God was less strident, but any idea of a link with the Catholics was guaranteed to arouse strong indignation.

The bearer of the news was our head teacher, Mr Hunt, a man not noted for humour, or open-mindedness.

'Not only that,' he continued plaintively, 'but he intends to allow any of those slovenly creek people to enter the church, if they so choose!' Mr Hunt always avoided calling the Aborigines by name when he could get away with it. Pa said the Education Department regional inspector had told him to avoid discussing the Aborigines at all, but if they came up, he must address them correctly in class. 'Everyone knows you can't teach the buggers, but it's new policy to avoid saying so,' Mr Hunt had said.

Ma was positively floored by the news. Pa was tickled pink. I couldn't see what the fuss was about. Ruth had been coming to church with us for as long as I could remember. Nobody ever said a word about it. Yet suddenly, the likelihood of black folk in white churches was the talk of Kurra. 'Did ya hear old Giles has finally lost his grip, allowing Koories into church?'

'I feel sorry for Amelia and David you know, poor, motherless kids.'

'They've got Miss Prinkett. I s'pose she's better'n nothin'.'

'Not if the Reverend's gone soft on the blacks, it ain't.'

And so they gossiped, idle tongues deepening the narrow confines of their narrow worlds.

We had a lovely service anyway, though Ruth was still the only Aborigine in church that day.

As life will have it, when the town folk had long since breathed a sigh of relief that 'all that Abo integration nonsense is done with', our wireless brought it right back. Rustling away before the easterlies had cut us into the winter of 1929, we learnt of the stirring of the natives.

An Anglican minister in Western Australia told a Royal Commission that 10,000 Aborigines had been exterminated by devious means over the past fifty years. Once the ABC had broken the news, Mr Barnawarren started a weekly bulletin, keeping us up to date with the latest findings.

'Totally irresponsible journalism,' Sister Mac declared, copying someone from the hospital more educated than she. 'We wouldn't be gettin' no trouble from the Koories if it wasn't for the whites openin' their big stupid mouths.'

Most agreed, but Figgy stayed with it, more out of defiance than good sense. Tempers flared and rumours ran as fast as our bush telegraph could carry them. The Royal Commission heard that when the natives became a nuisance, cyanide was put in their meat and arsenic in their flour. Murders in jail were commonplace. By June, they were averaging twenty a month, our *Kurra Mail* reported. Nobody knew what to believe, but a few of the old-timers fell oddly quiet.

Without warning, we got some first-hand information at Rosebery, and Ruth changed, seemingly overnight.

Sabella and Luther Prescott had never fully recovered from Black Tuesday. What with Mr Prescott's war injuries, and the shock and burns, he was forced to put the Cranberry Vineyard in the hands of a manager and move into town. Sabella's inheritance was of little use now – 'What good's money when your health's gone?' Ma declared. Stranded on a farm, without friends nearby, without Mackie at the ready? 'Luther's a proud man, a war hero, the best! He can't accept strangers in his home, paid for by his wife, for goodness' sakes!' she wrapped the situation up conclusively.

Pa stepped in immediately. The State Government

and the War Department agreed to let them renovate the disused barracks on our station acreage. It was still a barn, but Sabella and Ma prettied it up. The Prescotts called it home.

Unemployment was rising rapidly. The Government released some funds for reconditioning of the railway lines. At last Pa had work for casual linesmen, but Luther was too old and tired for such tasks. He and Sabella continued light duties two or three days a week for the new manager at Cranberry, but Luther acknowledged his days as a vigneron were over.

They stopped in often for tea. Mr Prescott looked older than I'd ever dreamt a man could look. He was thin and wily at the best of times, the legacy of surviving General Ludendorff's offensive at the rail junction of Amiens, Pa said. He looked like too much life had worn him down now; he had shrunk some more and his face was grey. The sparkle in his eyes had gone, a dull piercing stare in place of the mild amusement I'd always found so easy to like.

'They're employing them for a week's work, then ordering them to dig their own graves,' he stammered, barely before he'd sat down. The latest news bulletins of the black deaths story was obviously central to his mood. 'We have to stop them, Nathan, we can't stand by and let this happen, but I'm too weak,' he gesticulated wildly, his arms dropping heavily from the effort, or the thought.

'Slowly, slowly,' Pa urged anxiously, picking up the tea cup, holding it to Mr Prescott's mouth. 'A nice hot cuppa will help,' he encouraged fondly, as a mother to a sickly child. Yet, there was naught but manhood here. I had the strangest feeling they'd been through this before.

Mr Prescott sipped the tea and took some strength from Pa. 'Those mongrels managing Cranberry, Nathan . . . they're buying the blacks for a week's work,' he began again, shiny globules of sweat swelling up on his high forehead. 'They work them from dawn to dusk, digging new fields, then they move them to one end of the field and get them to dig a huge hole. When they're all in there, digging, they . . . they . . .' He slumped forward, sobbing like a baby.

Ma moved quickly, dampening a towel, handing it to Pa. He placed it behind Mr Prescott's fallen head. Mrs Prescott sat, unchanged, a blind pulled over her eyes, as though nothing had happened. It came to me suddenly that she was dreaming, not of our world at all.

'And they opened fire!' He was becoming hysterical. 'They opened fire, Nathan, like the Germans at Amiens!' he screamed, throwing the towel from his neck, raising his head like a wild dingo on the range.

Ruth jumped up, her chair flying behind her, hitting the icebox. The door flew open and the milk fell out, splashing wildly. The bottle shattered. She lunged forward, back across the table, her long brown arms outstretched. She grabbed Mr Prescott's protruding ears, closed her fists around them, black knuckles turning white. His eyes returned hers in abject fear, fixed, suspended in shock.

For many long seconds her eyes fired rounds of hatred into his. Then, suddenly, when the breathing had stopped and the madness peaked, or the barrel emptied, she opened her hands, her body lying halfway across the table, white streaked palms facing upwards to heaven. She was breathing heavily now; her face had drained. He began breathing in short, light chesty puffs; his cheeks were florid.

Nobody moved. The clock struck six. When the chiming stopped, Ruth stood up, smoothing her dress, absently picking up slithers of glass at her feet, throwing a cloth over the white puddle on the floor.

She stepped over it and walked out the back door. I stirred.

'Leave her be, Billy,' Ma said firmly. 'She needs to be alone.'

In an instant Ma was up, mopping the floor, making an omelette with left-over chopped lamb, chatting away about absolutely everything and nothing. Pa opened a bottle of Madeira he'd had since last Christmas and poured everyone a tumblerful, even me. Ma was cross because he didn't bother to go into the fortress room for the crystal. Pa said later he was afraid to leave in case Mrs Prescott came out of her trance. 'And in any case,' he'd added, 'there are some days when you need a tumblerful.'

Ruth stayed out that night and all of the next day. By mid-afternoon, we were worried sick. She was trained to our ways and had not gone walkabout since her return in 1923. Our nearest sheriff was an hour away in Tarrenbonga; no point in calling him. Figgy Barnawarren was the best bet. Ma was pleased to admit his strengths, ever since he'd brought about the downfall of Carter Pip. James rushed over when Pa discovered our town's demagogue had driven to Tarrenbonga, chasing a hot tip on the black murders story.

'Leave it with me for an hour or two,' James said mysteriously. 'I've got an idea. He'd galloped off, clutching his rifle to his thigh, inadvertently heightening our panic.

Like all the young men in Kurra since the fire, James had a confident air about him. He sat tall in the saddle, his bronzed skin offsetting a rush of long blond curls falling incongruously around his fine-boned face. Had his hair been short, in the new fashion of the day, he may have looked his age. As it was, he looked about sixteen, when he was nigh on twenty. He spoke like Joey spoke – used to speak –

with the polished accent of town living, not at all like the roughnecks of the bush. It was hard to figure, when we'd all been taught in the same classroom, by the same teacher.

I had wondered a lot about class. If James Barnawarren and David Moon had it, but the O'Ryans didn't, why did they all pack a rifle and mount a horse the same way? Why were they mates together, when girls of different class could never mix? 'You can't change your station,' Ma said, 'unless you marry up. Since men like to marry down, you're very fortunate to be brought up a stationmaster's daughter.' If class and a decent husband were based on Pa's profession, why did I need an education, I'd asked.

'A Presbyterian your age should know better,' I was told, firmly ruling out any chance of a satisfying answer to another of life's great puzzles.

James rode off heroically into the sunset, as far as I was concerned. I was passionately worried about Ruth, of course, but my heart told me she was safe. She was black and strong and beautiful. James was blond, strong and handsome and would rescue her, carrying her back sidesaddle on his horse, her red dress, cut on the cross by us the Sunday before, flapping wildly in the wind.

He told me about that day, many seasons later. Dear James, what a good friend he turned out to be.

He'd pulled up hard at Mini Mini, in the rubble of the old homestead. There were many changes there. A cabin had been constructed, rough and ready; three large rooms and two outhouses. The kitchen was a makeshift shed, no better than the rest, the stove smoking badly through the second-hand tin chimney. Spinster Jane, Mrs O'Ryan's sister, looked up from her crouched position in the yard, filling a rusty bucket that had once seen babies born. James alighted from his horse and stared blankly at the tank. He used to stare at tanks, hoping for rain. Now he stared at a boiling pot, burning human flesh until the stench was louder than the screaming flames. We all did.

'Who do ya want?' Jane acknowledged casually. Sister Mac said she was casual from her boots up and even worse than her sister used to be. Ruth said Mackie ought to know.

James raised his hat, following her succinct lead. 'Where's the blokes please, Jane?'

'Out workin', I 'spect,' she shrugged. She had no regard for town folk manners. Fancy riders on a Saturday afternoon.

'Micky in the main cabin with Ruth?' he shrugged back. It was impossible to call it Mini Mini.

'Might try the kitchen,' she begrudged. James said you could tell what she was thinking: the beautiful people reckon they're Christmas. But he tapped his hat, remounted and circled the debris, pulling up at the kitchen outhouse, slowly tying his horse to the post. Now that he had found her, what should he do next?

He knocked, tentatively. The door was not properly shut. 'Hello!' he called excessively loudly, pushing it open. 'Hello there,' he repeated. 'Anybody home?'

Ruth was half draped in a man's red and white striped robe, gaping at the top and crunched in suggestive folds at the bottom. She sat on a large iron crate, a depleted mug of beer in one hand, a half-smoked cigarette in the other. Micky was making art of the rolling of tobacco, his long, thin fingers neatly filling, lips poised to lick, both hands standing by to fold.

'G'day, Jimmy,' he acknowledged laconically, closing his latest *Flying Machine* magazine, lifting a pile of them from the nearest crate.

'G'day, Jimmy,' Ruth echoed. James helped himself to a beer and sat down.

'The Batchelors are worried about you, Ruth,' he understated the situation. 'They want you home.'

'I am home,' Ruth said, tossing back her thick mop of shiny black curls defiantly.

Micky sat up sharply. 'Hey, listen, Ruthy, you can't stay here. I mean, ya gotta go home, love.'

'I am home!' she repeated stubbornly.

Micky was visibly worried now. 'Hey listen, Ruthy,' he said again, 'I mean, you can stay a week or so if ya like, but it wouldn't do for no longer, you know, what with Isobella and Veronica and –'

'And what?' she pounced. 'I'm an Abo and they're working my people for a week on Prescotts' old property, then killing them. You want to bed me for a week then kill me too? That it, mate?'

'Oh Ruth,' James gasped, 'where'd you get such crazy ideas?'

'They're not crazy ideas, Jimmy,' she snapped bitterly. 'You live in the town and think you know all there is to know about the black murders from the Royal Commission. Why don't you tell your father to start investigating in his own backyard! Tell him, Micky, for God's sake tell him!'

James looked from one to the other, Micky turned away. 'What is this, Micky?' James reached for his shoulders, shaking him violently. 'What's she saying? What's going on here? Answer me!'

'It's bloody true, mate, bloody true.' Micky's eyes focused on his boots. 'Only found out about it meself, last week,' he added hastily, all hope of approbation dashed the moment it was said.

'How did Ruth find out?' James asked directly, suddenly unable to acknowledge her presence. Micky outlined the events of the evening past, as told to him by Ruth.

Ruth sat between them, staring blindly into her empty mug. Her face had hardened with the day, the light gone from her eyes, her body limp and strangely calm. She had no expectations from these young, white men, young white men who felt some shame but had no power to act. She had seen and heard too much to dream, or pretend it hadn't happened. She was old enough to understand Ma and Pa's position too, and smart enough to sense the dubiety of her future.

Because of her years with us, she was also proud and stubborn. Her first reaction had been to flee into the willing arms of Micky O'Ryan, neither seeing how her life would be, nor thinking through the fearful implications. Now, sitting in the kitchen with her two friends, and foes, hunched pitifully before her, the full force of life's cruel truths ascended. Instinctively, she straightened up, pulling the open gown around her breasts, cutting off all sexual favours lingering from the soft, black mounds of skin. Thus bodily secured, she closed her heart and opened her mind. Sharp and dispassionate, the Nemesis began to form. It was not quite clear yet, but she would work on it. She had nothing to lose; her conscience would not hold sway again.

Micky had finished talking. James' eyes were wet, though no tears came. He struggled for words, his mouth open for a moment, but there was nothing in reserve. They sat with their arms on their knees, heads drooped over, drinks forgotten. Ruth strode across to the main cabin, quickly dressed. She re-emerged resolutely, breaking the silence, and the mood.

'I suppose it is rather inconsiderate to disappear, just like that. It's not Mrs Rosey or Mr Nathan's fault that this has happened, is it?' The young men stared, wide-eyed. They had not expected this. Ruth seemed not to notice, standing tall and confident in the late afternoon light, her voice as inviting as her firm young body, now suggestively robed in the red dress with the full, circular skirt.

'I guess I owe them an apology. They treat me like their own really, and, of course, I am half-white, you know.' She paused just long enough to ensure the message had been firmly received. 'I'm an experienced telegraph operator too, and I'm planning to get a pilot's licence!' What an inspired thought, she flattered herself. This might even turn out to be fun.

'You're what?' Micky almost laughed. 'Girls can't fly, Ruthy!'

'When I've saved enough money, you'll see,' she smiled, wondering if she'd gone perhaps a little too far. 'Now I suppose we should head back to Rosebery, James. Save everyone worrying any more.'

James stood up eagerly. 'Well, I must say you're handling this rather well, Ruth,' he cast a furtive glance at Micky, 'and we're very proud of you.'

Micky was vaguely unsettled. 'Hey, wait a minute,' he scrambled for a line. 'Why don't you stay over, Ruth? Go home tomorra? James won't mind ridin' back and telling them you're okay, just . . . restin'.' He winked.

'No thanks, no thanks, Micky. This way, there's no need for them to know what we've been up to. You just took me in 'cos I was upset. But I won't be able to visit afternoons any more. It's not right,' she added with a new-found piousness that made her feel positively superior.

'Oh com'on, Ruth?' he started.

'No, I've been stupid, cheating . . . stupid. I can't imagine why I've been wasting time with the likes of you anyway. Why, I wouldn't marry a boy from Kurra if my life depended on it!' she said. 'See ya, Micky.'

'Marry . . .!' he began to laugh, then thought better of it. 'She'll be back, little black whore,' he spoke aside to James, consoling his ego easily. 'Puttin' on jam with the boys in Kurra won't get 'er too far. We've all kissed 'er, and 'alf 'ave bedded her, if a quarter the tales be true,' he added.

The more he thought about it, the more amused he became. Half-white? Well, he didn't know about that. That was a bit disquieting, but a pilot's licence? That was preposterous! And he told the male population of Kurra later that before James and Ruth were out of sight, he'd shrugged off the snub and was laughing happily to himself.

Ma and Pa were relieved by Ruth's return, though Ma mixed her relief with censure. I overheard her reminding Pa that Ruth had never been her idea of a good example for Rachel and she certainly hoped this was the last of such escapades. I was overjoyed, of course, but it was obvious my Ruth had changed. Tougher, sharper, she carried a fierce burden of outrage and sorrow at the Cranberry Vineyard murders, though in spite of lengthy investigations, there was to be no punishment for the guilty to help ease her pain.

As the days unfolded, however, Ruth found herself with a completely new direction in life, one that would change all of ours irrevocably.

# FIVE

# 1929...

I had made up my mind that if I should reach the absurdly ripe age of sixteen without getting my first period, I was going to join the Micks and become a nun.

Why my freakish, bloodless state had confirmed such a desperately logical juxtaposition was perfectly clear to me but when I dared think aloud to the women in my life, Sister Mac was the first to throw her head back and roar with laughter.

'An' if menstruation does 'appen?' she ribbed, in her best medical terminology.

'I'll guess I'll break into radio, then films,' I answered dejectedly.

Ruth was simultaneously languishing with a similar problem, though unknown of course to Ma and Sister Mac. I argued that at least she knew she could continue to be a woman of the world, regardless of whether the blood flowed in time, or not. When I asked her what she was going to do if her curse came – I couldn't bring myself to use Sister Mac's medical word – she sighed downheartedly and said she supposed she'd get her pilot's licence, then join Qantas or the Flying Doctor Service.

We did our chores and telegraph work as quickly as possible, both anxious to finish each task in order to sneak away to check for spotting on the crutch of our bloomers. If the station toilets were busy, or the men were lolling around on a smoko break, we'd be too embarrassed to go near, leaving only my bedroom upstairs or the bathroom off the fortress room. There were only so many times we could charge upstairs in a day without arousing suspicion, and since well-bred girls never went to the bathroom together *and* we had to pass Ma to get there, our days were long and agitated. The radio, local paper and weekly flicks were our only salvation. We had little spare time but maximized every moment, dreaming dreams that depended solely on the shedding of blood for implementation.

Our wireless had expanded to the far reaches of the nation with 300,000 licensed sets across Australia, guaranteeing an audience of more than a million people at any given time! It was difficult to comprehend. Talking pictures had arrived too. Al Jolson was our new hero. The Hollywood bigwigs decided the talkies were here to stay, setting up an Academy for annual awards to help the industry score world attention. Ma argued that was precisely the story they wanted us to believe. She said they were really hoping for the impossible – a House of Windsor legitimacy for America's fairytale kings and queens. When Mr Walt Disney created a cartoon character called Mickey Mouse and starred him on sound film, Ma finally conceded that they might perhaps manage to achieve the dignity of the British middle classes.

In Micky and Ruth's world of aviation, history was being made at a cracking pace. The first seaplane had long since travelled the round trip from Westminster to Australia. The Flying Doctor Service had finally been established, challenging outback settlers to accept a physical security they had never before dared to even dream about. When Amelia Earhart flew across the Atlantic, Ruth and I jumped and screamed so loudly, we missed most of her speech. 'Now we'll see who says *and pigs might fly*!' Ruth gloated wildly.

'Ruth!' Ma chastised.

'Well, it's true, Ma,' I rushed into the fray.' Don't you feel proud of Miss Earhart? I mean, really, really proud?'

'It's the most irresponsible thing any woman could do and I'm amazed you girls can't see it. Risking life and limb, taking incredible chances, and for what? Let the men do the exploring, I say; it's wrong for women to get involved. You will come to no happy endings entertaining the remotest thoughts on this matter,' she concluded on the same high ground with which she'd begun, foolishly switching off the wireless, as though that would confirm her predilection.

The *Kurra Mail* carried the story on the front cover. We read it again, studying more closely the soft face and shapely body of Miss Earhart. She did not seem at all masculine to us, including the fashionable flying trouser suit she was wearing. We'd been wearing overalls on the station for years. On page two, Reverend Moon had written a scathing letter, taking the same point of view as Ma. It occurred to me that he may have plagiarized her words, it sounded so similar. 'It is morally reprehensible for women to take up flying; their responsibilities are to their homes and families,' the letter commenced.

'We don't have families,' I said recklessly.

'Don't be flippant, Billy. It doesn't become you,' Ma rebuked.

We read on. He believed it was mentally dangerous for young women to be exposed to a larger world and the wicked ways of men. Women must be the strength of the nation and if they were permitted to do a man's job, outside war times we supposed, they would soon lose their superior standing in the home and become 'just one of the boys'.

'That's the first time I ever heard scrubbing floors and cooking meals referred to as a superior standing,' Ruth laughed cynically.

'I like being one of the boys,' I contributed.

The final point Reverend Moon made was women's lack of physical prowess to handle the job and there was the hint of suggestion that any women stupid enough to follow Miss Earhart's example may well find themselves developing male muscles and ruining their chances of fulfilling their ordained and Christian, biological function in life.

'Never knows when to stop, that man,' Ruth observed like a little old lady, reading the last paragraph aloud. '"Women who do men's work disinherit their gifts of feminity and the miraculous blessing of motherhood. They should not be tolerated; our law courts should take a stand now, to save these misguided, blasphemous women from themselves, and society at large."'

Ruth looked questioningly at Ma. 'How would he know? He doesn't have a wife and I sure didn't see him doing a man's work round here while all the real men were at the war. I saw the women taking the reins though! You can't seriously agree with him, Mrs Rosey?'

'That's quite enough, Ruth,' Ma said unsteadily. Like me, Ruth had been listening to Ma and Sister Mac for a long time.

When it came to sharing our dreams and secrets, Ruth was my blood sister. I had no perception of the double life she'd been leading, but I was aware she'd kissed every boy in Kurra and thought it simply marvellous. All the boys knew too, of course, but Ruth assured me none of the other girls did. True to her promise, she had borrowed *The Facts of Life* from the library for me and while it explained everything I needed to know about periods, the reproduction habits of the birds and the bees had left me more confused than ever. Since they didn't get periods, what could they teach me about humans?

With the taboo subjects of bodily functions and the differences between men and women suddenly being discussed relatively openly in our house, my arrested development had forced its way into my consciousness. I supposed I'd lived a sheltered life, but there had always been so many distractions, the days had rushed by in a frenzy of activities. Now they dragged interminably, each day taking me closer to my sixteenth birthday next year and the grown-up party Ma had promised. I became convinced that I was dying from an incurable, bloodless disease. There could be no other explanation. It never occurred to me that my body might be ripening slowly because of a sickly childhood, or that one day I would look back gratefully on such a late harvest.

Startled by the instant avant-garde approach to life now prevailing at Rosebery, I was gravely uncertain – about everything! It was not possible to contemplate a private discussion with Ma that might have alleviated my terror. I had not been taught to be open about such matters and anyway, she would probably laugh like Sister Mac and tell me to stop behaving like a girl. I'd made a promise to myself after Joe's death that I'd never behave like a girl again. I knew Pa would understand, of course, but how would I find the words to explain the situation to him? Ruth, my one true confidante, was sympathetic but preoccupied with her own predicament. We were a sorry pair.

If anyone noticed our depressed moods and furtive behaviour, they decided against counsel. Ma's bosom rose and fell with her eyes whenever she caught me staring into space. I could hear her muttering to herself, 'All things pass, given time.' I was certain this was the one occasion she would be proved terribly, horribly wrong.

The morning of Thursday, 24 October 1929 dawned like any other day in Kurra. The heat was already well up by seven in the morning, along with the chooks and cows and magpies and old Mr Prescott, who'd taken to walking over to our back verandah at first light and nodding off in Pa's old rocker until Ma nudged him awake with a hot cuppa. I staggered wearily down to the kitchen, feeling even more out of sorts than I had the day before. 'Can I stay home from school today, Ma?' I pleaded. 'I don't feel too good.' Ma put a thick, floury hand on my forehead. 'No temperature,' she declared. 'Don't dawdle, child, off and have your bath.'

At two o'clock in the afternoon, when class concluded for sport, I stood up from my desk and felt water trickling down my legs. I looked furtively behind me and saw the blood, my stomach curdling in my throat at the very sight of it. The familiar sensation that I was going to faint did not eventuate. A macabre fascination for the total plausibility of the blood rushing from my head down through my body, out of my insides and down my legs, shocked me into a sharpened consciousness. I sat awkwardly, instinctively burying my head under the lid of the desk, willing, praying that when I looked up, everyone would be gone.

I was in luck. Mr Merryweather had arranged a mixed cricket match that always guaranteed an eager exit to the oval. I eased my way out of the desk, a momentary nauseous lump rising in my throat again at the sight of the crimson puddle around me. I scrunched my old tunic up between my legs and staggered to the lockers. With only one hand towel (Ma was more frugal than ever lately, which puzzled me because her housekeeping must have stretched further since Joey had died), I realized it was going to take a long time to clean up. The trough was by the side door, the side of the toilet block.

Eyes fixed on the path, I rushed in and out, rinsing and mopping up, rinsing some more. Finally, I put the towel in my panties and studied my tunic. There was nothing to be done but take it off and wash it too. Nobody came. In my two-tone grey tunic, light at the top with a dark, spotty pleatless skirt hugging my legs, I crept around the back of the school house, my heart thumping wildly.

I had got my period! I was alive at last! I was free, free as the Kurrajong Ranges, free as the bellbirds and the brolgas and the bumble bees in the *Facts of Life* book, free to be the first woman of the radio waves, free to be famous and brave and strong, free to kiss boys and get a good reputation . . . free!

I took the long way home, singing to myself, shouting my secret to the cows by the roadside, pedalling uncomfortably on the wet seat with the folds of my tunic crunched tightly around me. But I didn't care. Blood is wonderful, I laughed to myself – this is no curse, this is no ghastly woman's lot. This is the beginning of my life! And yet my euphoria could not wipe away the mess of me, the bonds of respectability never far from sight. I could not go home like this.

I would go down to the point and watch the sea roll in. I would wait until evening, until my tunic was dry. Nobody would know I had missed sport and elocution. Nobody would know my secret. I needed time to think, to dream, to plan the way my life was going to be, to think about my body and what it means to be a woman. Yes, I would keep it all to myself, for just a little while.

I sat on my rock at Bunyip Point and thought about

all the people I knew and what it was going to be like to be a woman.

Jock O'Ryan was seventeen and still big for his age, though his shoulders had filled out to match his stomach and his red hair had turned a mousy brown, like the rest of the clan. Instead of the fair, freckled face of his childhood, he'd become one large freckle, spreading from his forehead across his face, down his chest and back, along his arms, up his slightly bowed legs. Two years in the saddle could do that to any man. Unfortunately, in spite of his improved appearance, he was still the same old Jock, protective of his sisters, terribly well-mannered, serious, religious, righteous! He was a bore.

It was Micky, now the oldest living O'Ryan, who captured our imaginations, the man about town that the boys tried to emulate and the girls wanted to marry. A crack horseman and the ringer of the sheds, he was now learning to fly aeroplanes. Tall, defiant, handsome and tough, he was our real life movie star, the epitome of romance and adventure. Ruth said he was more arrogant than defiant, more rough than tough, yet her eyes still glazed over when she spoke of him and I knew she was still in love with him, no matter how often she denied it.

Isobella and Veronica had long since taken up their duties at Mini Mini, feeding the men, keeping the shacks in order and doing the general chores around the property. If Frances and Sarah had not been burnt to death, they would have been fifteen and seventeen this day; Ma said the older girls might have had more chance if the younger ones had lived. I didn't know what she meant and when I asked . . . well, my timing was inappropriate.

James and Saucy Barnawarren had grown up graciously, much to everyone's surprise. Saucy was a stunner with her masses of red hair and flaming brown eyes that almost crackled when she was angry. More and more, she looked like her stepmother, Constance, whom Ma begrudgingly respected.

'I suppose she's done quite a good job on the youngsters,' she mused one day, following the announcement of Saucy's acceptance to Melbourne Teachers' College. 'Particularly useless trying to turn her into a teacher, of course,' she spurned easily, 'but it does show some degree of application on the part of the girl, I must say.' That's one thing Ma always did – give credit when it was due. She even suggested that Constance Barnawarren must have had good genes to step in, as she did, and 'turn those two wild ones into ladies and gentlemen. James rescued Ruth, after all!'

James was twenty and six feet four, 'blond and bronzed' as we'd been loudly observing for years, his fine-boned face, longish blond curls and pale smoky grey eyes still giving him the appearance of a growing boy. He'd completed his journalism apprenticeship, so Figgy declared anyway, and had joined the journalists' union – why exactly, nobody knew. It drew comment, but little ongoing interest. He was a quiet young man who knew the difference between right and wrong and didn't have an aggressive bone in his body: 'Undoubtedly, it's just a passing fad,' folk said. Pa suggested Figgy's overpowering personality might have pushed him into it, ashamed of his son's gentle manners and self-effacing personality. Ma reckoned it was hard for a boy to be tough when his father was so strong.

Amelia and David Moon, Ma could explain in finite detail, were another cup of tea altogether. Though I disagreed, I kept my opinions to myself. Amelia belonged on the cover of *English Woman*; her complexion was pale and creamy and her long blonde hair hung in willowy folds, as though the sun was shining straight through. She was five feet eight, slim, nearly thin, but for an unfashionable bust line. The flat look was in, but men still seemed to like the bulgy look. Of course, she was no brighter than she'd ever been, but she was so adorable, I couldn't help thinking only women seemed to notice her limited brain.

David Moon had just turned eighteen. He was six feet tall with thick black wavy hair and deep-set midnight eyes. He was handsome, in a slick kind of fashion – we couldn't appreciate his refined, cavalier manners. Instinctively, the roughriders style sat more comfortably with our country ways. He was leaving for Sydney University in the new year. His marks were not good enough in Matriculation for medicine, but he'd had twelve months' private tutoring from Mr Hunt and finally snuck in without a test. Reverend Moon had contacts in high places. The effort David had made could not be disputed, though. Ma said he was a nasty, scheming piece of work, born of a mother of easy virtue who'd abandoned him and his sister shortly after birth. This was not easy to swallow, given that Reverend Moon's wife was known to have died of consumption on the journey over from Southampton. I followed Pa's example and listened attentively. Right or wrong, there was usually an insight into human nature to be gleaned and if I was to become the first woman in radio in Australia, I was fast beginning to appreciate that I would need every bit of insight I could get. Nevertheless, if Amelia and David Moon were not destined for one Great Marriage and one Great Career, I'd swallow a tablespoon of liver oil every day for a month.

Perched smugly on my rock at Bunyip Point, thoughts came to me of the Dreamtime. Ruth said that once upon a time the bunyip was a monster, bigger than an elephant, like a bullock with eyes like live coals and tusks like a walrus. Legend had it they lived in the lakes and the rivers and the oceans of time. I was a bunyip, I thought, a miniature bunyip and Ma was a giant bunyip. She had been right to engineer the removal of Carter Pip from the station-master's job all those years ago. Pa was the most wonderful man in the whole universe. How long ago was that? It seemed like another lifetime, Joey and me, Ruth and Wendy Barr and Chocolate. No, Wendy Barr had faded away by then and Ruth was back in The Orphanage. It was just Joey and me. And Chocolate.

I wondered why we never got another dog. Of course, there were the station dogs, but they didn't count. Why hadn't Ma had another baby? Joey had been gone nearly three years now. Maybe if Ruth was pregnant, we could keep her baby. Pa would be glad. But no, Ma would never allow it.

The sun had changed colour suddenly. I ran over the rocks and hopped onto my bicycle, a chaotic mess of crumpled, stained grey tunic and glorious, unfettered pride. If I hurried, I'd have time to change before tea, without anyone being the wiser.

If I could have died, it would surely have been better than the embarrassment I fell into, head-on. Everyone I grew up with, and some others besides, were assembled at Rosebery that fateful night. Listening to the radio with Ma and Pa? Stockmen and jackaroos, linesmen and tradesmen were crowded onto the back verandah; Blondy had rigged up a speaker so they could hear the news from our kitchen wireless. Everyone else was crowded inside. Ruth said later it was just like a corroboree before the dancing started; she remembered from a long time ago, before the white missionaries and the Government men came to their creek shack outback of Stuart Town.

There were no signs of celebration tonight though, no painted Aboriginal dancers, no fiddles or accordions in sight. A sombre anticipation prevailed, each news bulletin more devastating than the last. I heard that a street had crashed. Dazed brokers wandering around the floor of an exchange, clutching wads of investors' instructions to *sell at any price*. My head was spinning, eyes blurred, no focus, no sense of reason. A street had crashed? Nothing more.

I woke next morning, stripped of all pride, aware that my appearance the evening before would have shattered the assembled throng, and probably nearly killed Ma. The station was still.

I climbed out of bed, tiptoed downstairs and turned on the wireless. Thirteen million shares had changed hands in New York yesterday. Police riot squads had been called in to disperse hysterical crowds. That it had occurred thousands of miles away made it no less disastrous. America was the wealthiest, most glamorous country in the world to us. Since the staggering success of Wall Street, anyone with fifty pounds to their name had invested on the Sydney stock exchange. Our interdependence on one another's lives and fortunes underwrote the panic that would spread along Oodoolay Street, down to the fishermen on the point, across the surrounding properties at the foot of the Kurrajong Ranges. Slowly I grasped the scene I had walked in on, and sat down on the back step and howled. While I'd been sitting on a rock in narcissistic bliss, the world had been disintegrating! What a selfish, irresponsible girl I was . . . when would I ever learn? Mostly, I was angry for missing out on the excitement, but my anger quickly turned to horror when the *Business Matters* programme following the news opened with America's Radio Corp collapse, its shares worth two hundred per cent less than yesterday. I came inside and sat down by the great machine and howled anew.

While I slept, my world had crumbled. No radio! The thought was unbearable. What would we do? What did we do before? And what about my career? 'I don't believe in You any more, God!' I sobbed aloud. 'You're a fake, You're cruel and I hate you.'

'My goodness me,' Ma's powerful voice sounded close by. 'It's not the end of the world you know, child.'

'But it is, Ma, it is!'

'Don't be a silly billy, Rachel, you've been fainting since you were very young and the boys would never have noticed the blood. You did a good job, cleaning yourself up before you got home.'

I looked at her in astonishment, initially missing her backhanded compliment. 'But, Ma, what about the collapse of Radio Corp? It'll follow here too, won't it?' My voice had shrunk, along with my tears.

It was Ma's turn to look astonished. 'My goodness, dear, is that all this is about?'

'Ma, how can you say that? My whole future depends on the wireless. I have no other plans!'

She brushed one hand predictably across her thin, prematurely greying hair and studied me seriously. I could sense that something very important was being decided, here and now. In my wildest dreams, I could not have imagined the challenge Ma had in mind for me.

'The University of Queensland offers scholarships every year for bright young men in the law and arts faculties,' she began obscurely. 'To celebrate the new decade, and perhaps because women are starting to make their presence felt in politics,' she paused dramatically, 'they're offering two scholarships for girls from 1930. You pass exams easily, Rachel. If you'd just knuckle down, I think you could win one of those scholarships. At very least, you should aim for marks that will give you accommodation assistance at Melbourne Teachers' College. Somehow we'll find the fifteen-pounds-a-year fees, if we have to. You'll need qualifications, Billy, if you hope to get into radio ahead of the men in the queue!'

The idea of leaving home to pursue an education had certainly occurred to me many times. I had thought of taking Pa aside and asking him how I would go about approaching Ma, but the whole proposition was too ridiculous to consider realistically. Ma would never hear of it – a tertiary education for a woman! The thought of it for her only daughter, Billy Rachel Batchelor, was somehow blasphemous, and besides, Pa would miss me terribly.

'What would Pa think?' I asked involuntarily, my view of the world topsy-turvy all of a sudden.

'He won't like it,' she said scratchily, her teeth grinding together in harmony with her hands. I wondered if she was beginning to rue opening her mouth at all. 'You get on with your studies, child, and leave Pa to me. I'll convince him your only hope is a good education. If he wasn't just a man, it'd be as perfectly plain to him as it is to me. Now, get to work, Rachel, get to those books!' she ordered, like an army major commanding a battle.

I did not wait to be told twice. This *was* my only hope. There was no doubt in my mind that Ma was right. At least I was going to be given the chance to be something better than a failure, or just a girl – or both? I couldn't ask for more than that, could I? And I couldn't help thinking this miraculous chance was because I was the nearest thing to a boy Ma was ever going to get now.

As I turned to my studies with a relentless vigour, determined to guarantee a hundred per cent in every subject, Ruth started vomiting in the mornings. Incongruously, the sicker she became, the bigger her stomach grew.

Not surprisingly, my mother was right onto it. As usual, Ruth and I hovered, overhearing everything. 'We'll have to get Doc Halliday to abort her, Nathan,' she informed my father. 'So much for our efforts to give her a decent home and a Christian upbringing! As I've always said, the genes will out.'

'I don't suppose you put any blame at the boy's door, Rosey, whoever he may be?'

'Of course not, Nathan! Probably some black middle-aged tramp from the creek bed . . . you know how they treat their girls.'

'Ruth is hardly a girl any more, Rosey. Billy's fifteen. That makes her twenty-three, doesn't it? We've kept her in an unnatural situation actually, when you come to think of it . . .'

'Well, I've no intention of thinking of it,' my mother replied. 'I'm not going to deliver a black bastard onto this fine station for love nor money. Mackie won't do it, damn Micks, though heaven knows she agrees with me. You'll have to get Doc Halliday over, Nathan.'

'Does Ruth have any say in it?' Pa asked pointedly.

Ma shot him a sideways glance. By this stage, I was standing on a chair, peering cautiously through the kitchen window. Ma knew Pa's current mood. It would not be wise to push him but she was nonetheless quite adamant a woman was in a better position to know the best thing to be done in a diabolical situation such as this.

As though reading her mind, Pa continued, without waiting for the inevitable counterattack. 'The only boys Ruth has mixed with in recent years, Rose, are white. This is probably the only chance she'll ever get of conceiving a half-caste, let alone finding a white husband. Since you're obviously, and extremely wisely, dear, most inconvenienced at the thought of losing the girl after all these years, I suggest we help her through her confinement. She can continue light housekeeping and telegraph duties, of course. (I'll need her if you insist on this madness of sending Billy to university anyway.) If the father doesn't come forward, we can have the babe adopted out to a good Presbyterian family the moment it's born. This would be much more Christian than taking up the butcher's knife, surely?'

Ma paced around the kitchen table a couple of times, clockwise, then anticlockwise. 'I suppose you're right,' she agreed briskly, as though she knew all along this would be the outcome. She lifted our large black kettle off the wood stove. 'I'm sure you're ready for a cuppa, dear?' she inclined her eyes.

'Why thank you, Rosey,' Pa affected surprise, like he always did. 'What will you tell Billy?'

Ma started, spilling the levied spoon of tea over the freshly washed floor. 'I certainly won't tell her the whole truth,' she replied grimly. 'What will you tell Ruth?'

Pa shook his head. 'I won't tell her anything, dear. She knows we wouldn't have her kicked out on the street.'

Ma's shoulders bristled, her bosom heaved. There was something wrong with his argument, kindly though it was. She did not have what she assumed to be the education to reason it.

Perhaps I would get some and teach her the things her brain could not fathom.

# SIX

# 1930

The Great Depression, the Great Pregnancy of Ruth and the Great Scholarship of Billy Batchelor descended upon Kurra as the New Year dawned.

Before we knew where we were, Ma was orchestrating our moments of history with a singleness of purpose and a relentless energy that almost upstaged the events themselves.

While 'The Soldiers of the Cross' and 'Waltzing Matilda' competed for equal space on our wireless, and the new heroes of our world were Amy Johnson and Donald Bradman, Ma seemed immune to the wider world as she gathered us up in her matriarchal bosom. Her hitherto unconquerable Christian faith however was showing increasing signs of faltering as she grappled with the realities of the changing times. For the first time in her married life, her whole life, she stopped going to church, sending Pa, Ruth and me off alone, always on the pretext of too much to do at Rosebery.

Certainly, there was a great deal to do; the dole queues grew longer every day and Ma had joined forces with Nan who, in addition to the boarding house, now ran the Temperance Tea House to provide daily lunches for the hungry. Nan was an odd friend, as Ma's friends went. She didn't believe in gossiping, had no dress sense whatsoever, and was extraordinarily fat – an endorsement of her excellent tea house, Pa said. 'Gotta 'elp the 'ungry,' was Nan's motto. That was enough for Ma. Our kitchen became an assembly line of soups, pastry, mince and sandwiches.

Ma's Religion Crisis was centred in the Holy Trinity and no amount of discussion with Reverend Moon could lighten it for her. On the one hand, she acknowledged that Christ was sitting at our table, aware of all the misery He had brought upon his people. On the other, she knew the savage tides of the ocean that lapped our shore were outside the Father's own mystery of life. Yet the Holy Spirit had gradually vacated her soul since Joe's death and only work could fill the void. She still mourned the young life, struck down before its time, and rose up to meet the inequity of his death that the Father had caused, through service to every other mother's son in Kurra.

She was angry with Ruth, yet oddly protective of her health and welfare, angry with God, the Father, and angry with Pa. Why had she allowed men to dictate her fortunes, her life, her very blood? What had they ever done to protect her and the things she loved?

Here was the Great Depression, dictated by anonymous men who knew little and cared less for the future of their women and children. Here was Ruth, birthing a white man's child . . . maybe Micky's child, or any one of our fair young men. All care from woman folk, no responsibility from men, except Pa, perhaps. Here was me, her daughter with the boy's name, reaching for the man's world, neither happy with her woman's lot, nor yet understanding the stupidity of the man's world she would take on. The only option was to subjugate, to be strong, stronger. To pull it all together, force them to succumb . . .

Encouragement from Pa, or perhaps the potency of habit or tradition, did see her attend church with us on Easter Sunday, along with nearly one hundred people from our small community. Chairs had to be brought over from the school to accommodate so many. As Ma appeared to me to be pulling away, most of the faithful were returning to the fold, finding comfort through tough times in moments of short ceremony, dedicated to hope for an ultimate reward in the next life, a reward that would surely justify the pain in this.

Pa's beliefs were undergoing change too, though he denied it. I said he had 'the Ruth' in him, the Will of the Dreamtime, because lately all he talked about was Jesus and the blacks. I got to thinking it was a pity I'd ever got my periods. If I'd still been of virginal inclination, I could have become a missionary and brought Jesus to all the Aborigines who hadn't heard of Him yet. But fortunately, or unfortunately, I was well on the road to a conflict of my own: how to remain an ace student while discovering the sins of the flesh.

Through Ruth, I learnt that fuck was a word that didn't appear in the dictionary, in the Bible, or in polite, white conversation. It was thrilling! Ruth said her people said it all over the place, but the whites didn't because they were afraid.

'Afraid of what?' I asked with the disdain of a newly confident fifteen-year-old.

''Fraid of themselves.'

'What do you mean?'

Ruth raised her shoulders. 'It's what your Mama thinks of the world, Billy. It's what the Mother knows of the Life . . . it's a motherfucker.'

'My mother would never use swear words, Ruth – she wouldn't even know any!' I declared loudly. Being so recently educated to the very existence of such words, I was quite sure I was right.

'For a bright girl, Billy, you sure are dumb,' came the retort, leaving me less wise than I'd been before.

It seemed that everything I learnt was just beyond my grasp, every opportunity one step further on. 'What do you want of your ma, Billy?' Ruth's white question punctured me. 'She's lived everyone's life but her own and has gotta be tired of that!'

'I wanna be a boy!' I exclaimed recklessly. 'It'd be a hell of a lot easier. I reckon Ma wanted another boy.'

'Stop talking bad English, Billy. You know better. Don't listen to me – I'm jist your black nanny, remember?'

'I thought you were half-caste!'

'Half-caste black nanny, what's the diff? Except we both speak good English, eh?' She laughed, a full-bodied laugh, a lifetime of laughs. 'Nobody ever wants a girl, Billy. Nobody ever wants nobody. You've got to want yourself. Your ma knows that, fuck does she know that!'

'Stop it! Stop it!' I covered my ears. 'Why do you talk so, Ruth? You're having a baby!'

She tossed her head back and laughed more earnestly than before. The throaty voice jumped out of her long brown neck, like a duck calling its babes to water. 'Oh, little daughter of Rosey and Nathan Batchelor! You think the baby changes everything? You think I'll become a lady because I have a child? Huh? You think if the father came forward and married me, that'd make me a lady – and my child white? Without no touch of the tar in him? That what you think, Billy?'

The trouble was, I didn't know what I thought. I had some comprehension of what she was alluding too, her mouth hard, her beautiful eyes looking past me, through me. My Ruth was not of my world any more. I loved her still, but my heart was uncomfortably suspicious of the changes in hers.

'How can you love a man so much that you want his baby, then turn away and have it on your own?' rushed out of my childish mouth before I could rescue it. Micky O'Ryan was handsome and strong. He was my new hero. He even looked a bit like Rudolph Valentino. He would surely want to know, want everyone to know, Ruth was having his baby!

I dreamt of the wedding, of how beautiful Ruth would be in flowing white lace Ma would sew to perfection; Micky in black tails, dashing, romantic. His horse would be cleaned up for the occasion, no scruff, no smells. The whole town would be there, singing and dancing.

'Why don't you marry Micky, Ruth? Ma and Pa would give you a wedding, if only they knew . . . I just know they would! If you don't marry him, Ruth, they'll take your baby to The Orphanage, won't they?'

For a moment, her eyes met mine, allowing me to glimpse a fragment of her pain.' There's no winning possible, Billy,' she muttered, more to herself than me. 'You know, my people have always married for genetic strength, not love, and now I know how right they are. I'd marry Micky O'Ryan if he was rich, but to give my baby a name? No sirree! Anyway, he wouldn't want no half-caste, would he?'

'He might,' I said, unsteadily.

'He can't have him anyway, 'less he's married to a white woman, thanks to the bastard white Government's Assimilation Act! Thank God I'm strong. This little one sure ain't gonna inherit much from his father.' She patted her stomach lovingly.

'It's all written in the Dreamtime, no matter what stinkin' white folks think,' she said. I wondered again at her terrible English, wondered about her opinion of Micky, so sure she was wrong, yet unable to address the important thing.

'Why are you talking like you haven't had any schooling suddenly, Ruth?'

'Good English ain't gonna do me much good now, is it? I'm what's called *reverting to form*, dear,' she added tartly.

'After the baby's born, you can help Pa in the telegraph office again and maybe even get your pilot's licence!'

'I won't be gettin' no licence now. Your Pa got no spare cash, and you'll be gettin' any he has to go to university, so praise the Lord and pass the ammunition!' she concluded more sarcastically than she'd begun.

'What do you mean?' I asked, wide-eyed.

'Billy, praise the Lord and keep your eyes on your ma. She's the one who'll be callin' all the shots.'

As Ruth's confinement continued, Sister Mac, Ma and Nan and just about everyone at church started knitting little clothes for the baby. When I asked Ma if she'd changed her mind and decided to let Ruth keep the child, she positively snapped my head off.

'Don't be stupid, Billy! Totally impossible, as you're quite old enough to realize. Don't mention it again.'

My heart ached for Ruth, the pile of tiny clothes growing at the same rate as her tummy. 'Stop them from doing it, Pa!' I pleaded. 'It's so hypocritical, so painful – it's just not fair.'

He sighed heavily. 'A good wardrobe might get the baby some parents right away, instead of being made a ward of the state.' It was women's business, he said; he would not interfere. Yet it was men who made the rules. It didn't make any sense.

For my part, I'd had enough of standing by, watching the farce as it built to its natural climax. I needed distraction, a new interest. Unsure what I intended, I wandered over to the *Mail* and found James in the front office preparing the editorial. Figgy and

Constance Barnawarren had gone to Witchitie for a week's holiday. James was clearly enjoying the freedom. His large feet greeted my face as I opened the door, set atop the old oak desk that was barely visible under the piles of papers and stamps.

'Hi, Billy,' he acknowledged me warmly, jumping up to unload a chair. His thick blond hair tumbled around his fine-boned face, rendering me quite breathless.

'My, have you turned into a stunner!' he whistled, grabbing my hands and twisting me around until his body was pressed against my back, his lips planted firmly on my neck.

'How dare you, James Barnawarren!' I shouted angrily, breaking loose. 'What do you think you're doing?'

He grabbed me again, this time pressing his firm, lumpy body against the front of mine. 'Hey, Billy, just giving you a little kiss. I could do all sorts of lovely things to you . . . make you feel so good.' I bit his lip. He backed away slightly. 'I don't want to hurt you, Billy, just let's cuddle, eh?'

He looked so dejected, I hesitated long enough for him to pull me back towards him. He was gentler this time. It occurred to me, all at once, that I was being kissed and fondled for the very first time. It did feel quite good, until his hands began to wander down my legs. I reached awkwardly to stop him, knowing it was wrong, wondering how it was possible to feel disgust and delicious pleasure, simultaneously.

'I'm not that sort of a girl . . .'

'Shush, okay, it's okay. We'll just cuddle and kiss.'

He wrapped his long, bony arms around my back and kissed me until my lips were burning and my skin began to feel like sandpaper. I pulled away again. 'You're hurting me,' I whispered demurely, unsure that that was exactly what I meant. He pecked my cheeks, my eyes, my neck and lips again, sliding his tongue between my teeth and thrusting it inside my mouth, reaching for my tongue. Completely dumbfounded, I allowed it, not at all sure that I liked this new sensation, though it seemed to improve the longer he did it. What my next reaction would have been can only be guessed at. The front door opened. Reverend Moon.

'Billy Batchelor!' he bellowed. James and I jumped, instantly stepping as wide apart as was possible, staring helplessly at the Reverend. 'Shame on you, you wicked girl. Get out of here at once and go home to your mother! And treat this as a warning, young lady. If I catch you kissing boys again, I'll tell your father. Speaking of fathers, where's yours, James?' he asked with measured civility, dismissing me without a further glance.

Humiliated, I fled. Who did old beady-eyed Moonface think he was? Some God he represented! Why were we made at all, if every good thing got burnt or crashed or adopted, and everything girls did was wrong and everything boys did was right?

Those first kisses awakened such strange sensations in my body, I didn't immediately notice the dampness between my legs, nor realize that my heart beat so fast, my small breasts were rising up and down uncontrollably. As I rushed along Oodoolay Street, all I could feel was the blood in my face, burning brightly. Certain everyone was looking at me, I averted my eyes, knowing they would give me away. I longed to hurry back to James and fling myself into his arms and decided there and then that I needed a lot more kisses to be sure I liked it. My heart told me though that James wouldn't want to kiss me again because I hadn't objected sufficiently. How was I to get more, without being called an easy mark, a common hussy – or worse?

If there was an answer to this, my biggest question in life thus far, Ruth would know it. When I arrived, she was sitting on the verandah, holding both hands to her stomach.

'Are you sick?' I asked anxiously.

'No, no. Feel!' I let her place my hand on the large mound of her stomach, pulling away quickly. 'It's . . . it's kicking?' I trembled.

'Yes, Billy, he's alive and kicking.'

'Does it hurt?'

'Not really. It feels like . . . like life. I wish I had your education, Billy. I'd be able to tell you exactly how it feels.'

'Then how do you know it's a boy?' I asked.

She looked at me oddly, the question puzzling. 'I don't know,' she answered eventually. 'Instinct I s'pose.' The whole mystery of instinct was totally beyond my ken. I wondered whether I had any and if so, when (or how?) would I know it? 'Maybe it's the strength of the kick?'

'I've never had a baby before,' she replied unnecessarily, 'so how would I know the difference?'

'Maybe you're wrong?' I persisted.

'No, I'm right,' she said firmly. 'It's a boy.'

Ruth was as strong as Ma when she'd made up her mind. I sometimes forgot that she wasn't Ma's daughter. Mostly, I thought she was a better daughter for Ma than I could ever be. In a way, I had the feeling Ruth didn't really understand how she'd come to be having this baby at all, yet in so many ways she was a woman of the world. It was all very difficult. Babies didn't become children to Ruth either. They were just babies that you had, and gave away. Then they were orphans, and after that they were liabilities or servants of white grown-ups.

'How do you get kisses without losing your reputation?' I blurted out the moment the baby stopped

117

kicking, precipitating another bout of it. 'Can he hear?' I whispered.

'I hope he can hear!' Ruth laughed. 'Why are you whispering?'

'I don't know,' I smiled.

'I don't know the answer to your question either. Maybe you can't . . .'

'You haven't lost your reputation, Ruth. You're having a baby! Pa says only good girls have babies.'

Ruth shook her head sadly from side to side, with the hint of a smile on her lips. 'I think you should listen to Mrs Rosey, Billy.'

It was my turn to shake my head. 'I don't understand.'

My brain felt trapped, like her baby kicking against the womb. How could she think my mother knew the answers to life's great questions? My mother had lived a bush life, a Christian life, without question. She was a cook and a homemaker, a wife and a firm disciplinarian. What did she know of our world, our times? She would never have allowed boys to kiss her. Never. It was true that she hadn't gone to school, but only because she was the only girl and had to nurse her sick mother. Why, she loved good music. She coped with all manner of people quite easily. And she was the most gracious hostess in the whole district! She had even got Pa his promotion, though of course he would have got it himself, eventually. The more I thought about it, the more I realized that perhaps I had underestimated her, a little.

Neither had it ever occurred to me before that Ruth was practised in the art of observation. It had not occurred to me that she questioned her lot.

Ruth took my hand again, this time holding it tightly in hers. 'Billy, your Ma knows that an education will lead you out of the Great Depression and help you become a happy woman, with a good reputation. You don't have to worry about anything except getting an education. That'll be enough, with everything else you've got.'

There were tears beneath her lower lashes, long black lashes, wet and shining. Her breathing was shallow, coming in short gasps. She pressed her hands to the boy in her stomach again. 'I think I'll go and lie down now,' she said softly. 'Would you help me there?'

My tears flowed freely as we staggered inside, arms entwined, noses sniffling, small half-laughs escaping our souls and joining us like blood sisters in some great purpose we knew not what.

The baby came in the morning, a morning two months too early, a morning when the light was so pure, it woke you from sleep.

She had the boy alone, on the couch in the fortress room, 'the makeshift stable,' Pa said later, for the little black girl who'd come from The Orphanage.

We woke to the baby's cry, or to the rarest of suns, and gathered around in our flannelette nighties and nightgowns. The sound of a horse's hoofs interrupted the cries; within minutes, Sister Mac had cut the long, bloody cord, issuing instructions all round. The big black urns I'd grown up with took on new meaning, emitting hot water one minute, and more comfortably, cups of tea the next. I realized once again that Ma was always right; she'd been putting an extra log in the wood stove every night before we went to bed for as long as I could remember, just in case it was needed. Even the Great Depression hadn't stopped her.

'He's weak,' Sister Mac proclaimed sardonically. 'Better light a candle, if it ain't too late.'

'Oh my Lord,' Ma sighed. 'Nathan, send one of the men for Giles.' Pa had already thought of it. Reverend Moon emerged through the sunstruck front door, a sanctimonious, godly duty beaming from his glassy eyes. I hated him, as I'd never hated anyone before. I think I hated all Presbyterians, right at that moment.

Quickly, the mood of love and joy dissipated with the clumsy mess of sheets and towels and urns. By the toll of Ma's grandmother clock striking seven, Rosebery returned to normal. Only the sleeping Ruth and the occasional whimper of the dying babe remained to be reckoned with. Sister Mac returned to the hospital. Pa went to work. I went to school. Reverend Moon went about his ministry. Ma? I don't know what she did, but when I returned mid-afternoon, Sister Mac was by Ruth's side, and the baby boy was still whimpering.

'Ya gotta lot o' Rosey in ya, Ruthy,' she cooed, as though she was talking to the baby. 'Ya little one 'as too! Reckon ya might just up an' show us all, eh?'

I could hear in her voice the Will of God, the Will of the Woman imploring God to be fair, just this once, please, just this once! It was like the wind across the ocean, seizing up, spent, begging one more wave to crash freely upon the shore. Would one more wave be too much to ask? Just give us this one, and we'll ask no more!

'Oh how temperate Thou art,' I heard her pray, words foreign to her usual vocabulary, all knowing to her Catholic catechism.

Ruth named him Than, though it was a little too close to the Greek God of Death for my liking. It was short for Nathan. Ruth used to call Pa Mr Than when she first came to our house.

He was very small for a long time, light brown in colour and gentle in mood. He rarely cried and began to smile at four weeks old, though his fate was still too uncertain for him to be so happy. We loved him instantly. We loved him so much, we hardly knew it. He was our lives, for as long as his slender life lay in the balance, it was all we knew. He was the pivot of our existence. We talked him, breathed him, closed ranks around him. I felt my life growing with every day he dared to live. I went to school dreaming of having a baby. I came home, changed nappies, cooed with Ruth, helped Ma with the evening meal, went to my room to study, returned to the fortress for goodnight cuddles and kisses with him.

He had a cleft palate. Nobody but Ruth and I kissed him. But we kissed him because, to us, he didn't have one. Doc Halliday came once and said it was hopeless. We didn't believe him. Than didn't believe him; he'd begun to giggle, his funny little twisted mouth laughing all the way up his cheeks, into his eyes and then his whole body would giggle and gurgle, feet kicking, hands punching, saliva bubbling from his precious half-lips. He was the happiest boy I'd ever known.

'What decision have you made, Rosey?' Pa asked one night after we'd all gone to bed. I was sitting on the stairwell, thinking about Eros and Thanatos, birth and death, and love and babies.

Ma was evasive. 'I haven't really thought about it, Nathan.'

Pa was very solemn. 'We can't put it off, Rosey.'

'If we can't dear, then I guess we're stuck with it.'

'What do you mean?' He sounded startled.

She began tentatively, but strengthened her resolve as she spoke. 'Well, we can't send him to The Orphanage, not as sick as he is. And nobody will want to adopt him. We can't send Ruth away either; she's got nowhere to go and she's not costing us to feed him after all! We'll probably have to keep him, for a while.'

There was a long silence. I could hear Pa's pipe

being tendered and the fire being stoked, almost in one movement. Oddly, Ma appeared to have put down her knitting.

'You know my feelings about short-term support, Rose.'

'Yes, dear, I do. We're stuck with the Depression and we're stuck with a daughter who thinks she can remain feminine while striving for a man's career. We're going to watch both those demons move on, but we've got a choice about the black girl with the abnormal child, for a while, anyway. I think we probably need Ruth and her boy for our sanity. I'm being quite selfish, Nathan. He's . . . he's God's way of giving us Joey back . . . a boy to nurse, to set on his way, until he's strong . . . I love him,' she said, her voice breaking pitifully. Pa rushed to her side. 'I've been so lost, Nathan, so lost.'

Her composure was low. She began to weep, then collected herself, almost as quickly as she had stumbled. 'I'd hate to lose them now. They may be all we finish up with.'

I wished I could see Pa's face then, but I could picture the soft warm lines of love and care and understanding, framed by the fine grey hair, what was left of it. His voice was tired when he responded, old like his face. I'd read in one of my books that the ones you love never grow old, but it was only fiction.

'We'll finish up alone, Rose,' he stated simply, 'and Than will be his own little man, just like Joey was his own person. But, we'll help him on his way, for as long as we can . . . We'll finish up alone, Rose. Then . . . then we return to the earth, dear. Nothing more, nothing less. I love you.'

'Nothing more? No heaven? No afterlife? Oh Nathan, my dear husband, have you lost your faith altogether?'

'I don't know, dear, I just don't know any more. But I haven't lost you. I love you,' he said again.

'Thank you, dear,' she cried softly. 'I love you too, and I'll pray for you.'

I crept back to bed, brimming over with joy that Ruth would be able to keep our beautiful baby Than after all. At the same time, I felt desperately sad. Would I ever grow up enough to understand my parents?

# The Great Career of Billy Batchelor

# SEVEN

# 1932

I was leaving my beloved sounds and smells, tastes
and sights and frugal comforts of Kurra Kurra in
depression, for an equally frugal and closeted university village.

My accommodation was secured in the Churchill
House, an austere room no bigger than our bathroom. Apart from Pa's old war suitcase, I was travelling alone and going to no one. When the time came
for me to board the train for Brisbane, I was not at all
sure I wanted to leave.

My bush orchestra would not miss me, but I was
already lonely for the loud, discordant cries of the
jackasses echoing throat to throat across the ranges,
laughing heartily at the harmonic shrills of my joyous
bellbirds. The hustle of the telegraph station, the
clicking and clacking, the alarm bells, the telephone
ringing . . . the huffing and puffing, the whistles and
the signals and the chug-chug of the trains . . . baby
Than giggling and crying, and everybody laughing
when he did something cute . . . church bells on
Sunday, Ma's dinner gong every day and the clatter
of silver knives and forks on Royal Albert china, for a
few moments rising above animated conversation on
a busy night at Rosebery.

Would I be able to smell the smells when they were
no longer there? Ma's kitchen, rich and sweet,
aromas pouring out of huge black pots that were
never idle, a backyard bigger than a cricket ground,

steaming with horse and chook dung, lemon trees and eucalyptus, salt from the ocean competing with the smoke from the fires when the Aborigines replenished the land. Was it smell or taste that I'd remember when a thin film of lazy pink dust oppressed our lives or when old Mr Prescott stumbled into the kitchen stinking of alcohol but complaining of thirst, or when a fresh log was put on the fire and the soup bubbled over?

Would I recall the moods of the ranges, the colours of my world? The blues, greys, lilacs, rusts, greens, clarets, browns. Would I remember the scorching yellow earth beneath stinging bare feet or the red and orange fires of sunset that lit the memory of Black Tuesday, and our Joey? White lace pillow slips, handkerchiefs, serviettes . . . hot charcoal iron rods wound around long black hair to make curls . . . long grey poles and aching arms, stirring off-white sheets in boiling water to bring them back to white . . . Ma's bosom heaving pink and creased . . . Ruth's pitch-black eyes and shiny brown skin nursing Than's light chocolate little body with the twisted pink mouth; would they stay fresh in my homesick heart? How much of my world would be the same when I returned?

Ma and Pa, Ruth and Than, Sister Mac, Nan, Reverend Moon and Amelia, Constance and Saucy Barnawarren all turned out to wave me off. I could not help continually looking back along Railway Parade for some sign of James or Micky, or even David, who was leaving in the opposite direction tomorrow, having obtained a place in the medical faculty at Sydney University. I felt like the bush plant waiting for rain. When it doesn't rain for years, there are no flowers for years. I thought about Ruth's simple philosophy, that every man, woman and child is born to cherish a dream. I wondered how I would concentrate on my studies while my heart was beating so desperately for a boy who didn't know I existed, except perhaps as some easy plaything who liked to be kissed.

The signal was up. We saw the dust and the flint stones flying before we heard the hoofs and were able to distinguish Jock O'Ryan charging up to the station verandah. He jumped off his old stock horse and tied him to the rails, taking the ground to the platform in one leap. He dipped his hat, unfolding the curly mop of mousy hair.

'Have a good trip, Billy, an' best o' luck with your education,' he smiled bravely, two top teeth missing from a fight at Pigeon Shaft's pub the week before.

'Thanks, Jock,' I managed, as the disappointment welled up in my foolish heart. Ma's face glared coldly beneath her wide-brimmed, Sunday best pink hat. 'Thanks so much for taking the trouble to come in and see me off,' I added hastily, with as much enthusiasm as I could muster. Jock seemed pleased enough. Ma's eyes softened. She came forward and gave me a short, crisp hug and peck on the cheek.

'Be good, sweet maid, and let who will be clever,' she repeated for the umpteenth time since my scholarship had been advised. I did not understand what it meant, but could not let on. I had studied contradictions and tautologies and felt sure Ma had confused the proverb in her memory. I intended to check out some of her favourite quotes in the university library at the first opportunity. At best, many of them were highly suspect.

Sister Mac and Nan gave me warm hugs and salty, tear-splashed kisses. Constance and Saucy politely pecked my cheek and 'God blessed' me.

Pa patted me awkwardly on the back. 'Goodbye, darling,' he said, two words having to carry the full weight of his emotions. I couldn't look at him, those eyes focused so sharply, taking mental photographs to remember every minute detail, every flicker and twist of the smiles and frowns of his little girl who was going to the big smoke, chasing rainbows.

The train pulled out suddenly. I leant over the window frame, waving frantically. Jock O'Ryan threw his hat in the air, plunged his fingers into his mouth and sent a wolf whistle resounding up the track, louder than Pa's station whistle that, for some reason, he didn't blow that day. I could have died of embarrassment.

My last sight of home was a blur of faces rushing handkerchiefs to their eyes. It seemed odd to me that they should be sad at my parting. I'd been sure they'd been looking forward to it for months.

'Swift's *A Modest Proposal* proposes regulated cannibalism,' Harry Carmichael began, swishing his black gown behind him in a gesture resembling the theatrical shenanigans of Reverend Moon on a special holy day.

'Swift recommended that one hundred thousand children of one year of age be slaughtered and offered in sale to persons of quality and fortune as meat for their tables. Such a proposal would have been shocking, had Swift not presented a plausible list of reasons why such drastic steps would solve much of Ireland's poverty.'

Professor Carmichael paused to take a fresh breath of equally deep proportions. 'You may think *Gulliver's Travels* is the Great Work of Swift,' he pointed menacingly, accusingly at his cowering first yearers. 'Lilliput and Brobdingnag allow Swift to show his contempt for the littleness of human nature and Houyhnhnms represents the disgusting spectacle of man without reason or moral feelings and only just with understanding . . . his horse gives the misanthropic ideal of man being immune to rule or duty, untouched by the principles of love!'

I took a deep breath for him at this point, wondering when it would be possible to commence note-taking. We'd had instructions on how to do it, when to do it, but nobody had warned us about Harry Carmichael.

'The population are starving to death,' this extraordinary man rushed on, without pause. 'Widespread famine, driven by a series of disastrous harvests that began in 1727, have created poverty and degradation for large sections of the Irish population. You may now pick up your pens and begin to take notes,' he said without punctuation, the monotonous voice lifting ever so slightly with the instruction itself. 'There were too many babies, treated like animals, left to starve to death,' he droned on, yet a physical shift in seats was discernible throughout the auditorium and the crackle of moving paper and pens dipping into ink wells heralded a changing mood of sceptical interest. He paused momentarily until we resettled, his voice still dry and flat, his eyes sparkling at our deepening horror.

'Swift merely proposes a radical solution for a radical problem. He shoots at the callousness of English exploitation of Ireland and indeed the lethargy and stupidity of the Irish themselves! He develops a cold, statistically backed argument for the systematic elimination of such children, an argument completely impervious to the monstrosity of the proposal itself and synonymous with the prevailing attitudes of the day.

'There are many parallels in modern history, ladies and gentlemen! Is the slaughter of babies worse than allowing them to starve to death? What do you think?' His long forefinger reached out over the podium, pointing like a gigantic prehistoric creature at his audience of absurdly dwarf-like green lepre-chauns, all staggering under the weight of hitherto impossible literal or metaphysical perceptions.

Without further bidding my thoughts rushed home to baby Than. How many of Swift's economical arguments could be dealt against him, making him *dispensable* under Swift's proposal? He was filling out now, enough to allow a butcher to flay the carcass and make gloves for ladies and boots for gentlemen; money from purchase would circulate among the wealthy, including growth for the owners of manu-facturing sweat shops. Swift's solution that if Than was killed off, Ruth would be more attractive for marriage and men might even become as fond of such a wife during pregnancy as they were of their mares in foal, sounded intolerable to me.

The thought of young Than being breast-fed for a solar year in order to increase his weight to twenty-eight pounds for the carcass to fetch ten shillings on the open market, was too much. I raised my hand to leave the huge lecture hall, but nobody noticed. I rushed for the women's lavatories, but reaching only the double doors of the auditorium, I was violently ill. Predictably, Harry Carmichael did not draw breath. Since I knew nobody, little interest was shown by anyone but the cleaning staff, presumably. It reminded me of my very first day at school, all those years ago, the shame and embarrassment the ruler had inflicted on my pride! Yet, oddly, to be violently ill on my first day at university had little impact on that pride. Was it the sea of strangers that lightened the horror, or something else, something less obvious?

By nightfall, I moved to my four-by-two-feet desk, pondering the predictability of my body and wrote up a summary of the day's lectures. Today's version of the truth was irreconcilable with previous versions;

how much were my attitudes destined to change, when my first day of tertiary education could shock me so?

Refreshed from two glasses of lemonade and a sense of achievement, I got up from my desk and looked distantly at the single bed. It was too early to turn in. How would I sleep after such a day? How would I ever learn to sleep in this dingy, dilapidated room, the white ants having eaten all the woodwork around one of the double windows and the lining of the walls so badly eaten in some places, the ventilator had been removed. The Oregon timber studs, plates and rafters were disintegrating before my eyes. I wondered whether the Churchill House would still be standing by the time I completed my degree.

I slipped a blue floral cotton jacket over my new sky-blue dress and wandered out into the quadrangle, across the gardens and onto the road that led to the swimming pool. It was dark, but the lights of the city cast a shimmering glow around the university buildings, catching walls and posts and windows in broken segments of gold and black. I was on the brickwork surrounding the pool before I realized I had company.

'Feeling better now?' the deep, articulate voice said from a large, dishevelled frame and on closer inspection, a crisp moustache and beard. Harry Carmichael.

'Yes, thank you,' I replied awkwardly. How mortifying! He was to be my tutor and I'd already been violently ill at his first lecture.

'Does Swift really conjure up such horror, Miss Batchelor, or is my style so bad it makes you sick? Or perhaps you were recovering from too much cake and soda at your farewell parties in swinging Kurra Kurra?'

His voice held the slightest edge of sarcasm, yet he smiled readily as he looked me up and down appreciatively. Ma had made me half a dozen simple cotton frocks in bright colours; it was grand to be out of the school uniform tunic, a cheap copy of masculine cuts, undoubtedly designed as a cover-up for blossoming womanhood.

'You have the most magnificent black hair, what a sensible woman keeping it long, I never liked the twenties' craze of the bob and the thirties so far are not much better but I do think the shorter skirt is more attractive and you wear it so well . . . do you mind if I call you Billy? Please call me Harry.'

I opened my mouth, but he continued before I could speak. His hand was at my elbow, steering me into the administration block and upstairs to the staff kitchen where a huge urn was bubbling. 'Tea, I suppose? Good country girl and all, yes, tea. Two lumps? Plenty of milk. Not as fresh as you're used to, of course, but you'll develop a taste for it – some other things besides, I'd be wagering. Why are you here, Billy? What's a cracking good-looker like you doing spending three years of her life in a university? Not going to marry? Well, can't blame you, really. Men aren't much chop for bright women, are they? Boring, selfish slobs, most of us . . .'

'Do you ever require an answer to anything you say?' I butted in.

'Very rarely, very rarely. I'm going to ask you an important question one day soon, however, so be prepared. We'll get you through the first week or two though, get you settled, orientated. How's your tea? Good. If you like Swift, I can't wait to see your reaction to Conrad. Read any? No, well, once you start, you won't be able to stop. *Heart of Darkness* will get you in; the abiding message, Billy, is that men put something of their baseness, some evil, into even the noblest cause. Darkness lives in the hearts of all men. Without society's laws, all men succumb to the rules of the jungle. What do you think about that, Billy Batchelor? What do you think my motivations are in paying special attention to you, eh? Light or dark? Good or bad?'

He stopped abruptly, as though he'd planned every word and now the game was over. I laughed. He was the most annoying, sophisticated, intelligent, arrogant, verbally fluent man I had ever met. I wanted to hate him. Instead, he fascinated and en-thralled me. He laughed too, his green eyes twinkling in the harsh white light.

'Com'on, Miss Billy Batchelor,' he took my arm firmly, 'I'll walk you back to your house. I'd prefer not to, of course, but we'll get to that later.'

He walked me home without another word. I sat on my bed and tried to untangle my first day, the most extraordinary day of my life. The systematic slaughter of babies, sold to the rich for their culinary delight – Than eaten alive by rich white folk? For even the noblest cause, men put something of their base-ness – Pa allowing the annihilation of Carter Pip's career for his own ends? And Harry Carmichael, the only person who had seriously noticed me all day – a harmless eccentric, or a lecherous academic? I had a good deal to learn.

In pursuance of this, my Great Education, I surren-dered to university routine quickly. It was easier, and harder for me than most, mainly because most were boys. They were distracted by the few girls on campus, but I was certainly not interested in them. They were childish and small, grossly under-developed compared to Kurra's young men.

'Bet they've never done a decent day's work in their lives!' I scoffed to my new friend Thea. Thea Bickley. Thea was no beauty, yet she was as tall as most of the boys, stunningly elegant in dress, exquisitely citified in manner. She studied the lads anew. Born and raised in Brisbane, she had no yardsticks from which to measure these white-skinned, flabby city boys. To my mind, they also lacked class, from basic common courtesies to everyday table manners. 'Are all boys from the city as rude as the ones we're stuck with?' I asked.

'Afraid so, Billy,' she sighed wistfully. 'Isn't Peter Caruthers gorgeous?' I found him obnoxious. The only thing going for him was a pretty face. He behaved like a crude, flippant sixteen-year-old.

'He's quite handsome,' I agreed cautiously. Thea had already shown signs of jealousy and I had quite decided I was not going to be side-tracked by boys anyway. If that meant keeping my distance from the few girls on campus, I would do it.

'Let's go to the clubhouse after tea,' she was urging me now, adding more make-up to the old, her soft pink complexion taking on a rubbery look.

'No thanks, Thea, I've got work to do.'

'You're really a bit of a snob, you know that? Everyone says so,' she smiled happily. 'Don't be stuck up, Billy! Come and join in the fun. You can't go through university studying, for heaven's sake!'

'I might come over later,' I hedged, knowing I wouldn't. She knew it too.

'Sure, Billy. See ya.'

Why I felt so different from my peers was still a mystery to me. My secure country upbringing had bred confidence and ambition, yet I was unwilling to become one of the gang. Life was as busy as it had always been, but with a singleness of purpose that made each day distinctly measurable. I was always first to the bathroom in the morning, last to the lavatory at night. Sometimes I wondered if I was dumber than my fellow students, that I had to work such long hours to keep pace, but mostly, I revelled in the challenge, the stimulus to my previously under-utilized brain. Anyway, the university social life simply did not capture my interest.

The recreation hall on Friday and Saturday nights was no more than a beer hall for the boys. My ability at sport was not strong enough to join any team. But for Thea, my spare time would have plainly been dull, taken up with study and washing and ironing. Thea was always happy to share gossip and laughter; we went to Saturday morning matinées and to her luxurious home for tea, whenever Mr and Mrs Bickley weren't entertaining society.

I had also discovered as much as I needed to know about Harry Carmichael to eliminate him from any romantic interest. He was a confirmed bachelor, and a rogue – no decent girl would be seen with him. Just as I was settling down to the life of a bookworm, he invited me for a Saturday afternoon flight in a friend's de Havilland 9.

'I couldn't possibly come flying with you,' I replied indignantly. 'My ma would die!'

'She won't if she doesn't know. Anyway, Billy, if anyone's going to die, it's you, literally speaking, that is. You know what I think? I think you're afraid – yes, tough little girl from the bush is afraid of flying! Well, who would have believed it? The lateral thinker, the girl who says black is white – she's afraid of taking her feet off the ground for half an hour!'

'You will take those words back, Mr Carmichael!' I declared. 'Give me a couple of moments to put on some suitable clothes.'

With that, I strode off across the quadrangle, feeling his amusement at my back. My heart fluttered like a kite in an ocean wind, rising up to my throat and down to my stomach in short, sharp bursts. If this was my state now, how would I be during the flight? The more I thought about it, the more I marvelled at his courageous invitation. If I could be sick in a lecture, surely I could have a heart attack in a plane?

As we pulled out of the staff grounds in his Model T, I asked him directly. 'Have you given serious consideration to how I might react to this joy ride?' It was almost enough to be riding in a car, even though the Ford had become commonplace since mass production. He laughed, as I might have expected.

'You don't understand yourself very well yet, do you? Trust me, Miss Batchelor. I have the feeling you're going to have the time of your life.'

The cockpit was open, allowing full view of the workings of our takeoff. 'If you can't call me Harry on weekdays, at least try to manage it on Saturdays,' began his lecture before we had even taxied along the pocked runway. 'Now what do you know about aeroplanes, Billy? Not much, I'll wager, though I bet you followed Amy Johnson's Gypsy Moth flight into Darwin, eh? Almost beat Hinkler, you know, not a bad effort for a woman.'

'Why does everything women do have to be compared with men, Harry?' I asked vaguely, not expecting an answer to the question I'd been asking since I was old enough to speak, realizing instantly that no question was ever left unanswered by Harry Carmichael.

'Because we're afraid you might after all be better, smarter than us. We have to get good mileage out of the smallest gains, Billy, in order to keep you from catching on that you can pass us any time you like.' He smiled nonchalantly, his eyes suddenly more grey than green, a flickering amusement softening his square jaw.

'If you don't want us to wake up, why are you educating us?' I asked.

'Aha! Good. The young beauty from the bush is thinking now! Yes, it's interesting, isn't it? Your Christian God, Billy, must be tearing His hair out, wondering how on earth He'll keep up the myth of wicked Eve and woman's inferior IQ fifty years from now, when we get enough of you educated, that is. Sorry I won't be around for that, but then, man's base instincts will never change, you know. You'll always have to use your bodies to maintain any real power over us, praise be to your God! Here, let me strap you in, Billy, make sure it's tight. We'll get some decent airpockets today with that southeasterly blowing.'

We took off like the wedge-tailed eagle, soaring high on motionless wings. It was 110° in the cockpit. We rose and fell to our ultimate cruising speed of 8,000 feet, my stomach dangerously loose from my body, held together by the seat belt and my hands clasping the open brown paper bag. The pilot was a strange little man with no front teeth, who held a wet singlet to his head for most of the flight, mopping up the sweat pouring from his brow in short, sharp pats. I thought of Ruth and wished she was here and I was there.

'Looks like the wench needs a bit of excitement to take her mind off her belly,' the pilot chuckled, an evil wink passing to Harry. He pulled the joystick forward in one swift movement, pointing us upwards, the clouds parting like the biblical sea, then dumping us in one huge crashing wave as we dived downwards to our deaths. On the way up I screamed. On the way down, I fainted.

We were landing when I came round.

'There you go, Billy, terra firma and another experience to add to your education!' Harry wrapped the saturated singlet around my neck. I felt his other hand tightly gripping my waist. His breath was hot and close to mine, breathing rhythmically, invitingly.

It was infuriating, but I suddenly wanted him to kiss me. As if he knew, he brushed his bearded lips lightly across the nape of my neck. A tingling sensation travelled along my spine, a little involuntary gasp escaping my parched mouth. 'We're down, Billy, and now I'm going to feed you and put some colour back into those luscious cheeks,' he yelled above the closing roar of the engine.

'I'm not going to lie to you, Billy Batchelor . . .' We were seated at a balcony table in the Stage Coach Hotel. The afternoon swill following the races was raucously underway downstairs but upstairs was strangely quiet, only one other couple sitting close together at the far end of the balcony. It was Harry's favourite pub. 'I want to be your lover,' he continued, poker-faced, his voice seducing me in the husky monotone he used in his lectures. 'I'll be good to you, take you out, help you with your studies, make sure you pass your exams, but I will not fall in love with you. When I say goodbye to you, I'll never see you again. Close your mouth, Billy, or I'll be forced to kiss you right here and now, and it won't be a schoolboy kiss, I can tell you.'

I obeyed unconsciously, turning my handkerchief over and over in my hands until my nails pierced through Ma's fine lace edgings. What an extraordinary thing . . . what a proposition! What a thrill! My very own Valentino. Could it be true? Did I hear right? Could I dare be so wicked, so absolutely grown up?

'Why me?' I whispered at last as the sun eclipsed the roof like a theatrical prop, plunging us into timely shadows. The distant sounds of men laughing, arguing, cheering a good shot of pool or a winning throw at darts, might have been a thousand miles away. 'Why me?' I asked more convincingly, the question now firmly lodged. Was this the opportunity I'd been waiting for, when all my Great Questions of Life would be answered?

Harry touched my hands, his long, broad fingers running across my wrists, slowly pushing deeply into the fine veins, pausing at the knuckles, then finger for finger pressing up to the nails, turning my palms out, tracing the heart line, rubbing the mount of Venus until I pulled away self-consciously.

'Because you're young and bright and have worldly dreams that make you uncomplicated to me . . . because I have no intention of ever being owned by a woman and once I've made you, I'll get bored with you . . . because you're beautiful and I love beautiful girls . . . because you're forbidden fruit, all tight and well brought up and virginal and I like to open up the new flower and watch it grow . . . because my ego needs to look down from the lectern and see adoration in the eyes of my pupils!' He laughed, an open, boyish laugh that thrilled me as it had done the first time I'd heard it.

'You're playing with me, Mr Carmichael!' I stood up uncertainly, looking around helplessly, no idea what to do next.

'That I am, Billy, but I'm also quite serious,' he said gently, his hands easing me back into my seat without false objection from mine.

'Listen to me carefully, Billy Batchelor. I'm offering you a smooth ride into womanhood. I'm an experienced man and I'll be tender and romantic, all the things a young girl dares to dream about. You don't want your first sexual experiences to be fraught with clammy young hands fumbling roughly over your body, learning the pleasures of the flesh at your expense, do you? Boys who treat you like a toilet because they don't give a damn for you and don't know how to control their own bodies? Boys pinching your nipples as though they were bottle tops to be screwed off –'

'Stop it, Harry, stop it!' I cried.

'That's better, that's better,' he nodded approvingly. 'You have no idea how much passion there is inside you, just waiting for release, do you? Perhaps, perhaps even I am going to be surprised . . .' he mused, more to himself than to me.

I straightened up in my chair, flicking my hair back in a concerted effort to regain control. 'I have not yet agreed to your proposition, Mr Carmichael. I shall have to think about it,' I said stupidly.

'Of course you will,' he agreed easily. 'I would not want you to take the first step spontaneously. That would bring us unstuck very quickly.'

'What do you mean?'

He took my hand and began stroking it. I was powerless to stop him. 'Oh, let's just say you're a strong-willed girl and like to make your own decisions. You'd be full of guilt and remorse if I pushed you into it before your head has reasoned it out. Take your time. We've got the best part of three years. That should be more than enough. We'll have another beer, thanks,' he called to the waitress at the door.

'Sorry,' she called back. 'It's two minutes past six.'

'Stupid Temperance Unions,' he muttered under his breath.

He rose, pulling back my chair with an air of acquisition. 'Okay, Miss Batchelor, I'll take you back to your room so you can start your decision-making without delay. Think about spending Saturday nights in bed with an appreciative man, eh? A man who's twice your age and willing to be lover, friend, even father when you need it, and I suspect you need a man in your father's image rather more than most. Yes, yes, you've really landed on your feet this time, Billy Batchelor!'

\*       \*       \*

142

Letters from home came thickly at first, but tapered off as my preoccupation with study and Harry Carmichael accelerated. 'We know how busy you are, dear,' Pa's letters opened virtually every week. 'How can you be too busy to write?' began Ruth's. I resolved to maintain one letter a week back. It was easily promised. The second semester was slipping away as fast as my correspondence.

A hasty note from Ruth pulled me up with a thud, two weeks prior to the break, a break I'd decided to spend with Harry in the grand pursuit of losing my virginity. I wanted to lose it as badly as I'd once wanted to get my periods. My developing obsession viewed its loss as the greatest potential gain of my life.

Ma and Pa's twenty-second wedding anniversary would fall on the first Tuesday of the holidays and half of Kurra's residents were planning a surprise party. 'Of course you'll be coming home,' Ruth wrote, 'but you must pretend you can't, so we can keep the secret.' On the one hand, I was homesick and wanted to see everyone; on the other, the ache in my heart and groins had reached unbearable proportions. There was nothing to be done but bring my weighty decision forward and take the plunge prior to returning to Rosebery for the party.

What troubled me most was whether the family would be able to tell from my face what I'd been up to. Sister Mac always said I couldn't hide a thing and should never ever attempt to play poker. Her words sat uneasily in my memory now, but the die was cast. I was destined to risk it. Raised in a small town, I was all too familiar with the saying that one man's business is every man's business. While the campus was considerably larger in total population than Kurra, geographically it was exceptionally small – and close-knit. It might as well have been Kurra, rather than a self-contained village in the centre of a bustling city. Since I had made up my mind rather more quickly than I imagined Mr Carmichael would be expecting, I wondered whether he would be able to make what delicate *arrangements* had to be made, in the time remaining prior to the mid-year break-up.

The more I thought about the risks of disclosure, the more tentative about the whole affair I became. I could not afford to be thrown out of university, with or without the scandal and ruined reputation such disaster would incur. My heart was pounding wildly, my dreams of glorious sexual conquests with the most exciting man I'd ever met all but dashed, when I arrived at our usual meeting place on the back steps of the library, right after history.

He was waiting for me of course, caught in conversation with several of the lads from the second year. My thoughts prevented me from ambling into the group in the friendly manner we had thus far developed. I dropped to the grass and opened a book, seeing nothing but a blur of faces, all gossiping heartily about that wanton, scarlet girl, Billy Batchelor, whose personal standards were so low, she'd seduced the English master in exchange for High Distinctions for her essays. Until caught, that is, after which she was sent home to her shattered mother and devastated father, both of whom aged twenty years in a week. With neither education, nor reputation left for her, the story of the little girl from the bush who squandered away her destiny in shameful sin became a myth of the Never Never, oft repeated to small girls showing early signs of blind stubbornness.

Harry sat down beside me. 'So serious, Billy? Troubles?'

I coughed. 'No, I mean yes.'

'Let's have it. Spit it out.'

'I'm terrified,' I blurted unexpectedly, sufficiently shocked to fall silent immediately. It had been bottled up in my heart, and held secret in my head. I had not even dared tell Thea. She was merely at the necking stage of her sexual experience; I was about to plunge into the main event, without any rehearsals. On top of that, how could I tell of my plan to give up my virginity to the English master, Old Blue Beard Carmichael himself?

'Of course you're nervous,' Harry's slow, steady voice began on its soothing path to absolute, rapturous success. 'All of your fears will fade quickly once you realize you do not have to undo any of your precious upbringing – you just have to sidestep it a little,' he chuckled wickedly. 'Let's go into the Stage Coach and I'll buy you an ever-so-discreet beer. That'll remind you how grown up you are and how the time is ripe for danger and adventure!' He was playing with me again, in the pseudosupercilious sort of way that was so much a part of his personality. I found myself charged with a fierce desire to throw myself on top of him, right on the lawn in front of the library, in front of the whole university! The sensation was so alien to me, the very fact of it was a driving force within itself.

When we arrived at the hotel, he led me straight into a small room off the upstairs passage. In the centre of the room was a single bed with a blue candlewick quilt, on one side a narrow wardrobe, on the other, a maple side table graced with a blue and white bowl and water set. I had read enough, knew enough, to realize this was quite ignoble, but it had totally the opposite effect on me at that moment.

'What on earth do you think you're doing, Harry Carmichael?' I attempted to protest, without the slightest whiff of insult or conviction.

His experience of life was thick in that room then,

stifling any chance of youthful argument from me. I felt bewildered and oddly powerful, as though it was I who was about to conquer him when surely nothing could be further from the truth? He pulled me to him, manoeuvring me backwards in order to ease me gently onto the wire-strung bed. The weight of our bodies unavoidably landed hard as the mattress sagged and groaned, swallowing us up like babes in a hammock. I began to giggle. The lumpy protrusion of Harry's lower body hungrily crushed against me just a moment before, now seemed to shrink and disappear as he regained some measure of control. My giggles turned to a mildly hysterical, nervous laugh.

'Bloody charming, Miss Batchelor!' he groaned, pushing his hands straight through the buttons of my blouse, ripping the top hole clean open from the seam. 'I'll buy you a new one,' he muttered sarcastically, smothering my shocked, open mouth with his tongue and hairy lips. I continued to laugh for a moment or two, stunned at my own amused acceptance of the incongruities of this first sexual experience. Harry's full mouth and middle-aged body were now rhythmically stirring my body into clammy harmony, his long sensitive hands circling my stomach, thighs, finally making deep strokes between my legs, but still rubbing, caressing the limbs casually as though there was all the time in the world to get to the pot of gold, or the rainbow, or both.

In the end I couldn't help myself. 'Harry, please?' I breathed heavily, thrusting my pelvis against his, simultaneously struggling frantically to undo the buttons on his trousers, not knowing precisely what to expect but in no doubt at all that I must have whatever it was, and fast. He smiled kisses into my neck and quickly removed his pants. He was inside me in one effort, starting that rocking movement again, but this time it was truly our sex organs, naked, wet, hot, hungry, in and out, up and down, round and back, back and round. My life and body were no longer my own and he was revelling in it.

There was something about it that was grotesque, ludicrous, as dumb as animals without a brain jumping one another in the paddocks out by Billadambo. When the spring came to the billabong, the magpie geese and water fowl paused in their incessant feeding to preen and pounce, long-necked turtles and screeching pink-breasted galahs and proud brolgas gathering at dusk to jump a stranger, silhouettes of once gracious birds and beasts, twisted and deformed for one physical jerk of life, one last chance at immortality. Would I really want to do this all my adult life? It seemed unlikely. Was this the ultimate exchange that had made me, made our beautiful baby Than? Was this the perfect freedom of my lately dreams, the answer to the aching in my groins, the longing in my heart?

'Where are you, little one?' Harry stroked my hair, turning strands of curls around his fingers, straightening then letting them loose again. He had been silent so long, I'd lost his presence, unable to relate the man I knew to the man inside me. Perhaps it was just another dream and I was back on my roof, looking down on two tangled bodies who would be people, if only they could be.

'I'm in gumboots, playing in the mud with Wendy Barr and Chocolate,' I murmured. 'I've just got my period and I think the whole world is waiting for me, now that I'm a woman. I've just topped the school in English and won a scholarship to university and Ma and Pa are proud as punch. I'm everywhere, I'm nowhere. I don't know where I am,' I stumbled on, my mind untangling as he slowly drew me up again, down again, and kisses deep enough for drowning.

It was over, suddenly. 'I'm sorry,' he said, though I couldn't imagine why. 'I knew you were different from the start,' he whispered, reaching for a blue towel, colour co-ordinated with the curtains once upon a time, before the afternoon sun had drained them of life.

I had the feeling everything had happened exactly the way he planned it. Today had not been my idea at all, had it? A part of me was angry, somehow reduced by the lack of control, the invasion of privacy, the destruction of my Dreamtime. I had given up my reputation to a man full of words, a man who had found no words to use during my initiation ceremony. All the romance, the excitement, the tinkling sounds of broken glass inside my stomach were gone. In their place, the reality of a sordid hotel room, with blue props, faded and paid for, many times over.

He got up quickly, excused himself. The rubber had to be disposed of in the toilet at the other end of the passage. He pulled on his trousers, but I couldn't look. I wanted to look, but I couldn't. He was back almost immediately, cuddling into me, kissing my neck again, gently massaging my back.

'It takes time, Billy. It's an acquired taste, a gradual obsession. Juliet and Desdemona knew less than you know now, but I suppose it's unfair of me to tell you that . . . we're so superior in our literary academia,' he preambled, the flat Carmichael soliloquy evolving automatically. A tiny spark flickered inside me, like a peep of sunshine following torrential rain. 'We sink our first year students into Swift and Conrad, Shakespeare and Austen. We give you the best and the worst of human nature and expect you to grasp the difference. In truth, we enjoy your confusion, but mostly, we've forgotten why . . .' he trailed off momentarily.

I snuggled into him, warm and secure at the big oak table in Rosebery, with the men of my childhood talking above one another to make themselves heard. There was Ma, boiling the kettle again, feeding and fussing and tidying, silently wallowing in the security of her impregnable domain. There was Sister Mac, grateful never to have to subjugate herself to a man, grateful for the family hearth Rosey and Nathan Batchelor provided. There was Ruth, sometimes sorry to be born, sometimes sorry to be aware of being grateful.

'You were born to find another path, Billy,' his words came back at me, poling the white sheets up from the copper, wringing them out with heavy, blistered station hands I knew too well, 'and find it, you will. I am the first chapter in the Great Career of Billy Batchelor,' he smiled ruefully, rolling me over onto his hairy body, forcing my legs straight out behind me, spread-eagled above him. I was at home then, oddly comfortable, unaware of Freudian undertones, totally aware of female calm as it relates to weight distribution.

'You feel more powerful now, lying on top of me?' he suggested cynically, typically.

'Hardly! But with all your experience, you would have to understand it's more comfortable this way, given the sag in the bed and our difference in body weight.'

'Touché! Out of the mouths of babes . . .' He thrust his limp body upwards, without effect.

'I have to go home for the holidays, Harry. It's Ma and Pa's twenty-second wedding anniversary.'

'Ah!' he sighed deeply, 'so that's the Why of it, eh? You go home to your country boys and your dreams of life as it was, but I'll be here when you return, understanding the pain . . . in a bellicose sort of way – the way you like it. Yes, just the way you like it, Billy.'

# EIGHT

## 1933...

My final year at university was approaching so soon, I couldn't help thinking if life continued to slip away so quickly, I would be old before I'd had time to be young. In two short years, my small world had expanded tenfold, shattering the shaded glasses of my upbringing, launching me onto a different stage.

I had been living with Harry for more than a year, lying to Ma and Pa that I was still in the Churchill House, confiding to Ruth that my conscience was killing me, but what could I do? They'd never approve. Harry argued, 'What they don't know won't hurt them,' and Ruth tended to agree, while adding to my guilt by reminding me that pain always follows deceit. The radio brought the wider world into our tiny flat every day, comforting me one minute that everybody deceives, horrifying me the next because the liar and the cheat usually came to a sticky end.

When news of the Nazis' landslide came through, I was swotting for exams at our kitchen table: the population of Germany had given their overwhelming support to Chancellor Hitler to walk out of the Geneva Disarmament Conference. At first, I felt the tingling of excitement, the thrill of success, the power of believing in yourself to such an extent that you could tell the Vatican itself: 'No one can resist us!' A small voice of fear inexplicably followed, pitter-pattering around the lining of my stomach until I could not read the page in front of me. I tried to crush the gathering gremlins and get back to *The Canterbury Tales*, but all at once the characters seemed trite, unreal, unfunny. Ultimate power to the man who believed in Swift's dastardly solution? What was happening? That was a theory three hundred years ago, wasn't it? Could it be happening, really happening, today? The sterilization of an imperfect race? Ninety-two per cent of an entire population agreed with that? Endorsed it, hailed the dictator of such murderous intention as a leader, a man among men?

My jumbled thoughts would not leave me alone. I got up and turned out the lights, pulling the door to behind me without thinking of the key. The air was cool, refreshing, a soft spring Brisbane night just minutes before the heat came in for its lengthy stay. I tossed my hair back and set into a brisk walk.

My mind floated free for a while, released by the shadows of the night. A man passed me and dipped his hat. A pregnant woman struggled to her doorstep, laden down with brown grocery bags too heavy for her advanced condition. Two young boys rushed past, one reaching out to grab my breast to win a dare, or maybe win the girl? My arm flung out to stop him. Too late. They disappeared over a fence, laughing obscenities. Crude boys, always rough and crude, reducing women, reducing themselves, growing up to be powerful men with good reputations. Killing one another then rewarding themselves with medals and even bigger reputations. Nothing changes, everything circles. What good an education? What value in a good reputation?

I had been vaguely aware of the passing of innocence for some time and oddly at ease with the speed at which I had thrown out many of the Christian values I'd been brought up to believe. I had learnt the arguments of the thinkers, who shot sound holes in a patriarchal church that preached and practised jobs for the boys along with tacit approval of sewing a few wild oats, while dictating quite a different scenario for girls. It had been relatively painless, after all that had led me to it and I marvelled at my good fortune in meeting Harry.

That which I had first thought was such a lot of secrecy about nothing, slowly shrouded me in the most heavenly secret I had ever had to keep. The girlish body, once so weak and sickly, had filled out with the unfettered juices of emerging womanhood. The world of childish daydreams, of famous aviators and handsome movie stars, had disappeared without trace; in their stead, a world of famous men of history . . . writers, actors, poets, and Harry Carmichael. Life was love and I was in love with life, with poetry and music, with cars and planes and restaurants, and Harry. My direction was firming – I wanted it all – the chance to be someone, do something important, conquer the world! Yet . . . my heart was unsteady, my mood swings unfathomable. *Was* I in love with Harry? Really in love? I didn't know. Was I still enjoying our clandestine life together, full of the dreams of literature's sway? We had fun, but I had the feeling it was not the fun of youth, living a lie with a middle-aged academic.

And Harry would not let me float too high, too long, pulling me back from the brink whenever the heat of irrepressible lust threatened to disrupt my studies or expose our secret. I hated him for it, as a child hates a parent or a friend who knows what's good for them. As the horseman learns to hold the reins to check the filly, he had my measure from the start.

The Christmas of 1932 was the first time I had returned to Kurra since the anniversary party. Cyclone Elsie was blamed, but it was clear to me that God had intervened on my behalf. Harry didn't believe in God, but he used to say to me that it wasn't easy doing without Him. 'If you really care about yourself, Billy, you're probably close to God anyway,' he'd say. He was always telling me to learn to love myself so nobody would ever be able to hurt me irrevocably.

'Don't you care about yourself?' I interrupted one day when he was waxing philosophical about Aldous Huxley's *Brave New World* – the literary sensation of the year.

'Not much, old girl.'

'You contradict yourself, Mr Carmichael,' I'd argued smugly. 'I know you care about me, so you must like yourself or it wouldn't be possible!'

'Don't believe everything you're taught, Miss Batchelor. You've got to start thinking things out for yourself,' he'd chided, knocking me down till the next time.

And the next time and the next time repeated and regurgitated, each punch gaining time on the last, strengthening my resolve to beat him at his own game one day. Perhaps I was a slow learner, or perhaps he'd mastered the game? In any case, he never expected us to last beyond a year. He told me so. They never had before. First yearers, every one, fast entry into sex with the awesome professor, fast exit into boyfriends with the hundreds-to-one choices open to a *nice*, secretly weaponed girl of nineteen or twenty.

'I've made you a prize for the highest bidder,' he said at the end of my first year. 'They all want you now because you don't need them. You can take your pick. I've just been keeping you safe from the mob, you see. What a good bloke I am, you do see that, Billy, don't you?' he'd laboured, predictably raising the shackles of my stubborn pride.

'You? Huh!' I'd jumped right in. 'You're afraid I

might just return to you next year and foul up your plans for another conquest. You're afraid of commitment. You're afraid to feel. You're afraid to grow up. All you know is how to make love, and how to talk!'

He had thrown his head back and laughed, truly laughed. 'Listen to my little protégée! Listen to her now! Are you complaining, old girl?' he'd faked a frown, stretching down to gather me up in his arms, throwing me forcibly onto the bed, barely getting my dress up and his pants down before attempting to plunge his way into my unprepared body.

'How dare you!' I'd screamed, pushing him back against the wall with a strength that surprised us both. His erection dissipated as instantly as it had come, all urgency flattened to the wall.

His heart may have stopped, but mine was pounding wildly. 'And you, Harry the Great Professor Carmichael, you even know how to rape! How stupid of me to leave that out of your long list of accomplishments!' I heard a voice say, a voice intent on revenge. 'No wonder you can't hold anyone for more than a couple of semesters! You're an egomaniac who sets up young girls, talks them blind, robs them of their innocence, then casts them off by treating them with less respect than a prostitute could expect! You want me to carry the blame for the end, don't you? Well, Mr Harry Carmichael, I'll be damned if I will!'

Fighting back the tears, I'd walked unsteadily into the hall and extricated Pa's old suitcase from the cupboard. It had taken only minutes to throw some clothes together and walk calmly, blindly, out the front door.

I cried most of the train ride home that Christmas. I cried at every private moment for the four weeks I was home. I cried before I got up in the morning and for fifteen minutes in the bath every night. It might have been different if the boys had been home. David stayed at Sydney Uni, studying. James was on loan at the *Tarrenbonga Daily* while the Editor recovered from a stroke. Only Micky and Jock were around that Christmas, working long hours to keep Mini Mini afloat. Though nothing was said, the secret was out; Micky had quite taken to Than, turning up without notice for boisterous cuddles and play. Ma and Pa remained taciturn to my obvious malaise, 'All things pass' repeated silently in Ma's heaven-bound eyes.

My desolate heart reached out to Ruth, who comforted and advised, whenever she could, as best as she could. But my world was not hers any more. Anyway, we had little private time, her days filled with work, our nights spent with Than and Sister Mac and the family.

When I finally got to bed, I lay exhausted, crying for sleep, praying for the return of my soul. When my prayers weren't answered, I remembered what I'd always known, that God was wise and true and had rightly deserted me for more hopeful causes. I returned to Brisbane as I had left, with only the memory of the energy it had cost me to hide my shame.

Harry was waiting at the station. He greeted me with uncharacteristic tenderness, flushing out in an instant the bottomless pit of unspent tears.

'How are your folk?' he began calmly, moving me forward through a sea of bodies and cases and crying children. 'Did you have a good Christmas? How's baby Than? Bet he's growing up now, must be gorgeous. I thought of you on New Year's Eve, all hugging the radio, waiting for the Vienna Symphony to begin, your ma's kitchen overflowing with people and cakes and hot bread, everyone wanting to see their little girl . . . how much the big smoke has changed her?' He paused, but still I pulled away, big solo tears plopping rhythmically down my cheeks. 'How's your pa?' A subtle lift in the tone of his voice caught me off guard.

'He's fine, thank you,' I answered with automatic politeness, as though my good manners might make him a gentleman.

'And James Barnawarren, the godly Moons, the O'Ryan boys? Did you catch up with them?'

'Oh Harry!' I collapsed in his arms. 'I missed you terribly!'

He pulled me into him and wrapped his arms around my shoulders, stroking my back, my hair, kissing my eyes, the nape of my neck, the palms of my hands. 'I missed you too,' he whispered, loading me and my case into the car. 'Second yearer, eh? Well, there's a first time for everything.'

Could that be nearly a year ago? Could I have understood so much then, yet plunged straight back into the affair for another year of my life? The truth was ugly. The shadows of the night were ugly suddenly and I wished I hadn't wandered so far from the flat, so far from home . . . It must be late. Most of the houses had faded away, lost in lonely slumber, disconnected from each other for a few hours of nothingness. I was alone with the blackness of truth. I was not a child any more and the night was all around me, closing in, irrevocably. Two years with Harry had not altered a moment of it, two years of fiery, enlightened education could not stand up against it. 'The truth will out,' Ma always said. My God, the truth . . .

Harry was a user, a shallow, educated fool. He'd called his own bluff so often, he believed it, seriously believed it. He was the child, I was now the adult. The cerebral affair had never been; what forty-year-old man took virgins to his bed to satisfy his intellectual ego? And how he justified it! Believing he was teaching me to love myself, saving me from clumsy boys with their minds on their carloos and nothing between their ears! What about their hearts, Harry, what about their hearts? What about my heart? They might have loved me, might have really cared, might have become my friends, to keep . . . how much have I lost while I've been with you?

My thoughts came and went, jumping over the cracks in the pavement, withdrawing under the streetlights, sadly rising in the long black stretches home. The lights were on. Harry was home from his lecture. He was not home from mine, though. I knew I had to say it all, the lies to my parents, the lies and the cover-ups on campus, the lies of my life. I did not understand that I was angry with myself, nor that I wanted him still. I had heard the truth over the radio waves from that man on the podium . . . not much different from Harry on his. The cold pride, the indomitable power, little men, lording it over the little people from behind fastidiously kept moustaches. I supposed I owed something to the German Chancellor for making me see it.

'Where have you been?' he greeted me with some concern. 'I was nearly going to call out the dog squad.'

'Rubbish,' I said lightly, surprisingly easily. 'You've never been worried about anyone in your life.'

'Hey, that's a bit savage, isn't it? I've had the kettle boiling for ages.'

'Oh I see, you just happened to notice the clock when you realized you were missing your evening cuppa?'

'I noticed you're having trouble with your *Macbeth* notes . . . good idea to go for a walk when you get bogged down. Can I help?'

'You've looked through my notes . . .?' I began,

then stopped. It was funny. It was actually very funny. Perhaps it was Chaucer or Shakespeare to whom I owed my life? I giggled, just a single, breathless giggle.

'No, I have no conflict with *Macbeth*,' I settled quickly, the natural actress in me warming to the spellbound audience. 'Macbeth had an honourable start in life; he was a man of thought and imagination. Proud and ambitious in high degree, he listened to malicious spirits and an ambitious wife with a heart of stone and was swept off his feet. He believed in a dazzling destiny that carried away his mind, Harry. He murdered King Duncan and seized the throne, changing the destinies and characters of his people to suit his own purposes. Plunging deeper and deeper into crime, he finally loses success, honour, love, respect . . . and life itself. That's about it, isn't it? I certainly hope it is, because I got it from a crib you wrote yourself. You should know!' I tried to laugh, but it wasn't as funny as I'd first thought.

'You're upset with me, Billy. Please tell me what I've done to upset you and I'll apologize. I mean, I really don't want to upset you and I am sorry if I've offended you in any way.'

'Oh Harry!' I groaned, angry and sad, wishing it was over and there was nothing left to say. 'You're such a smug, academic snob! So cold and calculating, so passionless! "I'll apologize! I'm sorry if I've offended you in any way!" What is that? A wind-up toy, responding to some preprogrammed cue?'

'Listen, old girl . . .' he started.

'My name is Billy. You haven't needed to call me "old girl" to undermine my youth for many a day.'

'I suppose this is it, is it?' he sighed unemotionally. 'I've been expecting it – for quite some time, if truth would have it.'

'Truth? Did you say truth? Blasphemous to the end. How stupid to think . . . well. You have made me smart, Harry, but you haven't made me wise. I'll have to learn that on my own. You have robbed me of my sweetness, my girlhood dreams and precious choices. I'm used, second-hand, like you ordered it, planned it. Like you. How could I look into the innocent eyes of a man who loved me now, knowing what I know? Being what I've become, what you've made me?'

'Very dramatic, Billy! Very good indeed. But, say, aren't you deluding yourself, just a little? Don't slip right back from whence you came – that would be a much worse negation of life than anything I've done to you. I once told you that you'd have to start thinking things out for yourself and you obviously are but do remember, Billy, nothing is all black or all white and no experience is wasted, if you learn from it.'

I reached for my suitcase. 'Don't bother to pack,' he said. 'You can keep the flat until your exams are over. I'll move back into the staff quarters.'

He tossed his key onto the kitchen table with a symbolic flourish. For a moment I imagined him in his black gown, the first day I'd ever seen him, the day I vomited all over the back seats and big oak doors of the Grand Hall.

I knew before I stepped on the train for my second Christmas at home that it was going to be as bad as the last.

The train was derailed a few miles out of Brisbane, causing a two-hour delay that obviously threw my family completely out of kilter. When I stepped off at Kurra, there was nobody in sight, except a couple of new linesmen taking a smoko. It was foolish to be disappointed, since Rosebery was only a hundred yards from the platform, but I couldn't help it. I sat down on an inside seat, and wept.

How long I had been there when Pa sat down beside me, I do not know. His thin, weak arms draped around me as he pushed my head into his chest and hugged me as he hadn't done since I was a little girl. He rocked me gently, periodically patting my hair and renewing the hug until I had cried myself out.

'Welcome home, darling,' he said at last. 'I'm so sorry there was nobody here to meet you. Ma's preparing a special dinner for you though, all your favourite things. Ruth's painted your room and Than can say Billy Rachel Batchelor in one breath now. She's been coaching him day and night. Sister Mac's coming over for tea too. She got your card last week. It was good of you to remember.'

'Are . . . are the boys home?' I asked shyly, wondering whether they'd remember me. I hadn't written to any of them all year. 'Micky is, but we don't see much of him. He's doing it hard, Billy, what with the floods last year after Cyclone Elsie. And the Depression. Mini Mini is all but washed up. Micky is surviving, just, but there weren't enough returns for two. Jock's gone south, teaching. Figgy and Constance couldn't keep James in work either. He got a job with the *Bulletin* in Sydney. He'll go a long way, James. David's struggling at med school. That's about it, isn't it? I would have written you about the boys if I'd thought of it.'

'I should have asked, Pa. It's a shame Ma never learnt to write,' I added unnecessarily.

'Yes. Yes. She would have kept you up with all the gossip, wouldn't she?' he smiled wanly. 'And we're keeping Ruth too busy to maintain regular letters . . .'

I didn't notice how sick he was at first, wrapped up in myself and my deflated ego, but he spent much of that Christmas in bed and I spent much of it sitting on

161

the commode chair, reading next year's texts to him. He had developed a stomach ulcer and a hernia and suffered excruciating migraine headaches. On top of this, his heart was weakened from the war, Doc Halliday said. He wanted to operate on the hernia, but Pa was too weak and Ma was terrified of the knife. She vowed that even if Pa eventually got strong enough, she wouldn't let an old quack like Halliday get near him with a ten-foot barge pole.

Anyone could see that my father was in a no-win situation, since there was no money to bring in a second opinion and barely enough to pay for his medicines. Sister Mac managed to slip a few free bottles of pills and mixtures his way whenever a pharmaceutical salesman visited the hospital, but such visits were few and far between and after a while, they halved her samples. 'The Depression,' they apologized.

Ruth took over the running of the telegraph station and did most of the paper work for the railway as well, with the result that we spent little time together. When there were moments to spare, we were too exhausted to reach beneath the surface for the friendship of our youth. Ma looked after Than during the days and I baby-sat him in the evenings. He was beautiful, but demanding. I began to look for Ruth to come off duty long before she was finished.

I saw Micky on two occasions. He was more handsome than ever, with muscles to die for. He only visited because of his fondness for Than, Ma said. I wondered if he'd ever been told directly that Than was his. Ruth said he would never trust her, even if she could prove it. He hadn't taken up with anyone else around town, though, going the way of so many young men on the land during the Depression, and seemed destined to be an uncle to everyone else's children. Veronica and Isobella had both married boys from Tarrenbonga and begun the reproduction of the clan. Ma said the boys they married were louts, but mainly held her tongue in check when it came to the O'Ryans. They'd been through enough, she said.

David Moon came home for three days and mean old Giles kept him cornered the entire time. He dropped in on his way to the train to wish Pa a speedy recovery, but I was at the hospital picking up some medicines and missed him completely. Ruth said he was incredibly good-looking and smoother than ever. Ma described him as less of a dark horse these days, mainly because he had no idea who he was, where he was going, or why. 'His sister fared better,' she said.

Amelia had joined the Presbyterian mission in old Stuart Town, or Alice Springs as it had recently been renamed, as a trainee nurse, a compromise that pleased her father. She kept it to herself that she was still determined to become a missionary. She was unable to get home for Christmas, and I couldn't help wondering if she'd begged for a Christmas shift to avoid returning to her father, though she still wrote to Prinky every week, as though she were her natural mother.

The Reverend was growing more belligerent every day. When I recalled to Sister Mac how he'd seemed to soften after the fire and the deaths and black uprisings, but was now obviously reverting to form, she put me smartly in my place.

'I liked ya better when ya mouth ran off with flamin' questions, child,' she snapped. 'Don't ya say nothin' bad about the old Giles ta me, young 'un. He might be a bit crotchety, but you would be too if ya'd had a wife of easy virtue who upped an' abandoned her babies an' then ya kids upped an' abandoned you too. Holy Mary, Mother of God, 'e does 'is best,' and with that she'd crossed herself and turned her attention back to folding bandages.

When the time came to return to Brisbane, I couldn't get to the train fast enough. Pa was out of danger and back at work part time, Ma was huffing and puffing about not turning her hand to make me some new clothes because of the work load she'd had to cope with, Ruth and Than were spending mornings together again and Sister Mac had taken a week's leave to attend her sister's funeral and wind up her affairs in Tarrenbonga. It stunned me that she had a sister. I didn't think she had anyone, except us. Why had we never met her, heard about her at least? Pa didn't know and Ma didn't seem to want to expand. I let it go. As Rosebery got back to normal, I realized it would never be the same again.

My train left at midday. Pa had an appointment at the hospital for tests, Ma was on duty with Nan, in the soup kitchen, as the Temperance Tea House had become, Ruth was on duty at the station, Micky had turned up to mind Than. We all said goodbye in the kitchen, Ma handing me the mandatory basket of goodies that would last about a week, Ruth and Than hugging and kissing, almost like old times. With Pa's improved physical condition, and perhaps because we were not alone, the old-fashioned tough fatherly façade returned, allowing an austere peck on the cheek and a brotherly pat on the back.

I longed to hug him, as he had hugged me just a few weeks before. Instead, I smiled wet eyes on all of them and left as I had arrived – alone and lonely.

The odd thing about being desperately unhappy and confused is that the moment you decide to accept your miserable fate, life starts to pick up.

I moved back into my old room in the Churchill House in the February of 1934 with a head start on the texts for my final year and a determination to knuckle down and prove that I could do at least one thing well. Though I felt very different from the little bush girl who'd arrived two years before, frightened and tremulous with excitement at the adventures that lay ahead, in every physical way, nothing seemed to have changed. The white ants continued their march through the ceiling and walls and windows, the bathroom was still empty when I used it and my only female friend on campus, Thea Bickley, still occupied the room next door. Somehow, the sameness, the ordinariness of all things familiar, comforted me. I settled in with a sense of coming home that had been absent from my life for a long time.

I had expected to miss the dinners in the city, the joy rides up the coast, the flat with its privacy and independence. I had expected to miss Harry and the boisterous dissertations into the wee small hours of the morn. I did miss the loving, the warm nights that flamed as hot as the logs in Ma's wood stove, or, more lately, as embers trying to sleep, with the callous draughts from the chimney fanning them into a long, slow death. Yet there was a sense of relief at being back with my own age group that made the adjustment easier, or perhaps it was the slow death of our affair that had prepared me for new life? I knew I should ponder the matter at length, but there wasn't time for deep post mortems. In any case, I was still angry with myself and tired of thinking about it altogether.

'The drama group are looking for a Katharina for the mid-year concert!' Thea burst into my room, puffing loudly from a dash across the gardens. 'I heard old Blue Beard telling Dove Wilson you'd be perfect for it. He's going to ask you at tutorial tonight. You'll do it, won't you? I think you'd be marvellous, Billy, simply marvellous!'

I wasn't sure whether it was Thea's increasing affectation that annoyed me, or Harry's presumption to stick his nose into my business and dictate what I did with my spare time.

'I couldn't possibly do it, Thea. My scholarship finishes this year. So do I, believe me.'

'You're such a brain, Billy, you'd have no trouble at all. And it's the leading role! They've offered me Bianca,' she added sweetly. 'Peter's playing Hortensio, the lover!'

She was still absolutely mad about Peter Caruthers, who remained impervious to, if not remarkably tolerant of, her blatant advances. Sometimes he let her buy him an evening at the pictures, which fuelled her hopes and improved his lifestyle but did nothing to ignite any romantic overtures from him.

I didn't know *The Taming of the Shrew* but had heard it mentioned as the likely choice, there being only two female roles to fill. 'Have you read the play, Thea?' I asked curiously.

'Well, no, but it's a comedy,' she replied authoritatively, as though that settled everything. I reached for my *Complete Works of Shakespeare* and quickly isolated the play. It took but a minute or two to read the compendium and the last speech, a trick Harry had taught me. It had never before served me so well.

'Perhaps it might be fun . . .' I smiled distantly, avoiding Thea's wide-eyed naïveté. 'Bianca has more than one suitor though, Thea. She's Italian and is wooed for her money.' I wanted to add, 'Good casting,' but thought better of it. It was hardly Thea's fault that her family were incredibly rich.

'And Katharina?' she pressed eagerly.

'Katharina is your older sister, the shrew. She's self-willed and violent, jealous of her mild little sister, but not as strong a character as she thinks she is. Petruchio, a bold gentleman from Verona who cares nothing for what others think, transforms her into a gentle and obedient wife. Do you really think I could act out such a role, Thea?'

'You'd be wonderful,' she enthused generously. 'Playing a total opposite would be much easier than playing yourself, like I'll have to do.'

I looked sideways at her face; her voice was mocking but her eyes were edged with a sadness I had not noticed before. Perhaps there was more to Thea than I had given credence to.

The irony of Professor Carmichael's recommendation that Billy Batchelor play the part of Katharina was lost on campus. Brusque congratulatory and shy good luck wishes were extended from young men I'd barely acknowledged previously. Peter Caruthers was particularly vocal. 'With your speaking voice and personality, Billy, there was simply nobody else in the entire university, possibly all of Brisbane, who'd be right for the part.'

Thea agreed wholeheartedly, without a hint of jealousy. 'Absolutely! Nobody else would be right for the part.'

I set to work to learn my lines, knowing there'd be little time near the season of the play; mid-year assignments would be due. Thea flirted with luck, on all fronts, and did her damnedest to distract me from study and serious rehearsal.

Breathtakingly elegant, Thea was still plain, short-sighted and generous to a fault (with her money and her spirit), but she lacked the motivation to achieve. She wanted a nice boy, preferably Peter Caruthers, a medical student, who would fall madly in love with her and by-the-by be grateful she could afford to keep him until he was established and successful. She'd been sent to university for precisely that purpose. She'd been boy crazy from an early age, and her parents hoped to delay the inevitable and at least improve her mind sufficiently to make her a good wife for a professional man. 'The days of the wealthy layabout husband are over,' Mrs Bickley had drummed into Thea's head. It made little sense to her, since Mr Bickley had worked such hours all her life, she barely knew him. Everyone else who entered the mansion seemed joined at the wrist to a briefcase too.

In spite of her singularly unattractive upbringing, it was impossible to dislike her. She was also quite insult-proof; when her affectation or incessant chatter became overbearing, a quip 'give it a break, Thea' was enough to silence her without offence for hours.

There was only one chance to develop my role prior to the six weeks of rehearsal that led up to the two-week season. I went in search of Professor Wilson, or Dove as he was called, even on campus, mainly due to his theatrical style. Established rules didn't mean much to him and I had the feeling he'd understand when I told him I had to put on the show of my life because I wanted to be an actress. It was a lie then, but by opening night it had become the truth.

Dove was six feet seven inches tall, as thin as Pa, but with firm, muscular arms and shoulders that belonged more to an athlete than a professor. Sloppy and dishevelled, he reminded me of Joey the way his clothes didn't fit, never quite sat well on him, even first thing in the morning when, presumably, they were clean and freshly ironed. Yet as an English master and drama coach, he was a perfectionist, encouraging, driving and dragging us ever upwards to a clearer view, a new approach, a sharper reason for thinking at all. His fiery enthusiasm would not accept failure, but he had the knack of making even the weakest students feel better about themselves.

'Why do you want to be an actress, Billy?' he

asked immediately, dispensing with preliminaries. Was there anything I could say that he hadn't heard before?

'Because I'm happiest when I'm pretending,' I answered spontaneously, unaware I'd succeeded in surprising him.

He eyed me quizzically. 'What makes you think you'd be any good?' The question shocked me. It hadn't occurred to me I might not be.

'Because I've had five years of elocution lessons and . . . and I've got a photographic memory and . . .'

'No, no, no, no, no! Answer the question! Don't give me reasons from your brain, Miss Batchelor. Give me an answer from the heart, that is, if you can dredge it up again after the damage that's undoubtedly been done to it.'

The blood rushed to my cheeks. 'What do you mean?'

He said nothing for a few moments, then flashed me one of those dazzling Wilson smiles that sent ripples of excitement through the female first yearers when he was charging up and down the aisles of the lecture hall. 'If you have a passion, the only way to satisfy it, is to pursue it,' he said quietly. 'Maybe you don't know what your passion is yet, but acting might be the best way for you to discover it. Let us find out, shall we?'

I paced the dressing room, trying to remember my opening line. It wouldn't come. There was nothing there at all. A nasty lump was forming in my stomach, getting bigger and tighter, pushing my breath out in short, asthmatic bursts.

Dove poked his head around the door again, the easy smile more tentative than it had been the last time. 'Five minutes, Billy. Chookers!'

'Dove, I can't remember a word! What am I going to do?'

'Take deep breaths. You'll be wonderful once you get past the opening line.'

'That's just it, Dove,' I gasped, forcing him to enter. 'I can't remember it . . . can't remember anything! I'm afraid I'm going to let you down miserably, after all your work and faith in me . . .'

He grabbed my shoulders with his large hands and shook me into silence. Mouth open, I looked up at his angry face in shocked confusion. 'Don't look at me for sympathy or support, Billy Batchelor. Pull yourself together and get out on that stage and perform! This is not a country concert and you're not a small-town girl any more either. This is the big smoke and you better start acting like a professional.' He wrenched his hands from my shoulders and stormed out, slamming the door behind him. I jumped, the lump in my stomach leaping to my throat, pausing on the way up to kick-start my heart again.

The curtain was up and the Hostess and Sly entered. I was in the wings now, whispering good luck to the Lord and the Huntsman seconds before their entrance. The trumpets heralded the approach of the strolling players. The first servant was speaking, the second, the third . . . and still the Page and the Messenger to come. Would the First Act ever begin? Lucentio with his man, Tranio. One long speech each, then Baptista, Hortensio, Bianca, Gremio – and Katharina.

Suddenly, the lump dissolved with the jellied nerves. The real world returned, more vibrant, more exhilarating than one single word uttered during the weeks of relentless repetition and thankless rehearsals. 'Don't take that line so glibly, Billy! Get up quickly, listen to what you're saying, Billy! Turn slowly, gradually, make your actions a part of your speeches, Billy! Timing, girl, timing! Feel it, feel it, God, when are you ever going to stop acting and start feeling it?'

The First Act was over, and then the Second. On we went, moving quickly now, too quickly. My last speech was looming, the one I hated in rehearsals; the metamorphosis of woman, a theme worn threadbare in Shakespeare's day. The lines sang to me now, as though they were mine . . . and it was all over. Petruchio said, 'Why, there's a wench! Come on, and kiss me, Kate,' we made our exits and the curtains closed.

They opened again. We took our first bow. Drew back again, holding hands; more bows. Then some-one pushed me forward. I stood there, like a fool. 'Bow, Billy,' Dove yelled from the wings. I obeyed, seeing nothing, hearing nothing. The footlights came up. Half the audience were on their feet. Suddenly, the noise was deafening. I stood back and we all bowed again. The curtains slowly closed. Everyone was laughing, shaking hands, patting each other on the back. Some of the players were hugging. Every-one wanted to kiss me and shake Dove's hand.

I wanted to escape, to rush to my dressing room and savour the night of my life. I wanted to hold it tight against my chest and keep it safe from their flattery and pride. 'Thank you, thank you,' I said to the left and the right of me. 'You were great too.' I remembered my manners, conscious of the rising narcissism in my heart. *It's only opening night, Billy. You may be a total disaster tomorrow.*

But the season was an outstanding success and the usual talent scouts were in our audience for the final curtain two weeks later.

'You have a rare gift, Miss Batchelor,' Brumby Gorman said, extending his hand with Dove's intro-duction. 'I'm looking for a Jessica for *The Merchant* later in the year at the Playbox. I'd like to offer it to you. It's not a big part, as you'd know, but it would give you a good start. It will pay five pounds a week, plus lodgings, for the run of the show. With the age-old hatred of Christian and Jew rearing its head again, we're expecting a long 'un,' he grinned, an avaricious, toothy grin that nevertheless held no malice. He moved away, dismissing me with a nod of the head and a deep draw on his expensive cigar. It was a large Havana with a gold band halfway along. Ruth and I gave a box to Pa one Christmas. The full-flavoured smell turned my thoughts swiftly home-wards.

Rosey and Nathan Batchelor's little girl being offered five pounds a week? It was impossible, unbelievable, totally insane. I could hear the old-timers in Shaft's pub rolling it around their tongues in bewildered awe. Who would be pleased and who would feel slighted, subverted by the rapidly changing world? A girl getting more than man's basic wage? The thought of it was enough to divide the town; at very least, it would create much business over Kurra's kitchen tables.

Harry Carmichael interrupted my thoughts. 'So you're on your way, little shrew, are you? Can't say I'm surprised, you've worked hard for it and you deserve it. I didn't think you'd do it, of course, but then, you've always been a contradictory miss, haven't you?'

His voice was more sharply laced with sarcasm than I remembered it in private conversation, or was it something else, more sinister?

'What didn't you think I'd do, Harry?' I ventured cautiously.

'Risk your chance of being Triton among the minnows for your degree, but then, you've achieved that in another way now, haven't you? I always said you were destined to track a different path, though I must admit I never thought you'd get your tongue around some of Katharina's speeches so convincingly . . . Why did you do it, Billy? I'd be really interested to know.' He was riding me, the way he always had, for his own deserts.

A part of me wanted to let him back into my head, tell him everything, how miserable I'd been, how I'd wanted him back, had taken the part to show him he'd never be happy with anyone but me; how all the young girls were wet behind the ears. I wanted to tell him I was capable of being enough woman for any man, that I was not just a wilful, stubborn girl from the bush. Fortuitously, the perfect part had landed in my lap, an allegory of the part I had decided I wanted to play in life.

Now, as I stood in front of the man who had inspired me to such passionate and calculating endeavour, I wondered what on earth I'd ever seen in him! Yet, this balding old man in his forties, with an ugly face that had to be covered with whatever hair still managed to grow to make him halfway presentable, was the catalyst who had manipulated me into growing up, plunged me into darkness, then, albeit unwittingly, dragged me back into new life, new hope, new beginnings. I marvelled that I had so lost my way, chasing the obscure comfort zones of my mother's existence, that I'd stumbled over the very dream I'd dared to dream as a youngster.

He was waiting for my answer. Which answer should I give? Mama's words 'be good, sweet maid, and let who will be clever' sounded from the prop boy in the wings. 'I decided it would take my mind off breaking up with you, Harry, give me something to do other than study. It's been great fun. I'm glad you liked my performance.' That's enough, Billy, I disciplined myself. Another word and he'll know you're lying.

As it stood, I could see he wasn't sure, but he gave me the benefit of the doubt. 'And will you take up Gorman's offer and tread the boards, Billy?' he asked emphatically, as though the answer was a foregone conclusion.

'It would kill Ma and Pa,' I replied in like manner.

'They know your make-believe world has always been more real than . . . well, the real world, Billy. I doubt it would surprise or shock them in the least.'

'And have you found your passion?' Dove's effeminate, lilting voice interrupted us, a striking contrast to Harry's soulful monotones. In stature, the contrast was greater. The old Blue Beard, tough Harry, looked decidedly small. I had never thought of him as short before. 'I think it would be fair to say I've rediscovered it, yes, but it's going to have to wait until I finish my degree. Would you tell Mr Gorman, Dove, or shall I?'

'I'll tell him,' Harry proposed with uncharacteristic brevity, moving away through the crowded room to the bar where the theatrical visitors congregated.

When he returned, he was strangely elated. 'What are you drinking?' Dove asked. 'It's working. What did he say?'

'He offered five pounds ten shillings and not a penny more. Want to change your mind, Billy?' I couldn't speak.

Dove shook his head. 'He's not a man to offer twice, Harry, but surely he'd understand in these circumstances?'

Now Harry shook his head. 'No, he made it clear she's unlikely to ever get another offer from him if she says no tonight. He's a bloody Pom and thinks women should be barefoot and pregnant.'

'But that's ridiculous!' I cried. 'He wouldn't be in a

job if there weren't any actresses. Who'd do the female parts?'

'He'd write them out of the scripts,' Dove groaned.

Harry quickly commiserated. 'Don't feel bad, Billy. You've been offered five pounds ten by Brumby Gorman. That fact can't be rescinded because you've declined the offer.'

Dove smiled jubilantly. 'That's right, Billy, that's quite right. Congratulations!' They watched my eyes fill and overflow, followed by the blood rushing to my cheeks. One day I would learn to control them both.

'When you're an international star and the whole world's applauding, you'll be able to shove it up Gorman!' Harry said crudely, patting me on the back like a man born of a different age.

But I wasn't at all sure I hadn't just turned down the opportunity I needed to get me there.

# NINE

# 1934

'Billy, Billy, thank God you're home!' Ruth welcomed on the platform, throwing her thin brown arms around me, hugging and clutching, tears instantly streaming down both our faces. 'Ruth, oh Ruthy!' It's wonderful to see you!'

A lifetime ago was just a minute away then; we gushed our way through a torrent of questions before I remembered my manners. 'Oh dear, forgive me, Thea. Ruth, this is Thea Bickley. Thea, this is Ruth. Thea's parents have gone overseas so I invited her home for Christmas. I couldn't let her sit around in her big house just waiting for results, could I? Ma and Pa won't mind, will they? Are you okay, Ruth?' I asked, noticing her appearance for the first time. 'You've lost weight.' She was never fat, but she had a womanly roundness about her, even before she'd had Than. I looked at her more critically as my words came back at me, realizing she'd lost at least a stone and looked gaunt and pale. 'Oh Ruthy, what's wrong?'

She gathered up my cases and one of Thea's, automatically slipping into the role model of long ago. 'Put those down at once!' I ordered. 'You're not a house girl now.' She dropped the large one in shock, then struggled to take it from me.

'That's all I'm going to be left with, Billy. Please don't rob me of it too.' Her voice was parched, her posture wilted like the grey gums along the track to Rosebery. It hadn't rained for five months.

Along the dusty track, under the glare of the hot afternoon sun, I could dimly make out an old man on a walking stick moving slowly, haltingly towards us. Could it be? My heart sank, then began to pound wildly. I started to run, but stopped a few steps away from him, unable to rush the final moment.

'Pa?' I whispered.

He lunged forward, throwing his arms around me, his stick thumping to the ground. 'I'm so glad you're home, Billy,' he gasped, his chest groaning with the effort. We rocked together, arms firmly entwined, until I heard Thea and Ruth behind us. I introduced Thea.

'Pa, Thea's parents went overseas last week and, well, she didn't really have anywhere to go so I asked her home for Christmas.'

Pa nodded sadly. 'You're welcome, Miss Bickley,' he said distantly, his skeleton body leaning heavily on mine as we staggered up to the back gate.

Ma's huge frame filled the kitchen door, white apron pressed tightly against a pink bulging blouse that gaped open halfway down the deeply creased pink breasts. Her once brown, silky hair was grey and frizzy now, yet she stood as tall as the mountains, authority intact and all-powerful, even stronger than I remembered her. Was it possible – or were the diminished statures of Ruth and Pa creating an illusion?

'I'm glad you're home, Rachel,' she said simply and I knew the news was worse than I had feared. She welcomed Thea briskly and instructed us to unpack, bathe and rest after the long trip. 'We have guests this evening, so you girls will need to dress.'

I waited impatiently for tea, knowing there would be no unloading of bad news before we were settled at the kitchen table and well into our meal. I wanted to apologize to Thea in advance for bringing her into a family crisis, but she seemed impervious to the brooding disaster around us. It occurred to me that anything that happened at Rosebery would probably be mild compared to what she'd seen in her own home.

Sister Mac arrived shortly after five and greeted me, as I was now coming to expect. 'We's real glad ya come home, Billy. My, I was worried sick ya'd take up that big offer in the city an' then where'd we be?'

When Reverend Moon arrived, I was convinced Pa was dying. They needed me home for the funeral. I wanted to scream at the top of my lungs, to throw something at the walls, to grab Pa and hug him so fiercely that my will to live would return to his body, breathe colour back into his sagging cheeks. Why did we have to go through this charade . . . this slow torture?

The house was strangely quiet without the radio blaring. I could barely remember when it hadn't been, nor understand exactly why it wasn't. Sister Mac, Thea and I sat chatting idly, useless conversation to fill in the time until tea was ready. We tried to enthuse about what we would do if we passed our degrees; my heart wasn't in it, and Thea really didn't expect to pass. Ma and Ruth would not allow any help on my first night home, but Ruth was getting anxious about Than. Micky had taken him riding and was late returning.

'Tell us all about him, Ruth,' I urged for the second time, looking for distraction on the one hand, hungry for news of him on the other. I was aching to cuddle him, jog him on my knee like old times, like nothing had changed . . . but she turned back to the stove.

'He'll be here soon. You can see for yourself.'

Why are we all being so cool and polite? Because good manners demand that we never make anybody feel uncomfortable, Billy! Because self-control is the most important thing. You'll never make a mistake you can't cover if you remain in control, Billy. You'll be respected by everyone and have a reputation you can be proud of. You'll never hurt anyone inadvertently. You'll never get bloody hurt either, because you'll never let anyone close enough to know your bloody feelings! Thus I lectured and castigated myself all afternoon, holding my tongue behind clenched teeth.

At last the sound of horses' hoofs cut through our stilted conversation. Ruth rushed to the door. Than appeared first, running as fast as his solid brown legs could carry him, falling into Ruth's outstretched arms in joyous reunion.

'Mushy, Mushy, we had a iceceam and I wode the pony!' He was kissing her, but his big black eyes were focused on the stove. 'I'm hungry, Gamma,' he tilted his head at Ma, a cheeky, pleading smile opening up his pixie face. I could not believe how beautiful he'd become, perfect but for the scarred red line running from his upper lip to the edge of his nose.

'Why, he's healed miraculously,' I cried in wonder, rushing towards him with hands extended. He shied away, burying his head in Ruth's shoulder.

'It's Billy, darling, we love Billy,' Ruth coerced. 'Give him a minute or two and he'll go to you readily.'

Micky entered quietly. He was taller than I recalled, and even broader about the shoulders. His face had filled out and was deeply tanned, the colour of the earth on the east side of the Kurrajong Ranges. Sister Mac said he'd pulled Mini Mini round, and he had the confident air of a station owner in good times about him, his walk slightly staggered by years in the saddle, or the unfamiliarity of drawing-room society.

'Welcome home, Billy,' he smiled shyly, a flush of colour charging into his cheeks.

Ma nudged me. 'Oh Micky, this is my friend Thea Bickley. Thea, I'd like you to meet Micky O'Ryan.'

Thea stood up, then sat down, blushing furiously. 'How do you do?' she stammered.

For a few seconds, nobody spoke. A burning sensation caught the back of my throat. Everyone was looking from one to the other, as the blood rushed shamelessly to both their cheeks. I looked furtively at Ruth, wondering what anguish their obvious attraction had caused her.

She smiled sweetly, as though she'd missed it. 'Thanks for giving Than such a great time, Micky. I'll see you out.' He mumbled his goodbyes and they exited to the verandah. I was stunned that he had not been invited to stay, but there was a sense of preordained order amidst the chaos that forced me to cut my tongue. When Ruth returned, Ma declared we would eat.

Reverend Moon had been remarkably silent but a plate of food in front of him was all he needed to embark on his latest hobbyhorse – the war drums beating in Europe. For the first time I became aware that the reason he was a sloppy eater was because he talked nonstop while his mouth was full, slithers of curried kidney sticking to his full grey beard like acne. Very soon, Ma's white starched double damask napkin was polka-dotted and ragged. Like me, I noted, Thea had to look away. How much worse could tonight get?

'The filthy Italians can't hide behind fascist façades for long, Nathan. The British will have to step in. The Germans have got the right idea. Banning the Jews from public life will ease the tension, they'll be able to consolidate and build a strong nation without them. It's all a matter of genes. Genes are destiny after all. You'd have learnt that at university, girls, I suppose?' he laughed capriciously, a supercilious edge to his voice that I'd heard many times before. But it was different now. Inside I fumed. Outwardly I smiled.

'Two can play, Reverend Moon, but you've certainly got us trapped.' I paused momentarily while he proudly stroked his beard. 'Our upbringing has taught us to be respectful of our elders and our education has taught us not to bother arguing with closed minds, so we'll let that pass if you don't mind, Reverend.'

I heard a short escape of air from Pa that fairly terrified me. In spite of the great advantages I'd been blessed with, I was still a selfish, thoughtless girl with no regard for his health or dying heart.

'I'm glad to see that education is not wasted on the young,' he said from the grave, though as I looked at him then, I thought I could see a little colour in his cheeks and the slightest twinkle returning to his eyes. 'What's the general feeling on campus, girls, about the Europe situation? Are your male counterparts excited at the prospect of war?' He sighed heavily. Whenever he recollected his own feelings before going to The Great War, they were inextricably linked to me; hating to leave, guilty for daring to feel glad he was going. I had been patient long enough.

'Yes, Pa, they are, but when will somebody tell me what's going on *here*? Please don't tell me I'm imagining it! I realize it's unfair on Thea to be dragged into a family crisis, but she's here and it would be extremely bad manners to exclude her now. Please? Sister Mac? Why don't you begin?'

Sister Mac shifted in her chair, then hiccupped. Ma poured her a fresh glass of water. Ruth rose and left through the fortress-room door. 'What is going on?' I stared at Pa, who focused on his pipe on the mantelpiece. Reverend Moon came dramatically to his feet, moving his plate away, patting his beard with the clown-like napkin. He might have been about to serve communion.

'The simple facts are these, Billy. Your mother and father, Rosey and Nathan, cannot continue to bring up young Than. Your father is not a well man and as much as Rosey and Nathan would love to adopt him, sadly, it's quite out of the question. The strain of a young boy around the house will only increase as Nathan gets older, not to mention the fact that your mother has quite enough to do . . . what with her increased duties at Rosebery and her service to the community, which as you know are without equal.' He paused judiciously, nodding at Ma with all the humility he could muster. As my panic rose, I hated God for giving the racist Reverend Moon more verbosity than the tolerant Harry Carmichael, though I had to admit it would be a close call. 'The facts are,' he continued with the conviction of a school teacher in a room full of five-year-olds, 'Than is a half-caste and as such, under the Assimilation Law, must be adopted by a white family, preparing for a white education. The Social Welfare inspector has most considerately given us a short period, six months, in order to find a suitable, sympathetic home for the child. Micky would like to adopt him, but, unfortunately, he doesn't have a wife.'

I bolted in my chair, spilling some tea in the saucer. Ma jumped up and wiped away the few drops with a great deal of unnecessary fuss. 'What . . . what on earth are you talking about?' I stuttered. 'Surely he can stay here, with Ruth? She's bringing him up, after all . . . in a white home!'

Sister Mac leant over the table confidentially, her voice lowered, her eyes darting towards the fortress room. She waved a hand at the Reverend, who sat down surprisingly obediently, wiping his brow with the curried kidneys.

'Billy, the laws ain't changed none since Ruth herself come to Rosebery in the first place. Ya know Than's gotta go to a married couple. Micky O'Ryan's turned out ta be a good bloke . . . 'e's pulled that station up by its boot straps an' got it runnin' good through the Depression an' all, so he's no slouch an' 'e don't wanna lose 'is baby.' It was the first time I'd heard an overt acknowledgement of Than's paternity in my home. Though I should have felt pleased, I was too shocked to feel anything. 'We been hopin', tossin' it around some, now that you've got ya education out o' the way, ya might be able ta come up with a way for us ta keep the baby in the family like, an' Ruth could be his aunty an' not 'ave to go through losin' 'im altogether, see? It'd be a truly Christian thing to do, if we could find a wife for Micky, an' the boy'd grow up good an' white.' Sister Mac leant back, seeking Ma's eyes for approval. Ma looked into her lap, cheeks drawn and grey. Pa nodded sadly, the resigned blue eyes rimmed with tears. I realized at last just how much his poor state of health had weakened his spirit.

It was difficult to accept the unspoken suggestion, but accept it, I must. Understanding would maybe lead me to find a palatable, happy solution. Ma had certainly not sent me to university, in order to marry me off to a country bumpkin, and a Catholic at that! But the men, even Sister Mac . . . did they still think an education for a girl was just a foolish female whim? That now that it's over and done with, it's time to be sensible, take up my role as a married servant?

'What does Ruth think of this?' I asked despondently, trying to focus on the reality of what had been proposed, wondering if I was having a nightmare, wondering if anything I'd ever learnt would ever return to my paralysed brain.

'She's an intelligent girl, is accepting the inevitable,' Pa replied. 'She knows she can't offer Than the advantages a white family could and is probably secretly relieved. After all, she'll have the best of both worlds, if Micky can adopt . . .' he added, unable to verbalize any suggestion of my direct involvement in the matter. He knew it was ridiculous too. I wondered if my whole family had gone mad. Was this any better a proposal than Swift's – or Hitler's?

'But what does she really think?' I asked again.

'Unfortunately, Billy, it doesn't matter what Ruth thinks,' Reverend Moon intercepted stoically. 'Under the law, she can't keep the child. We have to come up with a humane answer and finding Micky a wife is a perfect solution! If I may be so delicate, you could do worse, yourself. It could be a desirable marriage for you, dear girl, could it not? Wonderful thing to do for your friend Ruth . . . I understand, of course, that you may feel a certain disappointment that Micky is not, er . . . pure. But, if he could find a *suitable* Presbyterian, he has agreed to convert, in recognition of his sinful Catholic ways. He has promised to bring the boy up in the Protestant faith, thereby completely forsaking his past for his wife!'

My heart had stopped pounding as I looked around the table then. In the company of unquestionable allies, I grappled with the fact that they had taken a position on the side of right, on the stacked side of blinding Christian values. Oh Ruthy, what did we want to be when we grew up? Do you remember? How far from our dreams have we landed? I got up from the table, knowing I must seek her out and talk with her, that every minute I delayed would make the barrier greater, perhaps tip the scales against friendship for ever.

'Where are you going?' Reverend Moon started to his feet.

'Excuse me,' I said shortly, sending an apologetic grimace to Thea.

I entered the fortress room hesitantly. She was not there. The front door was slightly ajar.

I found her on the steps, staring out across the still black night. The wind had eased since our arrival. Large cumulus clouds had formed, hiding the constant moon and the River of the Sky – the thousands of babies that made up the Milky Way. I sat down beside her. 'He's having a rare night off,' I murmured without need of further explanation. It was written, in the Dreamtime; the face in the moon was the Father.

Ruth's lips barely moved. 'They're going to force me to take a lifetime off, aren't they?' she asked wearily, looking me squarely in the eyes. How much did she know? I regretted I hadn't paused long enough to find out.

'You know the law won't allow you to keep Than because he has a white father?' I asked as pragmatically as possible.

'Sure! That's how I came to be taken from my mother. I realize a lot of things now . . . and I'll find her one day. I've promised myself and I will. History repeats . . . I'm glad Micky wants his boy,' she nodded sadly, 'but finding him a wife won't be easy, if that's what they're thinking. There's nobody around any more.' Her instincts warned her something was not quite right. 'Is there a plan, a woman they have in mind I don't know about?' She lowered her heart with the movement of her eyes.

'They've decided I should marry Micky.'

'Oh.'

'At least, the men have, I think. They're hoping I might be satisfied with my education now, be ready to settle down.'

'Sister Mac? Ma? I can't believe it!'

'Sister Mac's prepared to go along – Micky's a Mick . . . Ma's counting on me coming up with a brilliant idea.'

'And have you?'

'Not yet.'

We sat close together, hugging the blessedly dark night in calamitous silence. We had never been closer together, yet plainly, never further apart. I understood Ruth would be searching the Dreamtime, searching the Never Never for answers that weren't there. Just another black woman reaching back for the roots denied her, about to be denied her son. How long would it be before there was nothing left to take?

I too struggled for identity, reaching back through the immutable power of white Australian history. I searched for answers of a frontier that had attracted a dubious mix of folk: Britain's best and worst, gold diggers out to make fortunes, underachievers trying to prove themselves, mercenaries looking for a quick buck, unskilled, unemployable men in their mother country. They'd claimed a stake in the Australian bush, dug a living out of iron wills and sweating brows, taken black women to their beds, birthed generations of half-castes – never wanted, never acknowledged. Then along came the missionaries and the Reverend Moons, devout in their knowledge that God's paradise awaits if only they can save the half-castes from their own inheritance, from this hellhole of blackguards, black sheep, black markets, black velvets . . . Black Tuesdays, Black Thursdays, Black, Black, Black, colourless black, obliterated from the light.

Why had the fair-skinned English women given up their privileged, genteel lives to come to this godforsaken land? Women who looked more like men a decade later, tough and weathered, pioneers in their own rights . . . Rights? Why, Pa's own mother had done it, Sabella Prescott did it, Micky's mother had done it! And the men of my world wanted me to do it. The only way to forgive was to excuse them their ignorance. They could not see that they were asking the same, asking for life to stand still, for progress to go away, for enlightenment to wither and die. Yet still the answer eluded me. What point the sacrifice? White women, black women: one bred sons to die for other men's land, the other bred sons to give away to other men's wives.

Was my education just a troublesome blackhead, a short pimply disease that had now passed, with the passing of puberty? You're cured, Billy, you've had your fun! Now it's time for the wake and you'll dress like Snow White and the old women will know it's actually your funeral and cry right through the wedding service. For love you must black out your dreams, little girl. You don't want change! How can you profit from change? You want exchange! Exchange is the basis of all family values. You take your husband's handouts and he takes your body and soul, and then conspires to kill that which you produce for some far nobler cause.

'I'm not going to succumb, Ruth!' The words tumbled out. 'At least Ma will be enormously relieved . . .' My arms crushed around her. 'I'll fight for your right to keep Than. A child should be with his mother – we preach that for our own, then convince ourselves that it's not God's will for you! I won't let them take him away from you, I promise, Ruthy, I promise!'

She smiled as she wiped her eyes, a tragic smile that believed in me but knew not to trust my words. 'Don't weep for us, Billy.' She stroked my hair. 'White folks are taught from birth to acquire wealth and all the images money can buy. Black folks are taught the opposite. We hunt and gather, we understand the world and its creation. We will survive in Dreamtime. And the dreaming starts with the baby's first kicks in the mother's womb, Billy, so Than's destiny is long struck. It will be his, uniquely, for all time. No white man can destroy it, nor manipulate it for his own misguided purposes. Than will survive because our laws are the laws of the universe.'

I stared at her with a new kind of reverence. How had she come to understand so much from such a dark, white sheltered world? How could my own family have so misjudged her private despair, her inner strength? As though reading my thoughts, she turned to me with a mischievous grin. 'Coons ain't afraid of the dark, Billy. Why, didn't ya know, we can see right through it!'

On New Year's Eve, the Bickleys telephoned from Paris to say they'd been invited by an old American school friend of Mrs Bickley's to cruise the Greek Islands on the royal yacht, as guests of the Prince of Wales. Naturally, they could not refuse. Would it be too much trouble if Thea stayed on at Rosebery for the holidays?

Pa had extended the first telephone line into the house just a few months earlier, to allow him a later start on the job in the mornings, so it happened that Ma took the call. She was so flustered and profuse in assuring Mrs Bickley that Thea was a delightful girl and ever so welcome, it might well have been the Prince himself on the other end of the crackling wires. So wound up did she become, I was certain she was about to drop the name of her distant cousin, the Earl of Rosebery. Fortunately, the line dropped out before Pa and I could die of embarrassment.

I felt sorry for Thea, as I'd done since the day I met her, yet she seemed strangely elated by the news and hugged my mother as I had not done since I was quite young. We expected our results the first week of January; I felt I'd done well, Thea was sure she'd failed and had no idea what she would do anyway, even if she passed. The idea came to me then, that her visit could well prove stunningly fortuitous, in the very way Mr and Mrs Bickley might dare to hope in their wildest imaginings.

Ma brushed Thea away awkwardly, slightly flushed, busying herself with a tray of scones that were already cooling, in no need of further attention. She ordered us all to the bathroom to wash our hands before high tea. 'Micky is coming over after tea, Billy,' she informed with some difficulty, quickly restoring her equilibrium with the business of laying the table with plates and napkins and jam.

'Why, Ma?' I asked nervously. The whole matter had thankfully been dropped following that fateful night before Christmas. Naïvely, foolishly, I'd decided they'd accepted my abhorrence of the idea of any involvement on my part, or that Ma had finally spoken up, dismissing the men's dreaming out of hand.

'I'm afraid Giles has been working on him, against my advice. Against your father's too. He's coming to ask for your hand in marriage. Whatever you have in mind, Rachel, I do hope, dear, you will try not to overwhelm him with your verbal superiority.'

It was an extraordinary thing for my mother to say and caught me entirely without retort. Her implicit support, and perhaps even Pa's, of my obvious unsuitability as a wife for Micky, restored my faith but helped not at all in the task ahead. I tried to steel myself for the event, ready to be kind, but I had no experience to draw on, to know where to begin.

Sensing my fear and frustration, Thea comforted me in the bathroom. 'Billy, you're the best actress I've ever seen. All you have to do is pretend it's a part, a gentlewoman's part. Tell him what you told Ruth, that you'll find a way to help him keep his baby.'

I stared at her wildly. 'My God, Thea! I've just realized something ghastly . . . something so obvious, I'm ashamed. Why? Why didn't I . . . why haven't I? Oh Thea,' I gasped, rushing from the bathroom in search of Ruth.

When I found her, drawing water from the tank, I shouted my questions at her. 'Do you love him? Does he love you? Ruth? Forgive me! Oh Ruthy, forgive us all . . .' Eyes imploring, I dropped to the ground, legs crossed, firmly planted there like we were kids again with big secrets to share. She dropped down beside me, drawing a circle in the earth with the end of the bucket rod.

'He's not much of a bloke, Billy,' she said simply. 'Born too pretty, loves himself so much I doubt he's capable of loving anyone else.' She drew a smaller circle inside the first one. 'I thought I was in love with him, early on – bit like you with Harry. He was a real charmer, in the beginning. I think I felt sorry for him, what with losing his parents and Danny and his little sisters, having to take control of the farm. Jock was too young to help much, so the responsibility fell on Micky. He's a hard worker, no two ways about that.'

'So what's wrong with him?' I pressed.

'Nothing much,' she shrugged. 'He's just a dumb man. He's a farmer, Billy. The only thing he's ever read beyond the price of sheep and Tiger Moths are the sporting pages of the paper. Well, he went to school so I suppose he read *Biggles*, once! He doesn't need a woman for anything other'n having his babies, cooking his meals and keeping his house clean. A black girl would do for that, of course, but he could never see it, even when I thought I wanted him. I'm not even sure he needs to make love. He only needs sex, like his animals really. He's pretty basic . . . after a while.' The coil of circles had run out. She dotted the centre.

'Most men stop kissing, Ruth, after a while,' I grimaced, knowing only too well. It was not even necessary to take umbrage at the black girl inference. It was the same for white women, given time. I weighed my thoughts carefully and tried one more question. 'If it was possible, would you marry him?'

'To save Than? I don't know. It's not possible. How can I answer that? He might be a good father, boys together. He does love Than. Pity he's got no interest in any of the Kurra girls. I've known we were running out of time, Billy – I know the rules better than anyone. School age looming, the drop of white blood means separation from his black mammy! Would I marry Micky for Than? Is it enough to have a good dad for your kid? Would I be the right mother in that situation? Just as well I don't have to make the decision, I think . . .' She shrugged again, pole-vaulting herself up, rubbing out our circling history with her bare feet.

My confusion compounded with every step I took. Was there a just answer – any kind of an answer? The idea of Thea marrying Micky was taking hold in my head – it had the potential to solve both their problems – yet Ruth's recommendations hardly proposed matchmaking as a friendly gesture. 'You can't get a rational solution out of an irrational situation,' I heard Harry Carmichael saying. 'Go back to the scene of the crime and apply some logic to it.'

Lost in thought, I returned to the bathroom to wash again. Thea was still there, curling her thin mousy hair, bending low with the curling wand. She was too tall for our mirrors. Than was at her feet, giggling about nothing.

'Well, Ruth's not in love with him,' I began, bending down to pick the child up, forgetting Thea had no idea that's what I'd rushed away to ask. Than whimpered and grabbed Thea's hem. 'What have you two been doing?' I asked coolly, vaguely uncomfortable with the way Thea had slipped into our lives so easily. As I looked at her then, I realized she was not as plain as she used to be, her pink complexion cleared of acne, her stick figure rounded out, proud, classy. Was I jealous of my rich friend with the generous heart and the parents who couldn't care less? Yes . . . perhaps I was. But why?

'Don't be unhappy, Billy,' she consoled. 'It'll all work out, you'll see.'

'How comforting to be surrounded by such wisdom!' I spat cruelly, wishing God would strike me down the moment I'd said it. She should have hurt, but she didn't flinch. She never did. She'd learnt to be tough.

'Nobody seems to want Micky, though everyone thinks he's a mighty good catch. So, why don't you help me land him? To be absolutely, truly honest, Billy, I think I fell head over heels in love the moment I laid eyes on him. And I just adore Than, and we really should all be thinking about him now, shouldn't we?' she smiled graciously, her head held high, a hint of girlish mischief in the unbelievably naïve, wide eyes.

Even as she said it, I knew it had been there from the start. Thea just needed a man, any man, and babies. She needed a home where she could create a family of her very own. Academically, she was average. Socially, she was rich. Emotionally, she was pitifully childlike, desperately lonely, hopelessly homeless, more homeless than Ruth or Than would ever be. They had their Dreamtime that even a white upbringing could not erase. Thea had parents who sailed in yachts with the future King of England. Thea had nothing.

* * *

'Micky, you deserve more than a wife full of doubts and dreams, full of stupid ideas about change and choices. I am not for you, old friend,' I said quickly, stalling his halting speech with concentrated tenderness, wondering if it was possible to overdo it.

'How could ya' want more than I can offer?' he rallied strongly. 'Sec . . . security, respect, friendship . . . love? We can find that. A lifetime of service, Billy, producin' off the land, bringin' up Than – and some of yours and mine? What man can offer you more than this?'

The moment he'd finished, his shoulders visibly dropped. It was probably the longest speech of his life; old Giles had coached him well. We walked silently for a while, *he* breathing evenly, relieved it was over, *I* struggling to find the right fork in the road.

'It's a real balmy night, Billy,' Micky murmured romantically, reaching for a hand tucked deep in my skirt pocket. 'Yes,' I said, pausing to move my arms expansively towards the heavens, thus avoiding contact. This could not go on. I suddenly saw Ruth's circles in the earth, starting from the outside, twirling inwards to the centre, like a Shakespearean tragedy that can only end one way.

'Micky, who first suggested that if you were to marry, you'd be able to keep Than?'

'Well . . . I can't remember. I think it might 'a' bin Jock when he was home on hols.'

I had not expected that, but maintained my course, altering the lines slightly to accommodate the anti-hero's forgetfulness. 'Did he recommend anyone in particular . . . I mean, did he suggest me, or merely say that if you were to find a bride, your problem would be solved?' I held my breath, wishing my fellow thespian had rehearsed his part more thoroughly. The night was warm. He pulled me close, his body heat sending electric shivers through my blouse. I drew away, old-fashioned decency ruling over his raw masculinity.

'Well, no. I mean yes, he said I oughta find me a wife, but Billy, you're puttin' words in me mouth. I mean, for heaven's sake, you're a beauty and we've been friends since we were kids and . . .'

'Micky, don't hunt for words to save embarrassment. I understand perfectly and am not offended, I assure you. You're quite right, we have been friends since we were kids – that's why it wouldn't work, don't you see?' I was dog-paddling through deep water now and prayed he wouldn't wake up to it. 'We'd be bored with one another in no time at all, and soon you'd hanker for a woman who was different, exciting, new . . . a woman who wants a husband and family as much as you want a wife, and Than.'

This was going very badly. I was splashing around, going backwards against the tide. His eyebrows raised, his voice hardened. 'What are you gettin' at, Billy?'

'I'm . . . I'm not getting at anything. I'm just saying that . . .'

'Billy, don't take me for a fool,' he exposed me sharply. 'You were always dreamin' when we were kids so maybe you don't know me at all, but I know you, and you was always jumpin' ahead o' yourself, so I'd wager a quid you got somethin' up ya sleeve right now?'

It wasn't in the script, but he was on to me. There was no malice in his voice, and more than a hint of curiosity. I began hesitantly, feeling totally miscast in the role of matchmaker. 'My friend Thea is available for marriage. She's a lovely girl who comes from a very wealthy family – and she loves Than and he loves her, and anyway, she's . . . she's in love, with you!'

Why had I told him she was rich? Why, why, why?

'I've always liked tall girls,' he laughed off-handedly.

Thank God he hasn't picked up on the rich bit, I thought to myself.

It took Micky and Thea less than three months to announce their engagement. Since the Social Welfare inspector had allowed only six months' grace, the wedding was planned for a month hence. I knew I would never be able to tell my children, should I ever have any, that my first proposal of marriage had ended harmoniously with my recommendation of a far more suitable bride.

The Bickleys gave their joyous consent to Micky by telephone from London, where they were holed up for the Season, not wanting to let down Mrs Bickley's American friend at such short notice. Mr Bickley was returning briefly to Brisbane to attend to business but unfortunately would not be able to get to Kurra Kurra for the wedding. Ten thousand pounds was deposited at the Bank of New South Wales in Kurra for the wedding (and any *little* extras that might be required), and Mrs Bickley was shipping a trunk of Paris originals for the trousseau. They were very proud that their daughter had captured the heart of a wealthy landowner; the Prince of Wales himself extended an open invitation to the happy couple to visit at Sandringham when they were next in England. 'Of course you will come to London for your honeymoon, dear, won't you?' Mrs Bickley gushed above the crackling line. 'Just because you're marrying an Australian doesn't mean you have to give up your British heritage, darling.'

'She doesn't belong in the real world, my mother,' Thea said philosophically, replacing the phone on its hook. 'I think I'd better take the train to Sydney and buy my own trousseau. She means well, but that trunk will never arrive.'

'Why don't you go with her, Billy?' Ma suggested. 'You might be able to pin down that theatrical agent and line up some work?' she smiled bravely. For the umpteenth time in my short life, I had the feeling I grossly underestimated my mother. Our exam results were long to hand; I'd passed with high distinctions, had been procrastinating on my decision to contact Brumby Gorman. Thea had failed, as she had expected.

Kurra prepared for the wedding with a spirit of camaraderie not seen since the aftermath of Black Tuesday. If any of the town folk suspected Micky had sold out, they kept their thoughts to themselves; Thea's money and stylish ways rekindled a sense of hope in the local business population that, albeit briefly, succeeded in pushing the Depresson onto a back burner. The atmosphere along Oodoolay Street was unquestionably prosperous, with not a mention of how old Ellie and William O'Ryan would turn in their graves if they knew their son was giving up his Catholicism to marry an outsider (a Pommy at that!) in order to keep his half-caste bastard. But when Thea agreed to sign over any children they had together to the Micks, it was a terrible blow to our Reverend's faith in an O'Ryan's word. I couldn't help wondering what God thought about it all.

Pa had lately taken up Ma's quote, 'the truth will out', yet in my heart of hearts I sensed this would be a good marriage, in spite of all that augured against it. Micky seemed in awe of Thea ('Not a bad start,' Sister Mac said), and Thea was madly in love with Micky. She had a rare touch with Than that was visibly growing before our eyes. By the day of the wedding, the men in my life were patting themselves most heartily on the back for the grand job they had done in orchestrating this happy union.

Thea's affectation had fallen away quickly in the down-to-earth atmospheres of Mini Mini and Rosebery, and her natural generosity of spirit shone through to none more than Ruth. Ruth fluctuated between glad and sad during the build-up of tension and excitement at the station and in the town, yet she managed to generate a philosophic mood for the most part, developing an oddly protective devotion to Thea. She looked out for her, running messages, teaching her the ways of country life. She picked up and cleaned too, causing Ma to become quite agitated.

'Don't make the mistake of becoming her servant,' I heard her warning Ruth one afternoon, just days before the wedding. 'These rich girls are used to servants, you know. Before long, she'll be treating you like one.'

Ruth had retaliated quite boldly. 'I've been your servant for a long time, Mrs Rosey, and you've never treated me like one.' I heard Ma gulp, but she said nothing. She'd grown more circumspect in her maturing years.

St Matthew's bells chimed at ten in the morning for fifteen minutes, then again at three to herald the arrival of the bride. The whole town and most of the surrounding district came out in strength, lining the footpaths of Oodoolay Street to catch a glimpse of the bride in the Paris original that had arrived courtesy of Mrs Bickley's third cousin, Lady Amy Mollison-Bickley. When she arrived on British Airways in Sydney two nights before the wedding, it made the world news bulletin from the ABC. For one brief moment, Kurra Kurra had become part of the wider world, the town acting as though it had a royal wedding on its hands.

Miss Prinkett was playing the organ as we entered the church. Thea on Pa's arm (she, holding him steady), dressed in millions of yards of crushed, ironed out silk and hand-made lace. Me, following, in thousands of billowing puffs of tulle petticoats and pink organza overlay, holding me steady in their own right. Than, alongside, in white dinner suit, baby hands stiffly holding the white Bible on a small satin, lace-edged pillow, terrifyingly close to the highly polished floorboards. Jock, in a suit at least three years old and likely borrowed, arrived an hour before the service and took on the much-needed role of best man; it was good to know he was close by. He was the uncomplicated O'Ryan, contributing an anchor to the bridal party.

Ma, Sister Mac and Ruth led the matriarchal brigade in sky blue, green and earth brown, a strange mix of mother, spinster and surrogate of both . . . 'Who knows anything about anything any more?' I whispered to God.

Reverend Moon read the ceremony intently, as if he didn't know it off by heart by now. 'You are performing an act of total faith, believing in one another to the end.' Sister Mac hiccupped. Than giggled. Ma wiped her nose, without any cause since she had not even begun to sniffle.

'As the bride gives herself to the bridegroom, let him be to her father and mother, sister and brother and most sacred husband.' I wanted to interrupt. I understood father and mother and sister and brother, but what definition a *most sacred husband*? 'As he gives himself to her, let the bride inspire and sustain him, let her unite with him in all the experiences of life to which their paths shall lead. The great moments and the small, that the choices of his shall be the choices of both, the successes of his, the successes of both. Let her obey him in all things, and success is theirs in this life, and the life here-after.'

I had never been to a wedding before. I thought marriage was a legality that freed you to be yourself, to ease, not restrict! It sounded like the husband got the freedom and the woman got the restrictions, according to God's law. I thought the legal making of love was spiritual and physical freedom, not owner-ship! Oh Thea, what have I done to you? Where have I been? Please forgive me . . . I didn't know. They didn't tell me you had to agree to obey, in God's Word! I should have found out, should have re-searched it, should have . . .

Pa stepped forward. 'I do,' he said, placing Thea's hand in Micky's.

'Michael William O'Ryan, will you take?'

Oh yeah, I'm takin' her, ain't I?

'Thea Elizabeth Carmel Juliette Bickley, will you take?'

No, I give.

'To love and to cherish?'

Yeah. I think she's a bit of all right.

'To love and to cherish?'

I will.

'In sickness or in health?'

She's strong. She won't get sick.

'In sickness or in health?'

He's been through a lot – alone. Whatever comes, I'll be there.

'Till death us do part?'

Of course, I'm a Mick. I understand that. I'll stick with it, no worries.

'Till death us do part?'

With all my heart.

'I now pronounce you Man and Wife!' Miss Prinkett missed the cue, but it didn't really matter. Everybody clapped, as if it was live theatre. There was barely standing room left at the back of the pews. We left with Micky and Thea to sign the register and Miss Prinkett led the congregation in the Twenty-third Psalm, a hymn I always thought was good for a wake, if indeed you'd choose it for anything.

When the wedding party emerged, the mood was predictably funereal, but Thea's handsomeness and Micky's beauty lifted the veil of descending gloom. The rice packets came out in the dozens. The town carnival that followed was a riotous affair, with most of Kurra getting quite tiddly, a few becoming highly inebriated and one or two, unequivocally drunk. It was the best party our town had ever known; very loud, very lavish, and the bride and groom sensibly left early.

Ma couldn't help commenting that a Kurra girl would have stayed a bit longer. Pa blamed Micky for showing his country bumpkin roots and being over-anxious. Sister Mac said the whole thing was too damn loud for her and Ruth went for a swim in the Pickle River, though there'd been no water in it for months.

I went to bed and dreamt of Wendy Barr and Chocolate, and Joey yelling at me to come down off the roof because Pa was home from The Great War. The past smelt sweeter than the future that day. My own future had been saved from Micky O'Ryan, but what was I being saved for?

# TEN

# 1936...

The air in the Tarrenbonga studio was oppressive, becoming almost unbearable.

The big black second hand of the clock broke the terrifying silence, ticking its way irrevocably around the blurred white face. I lifted the earphones to relieve the stillness, mopping the perspiration from my hair, instinctively pressing it back into place as though my audience would be able to see me.

'Thirty seconds,' called Lefty Fitzpatrick from the control room. I stared incredulously at the second hand again. Over and over in my mind reeled the opening lines I'd rehearsed so often, knowing in these last moments they were all wrong, terribly wrong. Why had I stubbornly insisted on beginning with a woman's memorial to King George V and Rudyard Kipling?

'It's a death story,' the general manager, Max Dorevitch, had said. 'Bury it later in the hour if you must.' Realizing he'd made a little joke, he chuckled proudly, as was his way.

'I think she's right,' Lefty had argued. 'Both deaths have dominated the news this month and we go to air on 3 February after all. She's aiming for the heartstrings right at the top, coming from an angle no man would think of.'

'What angle is that, Miss Batchelor?' Max sighed with an easy resignation. I had not met many Jews in my life, nor general managers for that matter; Max did not fit my image of either. I answered him confidently. 'Well, sir, the advent of the wireless made George V the best-known monarch in history, but he was a private man who hated the worldly attention. Kipling was world famous for most of his life too, yet he was denied the title of poet laureate and refused the Order of Merit. *The Unwilling Kings* has great female appeal. And this is a women's programme . . .'

'Quite so, quite so,' Max had nodded, digging around for his breast pocket gold watch for the fourth time since the meeting began. Why didn't his wife buy him a chain? 'You creative people seem to know what you're doing, so, er, keep up the good work.' He had risen clumsily and made his usual bumpy exit.

Now I wished I hadn't been so sure of myself. I fumbled with the script, blindly turning the pages. Everything was fuzzy. The typing was illegible; psychedelic stars zigzagged all over the stark white sheets – I wondered if I was going to faint. 'Fifteen seconds, Billy,' shocked away the stars and I stacked the pages back together, gripping the edges with clammy hands. The second hand was a time bomb now. Lefty breathed into my earphones: 'Good luck!'

It was happening too quickly, the deafening tick, tick, tick as I lowered the *On Air* switch. Years of working and waiting, and many more of dreaming, had brought me to this. Brumby Gorman believed in me, had sold me as a wonder girl to Dorevitch, convinced him he'd never regret being the first radio GM to put to air the first women's programme in Australia. So much depended on this premier hour. Brumby had argued for their very own show for my fellow country women, to fell the lonely hours and close the distance from neighbour to neighbour. I mustn't fail, I can't . . .

Pa would be sitting patiently in his old rocker, stacking his pipe, poking it unnecessarily deeply, afraid to strike a match until I'd begun. Ma would be flustering impatiently, buttering perfectly timed hot scones that nobody would be able to eat until it was over, when they could relax and say, 'I never doubted it for a minute.'

I was On Air. I'd planned the music to fit the story, to tug at the toughest heartstrings, to catch the most cynical listener. Lefty faded it out, and the faces began to fade too – those that I knew and the thousands I would never know.

The script was the only life force now, voice steady, warm . . . heart pumping loudly enough to wake the dead. 'Think about the words, Billy! Put your heart into it!' Dove Wilson echoed in my brain. Would he be listening, angry that I'd sold out to radio, country radio of all things, wishing he'd never introduced me to Brumby Gorman? Ten-second breather, 'Skye Boat Song' full volume. I fidgeted with the silver watch Ma and Pa had given me for my twenty-first birthday last year. It was a family heirloom, originally worn as a fob watch by my great-grandfather, Sebastian Batchelor, keeping time for him on the long treacherous journey to the new frontier from the Jersey Islands in 1872 . . . *Carry the lad, who's born to be King* . . . fade out.

To the second part of the first story, meant to stimulate debate, stir the thinkers, anger the old brigade: Are all women born to be subservient to men, any more than all men are born to be kings? The nervousness I thought had disappeared returned without notice as I set up the argument. I flicked the *On Air* button off for a second to clear my throat and gulp down some water. Why in heaven's name had I embarked on this dangerous course? What would Ma and Pa think of their daughter? Actually, perhaps *they* wouldn't be surprised. What would my own peers think? Would they agree with me?

The temperature in the studio reached the century as the hour rushed by. I loosened the red scarf around my neck and undid my belt, all sense of modesty in front of Lefty washed away with the perspiration oozing out of every pore. *Cavalleria rusticana* swelled to its finale as I reached the last page before me. The second hand of the clock was nearly there for its last cycle. Thirty seconds, fifteen seconds, tick, tick, tick.

'Great work, Billy!' Lefty called. The red light faded to black. 'Was it?' I whispered, relieved, panic-stricken, exhausted, bewildered. It was over so quickly, but would my listeners think so? I stood up and stretched, peering through the glass into the control room, now full of familiar faces. The red light came on again.

'What's wrong?' I gasped. 'We're not . . . back on?'

'You're on for a long run I would think, Billy,' Max Dorevitch leant down until his mouth was almost kissing the intercom, though his voice suggested nothing more than indulgent indifference. 'I've told the boys to take you to lunch. In fact, you'd better not go anywhere in Tarrenbonga without an escort from now on, Miss Batchelor,' he winked suggestively, preparing us for one of his little witticisms. 'I'm not entirely sure whether you should be afraid of the men – or the women.'

'You've got the perfect face for the thirties, Billy,' James Barnawarren greeted me admiringly. 'Soft black curls framing a round face, high cheekbones, full vermilion lips. Wow, you should be in pictures, not ordinary old radio!'

'Oh James,' I laughed heartily, admiring his thick blond hair and gentle, boyish face, 'as I recall, you always did have a way with the girls.'

'As I recall,' he said swiftly, pulling me towards his lean body in one firm movement, 'you owe me a kiss,' and so saying, proceeded to steal one. I did not want to stop him, but we were standing in the main street of Tarrenbonga. It would be the talk of the town! He understood my fear of public displays of affection, but not my repulsion. I pulled away coldly. He eyed me curiously.

'Come now, Billy, you're a modern woman of the world. What's this uncharacteristic coyness?'

'I hardly think you'd be any judge of my character, James Barnawarren, and I'll thank you not to maul me in public – or in private,' I appended hastily, noticing his eyes sparkle with the unspoken suggestion. 'Com'on, Miss High and Mighty, let me buy you a beer. You still drink the stuff, don't you, or is heady success maintained with French champagne?'

He was enjoying the tease and I had to admit it was refreshing, no, comforting? No! It was exciting to be in his company again. Was I dreaming old dreams, hankering for a simpler time when everything was straightforward and people's affections were genuinely . . . genuine? When kissing was the beginning – and the end? What point in pursuing the possibility, whatever it was? I was contracted for twelve months to Radio 2IZ; James was contracted to the *Bulletin* in Sydney.

'I've resigned from the *Bulletin*, you knew, I suppose?' he broke casually, seating me at a rickety table. The dining room at McNally's was dingy and sparsely furnished, but the food was excellent. Only five o'clock, it was already half full. I wasn't in the least hungry, but I didn't like to say so.

'No, I didn't know you'd resigned actually. Why?'

'My old man isn't faring too well these days.'

'I'm sorry. I didn't know.'

'Yep, heart. Your Pa's ticker is a bit sus too, isn't it?'

'Sus?' I asked stupidly.

'Goodness me, for a girl of the world you really have a bit to learn, don't you?' He looked askance, obviously weighing up whether it'd be worth the effort to teach me.

'Don't worry, James, I'm a quick learner once I get the general drift. Of course, it's often a complete waste of time to absorb what men think imperative to know,' I glowed smugly.

'I'm beginning to see the wisdom in that myself,' he smiled in an annoyingly off-putting way.

Why was every man I met lately intent on agreeing with me? No man was in favour of equal social rights for the sexes. In a way, agreeing with women was just another way of reducing us, like patting a child on the head and saying, 'There, there. You cry all you want and Daddy will make it better.'

'Who are you trying to fool, James, if not yourself?'

'Dear, sweet Billy. Are you always this obstreperous? Ah well, never mind, I like a spirited filly. Come to think of it, you were always your own distinctive creature. Beautiful creature,' he stroked my bare arms unashamedly, bringing a rush of colour to my cheeks.

'So you're taking over the *Kurra Mail* for your dad, are you?' I chattered on, in no way diverting him from his main mission. 'You'll miss the *Bully*?'

'Yes and no,' he straightened up, a smarting, watery glaze coating smoky grey eyes. He was five years older than I, yet it was only now that I could see those years. 'I suppose I should tell you I was engaged to be married to the daughter of the Editor. We broke up. I lost my job. It's fortunate Dad needs me; there's no work in Australia, though I dare say I could have found a foreign correspondent's job, with the world in the mess it's in. Do you think we'll be dragged into a war?'

'Yes,' I nodded grimly.

'So do I. It's inevitable. The Nazis have entered the Rhineland, the Arabs and Jews are fighting in Palestine, the Spanish are fighting one another and Mussolini's bound to take his troops into Abyssinia. It's all ahead of us, I'm afraid. Will you stay here, Billy?'

'No. I'd have to get involved, a programme for the "Orstralians" in London, or something?'

'Then we best make the most of these peaceful days at home. Let's have a wonderful time together, put the future out of mind for a while? I'll visit as often as I can and you get home most weekends anyway. What do you say, Billy?'

For the first time, I felt the sting of truth in all the warnings I'd ever been given about becoming too educated for my own good. Oh, I was in no doubt that an education was a great and wondrous thing. I had learnt how to think academically, to argue rationally, to reason logically. The trouble was, I was fighting an enormous battle to overcome the immediate, inherent desire to think emotionally. When my handsome young man propositioned me with such detachment, I sensed I had lost something precious.

I frowned unconsciously, wishing he would hurdle over the table, gather me up in his arms, kiss me with wild, outrageous passion in front of everyone, then whisk me out to the sidewalk and deposit me grandly in his brand-new Austin 7.

'What do you say, Billy?' he asked again. 'I know I'm not the most romantic bloke in the world, but I think the world of you . . . Sorry, I mean I think you're absolutely stunning and I know you've got your heart set on a career and all, so, well, this is the most mature, sensible approach, isn't it?'

'Yes, James,' I smiled pleasantly enough. 'I just wish you hadn't put it so, so . . .'

'Calculating, I suppose you mean. I don't know, I'll never understand women. You want to be equal but when we treat you like we'd treat a man, you're insulted. The answer's yes then, is it?' he murmured, licking my ear with his tongue.

Now that really annoys me, I thought through tight lips, keeping them shut to hold my own tongue steady until I could be sure of controlling what came out. Men! Cool as cucumbers, slobbering in your ear, ' . . . the mind is blank, the external organs are loaded . . .' What of love, what of romance, tenderness, intimacy of the soul?

'Men aren't comfortable with women who are bright,' Ma had warned years ago. 'And they don't like successful women either,' Sister Mac had proffered bitterly. I had wondered at the time how either of them would know. Now, somewhere below the surface of my developed brain, nestled the discomfiting thought that Ma might be brighter than Pa; perhaps illiteracy was more, not less?

Well, there was not much I could do about it. Any of it. James was available, intelligent, good fun, gorgeous. He was not a patch on his father – didn't have the convictions – but never mind. He would do for a while, perhaps until the war came.

Nothing had changed, yet everything was different; it seemed a lifetime ago since I lived in Kurra. I'd been flatting in Tarrenbonga since my radio career began.

Nan's Temperance Tea House was still operating as a soup kitchen and Pigeon Shaft's pub was surviving. The six o'clock swill had become the seven o'clock swill and the locals greeted James as a close friend and acknowledged me like a foreign visitor.

The clannishness of prejudice was greater than I remembered, with words like *nigger* and *coon* tripping from idle tongues as casually as good mates joke with one another about who they've laid or how many bullets it took to shoot a dingo. Mr Hunt and Mr Merryweather had long since been accepted into the fray on Friday nights, a concession traditionally afforded lowly teachers after ten years of residence, 'with a begrudging respect for putting up with everyone's raucous kids all week,' Father O'Donaghan aptly decreed.

Nevertheless, they appeared awkward and reserved when James and I dropped in. 'Me thinks the teachers are in awe of their students,' James commented drily.

'Surely not.'

'Why does that surprise you? We're out, doing. They've never left school.'

'But I think they love teaching, James, don't you?'

'Perhaps. Everything palls, given time.'

'You're such an old cynic! Maybe they're no different from us. Everyone needs heroes.'

'Not me!' he retorted smugly. 'Never met anyone yet who didn't let me down in the end. The higher your expectations of people, the greater the disappointments.'

I had to concede he was right. For all of 1936, and quite a lot of '37, I rued the day I'd set up the union of Micky and Thea. It wasn't that they weren't happy – far from it. Blissfully so, from what I could see, but Than was constantly sick with one ailment or another and Ruth was miserable. Allotted visiting rights for three hours on Saturdays, she would have had more access if he'd been placed in an orphanage. Pa increased her duties at the station, ostensibly to decrease his own work load, though everyone knew it was out of the goodness of the Batchelors' hearts: 'Turn to your work like it's all you have; perhaps it is.' Why, she was even receiving twenty-eight shillings a week now, unheard of for a black woman in Kurra, possibly even the whole of Australia. Yet the payment of a wage had made her an indentured servant, easing the conscience of her captors and trapping her more irrevocably than before. I kept my thoughts to myself. While I accepted that my radio success had alienated me from the cacophony of discourse and argument that used to greet me down Oodoolay Street, finding myself a closet outsider at our kitchen table on a Saturday night was quite another matter.

Concurrently, Thea and Micky had been released from regular social intercourse at Rosebery for more than a year. 'They need time to settle down,' someone had decided. Everyone had thankfully agreed. 'Altogether proper to let the young lovebirds alone for a bit,' Reverend Moon had attempted a little risqué humour, predictably generating not the hint of a smile from anyone. Ruth and I had cycled out to Mini Mini to see Than on many Saturdays past, but my erstwhile friendship with Thea was nonexistent. The best we could manage was a polite acknowledgement, the legacy of well-bred young ladies.

It was Ma who decided it was time enough for the detachment to end and chose the occasion of Kurra's 1937 Annual Show to bring them firmly back into the fold. Ma had never been a woman of half-measures. She never baked one pie or one batch of scones at a time, never embarked on long, rambling dissertations when a few crisp words would do, and never, absolutely never, extended hospitality without the maximum of pre-organization that allowed her to dispense it with the minimum of apparent effort. Thea, Micky and Than O'Ryan were to be overnight guests, joining us for Saturday night tea, a misnomer for a good old-fashioned Rosebery party, followed by a day at the showgrounds that adjoined our railway and telegraph station village.

Pa debated the jugular tactics mildly. It was expected. 'Are you sure, dear, you aren't trying to conquer too many birds with the one stone?'

'The expression is "kill too many birds with the one stone", Nathan, and no I am not. If a thing's worth doing, there's no point in doing it with a half-cocked gun.'

James and I arrived early, catching the tail-end of this final argument on the matter. By six o'clock, Ma was instructing Ruth and me about the seating arrangements; by seven o'clock, we were seated around Rosebery's fine oak table, all eighteen of us. While we shuffled chairs and plates and installed Sabella and Luther Prescott, now confined to wheelchairs, at the far corner of the table nearest the back door and toilets, Pa greeted the guests and Bluey tended the horses. There were as many cars as there were horses now, which was just as well since Bluey's arthritis had slowed him up considerably, though he flatly refused to admit it. As darkness fell over the Kurrajong Ranges, Figgy Barnawarren and Reverend Moon kicked off a lively discussion about King Edward's abdication in December, hoping to draw Thea out with her presumed intimate knowledge of the situation. The faintest flicker of suspicion inadvertently jumped into my mind about Ma's motivations for this expansive reinstatement. No, she wouldn't, would she? No. It was too utterly ridiculous.

'Will Mr and Mrs Bickley be visiting the Duke and Duchess in Europe during the coming Season, Thea?' Ma asked, breaking the men's impasse on Stanley Baldwin's handling of the constitutional crisis that had gripped the upper echelons of British power for months.

'I don't think so,' Thea smiled sweetly, looking prettier than a picture with her new short bob haircut, designer label jodhpurs and white Chanel shirt puckering suggestively at the third button, un-aided by an unbuttoned luxurious black velvet waistcoat. 'Europe isn't safe any more, so they'll stay in London. By the way, we're having a baby – a brother for Than,' she dropped upon us without cere-mony. So much in the one breath, Pa leant heavily over the table as the news slowly reached his compre-hension.

'Oh darlin',' Micky said hastily, 'you should 'ave given everyone a bit of warnin'. Mr Nathan looks bloody shocked!' Micky leant back, grinning augustly, flexing his shoulder blades and arms around the back of the chair. Thea blushed profusely, eyes cast downwards, then rising, darting around the table with the beguiling appeal of an ingénue. The two of them radiated such *amour-propre*, even Ruth, carefully positioned at the opposite end of the table, seemed swayed, though it was hard to tell these days.

Ma recovered first, reaching for the Madeira. 'This calls for a celebration, Nathan,' she instructed clearly. Pa dutifully responded, re-emerging from the fortress room with Ma's favourite silver tray of sparkling crystal glasses. His hands were unsteady lately; Sister Mac took over the male role of waiter like the sea-soned nurse she was. When the glasses were evenly distributed, Reverend Moon rose majestically. His beady eyes, now doubled through bifocals, stood out like four beacons on a white and battered knoll.

My God, I thought, what a lucky man he is to get these moments of theatrical glory in a plebeian town like Kurra Kurra.

'Ladies and gentlemen,' he began, with the metre of the opening words of the marriage ceremony, 'we are gathered together on this mild evening at Rose-bery, loving friends and family, sharing bread and wine in the spirit of Our Lord. We give thanks to Him for the joy of new creation, for the baby conceived in love by Micky and Thea O'Ryan. We give thanks also for the blessing of humility, for the strength of forgiveness, none more ever given than presides at the table of Rosey and Nathan Batchelor tonight, nor all the nights that have gone before. We pay homage to the Mother, Thea O'Ryan, for her love of the baby Than and her love for the new life, just begun.

'Ladies and gentlemen, please rise and charge your glasses to the King!' We all rose, apart from Sabella and Luther Prescott. Luther was asleep but Sabella made a sterling effort to lean forward in her chair, promptly splashing her thimbleful of Madeira in a horizontal pattern across Constance Barnawarren's delicate lemon chiffon-covered stomach. For some inexplicable reason, Ma and Sister Mac ignored the disaster, leaving Constance no choice but to pretend it hadn't happened. 'To the King!' we chorused, gulping noisily, though a sip was more the natural order of things.

There was something surrealistic about toasting the King that night, more important than Constance's blood-splattered stomach, more compelling than Thea's tiny growth emerging. The shy, stuttering Prince Albert was King of the Realm! Anyone could do anything, if they had to!

'To Micky and Thea!' Reverend Moon rushed on.

'To Micky and Thea!' we chanted, gulping some more.

Sister Mac was always good for occasion too. 'I'd like ta propose a toast ta Rosey an' Nathan, for keepin' the family an' friends together.'

'To Rosey and Nathan,' we chorused with renewed gusto. James took over the topping up of glasses.

'I'd like to thank yous all for your congratulations to the wife and me,' Micky slurred beautifully, white teeth gleaming immaculately out of his wide-open, sunburnt lips.

We drank again, slightly bemused without any prompt words to guide us. A short silence fell. Everyone looked at me. My turn?

'I'd like to drink to Ruth,' I said simply. Nobody moved.

A longer silence descended. Thea suddenly jumped to her feet.

'I'd like to drink to Ruth too,' she smiled, one large gallant tear struggling out of her right eye.

'To Ruth! . . . To Ruth!' hiccupped Sister Mac.

'To Ruth!' the echo followed, lighter and more comfortable by far than the first or second harsh sounds of her name.

Ruth's lovely face opened up as it had not done in many a year. The conversation grew easier, freer, until the last hour when we all turned in. I felt a sense of warmth and peace at that moment, as though we were commencing a new phase, a new era of a wider family; a state of belonging for everyone – Thea, Ruth, Than, everyone.

Thea, Micky and Than had Joey's old room, untouched like Miss Havisham's wedding breakfast since the day of the fire. Ma had finished mourning at last, her heart at rest since young Than's family life was set . . . that everything had turned out for the best. Ruth and I shared my old room next door, my weekend room, Ruth's weekday room since I'd set up in Tarrenbonga. Usually she moved to her old sofa in the fortress for my weekend visits but the sofa, in fact, the entire fortress room, was layered with food for the show. Pa had rigged up an elaborate fan system to keep the delicacies from curdling in the heat – he said he hadn't seen a room like it since the day he woke up in a Salvation Army hostel in London in 1914, the year I was born.

'Doesn't it bother you to be sleeping in the room next to Thea and Micky?' I asked inquisitively, the moment Ruth and I had closed our door.

'It astounds me, Billy, that your curiosity is stronger than good breeding and education combined,' she quipped. 'If I had your life, I wouldn't be sleeping with me tonight.'

'Who'd you be sleeping with, Ruth?'

'Sure as hell wouldn't be you,' she said.

'Well, I can hardly rush over to the Barnawarrens and crawl into James' bed to save you from this awful fate,' I laughed.

'Obviously not much joy there, or you'd do it, I'd reckon?'

'What do you mean, Ruth?'

'You didn't speak to him all night. He looks at you with those big cocker spaniel eyes and you act like a cat who's given up heat for Lent.'

'You've become very coarse since you've been paid for a living.'

'Money makes you tough, Billy, but once you're used to it, you can pretend to be all soft and feminine again. I'm in the transition period. Give me time and I'll be just like you!'

Men had spoken to me with that superior tone of voice, that all-knowing, sanctimonious one-upmanship: Harry Carmichael, Dove Wilson, James Barnawarren, even my father in a gentler, more time-honoured way. But never a woman. Ma could cut me up like lamb's liver and serve me to the work dogs, but I'd long since realized she was more bark than them. But Ruth? My Ruthy!

'"Hell hath no fury like a woman's scorn . . ."'

'"Like a woman scorned," don't you mean, Billy?'

'Shit!'

How closed my mind had been! I thought a woman's scorn only applied to men. Men put scorn on women like salt on potatoes so we didn't notice it after a while – but a woman scorned by another woman? It had never occurred to me. It was personal, intentionally savage, perhaps deserved. I feared I was being dramatic, yet it felt like I imagined a dagger would feel, plunging into my heart; shooting knife-like pains, charges straight through my body, real and unreal.

When she saw my face, her eyes moistened. She turned away. 'I'm sorry . . . uncalled for,' she mumbled to herself.

'Not at all,' I replied coolly. 'You've been down a tough road. I can't imagine how you must feel.'

'No, you can't. But you would have been able to, once.'

'What are you trying to say, Ruth?' My voice was taut, the natural mechanisms of self-protection warming up for retaliation.

'You've changed, Billy. I don't know who you are any more.'

She pulled the hairpins from her hair, dropping them on the dressing table, picking up her brush, commencing to unknot the thick black curls in long, rhythmic strokes. I was angry and hurt, but also completely stupefied. Where had this come from, what right did she have to accuse me of . . .?

'Ruth, what *are* you accusing me of? You've been impossible to reach for months. When I try, tonight, to bring you back into the fold, you reward me with this, this incredible . . .' My brain had seized and the words wouldn't come. I was quivering all over now and my right eye was twitching. I felt like a bird in a cage with the gate open, the worst place to be; trapped because there was no place to go.

Ruth's clouded face had paled, but she was in

control. She spoke to me through the mirror, sadly, painfully slowly, as though she was hurting herself rather than me. 'Do you remember the story of how the brolga came to be? Remember the young girl who loved to dance? She was beautiful and talented and one day the north wind saw her and decided to carry her away. I think . . . that's what's happened to you, Billy. You've let the wind carry you away, you've let it reshape you. It's turned your lush green heart into an arid brown desert, all worldly wise and resigned to it; too hot by day to care, too cold by night to feel. I love you, Billy. I'll always love ya, old girl. But you're outa touch with yourself since you left Rosebery and Kurra for the big wide world. You're more of a snob than Thea was when you first brought her home. Even then, you could still hear her heart ticking . . .' She closed her eyes for a moment and took a short, deep breath.

I walked unsteadily towards the mirror, my fists clenched. I think I was going to hit her, but she moved, her eyes finding mine.

'I haven't finished, Billy.' She stared numbly, the low voice picking up its powerful bush rhythm. I froze, confounded by my intentions and her unerring calm. 'You're using James, though he's desperately in love with you. You'll be a spinster for ever if you don't start thinking about what you're doing. You contribute nothing to Mrs Rosey and Mr Nathan's lives any more, too caught up in your own world. You're critical of everyone's beliefs and attitudes. You've become too big for your boots, Billy, and as I remember it, they were always two sizes too big for our feet in the first place.'

When my voice broke, it was shrill, pouring like an unleashed dam upon the river beneath. Ruth's motherly tirade had not yet reached my adult consciousness. All that had surfaced was the wounded pride of the child. 'For God's sake, Ruth, who do you think you are? I've fought for your life like you were my sister, I've never criticized you, I've stood up against the filthy racism and injustices you've been dealt and I put off following up a career on the stage in Sydney because I knew Ma and Pa and you and everyone needed me here! You've got a bloody cheek to think you can tell me how to live . . . too big for my outsized boots, eh? Well, what about you, little black orphan Annie? What about you?'

She slumped forward across the dressing table. The brush fell to the floor. Her shoulders began to heave and I staggered backwards towards her bed, my legs buckling when I felt it jump up behind me. I put my head on my lap, and wept.

We sobbed, separate, tormented tears for a long time. The terrible understanding that finally came to me was that Ruth was not crying for herself. We were both crying for me. All my loud protestations, my brave new world full of fame and equality for all, especially women and . . . even black women, killed with the involuntary dropping of a bomb planted secretly in my brain by enemies unknown. How had they crept into my soul unnoticed? Who were they? What other fatal damage had they been doing while I was busy elsewhere? Did I have to kill them, in order to survive, myself?

I wanted to get up, go to Ruth, beg her forgiveness, apologize for everything, anything, just undo what had been said. But it wasn't that easy. It wasn't even possible. There was too much to work through, too many emotions to deal with, too many issues too wide and too far reaching for a small apology. As if she sensed it, she came to me, wearing her courage and her love like the phoenix rising.

'Oh Ruthy,' I wailed as she wrapped me up in her

strong arms and rocked me like she used to do when I was a child.

'Just let out the sails, Billy,' she said. 'You can't direct the winds, but you can learn how to ride them.'

'How did you get to be so wise?' I blubbered. Her face shone brightly, as though all the pain had never been, washed away with a question so humble. I sat wide-eyed, watching the stars dancing in her eyes. She laughed, more of a gurgle than a real laugh, small drops of saliva bubbling at the edges of her rich, full mouth, just like Than used to do when he was a baby.

'Do you remember the end of the story of how the brolga came to be?' I shook my head. 'Two spirits, who lived in a nearby lake, saw the north wind carrying away the beautiful and talented girl who so loved to dance. They knew how much they'd miss her, were sad and lonely to see her go. They decided they must save her, at all cost, so they put their two heads together and dreamt of a plan so mystic and wonderful, even the Milky Way applauded. Do you remember now?' I nodded, in time with my tears.

'Ah . . . yes!' she acknowledged. 'The two loving spirits turned her into a brolga and that is why, to this very day, the brolga is still known for her beautiful dancing.'

It was show day in Kurra and I needed solitude. How on earth was I going to get through it? My life had been mapped out. Everything was going along just fine. I had a stunning career, a good-looking man who adored me, loving family and old friends, independence. Not to mention an exciting war and a big future on the horizon, whichever way you looked at it.

That was just it. I had only looked at it one way. What I really had, was a disaster.

My career in radio was a lucky break. I'd gone for an audition with the Royal Shakespearean Players and failed. 'Try again next year,' they'd said, 'or you might get into the Redfern Rep. They're only amateur status, but they're good and it would give you some adult experience.' Funny that I hadn't even been able to tell Ruth about that. Brumby had come out of the woodwork with an offer from 2IZ, saving my face, and my future.

James was a good-looking, egotistical bore, just as I'd known he would be. He was a lazy lover, with no idea of a woman's needs and no interest in finding out. In fact, I think he had a carloo complex, viewing his entire manhood through his capacity to get an erection at the drop of a hat. The fact that he couldn't control it was completely irrelevant. Anyway, what woman is flattered by a man who can get an erection at the drop of a hat? Perhaps it was a castration complex? Bring it out often so you know it's still there . . .

Ma and Pa. I have contributed nothing to their lives since I returned home. Nothing. I breeze in and out, full of my own importance and my little world, bored to death with their trivial problems and trivial lives. What am I missing? Why can't I get excited about being at home any more?

I like keeping house. My flat in Tarrenbonga is only a bed-sitter, but it's cute. There are no white ants because the landlord has it sprayed every six months. It's at the top of Carolyne Street, only two blocks from 2IZ and just around the corner from the Tarrenbonga picture theatre. I go at least twice a week, on my own mostly. Love it. People ask for my autograph and I feel like a movie star myself.

I don't like being a spinster, but I do live on my own quite happily. I suppose it's because I'm busy. Perhaps I'm not capable of falling in love?

I used to loathe war, insane men killing one another, and for what? A bit more land? It's a good way to mop up the unemployed, of course. Five bob a day in the army. Boys together, fighting the good fight, more comfortable with their own sex, playing with real guns, getting to travel to distant places, away from the drudgery of home. Feeling proud to be saving the Empire. A purpose, at last. And the other fella gets killed. Ah well, could be worse. Could be me.

Do I really want to go to the war? Get a radio job, selling men's propaganda to the silly fools who'll devour it like red meat? *Let out the sails, Billy!* suddenly scratched a thin scar across my cynical heart. You're being very hard on yourself and the world. You'd better learn some tacking before you go to the war.

The Twelve and Unders were highland dancing, but I didn't stop. I could hear the bagpipes in the exhibition hall. I wandered around aimlessly, staring at dolls' clothes and lace doilies, blue ribbons sashed across fruit cake and tea cosies. There was a red ribbon for an unopened jar of mulberry jam. How could the judges be sure it was the same batch they'd tasted?

The tree felling was underway, saws zigzagging wildly. The men wore only singlets and shorts, their muscles rippling and glistening under the midday sun. One huge arm carried a tattoo of a naked lady, contorted and dizzy, wishing she could get off. He was powerful to watch. Next door the shearers were at it, positioning a sheep like it was a toy, taking up the blades with strong backs bent as though they were still in the womb. A huge crowd gathered round the rifle shooting competition. Shooting for fun? Shooting to kill? Shooting to win? I couldn't see what they were shooting at. Guess it didn't matter. 'I love shooting,' a bloke in a slouch hat said. I passed by quickly, not able to think about it any more.

Suddenly, I reached the pavilion, bumping head-long into Micky O'Ryan. It looked like one of his pigs had taken first prize, a surly-looking beast who was not at all pleased with the blue sash around his underbelly.

'Congratulations, Micky,' I greeted him. 'Will this mean more money for a serve?'

He threw his head back and laughed raucously. 'It would if it was a male,' he continued to laugh, bring-ing a flash of colour to my cheeks.

I kept going. I had to find the chooks. Ma's latest rooster always won but it was important to say you'd seen it, all cooped up in its tiny pen, exercising its lungs as though the entire day was five o'clock in the morning. I heard it before I saw it, of course, highly agitated by another blue ribbon draped across the wire netting. The sight of it made me realize I hadn't checked Ma's winnings in the exhibition hall. I hur-ried back, trying to remember what categories she'd entered this year. I hadn't been listening. All of them?

The showgrounds were congested and noisy, yet I heard the running steps, or felt the presence of some-one covering the hard ground to catch me. I stopped abruptly, swinging around full circle. He pulled up too quickly, tripped and fell at my feet. The crack was loud, as he struggled to control his anguished face. Jock . . . Jock O'Ryan? It had to be Jock O'Ryan.

'Oh no!' I fell to the ground, kneeling at his feet, staring in horror at his ankle turning blue, doubling in size before me. 'Oh Jock, I'm so sorry. Dear God, it's a nasty break. Oh Jock, Jock!'

'I like the way you say my name, Billy. You've never said it with sympathy or tenderness before. My, you're even lovelier than I remember.' He smiled a full, warm smile, seeming oblivious to the disaster that had befallen him. People were rushing in on us now. The St John man arrived with his black bag open, ready for action.

'Oh my Lord,' he exclaimed, snapping his bag shut. 'Ain't nothin' I can do. Don't move 'im. I'll get the ambulance.'

'Stay still, Jock,' I said mindlessly. 'You must be in terrible pain. They're getting the ambulance.'

'It's not so bad. The adrenaline's flowing at the sight of you. My, it's good to see you, Billy.'

I shook my head incredulously. This couldn't be Jock O'Ryan, that crude, rude, red-headed monster who caused me to get the strap on my first day at school . . . who ordered me to stay away from his father . . . who came to see me off on my way to university? The same man, who stood up for Micky at his wedding?

Since Black Tuesday, I'd seen so little of him, not thought of him. He'd been teaching in the Mallee in Victoria for years – it obviously agreed with him. He was well-proportioned now, tall and solid, his hair thinned out and neatly styled around his smiling face. He had the look about him of a man you can trust, the kind of man who makes friends easily. The Depression and the drought had obviously been his godsend, forcing him to find his own way, far from the inappropriate inheritance of Mini Mini.

They found Doc Halliday, firmly ensconced at Shaft's pub. He always travelled to Kurra for the show, though he'd never walked into the showgrounds in his life. He came now, with the ambulance.

'Looks like Achilles tendon,' he said, rubbing his jaw thoughtfully. 'We'll splint it and get you to the hospital for X-rays. Sister Mac on duty I suppose, Billy?'

'Yes, I think so. Can I travel with him?' I asked.

James arrived on the scene and summed up the situation with the cool efficiency of a newspaper man who'd seen it all before.

'That's not necessary, Billy. I've got the car here. We'll visit him later when he's repaired and comfortable. How'd it happen?' He took out his notebook. The St John men carried Jock up the ramp and into a waiting wheelchair. I stood angrily between James and Doc Halliday, powerless to alter the course of events, not confident enough to override James in front of so many people.

The rupture of Jock's Achilles tendon was total, requiring surgical repair and immobilization for six weeks. He was in surgery when we arrived at the Kurra bush hospital and not allowed visitors before we had to return to Tarrenbonga. It took an hour and a half to drive back; James accepted my pensive mood, letting the starlit night be his company. When we reached my flat, I opened the car door quickly. Offended, he reached for my arm.

'Hey! Please wait. I'm coming around to get you.'

'No, James, not tonight. I need some time . . . I've got work to do for tomorrow's show.'

'Okay, okay, darling. But let me open your door, please?'

His lips were hot and dry when he took me in his arms against the parapet that supported the balcony roof. I leant against it heavily, submitting passively to his unspoken request. In so doing, he understood that I meant what I said. 'See you Wednesday night?'

'Yes, fine. Thanks, James. Goodnight.'

I knew I would have to finish my relationship with him, but there was no room in my head to think about it yet. Ma always said that blessings never came in twos, misfortunes never came alone. How right she was! In one weekend, I'd destroyed the trust of my dearest friend, broken the ankle of a friend I'd never acknowledged and come to the realization that I must break the heart of my boyfriend. God only knows what pain I'd been causing my parents, who could but stand by in the wings, watching and wondering where my path of destruction would lead me next.

Harry used to say that failure was largely a matter of not listening properly, or completely misunderstanding the question. Well, I was listening now and Ruth had plaintively clarified the question. I threw out the programme I had planned for Monday and dug in for a long night. I would open with a hymn of thanksgiving, '*Te Deum laudamus* . . .' The show would be a tribute to the people of Kurra Kurra, a celebration of the bush folk of Australia. I would ask, 'Who are we?'

My pen began to flow. The annual show was a good place to begin. Are we boater hats, derbies and berets, bonnets, capes and scarves, or are we slouch hats and bobbing corks and handkerchiefs tied up in knots to repel the sun and the flies? Are we poodles or working dogs, elm trees or eucalyptus?

I sat staring at my notes. They were not right. I ripped up the page and started again. Are we a young country, a babe in arms, struggling to grow up in a new, inhospitable land? Or are we an old country, old as the hills, older than our indigenous inhabitants who are not permitted to tell? Our detractors accuse us of being culturally inadequate, unwilling to modify our European heritage, willing only to damn our Aboriginal history. Can I get away with that? Yes, I can. Putting the words into the detractors' mouths will satisfy Dorevitch. He'll love it anyway, he's a Jew after all: 'Up the underdogs!'

Where do I go from there? Can we hope to develop a uniquely Australian identity until the dispossession of the indigenous people of Australia is acknowledged? I was getting off the track. I put the last page aside and concentrated on three short personal tributes: Sister Mac, the O'Ryan family and Ruth. I snuck a cheerio to Jock in the Sister Mac story, concentrated the O'Ryan saga on the courage of the young offspring following the fire and the coming together of two distinct cultures in the union of Thea and Micky.

I reached for the Bible for the story of Ruth and cried for the two hours it took me to write a few words about a little black girl who'd nurtured a white family to maturity. I shuffled the pages around, snipping and cutting, polishing, adding. It was coming together. But was I?

Lefty Fitzgerald greeted me with usual Irish exuberance. I had not been to bed and covered my ears dramatically.

'Not so loud please, Lefty. I've had a rough night.'

'You look it, dear,' he said forthrightly, taking the sheets out of my proffered hands. 'New music? Wow, we'll have to move fast to get these out in time.'

'Thanks, Lefty. New show too. I'm going into the studio to run through it and try to think of a title. That's all I'm missing.'

'You're running a bit close to the wind, aren't you?' he said nervously, shooting a fast glance to the clock in the studio that held our fate in its hands.

The second hand ticked around mercilessly. Ninety seconds. Instinctively, I knew the answer to my own question was hidden in the script somewhere. If I could find it, I would have the title and the opening of the show. Sixty seconds . . . ticking, deafening. I could feel the adrenaline starting to pump through my veins, telltale butterflies waking up in my stomach. The clock was panicking . . . thirty seconds.

Facing the wall, it came to me. It had been there, all along. The relief was overwhelming.

'*Te Deum*' burst into my earphones, bracing and passionate. The black hand spoke. 'Coming out in five seconds, Billy,' Lefty whispered anxiously. I lowered the *On Air* switch.

'We cannot direct the wind, but we can adjust the sails,' I began.

# ELEVEN

# 1939

My affair with James ended without acrimony. When I said I thought it was time we called it a day, he asked wearily, 'Will you give up your career and marry me?' I answered as gently as I could manage.

'Thank you, James, but no . . . No.' Since he knew there was no third party involved, his male pride had to establish my work as the Jacky in the wood pile. It despaired me, but I understood; it was the natural palliative where no other existed.

'For a man who was desperately in love, I must say he's taken your rejection very well,' Ma said later, having occasion to bump into him on Oodoolay Street.

'Men are fickle, Ma,' I said simply. James was clearly relieved to be free of a woman he could neither control nor understand, and Ma and the rest of Kurra knew he had already begun courting one of the nursing aides at the Tarrenbonga Hospital.

'Oh Billy, what's to become of you?' Ma heaved, her bosom rising only halfway to her chin. She was growing older. Nothing was quite as momentous as it used to be.

I had turned a whole quarter of a century on 4 July! What on earth *was* to become of me? Ladies should be married and raising a brood of youngsters by twenty-five. Not only did I lack the natural instincts that the author of nature had designed for me, but I had never been in love. In lust, yes. In love with love, certainly. But truly *in love*? No, never. If it was true that only by assiduously acquiring the arts of pleasing can a woman attain any degree of consequence or power, and hope to become an object of love and affection, I was on the sorry path of self-destruction. As hard as I tried, I could not be mild and conciliatory in order to please a man. *'Les hommes font les lois: les femmes font les réputations . . .'* The desire to please may form the basis of social connection, but it was all too shallow and silly for words.

In my old age, I acknowledged that I had developed my brain and a career of some note. Were these achievements to be the bane of my life? Though perhaps of small consequence in the greater scheme of things, surely it is an insult to God to deny His gift of the mind? He placed the balance of power on the side of the male by giving him a larger, more robust body, but I could not accept that He had endowed man's brain with greater resolution and more extensive powers; what other qualities of counterpoise could He give women to balance such superiority of nature? Beauty? Why, beauty was not given out equally, nor exclusively to women, and those whose chief attribute was the employment of decoration of their person were nothing but vain, contemptible characters. Charm? Could inexpressible strength and persuasion be attained without cultivating the mind?

And what of the insinuating word, the knowing look, the winning smile . . . were these the qualities of soft, insipid women? The intercession of the mother of Coriolanus saved Rome from impending destruction. Alexander was conquered, Caesar subdued, the fate of empires and kingdoms decided by the power of women. Liberally scattered through the pages of history, men seemed to prefer women of sense.

'I think I was born too late, Ma,' I mused wistfully, jumping up from the table to help her pour the marmalade into rows of sterilized jars.

'More likely too soon, dear,' she returned affectionately, her voice softening in a rare display of empathy. I studied her critically. She had aged, yet remained ageless.

'You've never cowered to Pa, nor behaved subserviently to anyone. You don't even have a sweet temper and I don't think I've ever heard you change your opinion to suit a man! Why should I have to? Why aren't there any men out there like Pa?'

She gave the jam another deep stir before ladling again. 'I sometimes wonder whether it was the worst thing I ever did to insist you got an education, Rachel.'

'You . . . you insisted?' I gulped incredulously.

'Of course, dear. Your father didn't want you to go to university. I fought him very hard, for months as I recall.'

'Why? Why didn't he? Why did you . . .?' I was dumbfounded. I vaguely remembered something, something other than her relentless driving force charging me to study harder to win that scholarship, but I had tucked it away, unwilling to examine it, unwilling to change my view of the way I thought things were.

She saw my confusion and disappointment and slammed the ladle down impatiently. 'Yes, yes, I insisted you get an education, though I do wonder why sometimes, Billy, for all the good it's done you! Your father didn't want you to fill your brain with all sorts of worldly things. He just wanted you to find a nice husband, settle down, be happy. He's proud of you, but he's disappointed too . . .' she trailed off, the anger spent in speaking the unspeakable.

'And you? What did you want, Ma?'

'I wanted you to have a better life than I've had,' she murmured sadly, wiping one hand across her face, picking up the ladle with the other.

'Oh Mama!' I threw my arms around her, abandoning a lifetime of propriety, so utterly amazed was I. 'It never occurred to me that you weren't happy with your lot.'

She pushed me away self-consciously, the full force of her body flicking the ladle out of the side of the pot. She turned awkwardly to rescue it mid-air as I leant forward to steady the pot. We collided, the pot hurtling to earth, splattering boiling lumps of jam all over her slippered feet. A small cry escaped her lips. She slipped to the floor, her dress and apron stuck together, piled up around her waist. 'Get the first-aid box, Billy,' she ordered calmly, her face contorted with pain.

I scraped off the jam and applied a compress of several folds of soft linen, dipped in cold water. Her right foot was the worst. It was obvious the burns were going to blister. 'You'll have to make up some pomatum,' she instructed, setting me to the task of mixing nutritum and the yolk of an egg, followed by rubbing well together two drachms of ceruse, half an ounce of vinegar, three ounces of common oil. Halfway through the procedure, her body began to shake.

'Why don't I get the Rocke Tompsitt Antiseptic Cure All, Ma?' I pleaded pointlessly.

'Absolute rubbish!' she scoffed. 'Nothing beats my mother's recipe. Just get on with it, girl, just keep rubbing.' When the pomatum was ready, I spread it across a fresh roll of linen and began to wrap up her feet. 'Here, let me do that,' she grabbed one end of the linen, 'and make me a hot cup of tea.' I reached for the kettle, climbing around her crumpled body and the unholy mess spread halfway across the kitchen floor.

Suddenly, she was crying. Not loudly at first, but steadily, uncontrollably. I would not make the mistake of putting my arms around her again, so I stood by helplessly, waiting for the kettle to boil, feeling the tears filling up my eyes, leaning hard against the table to stop myself from fainting. 'Turn on the wireless,' she sobbed, hoping against hope that Pa would not walk in now and see her in this vulnerable, immodest state.

The Sunday concert was nearly over, Beethoven's Fifth Symphony reaching an ominous crescendo. I wished she hadn't asked for the noise distraction. The cymbals and drums of the London Philharmonic seemed harsh and discordant, crashing into my scolded conscience for all the accidents I had caused the people who cared for me. Something always happened when I was feeling vaguely insecure . . . accompanied by dizzy spells and double vision, then the fainting, like I'd never quite grown out of my childhood weaknesses. And misfortunes came in threes. First I'd ruptured Jock's Achilles tendon. Now I'd burnt Ma's feet. What would be next? I lowered the volume. I was innocent, yet I was guilty, guilty of being a selfish, ambitious woman. These disasters did not happen to gentle women, women with low expectations and virtuous reputations. Ma was my innocent victim, even as she acknowledged her own unfulfilled dreams.

The back door flew open. Ruth and Than rushed in, followed closely by Pa and Bluey. 'Turn up the wireless . . .' Ruth began excitedly, her eyes pulling up sharply at the scene before her. 'My God, what happened?' she gasped, walking straight across to turn up the sound knob, her body unable to halt a previous message from the brain. Pa stood, transfixed against the doorway. Bluey put a firm hand on his arm. Than promptly sat down next to Ma, scooping up pieces of jam, proceeding to lick his fingers noisily.

The resonant voice of the Prime Minister, Mr Menzies, was making the announcement we had been expecting for weeks. 'It is my melancholy duty to inform you officially that in consequence of a persistence by Germany in her invasion of Poland, Great Britain has declared war upon her and that, as a result, Australia is also at war.'

For a few moments, nobody moved or spoke. Than stopped eating and sucked his thumb. The news rocked us as though it had come out of the blue. The reality, the finality . . . *Australia is also at war*. The past few months and weeks of anticipation, rumour and suggestion were dead and gone; 'What will you do if . . .?' was here and now, declared with the stroke of a leader's pen six weeks' sailing time away.

The rich aroma of lemons and oranges was strangely comforting in those shocking moments, but Ma's position was obviously not, her undignified and painful state taking on the appearance of a second-rate slapstick comedy. Ruth's heart rallied first, pulling up Than. Pa moved next and while Bluey helped him move Ma into the fortress room, Ruth set about mopping up. The kettle was bubbling away. I sat Than down and ordered him to be still while I made the tea.

'What's a war, Mushy?' he asked Ruth, his happy little face following her around as she worked. Since the birth of Thea's twins, Frances and Sarah, Than was thrust into Ruth's care every weekend.

'It's when men do things against their moral judgement,' she replied savagely.

'Ruth!'

'Well, you answer the question, Billy. How do you explain war to a young boy?' I took a sharp intake of air. We looked at one another anxiously, eyes searching

233

deep into each other's soul for a simple answer that would suffice. He sensed fear in our silence, his small voice pitched high when he asked again.

'Mushy? Billy? Is somebody died?'

Ruth swayed slightly, using the mop to steady herself. 'No, darling, nobody's died.'

I stepped in, setting my face in a half-smile of grim determination. 'A long, long way from here, right across the ocean, some greedy men decided that they wanted to . . . to own more land, so they've started a big fight with their neighbours.' I paused, watching his reaction. Perhaps that would be enough to satisfy him for the time being.

'Will they get hurt?' he asked, wide-eyed.

'Yes, some . . . some will get hurt.'

'Will they fight with fists or guns?' he persisted brightly.

'That's enough, Than,' Ruth interjected, thrusting the mop into my hands. 'We need to clean you up before tea.'

'Will anybody die?' he called to me as she led him out.

'Com'on and Join Up!' the posters shouted. 'Be in it, Digger – it's on again!'

Patriotism swelled in our breasts and broke the long, harsh insouciance, the ponderous outlooks and the unimaginative, dampened spirits of the Depression years. The drought had broken and once again we were active members of the great and powerful British Empire. We could trace our heritage to William the Conquerer and to all the Kings of England. We were descendants of Drake. We had whipped the Spaniards, the French, the Ruskies and the Huns – we could do it again. We were brave and strong and free, and free we would remain. We would spill the blood of our young men again for King and Empire!

'We will arrive early; we will be amongst the first to go,' I opened my show on the first Monday in September, as Judy Garland's 'Somewhere Over the Rainbow' faded out. Max Dorevitch was in the control room, pacing agitatedly, puffing and coughing intermittently on a newly acquired pipe. He would not like my lead story. The remains of his family in Europe had been persecuted unmercifully for years; he was impatient for us to be there, the sooner the better. But I had no choice. It was not personal. I knew he would realize that, as soon as the overflowing mail bags started pouring in.

'Last night, our Prime Minister announced that Great Britain has declared war on Germany and, as a result, Australia is also at war.' I paused for effect, my voice barely disguising my anger. 'Over a year ago on this programme, I paid tribute to the bush folk of Australia, in particular, some special people in Kurra Kurra. I asked you then if we were developing an identity of our own, an Australian identity born of the labour of convicts and indigenous slaves, of the vision and tireless energies of free settlers and the courage and unerring support of their women folk. Your response was overwhelming.

'We received 2,213 letters from you. Over 2,000 of those letters said you were fiercely proud of your new country, your new nationality! Many of you said it was time we stopped looking to Great Britain, since they had obviously stopped looking after us.

'Now, country women of Australia, you have been asked to send your sons and lovers to another war on the same battlefields that your own fathers and husbands fought and died on, less than a quarter of a century ago! Australia is not under attack, as it wasn't in 1914, yet we put up our hands first, in an insecure show of misplaced patriotism. Our Prime Minister abandoned our independence when he declared that we are at war because Britain is at war! He has plunged us back into the dark ages, sold us back to an Empire that didn't want us in the first place. We will pay with the lives of our young men today; we will pay with a lost Australian identity for many years to come.'

The control room had emptied, but for Lefty and the refrain of Judy Garland's pure, sweet tones that added some relief to the thick atmosphere. Max Dorevitch stormed into the studio, an unfamiliar air of outraged authority stalking his body as he tried unsuccessfully to slam the air-lock door. His soft eyes were red and glaring, his olive face flushed and taut.

'How dare you, Miss Batchelor!' he bellowed. 'You've gone too far this time. You've presented a political broadcast that will be seen as the voice of this station!'

Foolishly, I answered honestly. 'I had to take a side, sir. I always take a side . . . you know that. Most of my listeners will agree and we'll get heaps and heaps of mail, sir.'

'Don't sir me, Billy Batchelor. I've let you have your head once too often. You've got carried away with your little women's show. You're not a man, you're a woman, for God's sake! Only men on my station make political statements. I'll be the laughing stock at the club. A woman, inciting antiwar sentiment on My Station! It's positively indecent, unheard of, disloyal, ungrateful little . . .' He coughed uncomfortably. It was impossible for me to imagine what he had stopped himself from saying as he struggled to regain a gentlemanly stance.

He straightened his tie and pointed his pipe militantly to the left and the right of me. 'You're fired! You're fired, do you hear me? Pack up your office and leave your key with the commissionaire. We'll send you a week's severance.'

He turned to go, reaching the door with some difficulty. He looked back briefly. 'I'm sorry, Billy,' he croaked, leaving me to bury my head in my arms, and weep.

I moved back to Rosebery and had been moping around the station for several weeks when Brumby Gorman's telegraph came down the line. Ruth typed it up and rushed across the yard, waving it high above her head.

'Billy, Billy, it's your lucky day!' she yelled at the top of her voice.

I read the wire twice. It was vintage Gorman, full of theatrical flair like the old ham he was, but short on the important details because he loved the build-up and the negotiating game far more than the show itself. 'CONFIDENTIAL Arriving Friday if I can find bloody Kurra on the map STOP Have contract and passport papers for you to sign STOP Curtain up in two weeks REGARDS GORMAN'

Ruth's face beamed. 'There, see! I knew you'd land on your feet again.'

I tore the page into a dozen little pieces. Ruth's face fell and her eyes immediately glazed over. I wanted to do a Gorman on her, but didn't have the heart to carry it off.

'I can't possibly accept,' I began, dissolving into laughter at the sight of her face. 'It's supposed to be confidential, Ruthy, and more importantly, you left the last Stop off the wire. Gorman's a stickler for detail – he's still got the first shilling he ever made, so best we destroy this in case he sees it and demands your hide.'

'That was not funny, Billy,' she poked and pushed me, making me laugh openly for the first time since my career had come to an abrupt end.

We hugged each other, giggling and falling about

like two little girls of old. As the message began to seep beneath the surface of our mutual excitement, our merriment gave way to a new and frightening thought. We faced one another silently, slightly apart, considering a distant war, an unknown future. Without a word, we hugged again, tightly, desperately, as though for the last time. Predictably, Ruth broke the silence.

'It might only be Singapore, or New Zealand. And I'm sure you won't have to go until after Christmas.'

'You're such a good friend to me, Ruth. You're always so happy for my successes and there's nothing I can do that you couldn't do, if only you'd been born white. How can I ever thank you?'

'Just remember me when you're a big star,' she teased, hugging me again with a lighter grip.

When a Sydney entrepreneur of the reputation of Brumby Gorman announces by telegraph that he is making a visit up country, no confidentiality is possible. As the nation's most well-known guru of the stars, Gorman's flamboyant, larger-than-life reputation made his impending arrival the biggest news in the district since war was declared. By Thursday morning, when Ma sent me down to the general store for top-up supplies, all of Oodoolay Street was agog with speculation and congratulations.

Since my last fatal broadcast and instantaneous sacking, the town's sympathies had swung back in my favour. Anti-Semitic feelings ran high against Max Dorevitch as once again the Micks and Prodys joined together as one Christian body to support the stand taken by their home-grown prodigy. Their disgust at the Prime Minister's wordage was deeper than even I anticipated; Bob Menzies had won the election by a very slim majority and his many enemies included the Sydney press barons. 'It is not a matter of Australians not wanting to get into the fight,' they wrote. 'It is our PM's idolatry of all things British . . . and his outrageous submissiveness to the Crown that gets up our nose!' The city newspapers arrived a week late in Kurra, but were avidly read and usually followed. When James also ran a story in the *Kurra Mail* with identical sentiments to my fatal radio programme, our town unanimously agreed – the Prime Minister had sold Australia out.

It took me three hours to do the shopping. I staggered home with my parcels, mouth watering for a hot cuppa and the peace and quiet of Ma's ever-frenetic kitchen. I trudged wearily up to the back verandah, admiring the sparkling new Chevrolet parked by the horses' trough. Brumby Gorman opened the wire door.

'Domesticity is all right for a spell, I suppose, but I think you look better in grease paint, Miss Batchelor.' Smiling sardonically, he took my parcels seconds before I would most certainly have dropped them.

'Brumby! You're not expected until tomorrow!'

'Well, never mind, dear. I'm sure you can rise to the occasion.'

I shot a quick glance in Ma's direction, knowing she would hate this disruption to her plans. She smiled easily too, apparently unperturbed. Brumby's large presence and dry old British charm had obviously cast an instant spell. I had worried about how Ma would cope with Gorman, but should have known better. Neither minced words nor suffered fools gladly. They were like old friends.

'Here, let me do that, Rosey,' Brumby proffered, taking the large black kettle from her hands, flicking ash from the ever-present Havana cigar onto the hearth. Ma flushed girlishly, not even noticing. Ruth had been called in from the station the moment his car had pulled up and now she and I sat down with Ma, like ladies at an annual men's club dinner, while Brumby made the tea – and served it!

Such preliminaries from Gorman were rare indeed, but he was just warming up. 'I must admit,' he began gravely, 'I didn't know if I'd be able to sell you again, Billy, 'specially to the war moguls, though privately I suspect most agreed with your stance. How have the locals responded to your public castration? Do they love you – or hate you?'

'Country folk love the underdog. They love me more now than they ever did before. It's an odd mix of old hatred for the Jews and new fears of losing their young men. It hasn't got much to do with me, not really. I doubt it's even occurred to them that if I accept a position that is part of the war effort, I'll be selling out too, in a way.'

Ma's attentions were diverted by the stove and the conversation we were having, and the one she most badly wanted us to get on with. I saw her mind darting around, trying to redirect the course.

'Did you find out who's going . . . when? Where?' she asked plaintively.

It was as near as she could manage, without sacrificing all the rules of good manners and decorum. I nodded. She knew about most of them, but the question had to be answered. David Moon's results were due any minute. He'd signed up; if he passed, he'd go quickly. It would be a loud awakening for a new doctor. Micky was exempt because he was a solo primary producer. Jock was exempt too; his flat feet and the ruptured Achilles had saved him.

'James has joined the press corp,' I continued. 'They say he'll be off with the first ship, whenever that is. Mr Merryweather has signed on as a fitness instructor for the conscripts. He's leaving next week for a secret destination up north.'

'Conscription doesn't come into effect until next year,' Ruth sidetracked me.

'Yes, but they have to plan the programme.'

'When is Billy leaving, Mr Gorman?' Ma asked heavily, unable to contain the question until another drift in the conversation had run its course.

'Well, now, Rosey, it's a bit like Mr Merryweather really. My client needs Billy up front, if you will, in order to train her into the role,' he stated matter-of-factly, all theatrical affectation remarkably absent from his manner. 'She'll have to learn to toe the line, too. No ad lib political broadcasts on this assignment!'

'And who is your client, Mr Gorman?' she responded equally.

'The Government . . .'

'Which Government?' The shrewdness of her question surprised. He started slightly.

'Er . . . the British Government.'

Her innate intelligence had begged the question, but the answer stumped her. We sat in hushed silence for a few moments.

Pa's weary footsteps came across the verandah, sounding like the old soldier that he was. He entered without a word and pulled up a chair. Ma hastened to pour him a cuppa. He smiled his thanks wanly, extending a shaky hand to Brumby across the table. 'Where's Billy going?' he asked simply. The sight of him, living through his own private memories of the last hellish war, was too much.

'Now listen just a minute, everybody!' I began hesitantly. 'I haven't heard what the job is, how much it pays and whether I even want it,' I stumbled on recklessly.

Of course I wanted the job. Whatever it was, wherever it was. And I knew from hard experience that Gorman didn't ask twice, in the same year at least. But this was getting out of hand and he had no right, nobody had the right, to assume I would take just anything – even though I would. 'What *is* the job, Brumby?' I asked pointedly.

He leant back, puffing out his large chest until it almost measured the size of Ma's. 'It's a radio show for our boys! Before you tell me you'll want editorial freedom, Billy, I hasten to add that you'll have it, within a defined security framework, of course. I have to stress that – I did some hard talking to explain you weren't antiwar.'

'Anyone who'd listened to me for more than a minute would know that!' I scoffed, drawing Gorman right out.

'Oh, they listened all right. The War Office called for every show you ever put to air. They've issued a low security clearance – your superior officer will proofread everything before you go to air. Relatively standard procedure, of course.'

'Where is the job?' I reframed Pa's question.

'Unfortunately, my dear Miss Batchelor, I'm not at liberty to tell you that.' He was beginning to slip into agent mode. The big guns were coming. 'Classified, you know, but you'll be wonderfully safe. All expenses paid, including transportation and accommodation. You'll be paid twenty-five British pounds a month – a very healthy salary, far more than you'll need. Good chance to save,' he added for Ma and Pa's benefit.

'Thirty,' I smiled sweetly. 'Not a penny less.'

Ma choked on her tea. Pa wiped his brow with a grubby handkerchief that would have turned Ma pale, had the current situation not been more grave.

Brumby pushed his chair away and walked slowly to the door. His shoulders rose and fell perceptibly. He lit another cigar with practised ease and swung the wire door wide open. Half a dozen flies rushed in. Ruth reached for the swat; Ma was incapable. I fully expected him to ask if he could use the phone. If he drew it out much longer, Pa would have a heart attack. Perhaps he noticed Pa's increasing breathlessness, or perhaps the effect he wanted had already been achieved. He turned pretentiously, blowing circles of smoke into the air, his mouth doubling as a peace pipe.

'Thirty pounds, and not a penny more,' he sighed begrudgingly, shaking his head wildly, though anybody could see through the sham. 'Only God knows what they're taking on. If they knew, they wouldn't have listened to an old huckster like me!'

Even as he said it, I knew he'd sold me in as a tough act that could handle the heat. I was glad I hadn't let him down in the negotiating, but felt an unfamiliar stirring of blind panic in my stomach at the thought of what might lie ahead. 'You'll be fully briefed. Don't worry about a thing. You'll be treated right royally . . . think of all those men, eh?'

He took his departure as directly as he had arrived.

'Won't you stay the night, Mr Gorman?' Ma encouraged, hoping for a last-minute reprieve that might elicit some of the answers to the thousands of questions unposed.

He gushed extravagantly. 'Oh my dear Rosey, how lovely that would be, enjoying your homespun cooking and wonderful hospitality, but alas, the world awaits me.' He raised his head to the Kurrajong Ranges, a cloudy mist springing fortuitously to his eyes.

'You're over the top, Gorman.' I kicked him in the shin, regretting it immediately. With my record, it was the height of stupidity.

He stood firm, wincing only for my benefit. 'Yes, alas I must press on. Show business waits for no man.'

He gave Pa a brief demonstration of the vacuum-assisted gear shift and the pilot seat features of the Chevrolet and drove off into the sunset, just as he had planned it.

We all waved until he was out of sight, then stood in the aftershock, staring out cross our beloved country, tranquil and magnificent, no floods or fires to mar the view . . . only a far-off war that had now arrived firmly on our doorstep.

# TWELVE

# 1939...

The sun god Re, the great giver of warmth and life, beat down on our Commonwealth car mercilessly.

The outback Christian sun had ill prepared me for this cruel African god. It was 110° in the converted London cab as Gomah, the embassy driver, dispassionately manoeuvred us through the bloated streets of Cairo. There was not a drop of perspiration on his brow, nor an ounce of fear on his dark, handsome face.

Donkeys and camels jockeyed with buses and horse-drawn carriages while scantily clad herders moved cattle with long wooden prods, all vying for space on the great dusty highway. Men and boys draped in filthy white rags dragged carts laden with wheat and maize and huge piles of red ochre that spilled over onto the yellow dirt road; women smothered and veiled in black trudged along by the side of the road, juggling baskets on their heads and babies on their backs.

Beyond the road, the illusory horizon of obelisks . . . minarets . . . mosques, looked up to Allah without a care. An army truck blew its horn, a train of camels replied. Khaki-clad soldiers, barely out of short pants, clung onto the back flap of the truck and whistled heartily as they crawled by.

Our brakes screeched. We lurched forward, skidding into the gutter. 'It is nothing,' Gomah said easily. 'Just miss donkey.'

A small boy, about seven or eight I guessed, stood up unsteadily, using Gomah's door for leverage. He peered into the window for a moment, sad black eyes, far deeper than his years. He saw me in the back seat, clinging to the arm rest. The eyes appraised me, as a blue-collar man might from the scaffolding of a building in Brisbane. His hands suddenly shot to his mouth. Mine automatically rushed to my ears; I had always suspected the wolf whistle was international.

'Thirty pounds a month is not going to be enough,' I muttered caustically.

'Thirty pounds a month?' the boy repeated breathlessly, one hand remaining over his mouth, the other rushing to his distended stomach. His eyes filled with tears, and then he vomited, a foul-smelling mass of black lumps floating in dark brown liquid, splattering Gomah and the window, the donkey and an earth of decaying garbage and animal dung beneath.

Instinctively, I turned away, covering my nose with a white linen handkerchief, staring obliquely at the fine lace edging Ma had sewn with her strong, callused hands. A babble of hawkers passed by, selling gold and baskets of lapis lazuli. I had promised Ruth a bracelet of the rich blue stone but could not imagine ever walking these streets to shop. Gomah mopped up the bile that had stuck to his bright red shirt, turned over the motor and crunched the gears back into first.

'We're not leaving this boy here, are we?' I leant forward, spraying him with saliva thickened by sand and dust. 'My God, I'm so sorry,' I heaved nauseously, wiping his face with my wet handkerchief.

He smiled cognizantly, jockeying us back onto the road. 'No time at all, missy, you get used to it.'

'What about the boy? Shouldn't we take him to a hospital? He's very sick . . .'

'No, no, he okay, missy. We look after the little ones, but he nearly grown up. Young men tough in Egypt.'

'Why, he couldn't have been more than seven or eight!' I protested.

'Look of him, and what he had been drinking and smoking, he twelve or thirteen, missy. He quite able look after himself.'

We struggled on at a snail's pace. Commuters and shoppers and merchants dodged sewerage effluent as they ambled through alleyways overflowing with shining brass and silverware, vegetables and open barrels of herbs and spices. Gomah's eyes saw none of it.

'Look upward in Cairo, missy,' he instructed. 'The Citadel, our great modern father Mohammed 'Ali, he ruled 1805 to 1848. Spectacular mosque, yes? You must go to antiquities garden, to pyramids, to Old Cairo . . . but you learn Islamic tradition, then you know Arab world. Only way, missy.'

We had reached Tahrir Square. I had never seen so many buses in my life. A man spat on the flag, hoisted to the front of our car. Several British soldiers leant lethargically against a wall, unseeing, or uncaring.

'Centre of town,' Gomah informed mindlessly. 'We go south now, to Garden City. Most embassies there. Very nice, like Australia, yes? Further south, very poor.' The statement rattled me. I clung to the arm rests as we swerved to avoid two water buffalo. Could there be worse poverty and filth than this nightmare journey from the airport? 'My family, they southerners long time ago. We in British service two generations now,' he added inscrutably. Was he proud or sorry? I couldn't tell. I had a lot to learn.

We pulled into a courtyard, a clear blue pond to one side, meticulously landscaped with palms and lotus trees. Along the eastern wall, climbing roses bloomed profusely, reaching across to a wide latticed verandah. Two native girls were playing hopscotch on the pebbled path.

'We hear, missy,' Gomah opened my door, turning back to the boot to collect the luggage.

I stepped down thankfully, breathing deeply. The stench and chaos and pandemonium of the city fell away. The rustle of a Mediterranean late afternoon breeze whistled through the trees, spraying the perfume of the roses across the pond. The villa stood before me, intricately carved cream and green columns supporting the portico like an Aztec icon. A man in a pure white safari suit came towards me, hand extended.

'Welcome to Cairo, Miss Batchelor,' he said ceremoniously, shaking my hand vigorously, ushering me up the marble steps. 'I'm Terence Cardigan, first secretary to the Consul General. My good lady, Elizabeth, was hoping to be here to meet you too but unfortunately one of the servants had an epileptic fit this morning. Most unfortunate, most unfortunate. She's such a sweet thing, you know, taken the child off to her own doctor. Tiresome, these servants sometimes, yes, tiresome. Had an uneventful flight I hope? No sign of the Jerries? Skies of course are safer than the roads here though, aren't they, eh? Yes, yes, I can see you agree wholeheartedly with me. The suicide stretch we call it – airport to the city. Actually, it's a nightmare everywhere. Well, come along, dear, I'm sure you'll find everything to your satisfaction.'

I was greatly relieved that Terence Cardigan obviously required no response. My head was pounding and the shock of the air conditioning inside the spacious villa sapped my body of what little energy remained. I tagged along two steps behind him, barely noticing the splendid appointments and peering eyes that watched us as we marched. He was a short man, early fifties, carrying a lot of excess weight around his midriff. His hair was a steely grey, matching his laughing eyes impeccably. He spoke with the natural plum of the British aristocracy.

We walked across a small courtyard, garlanded by tiny white roses and entered a bed-sitting room. 'It's lovely,' I exclaimed, collapsing onto the settee.

'Excellent, excellent.' A young boy was ushered in with my suitcases. 'Put them down over there, lad. No need to unpack them now. Just run the bath. Miss Batchelor needs hot soapy water, food and sleep, right, dear? In that order I'm sure, quite sure.'

'I didn't thank Gomah,' I suddenly remembered.

'No need, no need at all. You'll have plenty of time for that,' he added hastily, observing my shock. 'Takes a bit of time to get used to handling the servants, but you'll pick it up quickly, very quickly. Don't make your bed or do anything silly like cleaning up after yourself, will you? Rob the locals of a job. We keep dozens of them in work, you know, and mighty glad they are of it too. Now I'll have sandwiches and a hot cup of tea sent in shortly. You just relax and have your bath and then you can sleep until you wake. Don't worry about a thing.'

'Thank you very much, Mr Cardigan,' I replied gratefully.

'Not at all, not at all. Actually, it's Sir Terence, but you can call me Terry if you like. Most of the ex-pats do.' He grinned happily and took his leave.

I fell asleep in the bath and woke four hours later. The water was luxuriously cold. I stepped out slowly, realizing the temperature was cool all over. The sandwiches were being enjoyed by two large flies and the tea had stewed. I fell into bed and slept for eighteen hours.

'Where is the war and when do I start work?' I asked Lady Elizabeth for the umpteenth time, ten days after my arrival.

'Plenty of time, dear,' she repeated crisply, the manner and tone more aggravating for its superior congeniality than that of her husband's.

'I don't mean to be ungrateful, ma'am, but I'm not here as a tourist! Couldn't you please ask Sir Terence if he would spare me a few minutes to explain what my role is and where I'll be working? I really must insist on knowing, Lady Elizabeth!'

'Yes, dear, I can see you've quite a stubborn streak, haven't you? I'll speak to him this evening before dinner.'

I sat down to write my first letter home, having only had time to send a postcard until now. There was much to tell. I'd been everywhere, seen everything; climbed ruins and toured mosques, ridden horseback across the desert to the pyramids, shopped in the Bazaar in Old Cairo. With the embassy staff on a nightclub crawl, I'd been spat on, pinched, abused and laughed at. Watched locals eating cats and being cudgelled to unconsciousness for a packet of French cigarettes. In the embassy recreation room I'd played pool with the Australian contingent while drinking Fosters straight from the can and gorging shamelessly on local delicacies. I'd had long, intimate conversations with men on leave from the desert, Europeans running accounting firms and banks, Egyptian royalty and a coterie of British journalists. The only war I'd seen was the ancient struggle of a disease-ridden, illiterate poor begging or stealing a piece of Utopia from the plethoric rich, perceived almost exclusively as white, and foreign. The constant demands for *baksheesh* rang in my ears before I went to sleep and were still there when I woke, more constant than the teeming, deafening traffic or the cold pealing of the air-raid siren.

I was beginning to wonder whether there was a job. Was this another bureaucratic bungle, of which I'd heard so many since I arrived? We were awash with top brass; swashbuckling generals, majors and colonels, professional soldiers and soldiers of fortune, rookie intelligence officers longing to unearth something important – battalions of corps d'élite. They all had plenty to say about everything, except what was happening.

'How long will I have to wait before they tell me what I'll be doing?' I asked an intelligence officer from Glasgow.

'No idea, lassie,' he replied.

'What do you know of the radio system for the Aussie troops?' I tried again with a communications colonel, on leave from Alexandria.

'Nothing at all, I'm afraid,' he said.

Were they refusing to answer my questions because they had no answers? Could I arrange a secret telephone call to Brumby? Surely he must know something? Confusion and speculation raged on every front around me, more incomprehensible than the complex mythologies that had reigned in Egypt through countless dynasties. I must get to work or I would go mad, or worse, give up my idealism and succumb . . . succumb to the ex-pats' Egypt, life in a bottle, no past, no future, just rumours and innuendo and all you can drink to keep from remembering that there's a war going on, and you're in it, though God only knows where. I felt a familiar wave of nausea and dizziness coming on, and determined there and then to force an answer from Sir Terence before the week was done.

That evening, dinner was a glittering affair with thirty-five guests. The upper echelons of Cairo society arrived early, not wanting to miss a moment of it. Cocktails were served in the ballroom. Ma would be so proud I'm here, I thought cynically, trying desperately to overcome my heavy heart. What had happened to me that I couldn't relax and enjoy this stunning good fortune?

'The world is smaller than I thought,' a smooth, confident Australian accent greeted me from behind. I turned swiftly, my full white satin skirt swishing luxuriously around me, upending a small Queen Anne table holding a tray of filled sherry glasses. The tall, blue-suited man reacted quickly, but the damage was done. Waiters rushed forward, gathering up the scattered crystal, making a gallant attempt to wipe down my dress. 'My fault,' the man said generously. 'I remember how accident-prone Billy Batchelor is! I should have known better than to surprise you.'

His face was oval-shaped, high forehead under a mop of unruly midnight-black hair. His eyes, too close together, shone iridescently, blues and greens and browns, the colours of the Kurrajong Ranges. His skin was fair, untouched by the sun god Re or the sun of the outback. He was older, perhaps twenty-eight or thirty. It had taken him a long time to get through medical school and it showed.

'David?' I whispered, amid the clatter of activity at our feet. 'David Moon? I can't believe it! What are you doing here?'

'I might ask the same of you, Billy,' he smiled again, the full rich mouth opening up like I remembered him as a boy.

'Frankly, I'm not sure . . . but for heaven's sake, tell me what you're doing.'

'Haven't you heard? The first convoy of Anzacs left Sydney Harbour last week. Troop carriers, warships, escorted by the airforce. A hundred thousand saw them off, though it's supposed to be a secret! The combined force is due here mid-February.'

'Here? You mean, Cairo?' I gasped.

'Well, Egypt. I'm not sure where they'll dock, maybe they won't? Anyway, I'm part of an Australian-New Zealand-British medical corp. We're establishing an army hospital, underground.'

'When did you land?'

'On Friday. Just slept off the five flights it took to get here, actually. All I know so far is that the traffic and litter are appalling but the locals seem friendly enough.'

I grimaced. 'I can certainly testify to that.'

'You don't like it then?'

'I'm beginning to. Shall we go in and try to get seats together?'

The servants were hovering, ushering us into the dining room. 'Sorry, Dr Moon, but you seated over there,' Bobby, the head waiter directed.

'Forgive me, please, but I wish to sit with Miss Batchelor,' he replied forcibly, leaving Bobby no choice but to rearrange five place names. 'Will our hosts mind?' he whispered as we were seated.

'Lady Elizabeth will say she planned it all along,' I replied.

'It's wonderful to see you, Billy.' He spoke his mind easily. 'I hope we'll see a lot of each other, that is, if you're going to be here for a while?'

'Yes, I think I am. All I know is I'm supposed to be doing a radio show for the boys. I can't understand why nobody told me they were on their way.'

'Security, I expect. From what I can see, there's a lot of important little generals wandering around pretending they know what hasn't even been decided yet.'

'I can't believe you've only been here a few days!' I

marvelled. 'How did you acquire such intelligence?'

'From a pious father and five years in the reserves; they have a great deal in common! They'll believe anything and they're great procrastinators . . . always waiting for someone higher up to make the decisions, I expect.'

'Let us all stand and toast the King!' the Consul General proclaimed above the polite buzz of preliminary social exchanges. We stood and toasted, followed by the hired trumpeters' mournful rendition of 'God Save the King'. 'Sounds like we're going to a funeral, not a war,' a large lady with red sequins dangling from her bosom declared. Several pairs of eyes chastised her ill-conceived crassness.

'Who's that?' David whispered.

'No idea,' I replied.

'What's the Consul General like?' he tried again.

I shrugged philosophically. 'The answer is much the same. I'm a guest in his home and assume that I'm here because he's a great-uncle of Thea's, but apart from being introduced to him a few days ago, I haven't seen him. He seems . . . dignified, don't you think?'

'I can see I've caught the indomitable Billy Batchelor in a somewhat unfamiliar, uncomfortable, uncertain situation. From what I've heard of your recent adventures, I'd better take full advantage of this rare vulnerability while I can. Will you show me a bit of Cairo tomorrow, before either of us get our orders?'

'You would place your life in my hands, Dr Moon?'

'Let us hope neither of us will need to call on my professional skills,' he grinned.

Lady Elizabeth woke me next morning. I clambered hurriedly out of bed, reaching for my gown and the alarm clock in one movement. Thank God! I hadn't overslept.

'I'm sorry, dear, but Sir Terence was so busy last night, I didn't get a moment to ask him about your job. Please just be a little patient, Billy. Everything will unfold as it should, I am ever so sure.'

'Oh, that's all right, ma'am,' I smiled sweetly, hustling her out the door. 'I'll be out today. Is there anything I can get you?'

'Why, dear, that's very thoughtful of you!' Her eyes lit up quizzically. 'Are you meeting that nice young man from Australia, a doctor, isn't he?' My heart warmed to her. She was all shimmer and show, but there wasn't a drop of bad blood in her veins.

'Lady Elizabeth, you're incorrigible!'

She laughed wickedly and left me to my toilet.

We set off by taxi, travelling through the suburbs of the privileged, into the chaos and poverty of the city. The green banks and muddy waters of the Nile were beckoning, the only place I could think where we might steal an hour or two of quiet intimacy. David hired a felucca. We set off, tattered sails half-mast, our guide assuring us the wind would do the rest. *Let out the sails, Billy*, Ruth's distant voice reassured me. I had already let them out and wondered whether my brazen interest would frighten off this handsome man from my home town.

We lay under the canvas, conversing in short bursts, content with long silences that let the past and the present traverse our thoughts. Snippets of news, fragments from each other's worlds, so far away, so close. Memories ebbed and flowed; memories of Joey. David was his best friend; bad boys, happy boys, growing up together. Fire, death, life goes on. Amelia. Beautiful Amelia, working as a missionary in the Congo. David's battle to pass medicine and get out from under his father's heavy hand; my battle to maintain integrity with employment in a man's world. The water lapped the sides of the felucca; our conversation trickled along, keeping the easy pace. We had discovered a code, verbal, nonverbal – a special language that only we would ever understand. He reached for my hand.

'It's so good not to have to explain everything.'

I traced my fingers across his soft, white palms. 'Yes,' I said.

I barely knew the boy who had become a man, yet at that moment it was as though we had been alone on this earth a long time. We were caught between two worlds, one of our parents' making, one of our own. Born and bred in the bush, we were weighted down with old-fashioned Christian values, not wrong in themselves, but stifling and narrow, immutable, unremitting. We had hoped an education would free us to be ourselves, to walk with the thinkers and turn those thoughts into bold, liberated actions. We dared to dream our questions would be answered, that All would become clear. Yet All was less clear than it had been before and we were more separate than we could ever remember.

We called Kurra home, but were no longer at home there. We were never quite at home in Sydney or Brisbane. We were foreigners in Egypt. For the first time in my life, I glimpsed through a porthole into Ruth's misplaced world and felt her isolation, accepted the intensity of her belief in the Dreamtime.

We drifted on, the magnificent, filthy Nile lapping gently against our thoughts. Now and then a passing felucca stirred us, children's laughing faces leaning precariously over the sides, waving and shouting, 'Hello, mister. Hello, missy!'

'Gidday,' we called back. Another word for their vocabulary, a word they would soon learn to add to *baksheesh*.

'I had a long talk with Gomah, the embassy driver, yesterday,' I remembered suddenly. 'He said, "For centuries we been ruled by foreigners. We had the best labour to make rugs. Turkey bought us out, now they make the best rugs. They get the money. We had the best linen. We were bought by England. Now Manchester has the best linen. They get the money. We wrote life down, going back to antiquity. The world copied us, then forgot us. We were pagans. Moses inspired Mohammed. The people saw a chance, became addicted to a new religion. But our empire is gone. It is too late. We let every nation take us, and now they fighting to keep us again. You think that odd?"'

David was patient, impossible to annoy with long-drawn-out dissertations. 'What else did he say?' he asked.

'He said, "Egyptians rise and fall and only the children know. When they grow up, it is easier to forget." Tears streamed down his face. "I give half my life to make one child smile. I give other half to make one person free. So you see, Billy, our life is not cheap like you think. It is very valuable because we value the right things."'

We fell into silence again, comfortable silence, two people talking between the gaps. The guide turned our felucca around and raised the sails. 'No good wind now,' he beamed toothlessly.

'No good wind now?' David repeated slowly. 'A very good wind now, I think.' He pulled me closer to him.

'Slow trip on way out, fast trip on way back,' the wise old sailor chuckled knowingly. 'You like hubble-bubble?' He pointed menacingly at the long rolled cord attached to the small brass teapot.

'No thank you,' we chorused, dissolving into childish laughter with the spoken affirmation of our oneness of thought.

'Egypt's obsession with death was really a

celebration of life,' David said suddenly, connecting back to his strict biblical heritage, 'and they do know the value of life . . . Dad always said you can't live unless you're ready to die.'

'Gomah thinks our two countries are similar,' I remembered. 'The annual flooding of the Nile, the lifeline for Egypt, just as Australians hug the coast . . . our obsession with sport, our adulation of half-clad women, our reverence for subservient women who stay at home and mind the children! "All Egypt!" he cried. "Desert and beer and towering monuments for the dead! Anzacs and Aztecs!"'

'Let's hope you get a show soon, old girl. I can hear the first programme is already written.'

At the embassy door, I hesitated. It would be in poor taste to invite him in, walk with him down the great hallowed hallways, across the courtyard to my private lodgings. Every bone in my body ached, every crease, every sinew, every orifice was alive and screaming to be nurtured, to be . . . loved. My God, was it possible? Was I . . . was I in love? I had been hit, struck, unbelievably knocked over the head. I *was* in love! Hopelessly, helplessly beyond help! Over the moon – over David Moon. Ridiculous, absurd, wonderful! I was the little girl I dreamt I'd be, all soft and panting, starry-eyed, vulnerable; beautiful, and desperate. It was true! Love at first sight really did happen!

He could smell me then, eyes hot, body tingling, anxious to be held . . . his firm hand into the small of my back. Do it now, David, I willed. And so he did. Standing on the doorstep of the embassy, he kissed me, neither too hard nor too long. I knew it was the same for him, yet his control was greater than his passion. I memorized it darkly; would his loving be thus, for all the days to come?

'I'm hopelessly in love with you, Billy,' he said.

I answered meekly, 'And I with you, David,' all urgency evaporating to the higher plains of reason and inevitability.

'There's no rush.' He combed my hair with his long fingers. 'We've got a whole lifetime. For the first time in my life, I know where I belong.'

'I'll dream about you all night,' I said.

'I'll be here in the morning when you wake,' he smiled, 'and I don't care what the servants think.'

But he was not there in the morning; he was not there for a month of mornings.

He was sent north, in a Decoder DC3, to Alexandria. An explosion in a local factory had injured dozens of men. A makeshift hospital was erected by the army; the injured men were operated on under the stars, a curtain-raiser for the main event. His environment was a disused rubbish tip, a junkyard for oil drums and petrol cans, barbed wire and sheets of corrugated iron, wooden huts and carcasses of vehicles used for beds. Instantly, an operating theatre for God's orphans, amputees, insanes . . .

I was sent south, on an antiquated British steam train, to Luxor. My mission was to see the Valley of the Kings, including the 3,000-year-old tomb of Pharaoh Tutankhamun. Fascinating. Ma would be thrilled, but where was the radio station, and where was the war? My escort was Gomah's brother, Nalbad. He had a higher security clearance than Gomah and I suspected an even more finely tuned capacity for philosophic meanderings.

'You need the power of Allah to help patience, missy. Only one big difference between you and us,' he rolled on, in time with the clop-clopping of our donkeys' shoes. 'We sure of ourselves, sure of our future, sure of our after-world. You not sure of anything. That is why you in such hurry. Silly, no? In big hurry to get there, but don't know where you going.' He chomped on a stick of tobacco, idling ahead of me nonchalantly. I dug my heel into the donkey's flank, puffing and spluttering like I'd never mounted a four-legged beast in my life.

'You don't understand, Nalbad. My life's slipping away and I'm powerless to do anything about it. I'm not used to being idle. I'm not an ornament. I'm not a city girl, I'm a country girl. Country people in Australia are always busy doing something worthwhile – like your people!'

'The big brass, they want you beaten so you fight more softly, no?'

'Nalbad, what you saying?' I stumbled unwittingly into his vernacular.

'I seen the brass do plenty much, tame green horns plenty good. You being soften up for the kill so hard to believe, missy?'

'Huh! It's too ridiculous for words,' I scorned, but his words stayed with me. I planned a showdown on my return to Cairo.

Perhaps it was the decision I'd taken, or Nalbad's advice sinking in at last? Perhaps it was Egypt, getting under my skin? Somehow, I couldn't remain angry and impatient, walking over vast populations of mummified humans and animals, sailing across crocodile-infested waters, breathing sand and eating God knows what, cooked to perfection. My work, my very life, grew smaller each day. Ancient Thebes, the capital of the kingdom, before Christ! Mammoth temples and forests of gigantic columns and tombs chiselled deep into the bleak limestone outcroppings, thousands and thousands of years old . . . I could not reconcile the paradoxes of modern Egypt, nor the great, dark realms of her human history, once more provoked by the threat of human destruction. Nalbad was right: 'The world gone mad, missy. God's book, the Koran, is only constant. Allah divinely inspired, all powerful, He give Moslems everlasting hope.'

The peasants working the fields along the lush green strips that flanked the Nile smiled and waved as we began the slow journey back. Thousands of miles of desert lay beyond, neutral, on nobody's side but its own, as it had been in the beginning. Now, trenches that were improvised out of foxholes by exhausted armies in 1914, were being dug out again by local soldiers, British soldiers, anybody who could lay their hands on a shovel. The endless round of spadework, all the way from the Nile to the Suez; latrines and telegraph wires going down, barbed wire barriers going up, British bare backs sweating under the savage Re, local backs covered in brightly dyed cotton rags. Occasional orange flashes in the terminal blue sky – did I imagine the screams of men? A column of trucks, armoured cars, more trucks, a couple of tanks, kept pace with the train for a hundred miles. When they left us, I wondered if they'd ever return, if they'd been there at all? And silly things, like whether the locals would be issued with uniforms when the big fight began?

Gomah was waiting for us outside Bab-al-Luq central station. I had changed into a sari I'd purchased in the tourist shop at the Winter Palace; his face lit up. 'It was amazing,' I answered his eyes, 'and I'd like you to drop me at the first secretary's office, please.' The two brothers slipped into a knowing silence, understanding my needs, relieved that my haughty impatience (or did they first see me as disdainfully self-important?) had mellowed appreciably.

When I entered Sir Terence's office, I was a deep tan, the colour of a thoroughbred. The sun strobed streaks of gold from my silk sari across his conservative, British green linen drapes. He jumped to his feet. 'My dear! How wonderfully rested and, and . . .'

'Indigenous?' I teased, cupping a spread palm on one hip, rolling my eyes coquettishly at the ceiling. There was another man present in the office, but I was so busy showing off, I continued my mannequin parade until Sir Terence collected himself and introduced us.

'Major Gib Dorevitch, Billy. Gib, I'd like you to meet Miss Billy Batchelor.'

'How do you do?' I asked, peering rudely into his deep, horn-rimmed glasses.

'Yes, yes, my dear, I'm Max's cousin. Morale, radio operations, entertainment and recreation officer, Jack of happy trades at your service, ma'am.'

'I'm very pleased to meet you, sir,' I nodded my head, then shook it. My being here had nothing to do with the Bickley family, everything to do with old Max at 2IZ. Maybe he hadn't wanted to sack me after all? Regretted his overreaction to a programme thousands had responded to positively? Under secret orders all along? How unbelievably neurotic! I said to myself. The diet of idle service people – intrigue, rumour, gossip and insinuation – had finally got to me. I could no longer think logically, only paranoiacally.

'You are as pretty as Max wired me, and no doubt twice as fiery! Must admit, I thought you'd have red hair, from what he told me. Hah, hah! Don't mind a little joke either, I believe?'

Sir Terence poured everyone an icy cold Victoria Bitter. 'You'll like this, old chap, yes, a great little drop. Only place in the world you can get a cold Melbourne beer from the fridge of an Englishman, I'll venture!' he joked heartily. Gib Dorevitch guffawed dutifully, reducing his mug by half, much of which seemed to remain briefly on his full red moustache and beard. 'Major Dorevitch has your orders, Billy. I'm sure you'll be most relieved to know you'll be staying here, working out of Radio Cairo.'

The Major took over. He was shorter and older than his cousin, more certain of himself and considerably more British, but the incarnate Jewish traits of businesslike efficiency and intelligent, piercing eyes left no doubt as to his character. When he had explained the situation, we took leave of Sir Terence. The Major's driver set to manoeuvring us across the city. We were heading south, through familiar streets. 'But Radio Cairo isn't in Garden City, Major?'

'Our part of it is, dear. You won't mind sitting through the war in the safest underground station in northern Africa, will you, Billy?'

I wondered about that, but shook my head frantically. I was in no mood to complain.

The guided tour did not take long. There were five rooms: two studios, one control room, one kitchenette, one operations meeting room that also housed the music library, and one bathroom. The equipment was modern and the staff of three seemed friendly and efficient. 'I'll leave you with Amy and Jefferson and Mr Mohammed now, Billy. An army driver will be called when you're ready to go home.'

Amy was a Welsh widow of the last war; she'd been with the BBC twenty-five years and knew everything about research and administration. She also typed at 100 words a minute. Jefferson was an Egyptian-born Australian, our sound and music man. Mohammed was Oxford-educated and head of operations. He was an Egyptian writer and film maker but a short minute ago, with the highest security clearance it was possible to have. He was older, a statesman of considerable intelligence and class. His dark good looks and charming manner would especially appeal to Ruth; I wished she was here, to share my good fortune.

I sat down with my new colleagues for the real briefing: length of programme, type of music, propaganda delivery to be naturally juxtaposed with selected stories from the daily news summaries wired from Australian and British Information Services. And we needed a name, a catchy name, a call sign of sorts.

'What about *A Batchelor in Cairo*?' Amy suggested.

'Sounds like a man,' Jefferson spurned, writing a few music notes on his foolscap pad. '*Cairo Calling*?' Nobody seemed impressed.

Mohammed scribbled Cyrillic letters on Amy's shorthand notebook. 'I'd like to see us tie in Billy's name with its unique Australian meaning. We could take the theme music "Waltzing Matilda" and come out each day with . . . what the men might be doing waiting for the show to start. " . . .Waited till his billy boiled?"'

'*Billy Blue in Cairo*?' I attempted.

'That's got rhythm!' Jefferson nodded, tapping his fingers on the table like drumsticks. Mohammed wrote and underlined 'BBIC/1' on Amy's pad.

Feet shuffled as legs changed position. Faces scrunched up and brains mobilized. I could feel a tingling mounting in my veins. The adventure had begun.


'There's a new moon over the old hills, and tonight's the night for me to be with you . . .' David's voice mouthed the words to the honky-tonk piano on Radio Cairo, rolling over to pull my head back into the nape of his neck. 'Hard to believe it took a war thousands of miles from home to give us the happiest days of our lives, isn't it?'

The transience of his mood still shocked me, as it

had been doing since his return from Alexandria, a lifetime ago. He held no long-term expectations. 'Even during that long month apart, I made love to you in my heart, Billy,' he'd said. 'I knew if we were never together, you were the one true love of my life.'

We'd been in Cairo well over twelve months. I had begun to indulge in daydreams that took us way beyond the realms of our temporary, tenuous term in Egypt. His 'live for the present' mood worried me more now, especially since our respective jobs were sheltered from the front in a direct sense. We had not physically experienced anything worse than spasmodic dashes to air-raid shelters. Yet we were at the front in other ways.

David was now assistant head surgeon, living with the gnarled, charred bodies arriving on stretchers every day from the battlefields, ships and planes in North Africa. Even old friends, new enemies were carried in . . . thirty thousand Italians were captured in Egypt following Mussolini's declaration of war on the Allies, the HMAS *Sydney* sunk an Italian cruiser off Crete before returning to Alexandria where the Mediterranean fleet were stationed, the swastika was flying from the Eiffel Tower and the Royal Navy killed a thousand French sailors to remove the threat of German takeover of the fleet. The battle of Britain . . . British and American freighters sunk in Bass Strait . . . the British land offensive in North Africa, Rommel to the rescue! . . .the siege of Tobruk. Where would it end?

'Sometimes I wish I was out in the thick of it,' David's sleeplessness stirred me. 'I spend my waking hours competing with God. It's the devil's own game.'

I agreed with him on that score, but kept it to myself. I lived with the constant warnings and diversionary tactics in advance of the action, holding me precariously on top of a waterfall that brimmed over, never easing up, a relentless, drowning farce. And my competition cut my listeners in half three days a week. Dubbed Lord Haw-Haw, the William Joyce broadcasts from Germany, designed to undermine public confidence in the BBC and the British press, meant of course that everybody had to listen. He had six million listeners, according to the surveys. My programme was strictly closed circuit to the boys, most of whom wanted to hear the factotum of the old British fascist leader, Sir Oswald Mosley. Why we bothered to broadcast across his time at all was quite beyond the army to explain. When the bigwigs took the decision, it was certainly not on their minds to offer our fighting men a choice of programmes. What was on their minds remained a mystery.

'Can't remember the bodies I've seen and the battles you've reported.' David wrinkled his brow, absent-mindedly flattening out my wakening head with his fingers. 'Each day rolls on like the one before. After a while, you can't even remember what they were fighting about, who they were fighting even.'

'Will we return to the bush, David? Would you take up a post at Kurra or Tarrenbonga?' I suddenly need to know.

He smiled uncertainly. 'Wherever you like, darling. I'll go with you wherever you like.' He pulled me towards him, an urgent bell ringing in his ears that every moment counted. His strength frightened me, like the strength of a child holding on to his mother as the fires swept around them. 'I adore you,' he kissed my ears, my lips, my eyes, my lips again.

'Gently, David, gently . . .'

'I'm sorry,' he released his grip on my neck, moving his hands over my body with indelicate haste.

'We've got tonight!' I burst through his kisses, gripping his hands that were ripping into my gown. He pulled back abruptly, resumed slowly, meekly. Was it passion, or panic? Was I a fool not to let it run? This man whom I adored was still as hungry for me as he had been the day we fell in love, yet it rarely showed, except in sleepless moments when fear ran high, when life itself held still.

'I'm embarrassed to say it's too late for me, darling.'

'You . . . you?' As we turned, I rolled into the telltale sticky substance on the sheets. He had not even secured the rubber. 'Should I be flattered?' I whispered.

'Always,' he replied sadly. 'In a way, it would be easier to die at this moment, than wait . . .'

'Wait? Better to die now? Wait for what, David?' My heart thumped heavily, all passion drowning in the deep conviction of his words.

'Now Athens has fallen, the Nazis will break their pact and invade Russia. After that, Egypt will fall. Nothing surer. I wish you'd go home, Billy, but I know there's no point in arguing with you. It would be easier, just easier, to die now, holding you and loving you as I do at this moment.'

'Do you mean, to love is to die a little?'

He stared at me. 'Possibly. Yes, I suppose that's what I mean, yes. To love is to die a little.'

# THIRTEEN

# 1941...

'The Desert Rats advanced fifty miles westwards from their starting point ten days ago near the Egyptian border,' I read, wondering how obtuse I was sounding out there on the front. Undoubtedly the actual scenario would be unrecognizable from this communiqué, but as Dorevitch had reminded us on a rare appearance last week, it helps the boys know that the folk at home are being fed good news.

'The feminine fingers of Australia's finest womanhood have assembled the Owen gun, the gun that passes all desert tests . . .' I read on, wishing I could break the story of the seven days a week these assembly line women operatives worked in abysmal munitions plants for less than half the equivalent male wage. Instead, I flipped the latest hit 78 onto the turntable and allowed it to close the show.

> 'She's the girl that makes the thing
> that drills the hole that holds the spring
> that drives the rod
> that turns the knob
> that works the thingamebob . . .
> And it's the girl that makes the thing
> that holds the oil that oils the ring
> that works the thingamebob
> that's going to win the war!'

I returned the *On Air* switch to off and stretched out

wearily. Today's real version of the truth was irreconcilable with yesterday's version, yet we just kept serving up yesteday's, pretending the war was going well. Raw data isn't raw at all! It's what we planned to find at the start. When some detail doesn't fit what we want to believe, we suppress it, or reorganize it until it does. And so the truth remains the truth, unalterable and unquestioned. We're winning the war. Japan is creeping down through southeast Asia, but it doesn't mean anything. All Jews over six years of age must wear the Star of David on their lapels, but that's all there is to it. It won't go any further than that. I fell heavily into my chair at the operations table.

'Our little antipodean feeling very downtrodden today, yes? Sunday blues? David not working this weekend?' Mohammed pulled up his chair and opened his AIS log book cautiously, wrapping his arms around some notes he'd made earlier.

We had all become similarly territorial. Our mugs were marked with different coloured dollops of paint, our sleeping bags were crudely, individually labelled, our earphones were Ours. Station RCUG (Radio Cairo Under Ground) was home and we were family. We knew one another's moods and idiosyncrasies better than we knew our blood family, yet we maintained our distance, sharing little of our lives above ground. We dealt in lies all day, disjointed days that drowned us in hypocrisy and sham. At night, we searched for peace and sanity amidst the blacked out, increasingly volatile city.

Why I suddenly felt so despondent, exhausted, drained from it all, I couldn't pinpoint. Radio was serving a fine purpose across the globe, offering the only entertainment available to millions of people in blacked out cities from London to Melbourne. Tommy Handley and Vera Lynn were all the rage in

London and Bluey and Curly had taken Australia by storm. In the tradition of the Aussie larrikin, the writers had just landed them in the Middle East to capture a fleet-footed Italian POW to train him for the Stawell Gift, the premier professional Australian footrace. The material was wonderful; I was using excerpts for *Billy Blue in Cairo*. A thousand more letters poured in every week.

'What is the matter with you, Billy?' Amy asked, expressing the question we all wanted answered.

'I don't know,' I said. Something in my manner alerted the Pharaoh, as we'd nicknamed Mohammed. 'Your eyes are not quite right, no?' he reflected, his pen doodling constantly. 'Your boyfriend, he hasn't noticed any change, no?'

'No,' I answered hesitantly.

'Ah! He has commented, yes?'

'Indirectly. I've always had dizzy spells, and fainting, but lately I'm just exhausted all the time. I've been getting headaches and . . . double vision too, and strange blocks of stars appearing out of nowhere, fuzzing up my right eye, for ten, fifteen minutes sometimes, as well as the nausea and dizziness . . .' It was the first time it had occurred to me there might be something seriously physically wrong with me, yet the symptoms jumped straight to mind the moment my eyes were mentioned. 'I'll go to the hospital on my way home,' I volunteered immediately. It would save the fuss I knew would surely follow.

We had nearly wrapped up tomorrow's show when the wire came through. 'Japan has attacked Pearl Harbor. America is at war. The US Navy caught with their pants down . . . thousands killed . . . simultaneous attacks in the Philippines, Guam and Wake Island.'

'Is it confirmed?' Amy whispered.

'Looks like it,' Jefferson struggled to speak.

'Will we have to do a misinformation job on this?' I ventured helplessly. It was so close, too close to home. The Pharaoh stared past me, his eyes focused on the world map on the wall. 'No, Billy, in the spirit of Hitler, this one's big enough to just tell the truth, I think. How do you want to begin?'

The enormity of his words was difficult to assimilate. We sat around the table scribbling words, crossing them out, starting sentences that tailed off without conclusion. Finally, the Pharaoh called it a day. 'We will all go home and start two hours early tomorrow,' he announced. 'And, Billy, you will go to the hospital.'

We stirred slowly, dropping notebooks covered in doodles and fragmented, scratched-out sentences into smart, diplomatic-issue satchels. Had we been living with our lies so long, we were incapable of absorbing the truth, of writing it the way it was?

The streets of Cairo were oddly comforting as my Jeep edged out of Garden City and headed across town to David's underground body shop. The filth and grime and incessant traffic, the spitting Moslems and the blistering sun offered a subtle, pervasive security against the images of purgatory in the Pacific. David would be working, but I had to see him, even though I'd lost all thought of having a check-up. I needed to surround myself in his strength and love to make this day believable.

As we pulled in to the camouflaged office car park, an American couple rushed towards us. 'Can you tell us, ma'am, how to get back to Talaat Harb Street?' the tall, floral-shirted man enquired loudly.

I'll make short work of this, I thought, as the realization hit me that the news would not be out in the streets yet, nor underground in the passages of death. 'Take a red and black taxi on the other side of the road to Tahrir Square. Talaat Harb runs off it,' I yelled above the sudden screeching of police cars, ramming into the car park.

Plain-clothed, olive-skinned men jumped out of the cars, guns brandished, positioning themselves along the rickety fence. They cordoned off the street, their target isolated to the two small terraces leaning precariously to the right of the office block. A team of men stormed forward, breaking in doors, smashing windows, dragging occupants out into the street. Children screamed, running naked onto the footpath. A dark man was beaten with a home-made whip. Two old people emerged in dressing gowns, young soldiers hustling them forward with black batons. Several shots rang out. Hand in hand, they fell to the ground.

'Get into the Jeep!' I yelled to the Americans. 'Take the back entrance,' I ordered the driver, new to the job and slow to react. And get your foot off the bloody brake,' I screamed.

We skidded around the side of the building and were swiftly cleared through the iron doors. In the bowels of the earth, we fell into the eerie silence, emerging into the light of Casualty. Two sisters going off duty waved to me. 'What the hell's happening?' two American women demanded aggressively from the back of the Jeep. I had been well trained. Somebody would tell them the truth later. I would give them the coded message. It was hardly surprising after all that the local constabulary were over-reacting. 'Obviously spies in the area, ma'am. Quick raids keep the panic down to a dull roar.'

We stopped abruptly. I jumped out. 'Where's David?' I called to anyone listening along the rows of camp stretchers.

'He's around . . . somewhere,' several voices responded variously. My heart was thumping. All life seemed to have drained from my legs.

'Darling, are you all right?' I heard him calling, shifting to the left of me, then the right. Why was he doing that?

'Be still, hold me, oh David, Japan has bombed Pearl Harbor. Thousands dead . . . half the US Navy destroyed . . . there's a massacre going on above us. We've got these four American tourists . . . David, hold me. I'm afraid,' I sobbed, and then I fainted.

'She's coming round,' I heard in the distance.

'What happened?' I whispered. He was close, too close, a blur of faces peering fearfully into my eyes.

'You fainted,' he said.

'Oh, is that all?'

'No. Not quite. You were seeing two of everything,' he laboured gently. 'How are you, old girl?'

My heart lifted with the familiarity of greeting. 'All right, I think.' I could see the CMO hovering behind him and felt a rising panic in my stomach. I tried to grip his hand, but my fingers were numb. They were speaking in hushed tones. I struggled to concentrate.

'She had rheumatic fever as a child, plus all the usual childhood illnesses. She's always been accident-prone, vomits easily, faints a lot, very tired lately, nothing sinister. I thought . . .'

'We can't do anything for her here, of course, David,' the older voice said gruffly. 'Any hereditary diseases?'

'Not that I know of. Father has a weakened heart from the last war.'

'The rheumatic fever won't have helped hers either . . .'

Oh David, please, please, be selfish now, my brain pleaded silently. I've just found you. Don't send me home. My home is you. But I couldn't speak. God, help me!

'Yet, I've wondered about the clumsiness, the nausea, dizzy spells for some time – perhaps a neurological disorder? I've been selfish. Blind . . . selfish.'

Madness reigned above us. The diggers were in the trenches at Tobruk. The Nips were on the beaches in Hawaii. It was a madness to be lying here with all the love and care a man could give while . . . while the diggers in the trenches of Tobruk were dying, alone and unrequited. There was nothing wrong with me. I'd been fainting all my life, been dropping things, bumping into walls, throwing up. Why, I'd been seeing stars for years! Too much imagination, too many nerves. That's when it happened – when I was nervous. It was nothing new, nothing untoward. It would pass. It always did. I was tired, just tired. God, I had never been so tired.

I clenched my fist around the strong, clammy hand, and hauled myself up, falling back heavily onto the stark grey pillow.

'We can't help her here,' the CMO repeated. 'She needs tests, specialist care.'

'Yes,' David said. 'I thought recurring infectious mononucleosis at first – the tiredness, but she won't rest; I'm sure she had that as a child too. Then middle ear . . . Ménière's lately, now this diplopia? God, I've been selfish!'

The CMO again. 'Any recent botulism?'

'No. She vomits when she's under pressure, always has, but nothing recent, that I know about.'

'Tumour?'

'God, possibly. We must get her home.'

'Do you want me to write the certificate?'

I hauled myself up again, every nerve in my body exposed and screaming with pain. 'I won't go home, David. I won't, I won't. I can't. I am home,' I collapsed again, his arms limp around me.

The CMO wasn't listening. 'You haven't had a

holiday for two years, David. I think we could arrange for you to escort Miss Batchelor back to Australia.'

'Did you hear that, darling?' David's eyes searched me like Mama's had all those years ago when she sat at my bedside and willed me back to life. All this time I had been reading into his words and eyes an obsession with his own mortality. I had missed the point completely; the fearful truth much louder now than my worst imaginings. He smiled grimly. 'I'll take you home, darling. You always said your stubbornness would win the day.'

'David, David, is this a win? It's an almighty vicious one.'

There were two worlds now, two Davids, two mes swirling in a cruel, black Nile, tipping our feluccas over into the mud and the crocodiles. The sails were torn into a million pieces. Then the wind was still.

Rosebery had known few visitors since we went off to the war; Kurra had shrunk to half its size. The occasional traveller passing through was welcomed heartily, leant heavily upon to stay and talk. Ma's table had shrunk too, but there was always hot bread and jam, and sometimes shepherd's pie for one more hungry mouth.

David and I arrived two days before the Christmas of '41, almost two years to the day since I had left. David's leave was open-ended. He would be advised when there was space on a returning troop flight. I prayed that they'd forget him in the Middle East and need him here, need him for the new front on the far north Australian coast. Rumours ran rife that we'd be next; my foolish heart dreamt it would be so.

I was ashamed of my thoughts, but could not blot them out. I did not want to sit out a war in a sleepy hollow up bush. To be stuck in Kurra, with spasmodic visits to Sydney for tests and treatments was unbearable to contemplate, bringing tears to my eyes that fuelled the very symptoms of my demise. That I would have to live it out alone, without David by my side, was more terrifying than death itself. He had foretold this hour. He knew it all along.

I would die inwardly, long before my body gave up the fight. Trapped between two worlds, a man to love but not to love, the babies to dream about but not to bear. I was to be shipwrecked in Kurra, with my back to the unnegotiable Kurrajong Ranges, my face to the unfathomable Pacific Ocean. Another dark stage in a Shakespearean tragedy, and I was perfectly typecast for a wasting body. My cup would overflow again on the battlefields of ordinary, everyday life in the bush. I would be there when somebody's brother died in a bush fire. I would know the old black layabout who got hacked to death by the AWOL sailor. A friend of the family would be killed at the Cranberry Vineyard crossing. I'd comfort the girl who flushed the unwanted foetus down the town's sewer. I'd help Ma turn a pound of mince into a meal for ten. I'd help Pa tell the untellable truth and send it up the wire. I'd push Sabella and Luther Prescott's wheelchairs out into the sun so they could see the sea and remember the days when they walked barefoot in the sand. I'd let Sister Mac bully me into taking my medicines and watch her stupid candles flickering, reminding me of my mortality.

For David's part, what peace for him, with death more real than life? What did he really cleave? Always another battle, another broken body, another dream gone wrong. Acceptance. Only the sheer futility of acceptance left to make some sense of it. But I could not lie down and die because he sensed it so! I could not, would not, must not! If only I wasn't so incredibly tired . . .

I forced myself to wake. We were at the last siding. The unseeing Kurra was just ahead, an afternoon easterly stirring up the dust that poured into our open windows.

'Whatever happened to the American tourists?' I spoke abruptly, as though I'd dreamt the question moments before I woke. He raised to consciousness quickly, moving along the carriage, yanking the windows down.

'Sorry, darling?' He kissed me lightly on my eyelids, as he always did when he woke. 'What were you asking?'

'I wanted to know what happened to the American couple, or was it couples?'

'They went for a cruise up the Nile.' He ignored the crude shot at my diplopia as though it were nonexistent. 'Amazing people, the Americans.'

'They what? I don't believe it! You mean, they just went on with their itinerary?'

'I expect they thought a holiday in Hawaii wouldn't be much chop,' he quipped sheepishly, his eyes flashing a much more powerful message. His was not a character that absorbed jokes or facilitated a light-handedness with repartee, yet his Egyptian experience had uncovered a paradoxical underground humour. It was cynical, and earthy. I laughed, as though I hadn't a worry in the world.

'Hey, beautiful,' he grabbed my hands, clapping them together forcefully. 'Will you marry me? You've got exactly ten minutes to make up your mind. I refuse to be delegated to the fortress room and this is the only reason I have now found the courage to ask!'

'Why, David! Anyone would think you were afraid of manifest accusations,' I rattled mindlessly, my heart leap-frogging into my mouth.

'I will make love to you in my heart, always,' I heard him saying that night on the embassy doorstep.

'There's no rush, we have a lifetime ahead of us . . .'
Oh David, David. Why now, when our futures are so
tentative? Tomorrow you'll be gone. Tomorrow I'll be
diagnosed. You're gazing at me, worshipping . . .
eyes pleading for my answer to guarantee perma-
nence, security, long life, happiness – health! Why do I
feel this desolation, now when I should be dancing
across the Billadambo like the brolga at dawn?

He knew my answer, but I couldn't give it now.
How could he ask, knowing what we knew? 'Say yes,
Billy. Just say yes. That will be enough.'

I could smell the sea, wafts of salt piercing the sand
and dust and diesel oil. We were close, so close. The
ocean waves rushed in to hug the shore, then hurried
out, afraid of death. He was watching my eyes. He
knew me too well. 'This is not a script, Billy! It's not a
play, with you in the leading role. It's life, with us
together and apart, sharing, being, in sickness – as in
health.'

My body trembled involuntarily, a foot leapt out
from the knee bone. My right eye began to twitch.
Please God, don't let me faint. Let me be in control for
once! Let me be normal in normality, just for a change?

'Pretend we're out on the felucca, Billy,' David's
voice wooed, 'drifting memories rippling with the
water's flow. Not having to explain, not having to talk
at all. The lousy world outside, you and I tucked safely
in our bed, no fears, no wants beyond what we can
give each other. I love you. I need you. There is no
point, without you. I love you because you're like a
rose on the . . . No. You're like a bird, circling the
earth, pausing for rest then flying high again. I'll never
ask you to be less than you are. Don't reduce me,
please?'

'It's a madness, being a woman and learning to fly.' I
hauled my heavy body up from the floor of the ocean
and flung it out the window. 'I'll marry you, David

Moon!' He hugged me, then pushed me back to arm's length. We were nearly there, a life's commitment suspended by the whistle of a train. We had come to the end of the line.

A motley group had gathered at the station. A bright blue banner stretched across the awning: 'Welcome home, David and Billy!' Two clusters of balloons and streamers billowed anxiously in the breeze. The high school band played 'Waltzing Matilda'.

'Good Lord! We're getting a heroes' welcome,' I groaned.

'Well, it's deserving for you, dear girl, but hardly for me,' he deferred humbly.

'I don't know that I'm up to this . . .'

'You'll handle it on a break, darling. Hello, Dad! Gidday, Miss Prinkett! (Glory be, the old Prinky's holding up well, isn't she?) Where are your folk?'

My eyes scanned the rows of faces. Bodies and arms pushed and shoved excitedly, close to the edge of the platform. We drew to a jarring halt. 'Pa, Ruth!' I screamed as we tumbled out, falling into one another's arms, laughing, crying, everyone kissing with reddened eyes and salty lips. 'Ma?' I shouted above the bedlam as backs were slapped and hands were pumped.

'She's not well, Billy,' Ruth yelled in my ear.

'Ma? Not well?' The mere suggestion offered no yardsticks on which to comprehend such news. At my insistence, we had not divulged my state of health. A small voice in the dark was calling, *Mistake, mistake!* 'What's wrong with her, Pa?' I gripped his sleeve, determined for an answer right this minute.

'A bad dose of influenza, dear,' he shook his head gravely. 'She wouldn't go to bed. Now she's got pneumonia, I'm afraid.'

'She's stable, Billy,' Ruth's voice was soothing. 'She'll get through it, she's a tough old girl. Come on. We're takin' you home. Reverend Moon will bring David over for dinner this evening. Mrs Rosey was adamant about that. She's running Rosebery from her bedside, wouldn't you know!'

David's hand clasped mine fleetingly as we were pulled in opposite directions. My eyes pleaded with him, but there was nothing he could do. We were outflanked, on every front.

'I'm afraid it's not a matter of whether you're getting married or not, Billy,' Pa's voice was strained and unfamiliar, his shoulders stooped, his face more carved in pain than I could remember. 'I cannot imagine what you were thinking of, dear. Your ma would never have agreed to David staying here in your room, for heaven's sake! Neither indeed would Reverend Moon!' He cast his eyes across the table, deeply shamed. Reverend Moon's eyes returned his pain. David sat still and white. Ruth stacked the plates and quietly left the room. 'I dare not imagine what gentlemanly opinion Giles can maintain for you now, Billy, but as the situation stands, it would surely kill Rosey if she knew. I forbid you to mention a word of it.'

'But Pa, we're adults! It's nearly 1942! We've been living together for the best part of two years. Would you have us lie about it? We love one another and we can't know the future – how much time we've got . . .' My breaking voice trailed off. The tears I'd fought back for twenty-four hours sprang silently to life, weakening my resolve.

I wanted to scream and kick and throw Ma's beloved Royal Albert cup and saucer at the walls. I wanted to accuse Pa of the two faces my diplopia was forcing me to see. Had he forgotten what it was like to be young? Had he forgotten what it was like to be in a war without the one he loved by his side? Had he forgotten the smell of death? I answered the questions as I asked them. He was blameless. He was a man for his time, a good man in the service of a God-fearing woman, who ruled her castle as her mother before her had done. I was the black sheep, the heathen, the fool. I had broken all the rules of my upbringing. I was guilty, as charged. I had thrown my reputation to the wind, enticing a pure-bred young man into my wanton arms. And worse, much worse: I had dared to flaunt the truth.

'Make me this promise, Billy?' Pa's fearful eyes implored. I wiped my tears and straightened up. An ill-begotten laugh escaped my lips. He shifted uncomfortably in his chair. David leant forward nervously. Reverend Moon closed his eyes in prayer.

'We will not disobey our fathers,' I said finally. 'Yesterday, you welcomed us home. You cheered and congratulated us. You treated us like a king and queen, like the soldiers of the cross! The band played. Pins and needles ran up your spines. How proud you were of our patriotic service, the sacrifices we have made. Oh yes, don't look shocked that we can acknowledge the sacrifices!

'It'll interest you, Pa, to know that my job involved telling lies. Every day. One lie after another: big lies, little lies, stupid lies – euphemistically known as propaganda. You'll be keen to hear of David's job too, Reverend Moon. Lies, every day. Comfort the dying, tell them they're going to live. Tell them we're winning the war, thanks to their capacity to believe the lie that going over the hill will save the world.

'Then there was the gigantic lie we lived together, surrounded by poverty and fear, luxuriating in magnificent villas with the locals looking after our every need. They were paid a pittance, of course, but we lived like the kings and queens you thought we were – could that be only yesterday? And this will give you a laugh, gentlemen,' I squealed painfully. David's foot. I had not lost control of the script, yet even David was frightened now.

'The one thing that kept us sane was the truth of our love. We knew from the very beginning we had found what we'd been searching for half our lives. There is no pretence, no game-playing, no lies between us. To come home and have to hide the truth in the interests of good taste makes a mockery of our lives, our love, our upbringing and the total education you gave us.

'How many days of your lives have held the bright promise of one thing and finished up something else again? And why? You are proud of the wrong things, gentlemen! You cannot reduce me to a scarlet woman and David to a poor, bewitched man without reducing ourselves.

'I will accept your ruling Pa. You are my father. Now, please excuse me.'

I left the table quickly, stumbling blindly into the night. The air was sticky, the breeze had gone. I propped myself up by the well and wept. I don't know how long I'd been there when I heard the footsteps. 'David? David?' I jumped to my feet. The world span out of control, stars darting around my face.

'It's me – Ruth,' the voice in the dark answered. I fainted in her arms.

She knew what to do. The night returned quickly. We were sitting on the ground, my head between my knees. I lifted my head slowly and managed a short laugh.

'We've been here before, Ruthy.'

The tears were streaming down her face. 'I heard

everything,' she said. 'I did your old trick and sat on the stairs. There's a fearful row going on now. Why didn't you write me you were sick, Billy? Why didn't you tell me?'

I stared hard into the clammy night, a new anger rising. 'David has told them about my health?'

'Has he ever! He's setting them straight,' she halted, hearing David's diversionary tactics, the mollifying words and their implications through my reaction.

'This has nothing to do with my health,' I breathed heavily.

'David told his father that he couldn't believe in a God who would separate him from the woman he loved. He said you were very sick and he could be called back to the front at any time,' Ruth volunteered desperately, adding no comfort to my heart.

We sat in hapless silence. The gentle lapping of the waves kissing the rocks at Bunyip Point disturbed me; I could not think why. My mind was blank. I had never been so tired. Ruth stirred with the sudden hint of a breeze coming up off the ocean.

'What are you going to do?'

'I love him, Ruth. He's the best thing that ever happened to me . . . if only he wasn't so scared of death, so scared of his father's wrath, so scared . . .'

She took my hands and held them tightly in her strong, hot grip. 'David is older than you and set in the ways of men. His religious upbringing was stricter than yours too. He's trying to make the peace for you; he doesn't mean to sell out. He needs to know you'll be cared for while he's gone.'

'My wise Ruthy! What you don't know isn't worth knowing. But men are so stupid! Talk, talk, talk. The hours are slipping by and all they can do is talk . . .'

The firm footsteps interrupted my anger. He lifted me off the ground like a baby, attempting to kiss me.

'I'm not interested in appeasing this bloody town's

sanctimonious morality, David Moon! Don't stand there talking at me! Love me, or let me be.'

'That's the spirit, old girl!' he swung me around wildly. 'How would you feel about a well-earned rest in the old cottage at Cranberry Vineyard?'

In the afternoons we strolled among the ruins of the vineyard, left idle by the childless Prescotts' departure years before, and the subsequent shameful management by the caretaker farmers.

The Pickle River was dry from the long, hot summer; nature herself seemed old and parched, sick and tired of all she surveyed. Now and then a squirrel or a rabbit scampered across the barren fields, a stray crow hovered for a day or two, and finding nothing, moved out. The lost tracks between the avenues of short gnarled branches of the ancient vines led down to the empty dam and back up to the old cottage on the hill.

In the evenings, we ate our tea under the stars. The stove didn't work because the chimney had caved in; David grilled chops on an open fire. I sat under the dead lemon tree, chatting away about Egypt and the war, and all things present. David was relaxed, almost jovial, taking great pleasure in small tasks that kept him close to me.

We had few visitors, but they were most welcome, breaking our days without staying too long. Jock came home for the school holidays and rode over with Micky to say hello. They were odds and evens, as brothers went; Jock, courteous, friendly and pale, wanting news of the war first-hand for his students, and Micky, rough and tanned in the saddle, still with no conversation short of the drop in the price of cattle and the interminable faults of the weather. Ruth sometimes rode to Mini Mini and brought Than out to join us. She talked of the loss of her son quite openly, told me she'd a good mind to have another to keep for her very own. 'I'm just a weekend baby-sitter, no more, no less,' she said.

Than was a fine young lad, boisterous and full of mischief. His deep-set, black eyes were ever busy, inquisitive of all things, his crooked mouth turned upwards no matter what befell him. He stirred up our grieving earth and played hide and seek by himself on Butcher, the placid old nag David had secured for me from the station. He was used to amusing himself. His twin sisters, Frances and Sarah, were not yet old enough to share the long, hot days.

In the mornings, when I was strong enough, we drove into Rosebery and sat with Ma. She was improving slowly, impatiently, insisting Doc Halliday was a stupid old man who knew nothing of women's health. On pumping Sister Mac, we learnt she had a prolapse that could be fixed with surgery. They were wearing her down bit by bit. The unmentionable had to be mentioned and her gross mistrust of the medical profession had to be overcome or she would never recover.

We saw little of Pa or Reverend Moon. David argued that Pa was preoccupied with Ma's health and since he had not been close to his own father for many years, there was no cause for concern. Ruth said time would take care of all our problems, regretting it the moment the words had passed her lips. Three weeks had gone, with no word from the army. The second hand of the clock was moving quickly now, ticking its way round to the end of our hour allotted.

My symptoms miraculously subsided, though I had not yet undergone tests or taken any medicines. The colour came to my cheeks readily again and my energy levels returned to normal. 'The irony of it all is that it's actually been an hallucination on the part of the medical profession,' I pronounced gaily one morning when even the birds seemed to have returned to our destitute oasis. I flung open the windows. 'See, world!' I shouted to an anthill, 'Ma was right again. What do silly old doctors know?'

'Hey, that's enough! Show some respect for the bread winner of the family!' David pulled me back to the bed, rolling me onto my stomach, beginning the ritual morning massage.

'I intend to find work, David, somehow. I mean, how else will I cope without . . . ?'

I was all tied up in knots, unable to voice the inevitable. We had become hesitant, qualified in our responses to one another. Our conversations were sketchy, as an early rehearsal of an unfinished play. We spoke in half-thoughts, stopped short by everyday issues that diverted us from the main performance. The days were flying by like the fork-tailed swift, yet we were weighted down like crabs under a rock.

'I think it's time we talked about it,' he said softly, rolling me over, licking my breasts like Than with an icy pole. I giggled. 'You are the most infuriating woman I have ever had the extraordinary privilege to know,' he murmured.

I could feel the quickening of his heartbeat as he closed his lips around a nipple. Muscular thighs manipulated my legs apart, beginning the slow, rhythmic crawl to love. My strengthened response aroused him more, increasing the tempo of the dance. It would be over soon, and he would sleep, more soundly than he ever slept in Cairo. I would still be awake, holding onto the wing, hoping, again, that life had been renewed.

We heard the wheels of the bicycle approaching before the music could reach its finale. Our hearts stopped, dead. Our bodies locked together like two cadavers, frozen to stone by a great catastrophe. Ruth's bicycle at 8 a.m.

She called loudly, making considerable business of a noisy arrival. We unlocked grimly, eyes meeting, acknowledging. David reached the door first. 'Come in, Ruth,' he said.

'Thanks,' she winced, edging her way across to the kettle. She put the wire down on the sideboard, started making tea.

'Hello, Ruth.' I stood numbly in the sunlight, watching her open cupboards, spoon leaves into the pot.

'It's on the sideboard,' she said to David.

'Yes. Thank you.' He took two steps, picking up the small yellow folded note. 'Read it out loud, David?' I asked calmly, startled by the resignation in my voice.

'Sutherland Flying Boat departing Darwin Saturday 8 pm STOP Connect seconded Qantas/RAAF Syd-Dwn Friday 4 pm STOP Assume similar previous assignment/briefing on arrival Dwn STOP Contact CMO Syd 2nd Div if any problems SIGNED BAXTER, CTO STOP'

'But today's Wednesday! You'll have to . . . you'll have to leave tomorrow.' I sat down on the wood box. My life was decomposing. It had come, as I knew it would. The second front.

'You've got an extra day, chaps,' Ruth proffered vigorously. 'Mr Nathan's putting on a special train 8 a.m. Friday. You'll make the 4 p.m. deadline.

She poured two cups of tea. 'I'm not going to join you, thanks. I'm going over to Mini Mini to tell Micky and Thea. They'd want to know. Mr Nathan will tell the Reverend. In the meantime, work out when you want to say farewells and I'll come out again tomorrow, around midday, get your instructions.' She walked to the door.

'Ruth?' My bottom lip was not my own. My eyes swam. 'Thanks.'

David sat beside me on the box. Then he stood up, bowing slightly. 'Thanks for a giving heart, Ruth.'

'Okay, okay,' she brushed away a lonely tear. 'You could always slip out without sayin' goodbye to the town, David. They don't know there's a train going at that hour . . .' She jumped onto her bicycle and pedalled hurriedly away.

David reached for the tea. 'I don't think I could manage it,' I said. Unsure whether I meant the drinking, or the physical handling of the cup and saucer, he let it pass and took my hand. 'Why don't you stay on for a bit? There are good memories here for us and you're close to home while your ma's recovering. You might even decide to do the place up, get the old vineyard going again? Your pa said the Prescotts have fifty thousand pounds in the bank for anyone prepared to restore the property. Think about it. You might even be able to call in the women's land army to help. Not too many radio jobs around at the moment and I'm not sure you're wrong about the medical profession – in your case.'

A fleeting whiff of salt air captured my despairing heart. We were ten miles from the ocean and rarely smelt a hint of it, yet I could almost hear it reaching out to the shrivelled, creaking hills. 'What do you mean, *in my case*?' Hadn't I heard it all, been up and down it with a shearer's fine-tooth blade?

He got up and quietly walked the small, sparsely furnished, dilapidated kitchen. His face was oddly loose and shiny, as though he had a secret worth the keeping.

'I don't want you to be a guinea pig,' he began at last. 'That's why I haven't pushed you to go for tests. Neurology's a new field, unexplored, unfashionable at the moment – medical scientists have been busy with popular diseases since the industrial revolution. They'll guess and poke and prod and write prescriptions without research to back them up. Compounding the problem, your symptoms come in waves and bursts, with long remissions. No consistency. I hope I'm not being emotional and selfish, but I think you should just get on with a simpler life and let the good Lord have a say.'

I did not know what had led him to this metamorphic trade in my management. I searched his naked face for clues of professional duplicity, but there were none. My voice faltered.

'Then you don't think I'm dying of a brain tumour?'

'No, I'm sure you're not. I don't think you're dying any faster than the rest of this crazy world actually.'

'Whatever I've got, it's just a slow crawl to the grave then?'

'It's slow . . . at least.'

A goods train on the way in from Tarrenbonga sounded its whistle. We got up silently and walked hand in hand into the simmering morning heat. The bleak landscape sparkled illogically. The sun burst over the gaunt blue hills and swept across the rotting fields. Flies buzzed on a few scattered dunghills where life flourished in vengeful abundance.

'Will you write often?' he asked.

'Every day.'

'Don't forget to number them.'

'I won't.'

'Let's say our goodbyes here, old girl, here and now, standing on this godforsaken earth with only God and the sun our voyeurs. I have known you as my wife, Billy, the most precious living thing in all eternity, for ever. I will make love to you in my heart, always.'

'I will make love to you in my heart too, David. Always.'

The old cottage came down like a pack of cards. Well, in truth it was just a hut but the locals had always referred to it as a cottage, out of respect for the Prescotts. And it was Prescott money that built my new house. I moved back to Rosebery while the building went up. I had dreaded the prospect, yet it turned out quite differently from what I expected.

Ma had recovered to full strength from her prolapse operation, an event that was never to be mentioned again, mainly because it was such an outstanding success. Like all women of excessively modest upbringing, life had chipped away much of the embarrassments of delicate female matters for Ma, but she remained stubborn to a fault in her beliefs that most doctors 'couldn't tell the difference between pneumonia and the common cold.' With renewed vigour, she attacked what she saw as the neglected tasks about the house and yard, redoing everything to her own perfectionist standards. She laughed often, cracking her well-worn verbal whip at anyone who got in the way.

I seemed to be the only one who could do no wrong as she forcibly hauled me back into the deep valley of her heart. She was so proud of me, it was hard to reconcile with the days of my youth. I felt at last that she was glad I'd been born a girl.

Pa and I picked up more circumspectly. The pain between us died slowly, the unforgiving remnants of my disappointed heart held together through the winter until the spring came – until I had moved into my 'Pharaoh' on the hill at Cranberry Vineyard. He had never left the station since he returned from The Great War, apart from the night he led the posse to Mini Mini, the night of the Great Fire.

I had been in my new house a week when he came. It was a morning like no other I can remember now. There had been no visitors, apart from one of the workers returning to pick up some tools. Micky and Thea had promised to come within the month and Ruth would be here as soon as Ma's Red Cross Week preparations were done. Apart from that, no one could spare the time, each too busy with his own, too busy surviving, like the old days. I didn't mind. I had David's letters, irregular though they were, and a wide, dead vista spread before me, waiting for me to kick it back to life. I had the old nag Butcher and a bitser of a dog who'd arrived during the building process and decided to stay. I called her Chocolate Two; silly really, since she was a spotty grey. It was good to be alone, just me and the animals, away from the fuss my returning symptoms would attract.

Chocolate Two and I were at the clothesline when Pa came. He rode up on a thoroughbred at an ambling pace – speed meant bad news. He'd never got round to buying a car. He didn't even have a licence, though he'd started his life driving trains.

'How are you, old girl?' he chuffed brightly, lowering himself gradually off his much younger horse. I looked up to him breathlessly, the world spinning, my heart soaring like an eagle. He couldn't know, would never know just what those words could do.

'Oh Pa!' I shrieked, dropping a sheet to the ground, along with my foolish pride. 'You've come!'

'There, there, Billy,' he patted my back sensibly, after we'd purged our congealed souls together for a few moments.

'How's it all going, dear?'

'Fine, Pa, just fine!' I steadied myself on his stooped, bony shoulders, unwilling to let go. He eased me gently onto the log fence. 'Let's get this washing out and have a cup of tea, eh?' He bent down awkwardly to pick up the sheet. Chocolate Two lost interest and wandered off, chasing flies. I sat under an uncertain sun, letting the retarded tears stream down my face. Transfixed in time, I watched him struggle with the pegs and the linen, learning a new skill women had known since the beginning of time. He took one handle of the basket. Gorged of tears, my face lit up with his raised eyebrows. I dragged myself up, took the other handle. We walked slowly along the path, past the dozen brave new vines growing along the verandah posts, and into the house.

It had four rooms, including an indoor bathroom and toilet, but was otherwise simple and airy. The kitchen was a large, sunny place with windows both sides. The carpenter had argued with me, but I'd refused to be swayed. Outdoor canvas blinds and the total verandah would keep the heat out in the summer and for six months of the year I'd be able to see the Ranges and the growing fields I dared to dream about, all at once. It was only a timber cottage, but it was home, at last.

Pa was clearly impressed. He limped about, opening doors and looking out windows, though the view was one he'd been looking at virtually all his life. 'Lovely, just lovely! Good-sized second bedroom for youngsters too,' he ventured, throwing all caution to the September winds. 'We had a card from David yesterday. He's well. Missing you.'

'Yeah! He's glad to be in Alexandria. Cairo reminded him of the past. He's above ground now too, right in the thick of it, but he's happier. Terrible to be stuck down there with no reason to come up. I've given up hope he'll be called back. They didn't call him to Singapore. If only we'd delayed just a few weeks coming home, Pa, he'd probably be firmly entrenched in Darwin by now.'

'Yes, Rosey and I have thought about that too, but *if only* pays no dividends, does it? As Ma says, what's meant to be, will be.'

'She seemed to lose that simple faith for a while, Pa. What brought it back?'

He sipped thoughtfully on his tea, juggling the question around in his brain, neither certain of where to start, nor how much to divulge. In the end, he said what was in his heart, brief and to the point. 'I didn't know my father, Billy. He died when I was five. My strongest wish as a boy was that I'd live long enough to see my children grow to adulthood. It never occurred to me that my own boy might not make it. I wanted a son so badly; when Joey was taken from me, God died with him.'

His voice had dropped perceptibly, but his eyes held firm. He pulled out an old faithful pipe and dug around his pockets for a match. I rescued the box and lit one for him. 'I always thought it was Ma who so desperately wanted a boy . . . who lost her way after Joey's death?'

'No, it was me. She shielded my heartache and disillusionment from you when she seemed to lose her own faith; she thought it would destroy you to see me as I really was. But even when she was heartbroken, her faith remained, in the end, invincible. She never doubted for a moment that I'd find mine again. She's a remarkable woman, your mother.

'We men are weak – weak at heart you know . . . but it was you, Billy, who brought me back.'

'Me? I couldn't possibly have.'

'Oh, not in a way you could poke a stick at, I'll grant you. No, no, no, much more subtle than that. Do you remember the last time we were close?' I didn't have to think about it.

'Yes. It was the Christmas of '33. Nearly nine years

ago! You were very sick. I used to read to you in the afternoons.'

'Yes, I remember that well. And you were nursing a bad case of lovesick blues at the time, not that you ever mentioned it.'

'It happened then?' I was mystified.

'On the day you left to return for your final year, specifically. It hadn't been much of a homecoming for you. None of your homecomings have been too bright, have they?' We smiled coyly at one another. Pa was not the master in our family at stating the truth succinctly, but he had always taken the cake for style. 'Do you remember how I tried to apologize to you for upsetting your holiday? You refused to accept an apology, convincing me absolutely that you had gained enormously from my illness. I'll never forget you saying how grand it was to have private time with your father, how you'd be ahead with your studies because you'd read me all the texts.'

'That's true – I was. It helped me get high distinctions, Pa.'

'See, it's in your make-up! You do it all the time; make people feel better about themselves, make them feel they've helped you when so often the reverse is true. All at once, I could see my Lord again, telling me how fortunate I was to have such a wonderful daughter. Telling me to put away my grief and get on with the present and the future. I started to get better almost immediately after that day.'

'So did I, Pa. So did I!'

My memory flashed back to the quick recovery my broken heart had made following the Harry Carmichael affair. I had not thought about it in years.

'Well dear, I must get back now. I've got Ruth training up a new recruit for the telegraph room. Thought it might be handy to have some back-up, you know?'

'Oh Pa! You're not poorly, are you?' I felt the flushed tinge of panic speeding up my heartbeat.

'No, Billy, never been better. Just precautionary for you actually. Your symptoms are returning, dear, aren't they?'

I studied the floor, fighting back tears. 'What gave me away?'

'Ah, I've been your father a long time now. When your energy is sapped, it's easy enough to see.' He got up slowly. 'I'm so happy though that your own little place is finished in time. You'll be content enough here, with Ruth in charge. Old Mackie will move in to help Rosey, so you won't need to worry about a thing.'

'Oh Pa, my dear Papa,' I cried openly.

'Remember, dear, it's not an ill wind blowing if you're forced to spend a few months resting. It's a time for renewing the spirit, for thinking vibrant, generous thoughts, for reviewing the past and planning for the future. Write up a diary, take the opportunity to make some sense of it all . . .'

'Thank you, Papa. I love you.'

'I love you too, Billy, yes, I love you very much.'

# FOURTEEN

# 1945

On 8 May, Ruth called the Flying Doctor Service again, as she had been doing since Doc Halliday was killed in the fires of '43.

Paul McNab had taken over my management 'from a great height', we used to joke. He was a dapper man, always bow-tied and jacketed, in spite of the temperature often hovering around 100° for weeks on end. He still had all his hair but suffered acute dandruff that made the early greying sections look like spotted dog. Short and overweight, he had a large nose, with lips too thin and eyes too close together; all this set on a florid complexion suggesting too much of the good life, he had, nonetheless, developed a warm place in my heart. His bedside manner was jovial, if not a little insensitive at times. I imagined him to be a good bloke to have around a bar; he knew how to listen and always laughed in the right places. I'd been bedridden more than three months, this latest bout; he visited whenever he could, and more often than my relatively stable symptoms demanded. Mainly, of course, he gave instructions through our combination transmitting and receiving radio, powered by a small generator driven by bicycle pedals. On this day, however, a new pilot delivered the doctor himself, landing the battered old de Havilland 50 on a partly cleared paddock.

It didn't particularly surprise us when a lanky

American stepped out with Paul McNab. The far north had been swarming with Yankees since the first bombs hit Darwin in '42. He was introduced as Flight Lieutenant Jay Childs, on temporary secondment from the Islands.

I was low that afternoon and Paul opted to sit by my bedside and talk to me about the war. He was certain it would be over any day now in Europe. He rambled on about how there were few opportunities for enlightened social and cultural discussions any more, apart from with other doctors and pilots, most of whom he found singularly boring. He was a jolly bloke who enjoyed a woman's viewpoint. There was little else he could do but talk to me anyway, so we slipped into one of our favourite subjects: the Government's outrageous news censorship of events occurring in the Top End and the Centre and the subsequent denial of the rights and liberties of all Australians.

In the kitchen, Flight Lieutenant Jay Childs was wasting no time making acquaintance with Ruth. He was a tall, handsome fellow, copper-coloured, his fuzzy hair bleached by the sun, with some obvious help from the bottle. The upper part of his body had been built by a football coach; the lower half was like a drainpipe supported by two smaller drainpipes. He was quite young, perhaps twenty-six or -seven to Ruth's thirty-eight years, but neither appeared to have noticed.

Eventually, Paul called loudly to the kitchen. 'Any chance of a cuppa, Ruth?'

We'd had rations for years, but somehow we never seemed to run out of tea, though now and then Ruth substituted coffee or Milo without explanation. It was one of those days. We all got coffee with fresh milk – Pa had given us a goat for Christmas. It was agreed we should move outside. The men helped, propping me between cushions and rugs in the canvas hammock on the verandah. 'Do her good to be out in the fresh air,' Paul said, and the air was certainly fresh. ' . . . *Can winter be far behind?*' He pulled his jacket closer to his well-padded body.

'Wow, y'all sure do it basic out bush, don't ya?' Jay shook his head in the direction of the chooks and our goat.

'Plenty do it basic in the cities too.' Paul started on his absolute favourite hobby horse, though Jay was plainly not seeking philosophic or educational communion. 'You blokes come over here, eat three steaks, six eggs and a huge pile of ice cream in one sitting, while our people queue for bread and ice. Why, some can't even get ice for their chests because you blokes are cooling your bath water! I'll be darned if you haven't changed the course of the war – and our lives!' he smiled fondly. It was an old and friendly argument between them. In a pub, anyone starting out to punch him would finish up turning around in their tracks and slapping him on the back.

Jay smiled patiently. He didn't mind how much he was ribbed, as long as we kept talking. His eyes had barely shifted from Ruth throughout the afternoon. When Paul started to make noises about heading off, he suggested we wait for the news and weather report, a cyclone warning likely, given the time of year.

Paul laughed good humouredly. 'Ah, the joys of youth! Why not, why not? I declare Billy's colour has lifted noticeably since we arrived.'

'And not only mine . . .'

Ruth's cheeks had lately lost the look of shining good health too. In fact, her life was dull and tedious. She had dreams for the future but was stuck nursing me in the meantime. She still longed for another baby, one she could keep, and she'd begun talking again about her desire to go back in search of her biological mother – in search of her roots. Perhaps the American in short pants would be good for some real dreaming, make a break from the mythical Dreamtime wanderings of her days.

She turned up the volume, praying for a cyclone. The Sydney ABC newsreader, Bryce Danielson, announced that he was crossing to a broadcast recorded from London in the early hours of the morning. Victory had been declared at 2.41 a.m. in a small red school house in Rheims that was HQ to General Eisenhower. V-E, Victory-in-Europe, Day! Two down: Mussolini and Hitler. One to go: Hirohito.

We screamed and shouted, kissed and hugged. Paul shook my hand until it hurt. Jay kissed Ruth, a long, lingering, tongue-lashing kiss.

Paul got up to rummage in our ice chest. 'One bottle of beer? Well, it's enough for a toast, then I suppose we'll have to go.' Jay separated his lips from Ruth's with great difficulty.

'There's a large bottle of brandy in the medicine cabinet,' she declared.

'Nobody will need us at the base tonight, Paul.' Jay took her lead. 'They won't even notice we ain't back, man! Why don't you stay here with Billy, have a shot or two of brandy, chew the fat and I'll take Ruth into town and get us some supplies?'

'Hey, that's jolly decent of you, old man,' Paul reacted quickly. 'You're quite right of course. Let's take the night off. Okay with you, Billy?' he reached for my hands and held them tenderly. I nodded, a touch nervously. There was a slight shift in his manner that vaguely bothered me, but I put it aside easily enough. David would be coming home soon! The war in Europe was over! I could almost feel my energy returning, though it had been many months since I'd been able to walk unaided.

Ruth and Jay departed on my old faithful Butcher. I had the distinct feeling we would not see them again until morning. I prayed Ruth would remember the rules, though it had been years since she'd had any cause to. Perhaps it didn't matter anyway. Did anything matter tonight, except Victory?

Paul resettled me on the settee, laying the chicken salad Ruth had prepared for us on the auto-tray. He sat down beside me, clinking his glass of beer against mine. 'Advance Britannia!' he toasted. 'Long live the King!'

'To Freedom,' I beamed. 'To David's safe return!' My heart was so light, I knew nothing could impede a steady recovery now.

'I suppose you'll marry as soon as your David returns, Billy?' Paul asked keenly.

'Yes, provided I'm well enough. Sometimes I think it's grossly unfair of me to marry at all, but no argument will convince my fiancé.'

'I don't blame him,' he said, downing his beer, repairing to the larder for the St Agnes Medicinal. He poured two glasses, a large one for himself. 'Bottoms up!' he cheered.

I was aware Paul had a soft spot for me, often taking more time than his professional calling demanded, but it had never before occurred to me he looked upon me as anything other than an interesting patient. He was drinking too quickly and there was a certain trepidation bearing down on me, alone in my house with no horse at the back door on which to escape. The fact that I would not have been able to get to my horse was not the point. The more my thoughts traversed these lines, the more I realized how absurdly paranoid I was becoming. Silly, sick old woman, that's all you are, I told myself firmly. Behaving like a frustrated spinster, thinking even your own doctor wants to do a Bogart on you! Utter nonsense . . .

Yet his hand tarried and his right fingers lifted mine to his thin pink lips. He picked them off, one by one. I drew back, horrified.

'Paul! For heaven's sake, what do you think you're doing?' I had known this man for two years; was it possible I did not know him at all? He topped up his glass again. If he was a little man with a big complex, how big was it? What level of control could I depend upon? Would he care about his reputation if his impassioned juices ran riot? Should I suggest he'd had enough to drink?

The arrival of the flying doctor and the seconded black pilot suddenly struck me as curious. Ruth had called for advice only. Normally it would be a day or two before we received a reply to a nonurgent request. The chance circumstances of Jay Child at the helm, plane in the area, work done for the day and on the way home? It was just a little too convenient. My heart steeled, my back stiffened. I would have to talk my way out of trouble. My situation presented no other options.

I moved my feet to the floor, attempting to stand alone. 'Paul, I would ask you to remember your position.'

'I'll help you to your bed, Billy.' His voice was easy, normal. Normal! I'd been imagining things, too much excitement for one day.

'Thank you, Paul. You may sleep on the settee and by all means listen to the radio. I'll be asleep in no time.'

'Ah, but I have no intention of leaving you to sleep alone, my dear. Your modesty has charmed me greatly, Billy, but two years is more than time to jump the bounds of social discretion. Let us throw caution to the winds and explore the joys and pleasures so long denied us!'

He lowered me onto the bed, returning to the

kitchen for the brandy. I breathed freely for a moment, but he re-entered the bedroom instantly, the bottle to his mouth, before putting it down on the dressing table. As soon as his hands were free, he fumbled at my neck unravelling the bows and buttons as I struggled to come to terms with what was happening.

'Paul, think what you're doing! Think, Paul! Stop this at once! You will sacrifice your career, your family – your reputation, your whole future . . . Stop now, Paul. I won't say anything – to anyone!' He flung himself on top of me, tongue reaching, hands pressing into breasts and thighs.

'Dr McNab! Have you gone mad? What fatal delusion have you . . .?' His thin mouth had grown thick, smothering mine, searching, tongue filling my cheek until I knew I'd be sick. I writhed beneath him, but I was a poor adversary. He dragged the untied gown from my body, ripping the top of my pyjamas away, rolling me onto my stomach, one arm hooked high behind my back. His teeth sunk into the elastic band in my pyjamas pants. 'Paul!' I screamed at the top of my lungs, though only Chocolate Two could hear, scratching wildly at the back door. 'For God's sake, stop it! You'll lose everything . . . Stop it! I'll tell everyone, I'll call the police, I'll tell you raped me, raped me, Paul . . . Paul, stop it . . .'

'Raped you?' A maniacal laugh exploded in my ears. He turned me over, my arm caught behind me, his face buried in my groin. 'You invited me to stay the night, bitch, you want me, bitch!'

He undid his pants, tried to rip them off in one movement. Heavily laced bush shoes were in the way. Momentarily I was free. I rolled to the floor, got to my knees before he reached me. His belt was in his hands, the buckle held like a rock about to be hurled. I cowered, fighting hysteria, pain and shock . . . disgust rendering me powerless. He picked me off the floor, hurtling me back onto the bed. His gullet was drawn, saliva oozing out of the sides of his mouth. 'Now, Miss Batchelor, we will see who is suffering from delusions, eh?'

His mouth closed over my lips again, cutting my breath. He moved to my nipples, and I screamed. Chocolate Two threw her head back and howled. The erect body began grinding its way into my defeated frame, using more energy than needed to still me. I fainted . . . must have fallen away from him.

When I came round he was shaking me violently, seething with murderous intent. 'Unattainable bitch! Fraudulent bitch! Who do you think you are, Miss Fancy Pants? You wanted me, you invited me in. You're a cunt, no different from the rest.'

I kept my eyes tightly closed. He dropped me heavily, flinging himself off the bed, miscalculating, hitting the floor, the buckle of his belt piercing his knee. 'Shit,' he groaned, repositioning, remembering. He lay there, unable to get up, the sway of tiredness, alcohol or pain pulling him down into unconsciousness.

His shallow breaths deepened. I lay motionless for a few minutes. Which way was I facing? I focused on the shadows of the room. The lamp outlined the kitchen doorway. I would never be able to walk to it, but surely I could crawl? I reached for my gown, could not get it on. What point anyway? It offered no protection. Forcing my body forward, I clawed my way into the kitchen. The matches were by the woodbox but my feet would not grip the floor beneath me. The radio had finished, a loud crackling arguing resolutely out of the speaker box. I reached up to turn it off, feeling the bruises rising in my arms and face.

When the back door opened, I was sitting naked on the floor, dragging Ruth's discarded sweater over my head. Footsteps approached. 'Get out of here, you filthy rotten pig!' I screamed.

'Jesus!' a new voice exclaimed.

'Who is it?' I gasped, blood rushing to my cheeks as fear gave way to discomfiture. I heard him reach for a match.

'Billy!' he rushed towards me, kneeling to the floor, throwing his arms around my crumpled, half-naked body.

'Jock? Jock O'Ryan, what on earth are you doing here?' Relieved and horrified, I leant over frantically for the unreachable blanket.

'I'll get it. Don't move.' He shied away quickly, reorganizing the blanket. He bundled me up and carried me to the settee.

The sound of a door squeaking lit my brain. Over Jock's shoulder I saw the belt swinging, gathering momentum, lashing around the crazed doctor's head. 'Move, Jock!' I yelled, pushing him to the right of me as the whip cracked through the air, missing us both by inches.

Jock was on his feet, eyes furtively seeking the room for a weapon. He reached for the fire prod, a long iron rod with a forked head. Paul stalked the settee, moved forward to one end of the table. Jock positioned himself at the other. I raised myself up again.

'Both of you, stop this at once. I will not have it, will not have it . . . You can't restore your non-existent honour, Paul McNab. Get out of my house and don't ever set foot on my doorstep again!' I leant back, exhausted. Jock closed his eyes for a moment, his shoulders dropped in relief.

Paul limped backwards to the door, one hand on the bloodied knee, mad dog eyes damning our souls to the devil. He turned to go, cursed under his breath, swung around, firing the belt across the room, the buckle torpedoing a crystal vase clean off the mantel, again missing us by inches. The shattered glass seemed to reach his brain; he turned back towards the door. Jock lurched forward, pitching himself at the lower part of his body, now midway through the opening. McNab staggered, trying to hang on to the door, jolting forward, falling, straight out, face down.

'Jesus!' Jock's face drained. A dark, unearthly moan rose up from the floor. Then the night fell still.

Jock recovered, moved towards the deranged hulk.

'Has he fainted?' I whispered.

He bent low over the chest. His lips parted. 'Heart attack?'

'What?'

He stood up as a sleepwalker, staring vacantly into the night. 'I think he might be dead.'

'D . . . dead?' I could feel the world fading out.

'Jesus,' he called again, before I went.

'Filthy bastard,' he was saying. 'God's justice.' I was coming around; the body was still at the door.

'What will we do?' I mouthed distantly, no sense of time or place.

'I think I'll just have to put him outside until morning. There's no way I'm leaving you here alone tonight. Ruth won't be back.'

The mention of her name returned me sharply to the present. What of her safety? Who was this Jay Childs? A friend of Paul's? 'How did you come to visit, Jock? My God, where's Ruth? Is she going to be all right?'

'Calm down, calm down. She's okay. She's with Jay Childs, the American pilot. He's just a boy. She could run rings around him. I met them at Shaft's, she told me you were here with Dr McNab . . . I wanted to share the news of the end of the war with you.' His voice dropped. 'One war ends, another begins? I'm back because I've just been posted to Kurra Primary. Mr Hunt's retiring. The world turns full circle . . .'

It was years since I'd seen him. He was older, but otherwise unchanged. He had always looked like a man you could count on. My grateful heart reached out to him, and my mind was full with the horrors of the situation I had placed him in, yet I couldn't help being glad I no longer had to face the repercussions of this night alone; couldn't help being glad I had a witness to all that had gone before.

Jock had answered all my questions and turned to the task of removing the body. 'We should call the police, I suppose.'

'Not tonight, Jock, please. They can't do anything tonight.' I shivered involuntarily, grasping the blanket tightly around my shoulders. It was enough for him.

'No, I guess not. We'll call them in the morning.'

With that decision, we took a fork in the road that would change the course of our lives for ever.

It was becoming increasingly clear to me that my upbringing had been largely successful.

Ma had warned many times that great intimacies between men and women are both foolish and imprudent. Under the sanction of friendship, even a man with the strictest, most honourable intentions holds his friendship with a woman as nearly akin to love. Wasn't it perfectly clear that I had courted friendship with Paul McNab, only to find a wanting lover?

The police actually had no desire to get involved in the unfortunate heart attack of the respected doctor from the Royal Flying Doctor Service at Port Hedley, no more than was absolutely necessary anyway.

They became involved, in part because we delayed calling them, but mainly because of Jock and Ruth. Jock's extraordinary attention to my physical and mental health disturbed them and Ruth's excessive guilt at taking the night off to have a fling with a *damn Yankee* (as Kurra quickly labelled him), set their suspicious instincts on red alert.

Rightly or wrongly, I had taken the decision that there was no profit to be had by exposing Paul McNab as a sadistic rapist. He left behind a wife and three children in Port Hedley and it was an absolute fact that he could not harm anyone again. When Ruth returned with Jay the next morning, we swore them to secrecy. Jay had purchased enough booze for us to cinch the plausible tale of too much excitement coupled with too much alcohol. That Paul had consumed a bottle of beer and three-quarters of a bottle of brandy would certainly show up in the post mortem, as would the damaged knee from his early fall on his belt buckle.

We tried to keep the cover-up simple. The doctor had a massive heart attack, right before my eyes. We left the shattered glass and dishevelled rooms, proof that he'd wreaked havoc staggering across the floor, prior to falling heavily on a piece of glass at the front door.

The following Sunday, Jay returned to see Ruth. The funeral had been an emotional affair; the mourning wife sobbed throughout the service, and one of the daughters launched into a screaming session that necessitated the funeral director and a driver carrying her out for medical sedation. Jock was visiting when Jay arrived, so Ruth made more tea and set up the table on the verandah. I had taken my first tentative steps in months and was able to get to my chair with the aid of a walking stick.

'There were two uniformed and a couple of

plain-clothes guys at the doc's funeral,' Jay informed us immediately. 'Ain't heard nothin' on the grapevine. Any idea why?' He looked around the table.

Jock sat up sharply. 'We've doubly covered the alcohol angle – he was overweight, and a known soak. Billy's an invalid, for God's sake! They couldn't, wouldn't . . .?'

'What could they have on any of us?' Ruth hastened warily. 'The looks of a fight? We covered that too, what with all the broken glass and everything. We just weren't where we normally are, doing what we normally do. Come to think of it, that'd sure be enough to raise the hair on the back of a black tracker, but white country cops? From round these parts? Well, I just don't know about that.'

'You travelled around with him, Jay,' Jock leant forward surreptitiously. 'Did you see anything in his life that might be of interest to the boys in blue?'

Jay shook his head. 'I only knew him a few weeks and, hell no, he was colder than a well digger's butt – until we came here, that is.'

'Unfortunate phraseology,' I muttered.

'Pardon?' asked Jock.

'Something doesn't fit. They know something doesn't fit. They don't know precisely what it is, but their instincts are telling them there's a piece missing.'

Everyone began talking at once. Chocolate Two started barking. It was bedlam. Ruth had something important to say and held up her hands to get our attention. As we calmed down to make way for her, we heard an engine in the distance. 'The police,' she said, too late.

'Goddamn it,' muttered Jay.

'Gidday, folk,' Jack Burger called lethargically, climbing out of his car at a snail's pace. He was a nuggety, second-generation Australian with a tough

German manner. He'd been on the receiving end of a fair amount of flack during the war; the locals had taken to calling him Little Jack Himmler. He tipped his hat.

'Hello, Jack,' I smiled wanly. 'What brings you out here on such a fine day?'

'Ah yes, I suppose it is. You're looking much improved, Miss Batchelor,' he commented wryly, instantly causing me to flush with guilt. 'I'm just going over one or two details of the, er . . . the death of Dr McNab.' He begrudgingly tipped his hat to Ruth, acknowledging Jay and Jock. 'Interesting group. Same as last Wednesday morning. Are we having a wake?' he enquired with exaggerated politeness, leaving no doubt as to his opinion of our characters.

I wanted to speak out, change my decision, explain the circumstances of that fateful night, but Burger was no pushover. To rush forward with explanations now, while we were all sitting together having a pleasant afternoon tea, would not serve us well. We were thick as thieves, and behaving like it. We would have to sweat it out. His questions were repetitive and banal – not worth the time to visit. He departed shortly, with a broad sweep of the arm.

Jay summed up the situation. 'He's either trying to scare the shit out of us because he's got nothin', or he's got somethin' on McNab, independent of us, and thinks we know about it.'

'And he's right . . . we probably do look a bit thick,' Ruth voiced my thoughts. 'You and I, Jay, are conveniently elsewhere for the evening. Jock leaves the pub immediately he runs into us to come out here and see you, Billy, knowing the doctor was already visiting.'

'What are you suggesting, Ruth?' Jock was the only one apparently unable to grasp the implications.

'He's got an idea you had the fight we know you nearly had. He thinks you're in love with Billy and may have killed Paul McNab.'

Jock's eyes searched mine, realization dawning slowly. He shifted slightly in his chair, but after a few moments pressed his hand on my arm. 'Well, I didn't, so we have nothing to worry about. The post mortem results must have clearly established heart failure. My guess is McNab had some other skeletons in his closet and Little Jack Himmler is out digging for anything he can get.'

'Human nature,' agreed Ruth. 'We know what a sick bastard he was; his attack on Billy would hardly be an isolated one.'

'Makes me wish I'd told the whole truth,' I said quietly. 'But, I didn't. Gentlemen, I regret this very much, but I think you had both better take your leave and stay away for a while. If the questions stop, we'll know we created doubt because of our somewhat immodest friendships. If they don't, I'll probably have to tell *all*. At least I'll be able to do so without unjust suspicions being cast on Jock's casual visit that night.'

'Are you asking me not to visit any more?' Jock's frown deepened. For a man with quick physical reactions, his brain seemed remarkably slow.

'Yes, I'm afraid I am, Jock. You understand, don't you? I'm engaged to David, who'll be home soon and, well, people don't understand friendships between men and women. I'm ever grateful for your kindness and protection, but it would be most unfair of me to abuse it by placing your future at risk. You've just secured your teaching post here. Imagine what the local parents will do to you if they're allowed to make something out of . . . any of this?'

I wanted to rush on, tell him he could visit as much as he liked once David was home, but better to be harsh now, for everyone's sake.

When Ruth spoke, her voice snarled, yet she appeared strangely at peace to me, her face barely disguising something resembling deep-seated relief. 'Does that mean Jay can't visit too?'

'Hey babe, just a minute! I'm back out to the Islands in a few weeks. Ya can't cut me off like that?'

'I'm sorry, Jay,' Ruth said mournfully, rather too quickly. 'My first responsibility is to Billy, and . . . we have to live here. You don't. You'll go back to the war and we'll be left to handle Little Jack Himmler, and the town folk. I'm sorry. It's been fun.' No one could doubt the finality in her voice.

Both men stood up uncertainly. My bottom lip was quivering. I prayed no one would notice. One word of sympathy now would reduce me badly.

Jock bowed slightly. 'I'll miss you, Billy, drop you a line occasionally if I may, just to let you know I'm thinking of you.' He walked dejectedly to his car.

Jay was less prepared to leave cordially. 'I could have loved ya, babe,' he said. 'Might have offered you a lot if ya'd let me in. Ya don't owe Billy Batchelor nothin'. What about your life? When are ya ever gonna start livin' for yourself?' He kissed her squarely on the lips and jumped into his Jeep, pulling out ahead of Jock, leaving a trail of dust in his wake. 'See ya, babe,' he called. 'You bet ya life ya will!'

'Good riddance,' Ruth whispered, reaching obsessively into her deep pockets for a cigarette.

'I didn't know you smoked!' I exclaimed. She choked on the first puff.

'I . . . I have done for years.'

'I'm shattered. I can't believe you've been hiding it from me all this time!'

'You don't mind?' she asked hesitantly, taking a short drag out of the corner of her full, dark lips.

'Mind? I think I could handle one myself right now.' She threw me the pack, without any overt surprise.

'David will be home soon and you'll be able to forget this whole nasty business, Billy,' she comforted, striking a match. 'And I'll be having a baby I can keep for my very own!' she added luxuriously, hugging her body with motherly arms.

'Ruth? What are you saying?'

'I've been waiting for a man, the right man, a pure black man – a father for a baby. One I can keep. It's part of my plan.'

'Your plan?'

'A baby first. Then I have to find its grandmother. My mother.'

'Ruth? Oh Ruthy? My God. A baby, Ruth? You planned this . . . how can you know?'

'I know. Believe me, I know,' she said.

The bunting and flag waving of V-E Day had just died down along Oodoolay Street when the Enola Gay dropped the A-bomb on Hiroshima and three days later, on Nagasaki. We stayed tuned to our radio, waiting for peace.

It came on 15 August, the day Sister Mac confirmed that Ruth was three months pregnant. We listened to the prerecorded broadcasts on the USS *Missouri* – and from Tokyo itself. The monarch was still worshipped as a god; a crowd had gathered around the Imperial Palace to beg forgiveness of their emperor. Radio Tokyo declared. 'We are moved to tears by His Majesty's infinite solicitude,' then the line dropped out.

'With all the gods floating around the world, Ruth, you'd think we might have been able to resolve our differences without annihilating entire populations, wouldn't you? At least you're doing your bit to replenish the earth.'

There was no animosity in my feelings towards her, nor towards the stand she had taken, yet I was envious of her in a way any childless woman of thirty-one might be; I admired her for doing what I could not have done. Though her sense of honour and obligation were deeply entrenched with a largely Batchelor upbringing, she had thrown off the shackles and attachments of traditional norms in regard to her feminine status. Perhaps she never took them on in the first place? She cared not for public opinion if it could not serve her, even less for the harsh reality of her life. Just as there had been no men around in the dusk of Sister Mac's heydays, there were none around for Ruth's.

'If we continue to hold wars every twenty years or so,' I commented a few days later when the death toll in Japan had reached 100,000, 'we'll have huge gaps in future civilizations and whole generations of women will have no chance of finding a mate, let alone reproducing.'

'That's precisely why I've taken the matter into my own hands, Billy,' Ruth had replied. 'I've bin picturing myself sitting here, twenty years from now, still waiting for something to happen. Probably bitter and twisted that motherhood had for ever passed me by too,' she'd said, beginning the knitting that would occupy every spare minute from now until D-Day.

As we talked, old Mugga, the only postie we'd ever known, pulled up in his battered truck, the pride and joy of his life.

'Gidday, ladies,' he called, getting out of the truck, walking up to the verandah to hand us our weekly papers and four days of mail personally. 'Nothin' from the good doctor in Egypt this week, Billy, but soon as I sees the blue lines, I'll come out special, don't you worry, lassie,' he assured. 'I's gotta a bluey for you though, Ruthy, yeah! Sure made a hit with the damn nigger Yankee, didn't ya? I'd kiss a Jap on Anzac Day rather'n see a daughter o' mine messin' with the likes o' 'im, but there y'are, there y'are!' His imitation of an American accent was more pathetic than his attempt at humour, but Ruth managed a small laugh. Mugga had never seen her as black. We settled into our respective worlds to read, and consider.

There was a letter for me from Jock. It was full of news of the school and the youngsters, especially Than. 'I'm probably biased because he's my nephew,' he wrote, 'but he's a bright kid with a natural intelligence and a keen wit, quite the opposite of what we were taught in teachers' college about Aboriginal youngsters, I expect because he's half-white. Frances and Sarah are little pets, but not a quarter worth of Than in the brains department.'

I pondered the news carefully, wondering whether this would be the right vehicle to launch into a matter that had been burning my soul for weeks.

'Jock says Than's doing very well at school,' I began.

'You think he gets it from his father, or his mother?' Ruth responded playfully.

'Obviously his mother,' I smiled. 'You know, if history does repeat itself, and you should have another son, he might be taken off you again, or conscripted for the next war. Do such possibilities not figure in your calculations?'

She laughed, a Ruth laugh that told me I was making mountains out of molehills again. 'I chose the father more carefully this time, Billy. Good and black. Whites won't be interested. As for the next war, no way will my full-blooded son be going out fighting for more territory for the whites!' Spontaneously, her midnight eyes spilt over with fresh sparkling tears. I stretched out my hands. She took them both, bringing tears to my own eyes in the simple gesture.

'Billy, I'm going back to my people as soon as my baby is born. I've got to find them, and me. I've put it off too long, wanted to take Than, couldn't . . . then couldn't let your folks down, always so much happening, so many demands; the years rushed by. I can't delay again, can't make the same mistake. I love you dearly, but once David's home, you'll be fine. I hope you'll understand and not make it any harder than it will be, please, dear friend, please?'

My heart sank. Her face was set, the eyes aflame behind the tears. She saw my resigned acceptance and sensed the fear I held for her before I spoke. 'It will be very difficult for you to live in the bush now, Ruth, knowing what you know.'

'What you're saying, Billy, is that European life has made me too soft to survive in the outback. But you aren't acknowledging the degrading, destructive European influences that drain my energies every day! I go shopping in Oodoolay Street and I'm still served last 'cos I'm second-rate. I'm an Abo, a col- oured, a boong, a nigger, a wog, a black whore, a munyi munyi . . . even a stonejack. I'd like to be just a person in Australian society, Billy, but your people won't let me.

'There just ain't no quality in white Australians' culture because you don't understand the Great Trinity. You think it's the fairyland Christianity! You struggle for worldly success under the cover of your invented, patriarchal God. Life itself knows the Trinity is Food, Water and Fire, matriarchal re- plenishers of the land – nurturers of all creation.

'I have no identity in your world, Billy. Your people can take away my child and deny access to my heritage, they can kill me in cold blood or send me to war without rank or wage. Yet I'm not even a citizen of your pure white Australia. I don't even get to vote!

'For a long time I denied my birthright, so ugly, so unworthy of the white man's world. I wanted to be like you, to have your self-esteem, to have your freedom to plan and plot! I got it too, but not in the way I dreamt. The education your parents gave me was a mixed blessing. I began to long for my own mother, my own Aboriginal family, my own piece of disinherited land! I gotta find the footprints in the sands of my Dreamtime. I have to find my past in order to go on with the present – in order to offer my baby a future.'

Ruth's long soliloquy had soaked up our tears. She had brought us back to earth, Mother Earth, and set us dreaming of a finer, more honest world. A gentle breeze drifted across the fields, rustling the branches of the rejuvenated lemon tree, lifting the sweet aroma of flowering jasmine into the spring mist. A faint memory, no stronger than the breeze, stirred in me then, a memory of a secret shared, never to be spoken of again. Yet it had risen up, as cream on milk, as the truth will out. . .

'Where do your people live, Ruth?' I asked, feeling a great sadness that I had known her all my life, yet couldn't even remember where she came from.

'My people are in the centre, the living heart! We are the Aranda people. My name is Nakamara. Just beyond the rolling dunes of the Simpson Desert, amid the shady gorges . . .' she floated high, nostrils quivering as though she could smell the tracks in the red land that would lead her home.

'Tell me a story of the Dreamtime, Ruth, like you used to when I was a girl. I think I'd better ask for one every day from now on so I'll have a store to remember when you've gone. And, and Ruth . . .?' my voice broke, 'I'm so sorry we let you down.'

She reached out for my hands, holding them close to the new life growing in her body. 'Oh Billy, *you* could never disappoint me,' she said.

'This is a tribal story of the evening star and why it is always the first star to appear in the sky.

'The evening star is a beautiful young woman who rises from the peak of a mountain at dusk and rides across the night sky until the early morn. At first dawn, the beautiful young woman descends to a distant peak as an old, old lady. There she must wait all day in the scorching sun and waterless land until a new evening wakens to transform her back to her youth. I think you and I, in our different ways, are the evening star in the Dreamtime, Billy.'

'Miserable old days, Ruth!'

'Young, starlit nights, Billy!'

'You're incorrigible,' I laughed, leaving her to skip down the path, hopscotching over the grid where the old bayonet gates used to be. Mugga sat tall and proud in the old delivery truck. 'Gidday, Mugga!' I bellowed above the roar of the engine. He waved two blue-lined envelopes high in the air. 'Thank you, thank you,' I ripped them from his waving hand. The familiar writing on the first envelope was from James Barnawarren. He was on his way back from New Guinea and would be home on Friday. May he have the pleasure of calling to pay his respects? The other was from David.

'But, Mugga, it's dated 2 October. It's a month old!'

'I know, lassie, I know. It's those Arab buggers at the other end. They couldna tell the time if the town hall clock fell on top of 'em.' My quizzical expression did not phase him. 'Suppose you ladies bin sittin' close to the wireless listenin' for news of the riots? Bloody Jews and Arabs fightin' over some anniversary of somethin'? Good thing the good doctor ain't in Cairo no more, lassie. Hundreds injud.'

I thanked him and returned pensively to the kitchen.

'Ruth, turn on the radio.'

'Something wrong?' Her eyebrows raised slightly. The previous letter from David, postmarked Alexandria and received last week, had warned of possible riots with mass demonstrations expected for the anniversary of the Balfour Declaration. 'Riots in Cairo,' I explained simply.

Ruth shuddered. 'Will the Jews ever be allowed to have a homeland?'

'David thinks not, when even Jerusalem can still be questioned.'

'Wouldn't you think they'd have had enough bloody fighting? Jesus, Billy, I wish David would just get the hell out of there and come home!'

'Ruth! Your language is becoming as expansive as your stomach lately. He'll be home by Christmas. He's promised.'

'You're far too understanding, Billy. The war's been over nearly six months. He's more than paid his dues.'

'How many of our boys are home, Ruth?'

'That's irrelevant.'

'I think not. He'll be here by Christmas, or when the last wounded Australian soldier is shipped out – whatever comes first.' There were some conversations we mostly left alone; why David didn't come home, why he felt compelled to stay to the bitter end. I understood no more than she.

There was no Egyptian item on the six o'clock news; we breathed more easily, continuing our normal routine about the house and gardens. My health had bounced back at last and with energy to burn, I determined at least to put the immediate paddocks to work before David arrived. With the help of Pa's linesmen, two days a week, we'd begun to clear the old vines, but the task was bigger than us. 'I'll have to ask Mr Prescott for some special funds. We need a couple of full-time jackaroos to hack through this.'

'Koories?' Ruth asked.

'Why not? Know any?'

'Sure,' she replied.

It never ceased to amaze me how close we were, yet how many secrets Ruth managed to keep. A day later, two burly-looking blacks turned up, equipped with shovels and hacksaws and an impressive array of clubs and spears and kalis and boomerangs. Following intimate greetings with Ruth, and formal giddays to me, they set straight to work.

'I had no idea you knew any of the local Aborigines, Ruth. Where did . . . how did you come to . . . ?'

'The local clan helped me track my family,' she revealed decisively. The matter was closed.

We worked with the men for the first two days, stacking, loading, clearing behind them. They were hardy blokes, tough as the sun, unbothered by incessant flies and soil set like rock. Their names were Banduk and Jabaljari. On the third day, they ordered us to remain indoors. 'We burn off far hills,' Jabaljari explained simply. 'You keep good lungs, no smoke in chests.' We closed the windows and attacked a spring clean. When the dust from our cleaning and the invasive smoke from the fields was seeping through the cracks in the window joints, Ruth called a halt, putting on the kettle, lighting a cigarette.

'Should you still be smoking with the baby so advanced?' I asked.

'What's the difference?' she spluttered, soaking a

couple of towels in the trough to drape around our necks and faces.

At the height of the smoke, we heard the horse approaching. 'Oh my God,' I gasped. 'It's Friday, isn't it? Wouldn't you know I'd be caught looking like this when I haven't seen James in years!'

Ruth responded instantly, combing my hair, mopping my brow, thrusting a clean white blouse upon me. 'Quickly, pop this on and put on some lipstick. You always come to life with lipstick.'

I did as I was told and was well done over when the door knocker banged.

Ruth hustled him in, slamming the door behind him. He stood tall and fair, his lovely face hardened, aged by the savagery he had seen. I stood up to greet him, but sat down heavily, unable to steady my feet on the moving earth. 'James?' I murmured expectantly, of what, I couldn't think. He was staring at me, holding a folded, yellow piece of paper in a clenched fist. Ruth's hand rushed to her mouth, but no sound escaped.

His fist opened in slow motion. He handed me the wire. My body moved in slow motion too. There was no rush.

'Will you have a cuppa, James? Ruth, we're being most rude. Let's get that kettle on.'

'It's . . . on, Billy. I'll just make fresh cups, if you like?'

'Yes, Ruth, yes, I would like. Thank you. Do sit down, James. You've had a long war. We read your stories on Saturdays, you know what it's like here. Impossible to get the dailies most weeks, but we rarely miss Saturdays. Not much you didn't see, was there? How's your health? I saw Figgy and Constance the other day. Constance said Saucy dropped in on Amelia in the Congo last month. Isn't it wonderful that Saucy's taken up with an American sailor, a rich one! Good luck to her. Extraordinary small world, isn't it, now that the war's over . . .'

'Stop it, Billy!' James' voice shot through me like a bullet. Ruth jumped and spilt the tea. James moved forward to help her mop up.

I stood, turning my back to them, opening the wire.

'What does it say?' Ruth's small voice, pleading, somewhere over the Kurrajong Ranges.

'"The CMO deeply regrets to inform you Dr David Moon fatally wounded in riots outside Alexandria on Thursday, 1 November."'

I concentrated hard on the yellow piece of paper, folding it carefully back into its predetermined creases. It came to me then that I'd just read the book of life upside down. The smoke engulfed me. I fell to the floor.

# The Brolga

# FIFTEEN

# 1946...

'O who could have foretold That the heart grows old?' I closed my copy of Yeats and reopened my diary.

I had been travelling for many months in the imagination of my past life, circumnavigating the globe while ministering to my vegetable and flower patches in the old vine tracts of Cranberry Vineyard.

The slushy thick mud from the new sprinkler system gave me weeks of exploration with Wendy Barr and Chocolate, making mud pies and guzzling them out of Mama's willow pattern Royal Albert bowls as the perfectly bred young ladies that we were. We stomped through the blackberries in our outsized boots, charging into the old house with its passage of polished boards, 'lifting our feet' when Mama bellowed. What days they were! I cried – when they were over.

The pedal radio, the telegraph lines, the distant trains that would carry our goods to market one day . . . old days, sitting in the telegraph station, learning the dots and dashes from Blondy and Clay. 'But what good is it to you girls, if you can't type it?' *Asdfgf;lkjhj. The quick brown fox jumps over the lazy dog. Billy Rachel Batchelor, Billy Batchelor, Billy, Billy, Billy. .* . Over and over and over again.

But the midday news followed; my escape was growing up, spiriting me away to university, to my first love, my first airplane ride, my first play.

Independence! How young I am! I can hear the clatter of Brisbane's city streets, the endless harangues of Harry Carmichael, the white ants eating away our Churchill House, the applause in the Great Hall. My heart breaking when it was finished. I was just getting it right and it was over.

In the mornings, the plump green rows of lettuce sparkled in the frosty dew, nearly ripe enough for picking; a microphone and a chance to spit it all out, make a difference . . . Wow, did I give them a run for their money! Lefty Fitzpatrick, wild colonial eyes bulging through the control room window, 'Lordy be, what'll she say today?' Max Dorevitch, conditioned for his time, unable to openly acknowledge his sympathies with female logic, forced by conscience to open the next door for me . . . Retribution? And James, handsome James. Gentle, mealy mannered James. Scared, intimidated – a woman with a mind! Hiding behind union meetings and a tough political pen, naturally replaced by the front of a tough war correspondent, filing chunky bits of history on the wire. A second-rate Figgy, Ma used to say; successful men produce mediocre sons, mediocre fathers produce successful sons . . . My mind was focusing too close to the present. Only the past mattered. Shut out James. You have no place.

The evening news followed; my imagination was growing old. Every day, working out in the sunshine, feeling the heat and the sand pressing down, swirling around. Egypt, our Egypt. David's and mine. The sails of the felucca half-mast – on the way out. Time to talk, to dream. Time to be silent and let life merge with the ripples of the Nile. Let out the sails completely – on the way back. Hurry to love; it's waiting on the shore. Enough water on the plants. Come inside for a cuppa.

At last, on 1 May 1946, the late news got through.

'Fresh unrest broke out today in the Holy Land. Arabs and Jews alike are indignant at the British mandate calling for partition of Palestine. Britain recognizes Palestine as a Jewish national home, but the Empire will never accept it as totally Jewish since it lies at the crossroads of the Arab world.' My circumnavigation was over; dark, sunlit months of exploration in my mind. There was nothing new to see, no morning left to mourn. The world kept turning, life following death following life.

The remainder of '46 came into focus. We planted, watered, sprayed, weeded, cut, boxed and sold to the Sydney markets. Pa stood proudly by the goods carriage as our cartons were loaded. 'Turn her hand to anything, my girl,' he'd say.

And all the while, the only thing worth more than twopence in our lives was Rosa. Ruth's Rosataca. She bloomed as fair as the morning frost, her sparkling black eyes beaming out of her shining black face. She was plump and mellow, barely crying, seemingly amused by life itself. Whenever I cried, most days during her first few months, she'd giggle and splutter, little feet kicking the air wildly, tiny arms waving madly in her first struggles for freedom. She was a charmer, a wisp of light, a great leveller. We moved hopefully into '47; everything was growing again, just as we knew it would.

Our little cottage, so long struck down with illness and death, seemed to spring up to meet the grandness of its Pharaoh name, greeting visitors on a daily basis. The climbing roses had overtaken the vines around the verandah; in the closing afternoon light, I could picture David and me sitting in the courtyard at the consulate, sipping our Fosters beers, discussing the war gossip, the radio station, the hospital, the embassy.

I put down my diary almost as instantly as I'd

picked it up. Yeats lay open alongside it as the conversation set in. My high tea guest was in questioning mood. As was usual then, I responded blithely. '"O who could have foretold That the heart grows old?" Yeats asked. Who indeed? No, I shall never marry now. It would be a mockery.' It had probably taken her days to pluck up the courage to ask and here I was, dismissing it out of mind.

'I dunno. Sure can't make ya out, Billy. You don't seem bitter but maybe you still suffering a dose of the conspiracy theory?'

'No, no, Sister Mac,' I laughed naturally enough. 'I've accepted it now. The best of him he gave to me and I've realized I've still got that. He could not give me more, were he still here. It is enough.'

'My dear girl,' she held a loose reign on her impatience with me, 'he's bin gone eighteen months now. It's time you started livin' again. Ain't natural, cooped up out here, growin' flowers and veggies. Ya should be growin' babies. Ain't fair on Ruth neither,' she added unfairly.

'I'm not going to marry James, Sister Mac, or anyone else floating single around town, just to make the family feel better, or relieve Ruth of her duties. She's free to go any time and she will when she's good and ready. The baby's still at the breast, for heaven's sake!'

Everyone had attempted to sway me, and no doubt this Sister Mac push was a last-ditch attempt on Ma's part to shake some sense into me. The unspoken message: Do you really want to finish up like her? Well, from what I could see, Sister Mac's life hadn't been so bad. She had satisfaction from her work, good friends, other people's children she could hand back when she'd had enough of them. She had freedom and independence!

'Do you feel you've missed anything, remaining

single, Sister Mac?' I questioned finally. My lack of response would be regarded poorly by Ma and Pa. The least I could do was dignify her visit with some old-fashioned manners and respect.

'Not in the baby department, that's certain! Delivered enough of the little buggers to last me two life-times! Seems to me not too many gets it right neither, the parentin', I mean. The young 'uns get forced to be extensions of their folks, so they never gets to belong to themselves. You'd think it'd be gettin' better, but it's gettin' worse. Ruth's right. Take little Rosataca back to the bush. She'll be 'eaps better off there, though God knows we'll all miss 'em, sure will.'

I did not need to be reminded of that. My own motherly instincts had risen dramatically in the last few months. It worried me greatly.

'Do you miss the security?' I asked politely. Ma would know I was not even listening if I didn't ask the Big One.

Sister Mac threw her head back and chuckled liberally, a deep throaty gurgling sound rumbling around in her primitive soul. 'Security? Ha-ha, ha-ha! Ain't no such thing. Never has bin. What security you ever seen stand up against an old worldly disaster, eh? More money ya get, more you's threatened by the loss of it. More kids ya has, more they all grow up different, less you sure you did the right things bringin' 'em up. Marriage ain't no offer of security, Billy. No, ma'am. Women got less in a way when they's married. More menial, unpaid work. Handouts like two names on the property only sets up payola for later. Husbands die or go off with a youngie and you's left with the kids, far more lonely an' insecure than ya woulda' bin if ya hadn't done the deed in the first place!'

'Why do men try to take everything from a woman, Sister Mac?' I asked unexpectedly. I had wondered about that for a long time.

'Ah! 'Cos women act so desperate for 'em to 'ave it, from what I can see,' she said.

I was now intensely interested in her responses and quite flabbergasted by her modern understanding. 'Why do you want me to get married then? I can't comprehend it!'

'Because you's got the goods to be happy in the estate, Billy. No man'd take you for granted now. Ya wouldn't let 'im. Ya wouldn't be lookin' for a bargain marriage what don't exist – you's got your emotional security in your own achievements, in your own soul.'

'Let me get this straight, Sister Mac. It's no fun having kids, there's no security with a man, but I'd be happy in the married estate? Why bother? You didn't! Why should I?'

She hiccupped, swallowed some water, quickly pulled herself together. 'My young man died too, but there weren't nobody else hangin' around. You got a choice.'

I felt terrible, but what could I say? She was philosophical, though I had obviously disturbed a long-buried scar. 'I'm sorry, but I've got to ask: What would he have given you that you haven't been able to achieve for yourself?'

'He was the only man I ever met who loved me for meself. He didn't care nothin' for wantin' me to stop work and look after 'im or anythin'. He didn't try to possess me, so I never lost me poise or me personal responsibility for meself. You an' me is lucky.'

'How's that?'

'I met mine once, so I knows how good it can be. Ruthy never met 'ers, maybe never will. She's smart though. She knew Micky would be a bad bargain all right, as well as the Yankee.'

'Thea's happy, isn't she?' I persisted, trying to hold back the tide.

'If ya like bein' in bondage, I 'spose. 'E lives up to 'er expectations for the time bein', maybe for all time. Wouldn't suit you though, not from the start. Would never 'ave suited Ruthy neither.'

Silence fell between us; Sister Mac had lost her train of thought. A part of me wanted to direct her, another part was fearful of where she was heading. We moved inside, stoked the fire. The nights were cool now. Winter was almost upon us.

'You're lucky, Billy, 'cos ya can 'ave your freedom an' the love of a good man too.'

'He's dead, Sister Mac, he's dead!'

'No, 'e ain't. David's dead. Ya was goin' to 'ave a big love for a short time, you two. Ya was opposites, all caught up in each other's shadows. The chips was already showin', before 'e went back to the war. 'E was always gonna be insecure, Billy. 'E would've had to cut ya down, sooner or later. No good for the long haul, Billy, no good for you.' I stared anew at her big, brown eyes. They were not her best feature; actually, none of her features were strong, taken separately. It was the combined force of personality and inner calm that lit her face. Always had been. Age had not diminished her presence, rather widened and deepened it.

I collected myself and mocked amusement, pealing a light slither of laughter off my chest. It made no impact, but my defences had only two choices and it would not have been appropriate to enact anger or disapproval. 'So you seriously think I should accept James' proposal? Simply because he's asked again, and probably out of sympathy at that?'

'No, I seriously do not!' She was angry with me! 'Jock O'Ryan's ya man. He loves ya truly, no conditions, no naggin', no obscenities about who's the man an' who's the little woman. He needs ya. 'E needs ya joy an' laughter an' strength an' he'll give it all back, ten-fold. 'E won't be a stick in the mud neither. 'E'll make a good lover 'cos 'e'll be free to grow. Ya can grow together, not in each other's shadows. 'E'll be a good carer when you's sick too.'

I couldn't help smiling. So that was the motivation! She had my love life all organized because my health was at stake, just as she'd held all our lives in the palms of her hands so many times down the years. She began packing her knitting, preparing to go.

'Thank you so much for the visit, Sister Mac,' I said. 'I'll give your love to Ruth and Rosa. Stay for supper and catch up with them? They'll be so sorry they've missed you.' She put a stiff hand on my arm. 'Keep a little love for yourself, Billy. Give James the boot and receive Jock when 'e comes a-courtin'.'

'Why, Sister Mac! Are you playing cupid in your old age?'

'I'm doin' nothin' of the sorts,' she snapped, climbing rapidly onto my old bicycle, now her regular mode of transport. 'You an' Ruthy an' Rosataca is expected for tea at Rosebery on Sunday. Don't be late. Ya know 'ow ya Ma 'ates tardiness.'

'Eenie, meanie, minie, mo . . .' Than pointed at Frances, then Sarah, then himself, back and forth, back and forth, while baby Rosa sat in the dirt in her thick grey napkin, bare-footed and bare-chested, giggling as usual.

Ruth unpacked the basket Thea had sent. 'Her cooking has improved,' she commented tartly. 'Micky, Jock!' she screamed into a crevice in the ranges, her voice booming into the chasm above and echoing down to the rock stream below. 'Tucker's on!'

'Stupid really,' she mumbled aside to me. 'We should be cooking our lunch, fresh, not unpacking a picnic basket. What will Than ever know of survival?'

'I don't suppose he'll ever need to,' I said.

'Eenie, meanie, minie, mo . . .' Than had made Frances *It* again; she was protesting. Dear, simple little Frannie, 'not quite the full bob', as Mugga aptly described, but a tender heart and winning ways that charmed us all, all except Than at any rate.

'Don't nag, Frannie. Somebody's got to be It.'

'Why does it always have to be me?' she wailed.

'Well, he may need survival skills if we have another war, Billy. By your reckoning of man's stupidity, that'll be on again before he's too old to go.'

'Frannie! You're not looking hard enough. You're no fun at all,' Than yelled.

'Does it bother you to see Than being brought up like his father was?'

'What do you think? Sure it bothers me, 'specially now he's started working on the farm full time. A bit of sense might drop into the bucket with Jock around but that's the only chance – once I go.'

'When will that be?'

'When you come to your senses I expect. Seems I'm just hanging around waiting for everyone to get wise,' she chuckled in one breath, raising her voice to screaming pitch with the next. 'Micky, Jock! Come and get it!'

'Who set up today, Ruth?' I suddenly needed to know. There had been so many possible set-ups, yet they'd all been passed off as my 'coming out' phase. Was I out now? 'Was it you, Sister Mac, Ma, Pa or Micky? Just a minute, who have I left out? No, certainly not Giles, although no doubt he'd prefer me married than on the loose, so to speak – a threat to all the happily married women in Kurra!'

'Are there any?'

'Eenie, meanie, minie, mo . . .'

'Am I *It*, Ruth? The rules of the game are that

somebody has to be It, aren't they? Game of choice, or game of chance?'

'Micky, Jock! This is the last time I'm calling. If you're not here in exactly one minute, I'm giving your share to Chocolate Two! Game of choice in our minds, of course, but there's always lots of chance involved, isn't there?'

'So, you finally deign to inflict yourselves upon us, gentlemen,' I berated the men, arriving with one dead barramundi.

'They're only here to inflict themselves on the food,' Ruth scoffed.

'Hush now, Ruthy! Hush your mouth. These are the brothers O'Ryan from Mini Mini, one of the finest cattle stations in the land! Do you think they would be so uncouth in the presence of ladies?'

'Shit,' said Than.

'What did you say, young man?' Ruth choked.

'Shit, shit, shit,' grinned Than.

'My God! What age is he, Micky? What age is he?'

'Shit, Ruth, what's that got to do with anything? You should know. You had him!'

We all began to eat. Micky opened a bottle of home-made beer and filled our tea cups. He was not one for conversation, but as he raised his cup in salutation, I had the feeling he was going to make a speech. He cleared his throat. 'Thea's got another bun in the oven,' he said proudly. 'Here's to me Number One son!'

We sat, stunned. His cup was raised but nobody moved.

'Here's to me Number One son!' he repeated, his beautiful eyes questioning, unable to grasp the irony, the tragic connotations.

'Aren't you buggers gonna drink to My Son?'

Ruth lifted her cup. 'Here's to your son,' she said

334

brightly. 'Congratulations, Micky. What a wonderful thrill for you. Fancy, expecting a son!'

Micky burped. 'Excuse me,' he said automatically, topping up his cup. Frances copied him, burping rather more loudly.

'Excuse me,' she sighed sweetly.

'What ya do?' Than piped up, licking his fingers with great concentration.

'Don't be rude, Than,' Micky rebuked. 'Pass me the salt.'

'Please!' corrected Ruth.

'Christ, Ruth! What do you want him to finish up like, a bloody wench?'

'Manners are not the exclusive prerogative of women, Micky,' I intervened, 'though one could be excused for thinking so, in O'Ryan company!'

'Hey, that's not fair . . .' Jock rallied momentarily, unable to follow up.

'Why don't you two go for a walk while I have an all-out brawl with Micky?' Ruth suggested cheerfully.

'I'll come with ya,' Than volunteered hastily.

'You'll be lucky if you get a brighter one than Than,' Jock commented pointedly, helping me up from the gingham tablecloth spread over the ground.

'Billy, Jock, sit down!' Micky ordered, startling us into compliance. He had always been able to do that, since he was a young boy. It was odd that we had all changed quite dramatically since we were young- sters, yet we still bowed to Micky, who had not changed at all. He had not even aged as we had, his bronzed, handsome face lined only by the sun, his manly physique unaltered by married life, though Ruth declared it was Thea's cooking that kept him slim. He had a coarse, uneducated Clark Gable air about him and though there was no evidence he was a ladies' man, heaven knows he could have been had he once felt the inclination to learn how. Trouble was, he rarely had anything worthwhile to say. Outside his devilishly stunning presence, brute strength and patriarchal power were his only means of communication and we were all growing a little weary of such shallow attributes. Still, he held us by tradition, or fear of what we might find wanting in ourselves, should we stand against him.

We sat down. Jock's eyes sought mine, an intimacy there that had been absent for a long time. Since I had sent him away after the death of Paul McNab, he had maintained a physical and emotional distance commensurate with a knock-back for life; his lightweight letters were the only link. Where most of the older men of Kurra had the propensity to be as lecherous as Willie O'Ryan had been, Jock was studiously reticent to impose himself upon a woman where no invitation was first extended. I was certain there had been some recent clandestine input from Sister Mac on my behalf, but the furthest thing from my mind was a push from the entire clan.

Micky leant back across the log he'd made his own and guilelessly, without preamble, presented his case. 'I proposed to you once, Billy Batchelor, and you right proper knocked me back. Did me a good turn too, hitchin' me up to Thea. Now I'm gonna do you a good turn. My brother, Jock, don't mind a spirited woman and he's been in love with you so bloody long, it's almost indecent. You're not gunna get a better offer, so you'd better accept his proposal and get on with it. You ain't gettin' any younger and it's time you had kids of your own. What do ya say?'

'Micky!' Jock exclaimed.

'Hey, Dad!' Frances yelled. 'Than's always making me It. I don't want to be It any more. Mushy, it's not fair.'

'Shut up, both of you,' Ruth silenced them. Rosa began to scream.

'Do you think you could stand it?' Jock asked me helplessly.

Micky put his teeth to another bottle of beer, spitting out the lid, refilling our glasses. Ruth turned away and put Rosa to her breast. Than and the girls sensed the sombre change of mood and ran off into the ravine.

I had a most awkward lump in my throat that kept me from speaking for a few moments. I was not in love with Jock O'Ryan, never had been, probably never would be. Yet we had much in common; our love of literature, our love of the land of our birth, our lifelong friendship . . . was it honourable to marry, knowing he would care for me as I could not care for him?

He knew my heart well, reached for my hands. His eyes told me he understood. I drew a deep breath. 'I suppose it's my turn to be It?' I said.

Kurra Kurra was fairly shocked when they learnt I planned to be married in the late afternoon. Nobody had ever, absolutely ever, held a wedding at dusk before.

The banns were posted in the usual way, of course. The date was heralded as a good omen; Monday, 1 September 1947. The community were unsure about a Monday, but the first day of spring set their hearts a flutter, capturing even the most hardened, battle-worn spirits in the grip of new life, new beginnings. Where a mid-thirties spinster and a late-thirties bachelor could find a mate, 'God's in His heaven, all's right with the world.'

I had chosen the dusk because the awakening milky way held more promise than the heat of the day to me. It was a simple decision, not meant to confuse the local population. Neither was I trying to prove anything when I asked Ruth to be my Matron of Honour. Everybody loved Ruth, in their way, but a Matron she was not and attendant to Kurra's most desperate bride, I heard tell, was singularly inappropriate. 'Don't worry,' I assured Ma, who kept her thoughts and feelings close to her chest these days, 'if I didn't ask Ruth, I wouldn't ask anyone.' It was her kind of logic and I knew if she understood, the whole affair would go off smoothly, regardless of the town's disapproval.

It had finally come to me that my mother, Rosey Batchelor, was a very nice woman. I don't mean that as cold praise, as people often do who refer to someone as 'nice' or 'good'. She had the wonderful capacity to adapt, graciously, to whatever wind was blowing. Black is black and white is white, yet when the wind blew strongly enough, she bent with it like a young tree. When I was young, I thought she was old. Now that I was older, I could see she was not old at all. If I could be half the mother . . .

A proud moon promised to rise high over the Kurrajong Ranges on that first day of spring. It was nearly full, beginning to light the sky and Oodoolay Street, though all the electric lights had been turned on early. It was the custom in our town that everybody was invited to the service and it had not been forgotten, regardless of the fact that there had been no weddings for nearly a decade. Small groups of old timers tut-tutted as I rode by with Pa in the old-station gig, presumably because I was dressed in white. 'Is she trying to pretend she's a virgin?' they whispered above the applause and clackety-clack of the horses on the recently tarred road. 'How disgusting! What a shame for Rosey and Nathan,' they chastened, revelling in it all the while.

Reverend Moon had agreed to perform the service, without compromise. There was a moment during rehearsal that I thought to ask for his theme of sermon, but somehow the opportunity had slipped by. As Pa and I walked down the aisle, with the 'Trumpet Voluntary' badly played by Miss Prinkett on the tuneless, dust-ridden organ, I remembered again the question I hadn't asked. It was all too clear.

Old Prinky could play, 'Here Comes The Bride', the extent of her matrimonial repertoire; her 'Trumpet Voluntary' left much to be desired. Old Giles could see his ex future daughter-in-law in hand-made lace; I feared that was the extent of his. I looked straight ahead and saw Jock standing there, with Micky close by, and sent up a small, useless prayer.

'We are gathered here, in the sight of God . . .'

I knew, absolutely knew, that I should never have allowed this wedding to happen. I was captive, unable to answer back. No education, no reputation, no worldly experience could save me now. Draped in white, I had surrendered. What fool me, that my last independent decision had been to wed at dusk, to wed in white – to wed at all! Marriage? What did it offer me? A respectable means of meeting my sexual desires and the opportunity to fulfil legitimately my maternal instincts? But at what cost, these age-old needs?

The people who had made me held great stock in names. I have a name, a proud name. I am Billy Rachel Batchelor. I was being given away, as though a man could give away his name, could give away the daughter of his name! To another man. With another name. As though I could become another person . . . as though I had been called to war, to sacrifice my life for my liege lord. Ask of me anything, my heart screamed, but don't ask me to be a second-rate you!

'I will,' I said. And it was done. I had agreed to

love, honour and obey. Reverend Moon would have his day, as though God's manly words were not enough. 'Ladies and gentlemen,' he began, predictably, 'I am not going to read from the Scriptures today. The world has changed, and we must change with it. This day, we celebrate the union of two people who have lived through these changes, in their own separate ways, yet found a meeting point in the midst of world turmoil and personal tragedy.'

I breathed freely. It was going to be all right after all.

'The miracle of this marriage should not be lost on any of us, nor undermined, nor threatened by our own small scopes of thought. In as much as Billy Batchelor and Jock O'Ryan have consented in marriage, I ask you that you give them all the love you have to give and wish them every joy that life and hard work dares squeeze out for them, for you know, as I know, that there are no guarantees and squeezing out the juice is about the best we can do . . .'

My God, he was going overboard. It didn't sound like our Reverend Moon at all. Could I have completely misjudged him, all these years?

'If I had my life to live over, I would run barefoot in the fields on the first day of spring. I would give in to the delights of dancing, I would go to the circus in the autumn and ride the merry-go-round and I would pick strawberries in the early light of summer. And when I travelled, I would travel lighter, packing less, accumulating more . . .'

The congregation shifted discernibly in their seats. There was no telling where he was heading, but all who had listened to his hellfire and brimstone sermons down the years had no source of reference for this unprecedented swing of style and mood. He cleared his throat, dabbing the beads of perspiration gathering on his brow before continuing. Several of the guests unconsciously followed his lead.

'If I had my life to live over, I would hug my beloved son David and approve his choice, even if I didn't understand it. The Bible says that God gives us no pain too great to bear, but coping with death is a very hard business, especially when you are carrying guilt for the dead . . .' He swayed slightly, leaning his elbows on the lectern. His eyes grew large. He seemed to be fighting back tears. Somebody should stop him, but how? A deepening horror filled the church with forbidding silence, broken only by a stifled hiccup from Sister Mac. I looked around quickly. Ma and Pa were ashen.

'Yes. Dying, ladies and gentlemen, is a very hard business – for the living. When the will for life has gone, how do you reinstall it? A glimmer of hope cannot be given. It has to be there. Encouragement can make an enormous difference, but the best efforts in the world cannot make it so. When a person has given up, it's a lost cause that runs so deep, you just can't fathom it. You just can't bring it back to life!' He leant forward, tears streaming down his tortured face. Pa stood up tentatively.

'Sit down, Nathan!' Reverend Moon thundered in a voice of old. 'I'm getting to the point. My point is . . .' His eyes rolled around the old rafters of St Matthew's, as though heaven could help him now. 'Why do some people still have that will to live, to be, to strive, to have another go, to walk again, to speak of love again, while others take defeat as the only course, the only option? "I'm done," they say. "This is all there is." How can a parent instil in a child the capacity to believe in the fight, without killing themselves in the battle?'

He stood tall again, straightening his flowing robes with practised skill. His eyes softened, his voice returned to its usual volume. Sister Mac hiccupped aloud. The congregation breathed a communal sigh of relief.

'My son, David Moon, had chosen well and it will be my regret, my anguish, to the grave, that I never told him so. Too full of my own ideas, my manly pride, my stilted, inflexible Christian ethics! Now, I must bless the day that Billy Batchelor has risen up to embrace new life, that she has seen fit to share that new life with another of the fine young men of Kurra Kurra. Ladies and gentlemen, our own Billy could have chosen a man of the world, a man of position and wealth. But no! She has chosen a simple man of humble faith, a man of her own kind, a man of the children, our own Jock O'Ryan!'

My heart had stopped. Please, Giles, please, I begged with my eyes, cut now, before you reduce me, before you reduce Jock, before you erode the compassion of your broken heart.

'Let us celebrate the Lord! Let us celebrate the immeasurable blessings of the Father and the Son, life everlasting, as it was in the beginning, now and ever more. For ever and ever, Amen,' he canted with a wide, theatrical flourish of the hands, his black gown swishing behind him like an English professor, long, long ago.

The choir stood to sing my favourite hit of the year, 'I'll Dance at Your Wedding'. Jock took my hand and led me towards the vestry. Ruth, Micky, Ma and Pa followed. Reverend Moon stepped down, collapsing softly to the floor. We turned around, aghast. He coughed, one short, light cough. His beady eyes rolled back, remaining open, staring up to the rafters, up to the heavens from whence he came.

Sister Mac rushed forward. 'Myocardial infarction,' she murmured incomprehensibly, shaking her head, cupping his in her strong, bony hands.

He took his last breath there, at the foot of his pulpit, before 'I'll Dance at Your Wedding' was over. It was an incalculable omen.

# SIXTEEN

# 1948...

For as long as I can remember, I have been a woman who, once an idea takes hold, must proceed to develop it. Pa believed I learnt it from Ma. She loudly proclaimed it was an hereditary trait in all women of good upbringing, a standard mixed metaphor from Ma that required no correction.

It was Jock who planted the idea in my head. The untimely death of Reverend Moon had cast Kurra into an eerie melancholy that felt horribly permanent. It had also settled heavily over our union, paralysing our marriage.

We were both sleeping badly, Jock in Ruth's old room and I in mine, as we had been since the day of the wedding. Jock suggested it initially, with due consideration for my feelings and a natural hesitancy on his part to attempt to consummate a marriage with a woman thrown so tortuously back into her past. But there was more to come. Sabella and Luther Prescott died within a few weeks of each other – she of a cold, turned to pneumonia, and he, of a broken heart. Though they had not lived at Cranberry Vineyard for many a year, their deaths cast a shadow across our path. Our marriage seemed destined never to begin.

Since that fateful night when Jock had re-entered my life, death had stalked us with a cruel irony we could not ignore. Dr McNab's sudden demise had opened the door to our friendship, a friendship that was viewed so suspiciously, we had broken it for many months to appease the town. Reverend Moon's last words from the pulpit had actually closed the door on my past, a past that would have been difficult to let go while he preached to us every Sunday, baptized our babies and buried our dead. As sole heir to the Prescotts' estate, I inherited a tidy fortune in property and capital on Sabella and Luther's deaths.

Immediately following the wedding we were inundated with visitors, the town folk arriving at Pharaoh to pay their respects. They brought small gifts of home-made jam or chutney, 'just to wish the newly weds well'. They skirted around the tragic heart attack of the Reverend, making small talk in subdued tones.

And then, after the funeral, Ruth and Rosa left for the centre. 'It's time for us to go, old girl,' Ruth said, simple as that. 'If we stay another day, we'll never leave.' How right she was! As things turned out, I was glad they'd gone before the next tragedy, or heaven knows, they'd probably never have got away.

I cuddled and kissed Rosataca, and wept openly in Ruth's arms. 'Oh Ruthy, what am I going to do without you?' We rocked together a long time, hugging fiercely, holding our dreams for each other within our tightly entwined arms. 'I'll think of you every day, write to you every week. Write back when you can, tell me about the search, tell me everything about your mama, tell me when you find her?'

'Of course I will! I'll miss you, Billy, more than you know. You've been all of my life. Soon Rosa and I will have a wider family, but you'll always be my Billy . . . I love you.'

After the Prescotts died, the visits slowed; within weeks, they stopped altogether. I missed Ruth's strength and companionship more deeply than ever. As analogies and connotations of the deaths clarified in the minds of small-town folk, the gossip gathered its own momentum. We became social outcasts, as though some ancient curse had been placed upon us. While the consensus of opinion put the ill-defined guilt squarely at my feet, Reverend Moon's last words in my defence all but forgotten, it was Jock who suffered the real sting of their tongues. Parents no longer wanted to talk to him about their children's progress, nor accept the discipline he measured out where it was due. Some said he had no right to be teaching at all, taking up a precious job when his wife could well afford to keep him in gentlemanly estate. He was no longer welcome at Shaft's, conversations reducing to polite acknowledgement whenever he had occasion even to pass by.

With the natural mateship Jock had shared in Kurra throughout his youth all but over, coupled with the utter isolation and desperate loneliness I was suffering, we were a sorry pair. Jock took up part-time study for a Bachelor of Education, determined to improve his station and earning capacity, though we certainly didn't need the money. In the late afternoons we tendered the chooks and the few rows of market garden I managed to keep alive. Our evenings were spent apart. I listened to the radio and read and sewed. Jock buried himself in the second bedroom, converted to a study.

The world news did nothing to lift our spirits either. There were riots in India after Gandhi's assassination, the death toll in Jerusalem was rising as the Jews and Arabs continued to clash, the communists had killed unknown hundreds in the Czechoslovakia coup and deaths were steadily rising with the Russian blockade in Berlin. Some nights I simply turned the radio off and wandered around the property, taking comfort in the anonymous nights and the cluttered skies. I'd think about how much

Jock and I had seemed to have in common, before we married, and how wrong I realized I'd been, after the event. I wondered if we'd ever find any common ground on which to overcome our harsh beginnings.

That my husband could leave me alone so long after our wedding served to highlight the huge chasm forming between us. His attitudes were narrow, restrictive; teaching had done little to expose him to the world. He had gone from school to the farm, and back to school. He had not been to war, nor been involved with a woman before. We were more like brother and sister than husband and wife, and I did not know then that our grief and worldly alienation was meshing us together, as two prisoners who share the same manacles.

When I applied for a position at my old radio station in Tarrenbonga and was knocked back on the grounds that I was a married woman and didn't need the job, months of fear and indignation, rancour and isolation spill out of my lonely heart. I sat on the steps of Pharaoh and sobbed, oceans of emotion overflowing onto the dry earth. When I could cry no more, I was violently ill and cleaning up after myself when Jock arrived home.

'Oh my Lovely, what's the matter?' his kind arms stretched out for me. I fell into them and the floods rose again.

'What am I going to do? Nobody will employ me because I'm married, and rich, and should be home having babies. I didn't want to be rich! I didn't want anyone to die. Why are they still ostracizing us? Why can't we just be allowed to get on with our lives, Jock? Why do I feel so guilty? When will the next death come?'

He patted my back, brushing his hands gently over my head until the sobbing eased. 'There won't be any more deaths for a long time,' he replied at length, sitting me down inside, pouring us a sherry. 'Pa reminded me last week that deaths come in threes and once they're done, the cycle is broken. I'm afraid you'll have to accept the employment situation though, Lovely; it's against the law for the public service to employ married women – you knew that. Doesn't mean you can't employ people yourself though, does it?'

My eyes widened. 'What are you getting at, Jock?' He had a way of dropping things on me nonchalantly, as though what he was saying was probably quite unnecessary to even bother to mention.

'Well, as you said the other night, you're not going to be approved of, no matter what you do. So I just thought you might be thinking along the lines of using some of the money to build a house large enough for our future children. Pharaoh won't go to waste down the track. I'm sure you're right and Ruth will return in due course.' My heartstrings pulled at the very sound of her name. He continued, unaware. 'And we might put the vineyard back on its feet when the probate's settled. Be handy to have quarters already established, for the help. Take the wind out of the locals' sails too – spreading the money round a bit.'

I stared at him in quiet awe. There was nothing fancy or particularly polished about him, though he was well read and loved poetry, but he had Pa's knack of bringing out the spirit in me. He was solid, irreducible, sensitive, gutsy. Not particularly 'a man's man' as tradition would have it, his manners and mouth too mild and philosophic, his humour more akin to the subtle, bitter wit of women. Now I began to understand why he had asked nothing of me in those first anguished months of our marriage, nothing more than friendship and a certain tenderness of touch.

I thought about the words of the burial service and was filled with an odd sense of wellbeing. *Man that is born of a woman hath but a short time to live, and is full of misery. He cometh up, and is cut down, like a flower.* Why do we make ourselves so unhappy when life is over in a moment, when death is the only mystery worth contemplating? A flash of lightning struck the darkening night, seeming to deliver the message I was receiving straight through the window and into my hands. Suddenly, there was no anger, no confusion, no insecurity. Out of the tragedies of our recent days, I felt a new courage, a new resolution. My heartbeat quickened. I reached out to Jock, impatience overwhelming me as it always did when the path was clear – the idea good. I wanted to get started immediately, plot the sort of house we would have; a large, large house to rival anything in the district. It would sit tall and proud on Cranberry Hill. We would stand on our verandah at dusk and wave to the peasants on the dusty road below. 'Oh, the ego of the girl!' I could hear Ma's lament repeating in my conscience.

'Slow down, slow down!' my husband urged, watching my animated face coming to life for the first time since I had taken his name and become his wife. 'We have some loving to do first, my Lovely. Tomorrow we will begin to plan the foundations!'

For the first time since our wedding day, I realized I wanted to love this man, wanted to share his bed, wanted to have his children. Perhaps I already loved him? The future was no longer desolate, but I would need many days of bright morning light before the memories of old passions and old heartaches could be called up without remorse.

For now, it was enough that hope had returned.

The first cottage I had built was far from grand, due to my preoccupation at the time with spending the minimum amount of the Prescotts' generous funds possible. Why I had called it Pharaoh had more to do with my imagination than reality – it was a worker's digs. Now I wanted the real thing and set about the task as though my life depended on it.

I wanted to create a new kind of house, one that combined the best of Egypt's luxurious style with the best of the Australian outback's unpretentiousness. I called in an architect from Port Hedley. John Brosolo was the son of Roberto, the stonemason who had built Rosebery and made the tombstone for Joey's grave. He immediately advised that what I wanted could not be done. He was silly enough to laugh – that really did it.

'John, if you feel you can't handle it, by all means say so and I'll find somebody else,' I advised him in my most reasonable tone of voice.

He settled down quite quickly then, making a few sketches alongside my sketches. 'It's going to be a big job, Billy. Take a lot of men.'

'That's good, excellent. Half the population are still unemployed.'

'The money will be in the labour all right, since most of the material will be coming from the hills. Are you sure it's all still up there?'

I hadn't explored the Kurrajong Ranges since I was a youngster, but had taken Butcher up there the day before our meeting. The wildlife wasn't as profuse as it used to be when we learnt the miracles of nature on our trusting bicycles, but the trees were whiter and the great boulders and cradled sandstone rocks were more richly coloured than I remembered them. 'It's all still there,' I said.

And so we began. For a fortnight, Brosolo and I sat at the kitchen table, huddled over our sketches and lists and costings. When Jock came in from school, we'd break for tea, explaining our day's workings to him. Sometimes we'd get so excited, he'd have to ask us to stop talking at once. I had agreed, with some misgiving, to allow Brosolo to put his own builder in charge. The only builder in Kurra simply didn't have the experience.

'Might cause some problems,' Jock warned quietly.

'Yes, but what can we do?'

'Cope with the flack,' he chuckled encouragingly. 'We've got a bit of experience at that, haven't we, Lovely?'

'The worst of our problems will be the weather,' the turncoat architect warned. 'We need a mild winter. Have you got any influence in that department, Billy?'

I was not at all confident that I did, but once I had felt the power of two gods and somehow knew I would have to will them both into action now. We need no accidents on the job, please God, no accidents. We need sunshine, lots of weak sunshine. We need a grateful population who will put aside past suspicions and grievances and rejoice in a brave, new future. I need continued good health, God; perhaps I should ask for that first, though I was in no doubt I could run the operation from my bedside, if worse came to worst.

It occurred to me that I had far too much to ask of one God anyway. Perhaps I could divide up the requests? The sun god Re would surely listen to Brosolo's plea, though how the Italians stood with the Egyptian god these days was another matter. Accidents were second nature to both gods, so perhaps I should just trust to luck on that one? How would the townsfolk view a city builder? 'Typical outsider,' I could hear them saying. And which god should I entrust with my health?

My confidence was severely dented by the time I confided my thoughts to Jock. He threw his head back and laughed heartily.

'I suspect you might be confusing the gods something fearful,' he said. 'Why not keep it simple?'

'Well, what would you suggest?' I snapped: ' "It's a lot to ask of you, God, but it is our turn, don't you think?" '

He laughed more thoughtfully, 'Why yes, Lovely, I think that would probably do very well.'

Whether God, or the gods, had anything to do with it, I can't say, but the sky stretched tight across the winter, shedding soft tears now and then in the evenings when the workers were home soaking in hot baths, and enjoying their first continuous red meat suppers for many a day. My energy held up and Jock came home late on Friday nights, having been invited back into the school at Shaft's pub. We lost a wall the week our builder had to return to Port Hedley for a funeral, but nobody was hurt and the respect afforded him thereafter was almost comical.

My job as chief overseer, cook and first-aid attendant kept me busy from sun up till long after dark. I revelled in it. The men relaxed after a couple of weeks, joking and chatting to me during their smokos, telling me of their families and how they'd got through the Great Depression and the war. We were friendly, but never close, avoiding the dangers of overfamiliarity between worker and boss. It was good to be working with men again, though it was different from what I had known. They called me Mrs O'Ryan. I liked it well enough. I still thought of myself as Billy Rachel Batchelor, yet I was beginning to feel that secret pleasure only women know, when men divulge a humbled sensibility to the non-threatening status of the married woman.

Pa maintained his weekly visits. When he had the time, he'd stop for a smoko with the men, telling them about The Great War, comparing notes, reminiscing over old times. I left them alone on these occasions, pressing on with my cottage chores, never catching up but getting by somehow.

'The men want to know what you're going to be calling the house. And they're calling you a chip off the old lady's block,' he said one day, wandering into the kitchen for a cuppa.

'Is that so, Pa?' I asked off-handedly, dying to know the extent of it.

He understood. 'They say you exact the same standards of others that you demand of yourself. They say there's no greater censure than your cold silence when something isn't done exactly the way you've planned it.'

'That sounds awful! I'm not that bad, am I?'

'They say you are incredibly stubborn but your sense of humour always saves the day. I don't think that's such a bad compliment from a group of tough working men, Billy. I am feeling mighty proud of you, dear. What are you going to call the house by the way?' he stumbled on quickly, covering his display of emotion.

'I honestly don't know, Pa,' I said, and cried a little then. His words were sweet and rare. To be perfectly honest, I was actually feeling rather proud of myself!

A tiny warning voice sounded in my heart, the adage oft times sounded by Ma so long ago: Beware of pride. It goes before a fall. But I was too happy and too busy to give it much thought. I was a married lady. I had a loving husband and a wonderful family. We were respected by the town at last and I was enjoying the best of health. I was building a beautiful house that would be finished on time and my period was three days late. All that was missing was Ruth, and she'd write soon, I just knew it.

'Thank you, gods, for everything,' I sang to myself. 'I'd better thank you both, hadn't I? Must have taken at least two of you to get this much right!'

353

The very next day, the long-awaited letter from Ruth arrived. Mugga had taken to leaving his truck at the top gate, walking up the hill to check on the builders before dropping in the mail. It annoyed me, but I couldn't find a way to tell him. It was hard to complain though he was arriving later than ever before. We had become the last drop off, rather than the first; he could then report to all his favourite customers the next day about the progress at Cranberry. I suspected from the post dates that he was also holding letters back if there was more than one a day, in order to ensure he had a delivery most days. What could I do?

This morning he came early, parked at the cottage gate, walked straight up to the kitchen door. 'Letter from Ruth, Billy!' he called, his gravelly old voice pitched an octave higher than usual. 'It's anuff ta knock the dags off a sick canary, eh, girl? I'm just gonna go up and say a good mornin' to the lads an' I'll drop back down if ya don't mind, just see 'ow she is, an' all?'

I turned the envelope over several times, post-marked Alice Springs. It was small, but felt thick and newsy. The familiar printing set my heart fluttering wildly, as though I held the whole world in my hands. 'God, I've missed you, Ruthy,' I said to the kettle, moving it back onto the ever-burning stove. I looked out the window up to the hill. Everything seemed normal. I went to the toilet. The kettle was boiling when I returned. I made a cup of Milo. I hadn't had Milo for months. I furrowed around for a cigarette, pulled up a chair. The envelope opened easily. A teaspoon of red soil fell onto the table. I scooped it up on a saucer and opened the dusty pages.

'Dear Mrs O'Ryan!' she began cheekily, walking right into the kitchen, pulling up a chair beside me.

How are you, Billy Rachel? I think of you every day and I know how you are 'cos I collected all your letters from the post office when I arrived. I've just finished reading them – it took three days!

I'm glad we didn't come to town earlier. My heart would not have coped, you knew that though, didn't you, old girl? When I read of the Prescotts' deaths and all, and the next letter telling me how hard things were for you and Jock, I rushed to the last letter. Thankfully you remembered to number them. I was so overcome with how well everything is going at last, I just sat down and wept. Then I read all the letters in between, and now I know you've regained your spirit. You must promise you'll never let it slip that low again.

What a stunner of a house you're building, Billy! Sounds just like you. I can see the tall white ghost gum pillars from our own Ranges, the thick stone walls, the huge windows standing high above ground, tall and proud on Cranberry Hill. I can see it in my mind as if I was there. I remember how stubborn you were about windows for the cottage. This house will dwarf the cottage, won't it? What's you gonna call it, Billy? It wouldn't surprise me if you came up with a real small name, opposite of Pharaoh. That would give the locals quite a turn, as Mrs Rosey would say.

I was sad there was no mail from your in-laws, 'specially Than, but it's hard for a growing boy to remember when I'm not around, I know. Thanks for telling me about their doings anyway. I was sorry Micky didn't get his son, but another set of twins is a great blessing, I'm sure. I laughed when you said they should have another set of twin girls so they could call them Isobella and Veronica and get it all over and done with, and bugger me, they did! You haven't changed! I wonder Thea didn't want some names from her side, though as you once said, best thing ever happened to her was to be rid of her kin.

It's hard on white kids, having to wear dead people's names, though. It's different with us, we have a terrific system. There's sixteen in our clan family – the boy babies have one name and the girl babies have my name. The system for marriage has been worked out so it isn't possible to marry closer than a fourth cousin, provided you obey it, and you have to 'cos it's the law. I'd love to see your reaction to that! I can hear your scathing attack on the 'cultured' English world producing awfully deformed offspring for centuries, while the dumb, primitive Abos have been getting it right for thousands of years. What a pity you don't have a radio show these days. I could really give you some stories, though most of your people are not ready to hear them. That never stopped you, though, did it?

Well, I haven't mentioned my Great Search, have I? It's real frustrating, I can tell you. I've found my family – cousins, uncles, aunts, nieces and nephews for Rosa (golly, I haven't told you about Rosa yet!), but my mother isn't here, Billy. She went bush with a bloke from the west last year and nobody's come through our camp since to tell us where she is. In every other way, I have found my life, the meaning, the spirit of it. There is so much to tell you. I wish I had your gift to explain . . . I'm writing in the diary you gave me, though. When I visit, I'm going to give it to you to keep. I won't need it, 'cos I'll have the words in my heart, with all the memories and all the days of our lives meshed together. Hopefully my mother will come back soon and I'll be able to complete it. If she doesn't, I'm going to hitch a lift to the west and find her. If I have to go, I'll leave Rosa with her new family – she has many mothers now.

She's healthy and strong, blacker than ever, full of mischief like Than, but more temperate, I think. She's learning the ways of the bush and loves the big rock, Uluru. I told her it was so old, nobody knew how many millions of years it'd been there. She's bilingual (fair dinkum!) and asked in our tongue: 'Old as Billy?' I know she was just putting words together (mimick- ing? you know what I mean) since she's too young to know better, but she is real bright. It's hard not to be

356

bright out here (not Alice Springs – the whites treat us like dogs, worse than the old days in Kurra), but there's so much to learn, the culture, the spiritualism of our people is rich as the red earth and the blue sky.

You've always been searching to be free. I wish you could come out here where you can feel it without trying. The wind and the heat make the days seem like for ever. Life is longer, bigger somehow. There's no clock ticking out here – you might miss that (?) – but you'd love to stand in the middle of nowhere and scream and yell at the top of your lungs and not a single soul to hear. It's freedom, Billy.

I suppose you'll be pregnant soon and that'll end any hope of coming out to visit? Never mind, perhaps in another life. But you loved Egypt so much I just wish you could know the real Australia, the raw, uncultured one!!! I can tell from your letters, though, that you've got to liking Billy Batchelor now, and that's the most important thing. You know, I never liked who I was? For a long time I couldn't fathom what you had to dislike about yourself. Now that I know who I am, I can understand how anybody, even you, Billy, had to go through some pain to get there.

I've started a school at our camp at Katatjuta (the Olgas, it means the place of many heads). There's change a-comin', Billy, tourists, I think. The welfare people and the missions and the travel agents have been active round Alice for yonks, but the buses are starting to come out more often. I don't think we'll be alone much longer. My people will need English, sooner than later. I was gonna try and get a grant from the Government, or someone, but nobody's organized and it just looked too hard, so I thought, I'll just do it, under the drooping desert oak where we rest during the day. I had eighteen in class last week! They come from everywhere, by camel, on foot, sometimes even by truck. Isn't that amazing? (You can tell old Mugga about that.)

It's the children who will rewrite our history, Billy – in time to save our race, hopefully, and our beautiful, beautiful country. Some of my children say, 'Naka,

357

but God made the world!' and I think to myself, these are kids who've been to mission schools and learnt white ways. I say, 'Yes, that's the white man's religion and each to his own. But who is God?' I ask them and they don't know, 'cos what has white man's God ever done for them? I show them the netted lizard, the red bud mallee bush, the blackfooted rock wallaby. I show them how to find the witchetty grub and native fig and the beantree with its red kidney seeds. Then I teach them the alphabet and tell them stories from the Dreamtime about how the desert came to be and how the kangaroo got its tail, how the sun was born and . . . do you remember, how the Brolga came to be . . . ?

You were my Brolga, the beautiful girl who loved to dance. When I first told them that I knew the girl of the legend, they pestered me so, I dreamt up a real fun story called 'How Billy Rachel Batchelor O'Ryan Got Her Names'. The little ones love it.

Be happy and healthy, dear Billy. I love you. I'll keep on with my diary, as you must keep on with yours. Love to Jock and a big kiss to Than, please. Rosa sends heaps of big kisses (very wet and sticky) to you both.

Your best friend,
Ruth.

Mugga had interrupted at the first page. I sent him on his way, assuring him that Ruth was very well and enjoying life enormously – he could have more detail tomorrow. As soon as Jock arrived home from school, I insisted he sit down and read it. 'You read it to me, Lovely. I've been reading all day . . . I'd love you to read it to me.'

My wise husband! He knew I was dying to read it again and supper would definitely have to wait until I had. So I began, reading more slowly this time, taking in new insights at every line. When I had finished, he was strangely pensive.

'What's wrong, Jock? Doesn't she sound wonderful

358

– well, apart from the disappointment of missing her mother?'

'Yes, yes,' he nodded uncertainly.

'Then say it, dear!'

'She seems to be discarding her past rather quickly, I would have thought. I know she never felt any empathy with the Christian religious teachings she had with your family, but I hope she isn't going too far with this alternative lifestyle business, that's all.'

'Why, Jock O'Ryan, I can't believe you said that! *Alternative lifestyle business!* What on earth are you talking about? She's gone home, Jock, back to her people, back to her roots, back to where she had every right and reason to be in the first place! We just had her on loan, Jock, a long "stolen" loan at that. *We* are the alternative lifestyle, Jock, not her. Surely you can see that?'

I was waxing flushed and angry, though not as angry as I was destined to become. I had never seen Jock angry, but he too was flushed and looked ready to explode. 'Billy, you've got a distorted view of Aboriginal intelligence because of one friendship with a black woman brought up in your own home, with all the benefits of white culture and education. You know as well as I do that the Aborigine has a smaller brain than us and consequently, a lower IQ. What Ruth is doing to Rosa is unforgivable.'

'My God! You really still believe that? I thought, *dared hope*, such ignorance went out with Ma and Pa's generation.'

'I can tell you, Billy, I have a lot of black kids through my class room. You can't teach them. They don't pick up on anything quickly and as soon as you think you might be getting through in the smallest way, they up and go walkabout.'

'Has it occurred to you that it might be your teaching skills? Ruth doesn't seem to be having any trouble!'

'That was beneath you, Billy.'

'Not at all, Jock! You seem to have forgotten you once said Than was one of the brightest kids in school. A drop of white blood alters the entire hand-out of brain cells, does it? Like your own father, eh? How do you decide who's got a drop of black blood in their veins that's acceptable, and who's got a drop of white that isn't? Fascinating really. Is there some secret academic method you use that we lesser mortals would not understand?'

'You're out of control, Billy.'

Funny how Ma always called me Billy when she thought I was wrong and Rachel when I was thinking the way she wanted me to think. Now my own husband was calling me Billy because he felt threatened; he called me Lovely when I was sweet and malleable. The idea that Ma and Jock held identical traits served to make me madder.

'You know, I used to think it was a terrible shame Ma never learnt to read or write, but now I can see that an Anglo-Saxon education is no panacea for understanding, or lucidity for that matter. You both resort to labels when you're not getting your own way, as though all of life can be defined in little boxes, according to the way you've been taught to think!'

He looked at me oddly, as though puzzled. 'Well, it can be really. You make it sound terrible, but we have developed our brains to be able to research the facts and draw definite conclusions. The truth is the truth and your life, Billy, would be far from what it is now, if this were not so.'

My mind darted around in frustration, trying to find a path out of this breakdown in our communication. Of course I knew Jock's schoolteacher attitude to the blacks, but . . . a racist? I did not even know the range of my own thoughts on this dark, complex subject. I looked up to our wonderful house taking shape on the hill, wondering if the hedonistic nature of white ownership was too firmly entrenched in lifestyle ever really to change.

But surely there must be thousands of people like me, asking the questions, pleading for answers that nobody wants to find? I had no women friends of my own vintage to talk with. I was isolated, like country women had always been. Was it just possible that nothing had changed? Because we, who saw the blacks close up and came to know them for what they really are, have never had the strength of numbers to raise the consciousness of our men?

I thought long and hard before I spoke again, calming my voice appreciably. 'Jock, we've never argued before. I don't like it very much, but I can't agree with Ma and Sister Mac that there's some things best left unsaid. That's probably why change was so slow in their day. "Don't rock the boat, don't rock the boat!" How many times were you told that, growing up? If you hadn't rescued me from your own father that day at Bunyip Point, where would I be now? You nearly fell out of the boat as I recall. You could have fallen and cracked your head open on a rock, but you didn't think about that. You spoke up, to save me.' He smiled gratefully. I could see the relief on his face, as though I had changed the subject completely.

'Any man would have done the same, knowing what I knew.'

'Knowing what you knew?' I repeated slowly. 'Does that mean that any man will fight to save the innocent and vulnerable from the strong, the oppressor, provided of course he can see that that is the situation?'

I had gone too far. I had not let him win; worse, I'd thrown his own words back at him to make him appear foolish and ill-considered. His face clouded over. He got up without a word and went outside. I put Ruth's letter away and began to make tea. A terrible thought dropped into my head that I could not dislodge. I wished we had lost the war! I wished our men had learnt how to lose! The only losers on our side were dead. If they could just live and lose once, at something big enough, maybe they would drop their bravado and massive superiority complexes and come down to earth where the real world admitted confusion and uncertainty, about everything!

When he returned, my heart was heavy but I had calmed down. He seemed relaxed, as though nothing had happened. I knew I could hate him then, wondered if it was true that hatred could hold two people together more strongly than love.

A few days later, my period arrived. When I told him, he nodded knowingly. 'Ah!' he said.

'What does that mean?' I asked stupidly. 'You don't sound very disappointed.'

'Oh sorry, Lovely. Of course I'm disappointed, it's just that, well, you haven't quite been yourself and I can certainly understand that now.'

I was so shocked, I burst into tears. Chocolate Two was at my feet and began to whimper. Jock put his arms around me.

'Leave me alone,' I shrugged him off, running blindly to the bedroom. I wanted to die at that moment. I would have been glad to be out of it. How stupid of me! Double stupid! Triple stupid! I thought his gentle manner with me in recent days was because he was thinking about what I'd said, perhaps beginning to understand. But now, it was my period coming that had caused me to defy him and argue about nothing! Now I had burst into tears, confirming his opinion, undoing whatever good I might have done. On top of that, I had run like a spoilt child from his arms, no doubt convincing him I'm deeply disappointed we're not having a baby. God, no wonder men don't understand women.

He came into the bedroom and lay down on the bed beside me, letting me cry myself out. 'We'll just have to keep trying,' he said softly, making no attempt towards intimacy.

Then: 'You know, Lovely, I've been thinking about Ruth's letter quite a bit this week. I can't help agreeing . . . she does seem to have found a new vision for her life. There's a lot of special value about dreaming. Dreaming is the field of creation to the Aborigine and I think you've got quite a lot of it in your soul, quite naturally.'

'That's a nice thing to say,' I sniffled begrudgingly.

'And she's right about teaching the kids English. Perhaps you should begin a fight to make their language compulsory in our schools? History suggests when we can communicate, we lose the need to fight.'

I turned side on to face him, hearing the peace, ready to talk it all out calmly, rationally. He put his fingers across my mouth, followed by dry lips, in search of life. I decided there and then that making up is one of the best parts of marriage.

We moved into The Brolga just in time for our wedding anniversary. I had not seen a brolga in years, but it was their breeding season and we kept our ears open, hoping to hear that deep trumpeting call down by the Pickle River, flowing again, at the bottom of our property.

It was a beautiful house, tall and stately, solid as the rocks that made it. It had four bedrooms and two bathrooms big enough to hold a small army, plus a monstrous kitchen with a twelve-foot oak sideboard running right down the centre. One side was my work area and the other was our sitting room-parlour. It was like an entire living room in its own right. I was especially proud of it because Brosolo had been dead against it. 'Why would a woman want people in the same room where she's working?' he'd asked incredulously.

'You should see Rosebery on a busy night,' I'd derided. 'Ma can hardly breathe for everyone hanging around. People love kitchens. Women like the company too, but since you men design houses, it would never occur to you to give us more room, would it? All you think about is the food coming out of the oven and you want to be there to make sure you don't miss out.' He'd gone along with me after that. He later had the grace to tell me he was designing all his houses from now on with lots more work room for the women, making me question my own temerity in fixing the idea in his head. How many of my modern sisters would be grateful for another reason to keep them at home?

There was much to be done, what with decorating and titivating inside and clearing and landscaping outside. Christmas came and went with the usual round-up at Rosebery and the New Year saw us ploughing up the fields, wondering what we were going to do with them.

During the long school holidays, Jock read everything there was to read on vineyards. One day he decided the climate had always been too mild to grow good vines, the next, certain varieties may well be successful. A week later, after yet another tour of the land, he became worried about blight and mildew, pests, depressions and Government changes. Bottle shortage was another problem. 'In the last century, they had to content themselves with old porter, ale and vinegar bottles,' he told me wearily. A few days further on, he decided the soil had been neglected so long it would need years of rejuvenation before it could handle anything other than dumb sheep. I listened, nodded, shook my head, asked questions and suddenly, the holidays were over and Jock was back at school during the daylight hours – and in his new study at night.

I stood in my big kitchen, looking out at the desolate, smooth fields of turned earth, wondering whether to buy more goats and a mate for my old nag and see if they could do something to populate the land. As mating went, we certainly weren't having any luck and I wasn't getting any younger. It was my thirty-fifth year, borderline, possibly dangerous, my gynaecologist in Tarrenbonga warned. Dr May Ling, a third generation Chinese Australian, was a straight talker and one of the first women doctors to specialize in women's medicine. 'You had better get on with it, and smartly,' she advised, proceeding to question me in some detail.

She drew an initial conclusion that we were not making love often enough. Was there a problem? No, there was not a problem. I didn't think there was a problem. Jock and I did not have a passionate relationship, no, not passionate at all. We were more friends than lovers. Didn't that happen in all marriages, after a while?

'But you have only been married a short time, Mrs O'Ryan.'

Well, we got off to a bad start. No, that's got nothing to do with it. Not much anyway. I didn't fall in love, if that's what you mean. I grew to love him. He's a good man.

'Are you lonely, Mrs O'Ryan?'

'I have no reason to be.'

'Reason usually has very little to do with loneliness – or guilt for that matter.'

'Will it make me fall pregnant if I acknowledge it?'

She laughed, a sweet, lingering laugh that softened her austere, professional manner. 'It might be a start in the right direction. If you badly want a baby because your life is looking rather empty right now, you're unlikely to conceive. Come back and see me in six months. We'll run some tests, if necessary.'

I thanked her, paid the bill and drove our brand-new Holden home. I took the long unmade road, avoiding Kurra, skirting Mini Mini, stopping for a walk by the Lake Pickle salt mines. Ruth and I used to ride out here and catch tadpoles. We used to run up the lower slopes of the ranges and sit perfectly still by that big ghost gum, watching the kangaroos feeding their young, listening to the opera of the bellbirds and the harsh call back of the red wattles.

But they were silent today, and the earth was barren.

Micky had been so busy at Mini Mini, with cattle sales and one thing and another, Isobella and Veronica O'Ryan were nearly twelve months old before they were christened.

Thea decided to hold a large party in the Botanical Gardens one Sunday after Mass; the entire town was invited. It was as well to ask everyone; they would come anyway. She had wisely refrained from a party for Frances and Sarah's baptism. The food rations and severe financial straits of most at the time would not have been well received since it was traditional for the men to supply the beer and the ladies to bring a plate. It was the first big party in Kurra since our wedding. Everyone prayed for an uneventful day.

The night before, we had the first heavy rain in months but the morning beamed bright and promising. The grounds would be soggy underfoot; the children would stir up the mud once they began playing, but the mothers would bring gumboots and a change of clothes. It was no cause for concern. Christenings were grand celebrations. The youngsters were allowed to run wild, leaving the adults to get on with some serious drinking, particularly since it was a Mick party and Thea and Micky were throwing in a keg, just to be on the safe side.

Amelia Moon wired Miss Prinkett she'd be arriving home the day before, adding great excitement to the event. Why she was bothering at all was the talk of the town, since her family were dead and her ties with Kurra were cloaked in tragedy. She had maintained a correspondence with Prinky, but as far as anyone knew, had not kept in touch with anyone else. Stationed in the Congo since she left Sydney sixteen years ago, she'd sent flowers to David's memorial service and Reverend Moon's funeral and written Prinky she was visiting her brother's token grave in Alexandria on her way home from Leopoldville.

Apart from the usual births, a few expected deaths and the building of The Brolga, nothing very exciting had happened in Kurra for some time. The imaginations of the town folk bloomed quickly. Before the week was out, they had conjured some wildly eclectic possibilities.

'She's finally got malaria and has to come home for complete rest. Is it contagious?'

'Reverend Moon planted a rose bush in the gardens in David's memory; perhaps she just wants to pick a rose?'

'She's dying of consumption and wants to be buried near her father.'

James Barnawarren had not married and someone had overheard someone talking to Prinky. They were absolutely certain she said Amelia was tired of being a missionary and wanted to be a wife before her biological clock ran out.

It all seemed harmless enough until I realized I was hanging off every new story Mugga brought to my kitchen door. I'm becoming like my mother, I thought, desperation gripping me. 'There's nothing wrong with your mother,' I talked to myself, 'but surely you've got more to do with your life than just hang around waiting for the next bit of gossip?' Nevertheless, I was deeply curious about meeting Amelia again and looked forward to the christening with an impatient, mounting excitement. Since the war, there were three girls to one boy being born in our town, but there were no women of my ilk, apart from Thea. I hoped Amelia planned to stay, though I could not think why she would want to either.

We met quite by chance on the big day, appropriately beside David's rose bush. Perhaps I was lingering? There were three hundred people in the gardens, including the children. It was bedlam.

'Let's go across to Nan's Tea House, find some peace,' Amelia suggested almost immediately. She was obviously not used to crowds.

When we were seated, I looked at her more closely. Her once fair peaches and cream complexion was dark, dark brown and lined with toil. Her once fair blonde hair was stringy and dull and had turned quite grey. She was dressed in a loose, drab corduroy tunic affair that was far too large. She looked fifty, or more, yet her eyes sparkled and the childhood sweetness of expression had deepened and mellowed on her, like full-grown blossom. 'You're still beautiful, Amelia,' I admired her breathlessly.

'Oh no, Billy! I'm old and weathered now. Anyway, you were always the beautiful one – and still are! I was just the pretty little thing that tagged along behind you, hoping I could catch a bit of your confidence.'

'No!' I gasped.

'Why yes, of course! We all did. I picked up enough too. You taught me that I could do whatever I wanted to do, provided I wanted it badly enough. Father was desperate for me to be a nurse, you know.'

'No . . . yes, I think I did.'

She laughed, remembering. 'I suspect he didn't want any competition in the family. He believed he had an exclusive hold on God. I'm so sorry, Billy, that you lost David. I must admit I was stunned when I heard you two were together. I would never have thought you had anything in common. Life's odd, isn't it?'

'Yes, it doesn't seem to follow . . . Why did you think we had nothing in common?'

'David was a bit of a Jekyll and Hyde, you know. What am I saying, of course you know! You were always so, well, straight up, predictable.'

'I was? He was . . . ? Forgive me, Amelia, but I don't know what you're talking about. I've always thought I was a complicated, confused mess. I thought David was totally cut and dried.'

Her warm, lush eyes studied me carefully, a sympathetic awakening dawning in their lights like our winter sun rising over the ranges. Her life was in her face; I knew nothing of it, yet one look conveyed the character she had become. 'David was a goody-goody on the surface, always wanting to do the right thing and score points with Father. Behind his back, he was a terror. He told incredible lies, boasted about cheating to pass his exams and was always trying his luck after school with the Catholic girls, down by Billadambo. He and your brother, Joe, got up to some terrible pranks.' My heart jumped at the long-forgotten memories, pushed down firmly, out of sight, out of mind. She continued comfortably, unaware of the memories she was stirring. 'David suffered more than I from our mother abandoning us.

You remember how Father told the world she died of consumption – sometimes I think he actually believed it – but he used to tell us she was a loose woman and we were well rid of her. And everyone knew. Poor old Father. His heavy-handed upbringing naturally created enormous psychological pressure on David to succeed.

'Miss Prinkett was the best thing that happened to us in many a year. Your mother did us a great service when she had Carter Pip excommunicated from the town so your father could have the stationmaster's job. We wouldn't have got Prinky if Mr Pip hadn't summoned our first nursemaid to Queensland. We wouldn't have got her either if Pa hadn't been so racist and refused to have Ruth. Were you aware of that? No, I don't suppose you were. Prinky was the one who really took David in hand and taught him that cheating would not get him the success he so desperately wanted. She knocked him into shape and made him like himself enough to believe he could get a woman without having to use brute force too. Didn't you ever wonder why it took him so long to get through medicine? He'd skipped so much school, he came from a long way behind to make the grade.'

'Yes, I did,' I whispered, wondering how I could have missed so much, blocked out what I did know, remained ignorant, even in death . . . 'Amelia, how could I have acknowledged so little about the man I fell head over heels in love with?'

'Simply that, I expect! Intelligence and education have never been a hindrance to falling head over heels in love, my dear. Accidents will happen,' she smiled, that haunting smile again, as though the harsh words she had spoken of her brother were no more than simple truths that held no sting.

'Tell me all about you, Amelia! Tell me about the

Congo and why you're here, what plans you have for the future?'

'I'll answer one of those questions now, and tell you all the rest over the next few days. I need a favour from you, Billy.'

'From me?' I started. The idea was extraordinary.

'I'm having a baby. It will be a half-caste. I couldn't remain at the mission in the Congo; it would offend my fellow missionaries' morality too deeply. Prinky wrote that you know where Ruth is – where she's teaching in the centre. I want to join her. I couldn't stay in our culture, Billy – it would be too hard on the child, perhaps, mainly me. After sixteen years in the Congo, I'm tuned to a different way of life – harsher, lonelier, but . . . more honest, for me. I want to continue my work and I know this is the right solution. Will you help me?'

I reached across the table for her hands and clasped them tightly. 'Yes, yes, of course I'll help you. But you'll find it different from life in Africa, Amelia. The school system alone . . . and the Alice is quite racist. Out bush, well, perhaps that's an inspired solution. What an incredible species we are, Amelia – how far from those early, carefree days did we land? Ruth will be thrilled to see you, have your help in the work. There's a whole family of mothers to help you too, when you have your babe.'

'I know,' she smiled, 'I've been reading up about it. It's richer than the African culture, no doubt partly because it's older. My child will have a better chance as a native black than being half-caste of a single mother in our white society.'

At the back of my mind, Ruth's voice was calling, urging me to warn her some more of the down sides, of the changes coming to the centre. But we were disturbed by Ma, who shook her hand firmly. Because of the speed with which Ma moves, we were pretty sure she had not heard the tail end of our conversation.

'Welcome back, dear,' she said efficiently. 'You will join us at Rosebery for supper, I hope?'

'Why thank you, Mrs Batchelor. That would be very nice.'

'That was close,' I said when she had moved on. 'Everybody seems to be having babies but me, Amelia. Maybe you can help?'

'I'd love to, if I can, but let's wait until we're absolutely alone. Nobody else need know about my baby because I have no intention of ever returning to Kurra. If at all possible, I would prefer not to upset your ma and pa's memories of the Moons and their fine reputations!'

We laughed as we used to do, when we were girls of six or seven, though there was the women's edge of cynicism framing our amusement now. Having missed the christening party altogether, we walked slowly back to Rosebery, along Bullock Creek where the blackfellas lived, and over the Birrie Bridge.

Amelia's life was all worked out now. But I was still waiting . . .

# SEVENTEEN

# 1950...

The views were glorious from the master bedroom of
The Brolga. To the east, I could see clean up to the
very tip of the Kurrajong Ranges and to the west,
down the hill to Pharaoh and an assortment of barns
and pens and outhouses.

We had planted an avenue of Australian gums and
English poplars leading up to the circular drive into
The Brolga; when I sat up for meals, I could see the
bottom half of the small plants growing stronger
every day and the top half of my vegetable and
flowerbeds overrun with weeds, dying from neglect.
At the very edge of my western view I could glimpse
the river of my childhood, watch a new generation of
youngsters racing their bicycles straight over the
banks into the shallow water, splashing, crashing,
laughing and dunking one another until they grew
tired and irritable. Usually the biggest boy of the
group would start the fight, but once it had begun, it
was all legs and arms and bicycles with nobody appearing to win. In our time, the boys always had to
have a winner, but then, times had changed.

'Like a cuppa, dear?' Prinky called from the
kitchen. She had turned up a few months ago when
she heard I was poorly and seemed in no hurry to
leave. She was a sulky old stick, but her heart was in
the right place. It certainly saved Ma having to worry,
about Jock's meals mainly. We'd re-employed
Banduk and Jabaljari to do the household chores,

washing and the like. It was the first job they'd had since Ruth had employed them for me, how long ago was that? Years anyway. 'Thanks, Prinky, I'd love one.' I repositioned myself and the dailies scattered around me.

The problem with change is that it always seems to hit you as having come on suddenly, when in reality, it takes its time and far too much of it, at that. Men were used to working long hours for little money. They were used to going off to wars and fighting on near empty stomachs for some other bloke's country. All they dreamt about was returning to the security of home where everything remained the same. But it didn't, not this time.

Women were valued during the war. They were needed for men's work. Their self-confidence went up; they began to realize they could think. I say *they* because, apart from my two years in Egypt, I was pretty much out of it. In any case, I was one of the privileged few who'd already had an external shot of brain stimulation via a university education.

When it was all over, we weren't even recognized on Anzac Day. We knew, once and for all: we were nowhere near as important as men. So we all got busy again, producing babies . . . well, anyone who could, did. Just what would trigger the revolution I could hear humming and circling like a whirlwind caught between two rocks in a desert storm? Would it be the interminable boredom when the youngsters went to school? Would it evolve because the men had had all the fight knocked out of them? Would it be the memory of those fat Yankee wallets that could buy a girl the little extras that made the difference to a dull and menial existence?

My tea arrived. I folded the newspaper over and propped myself up. Prinky fluffed up my pillows. 'Thanks, Prinky. Have you got a minute?'

'Certainly, Mrs O'Ryan. What do you need?'

'I don't need anything. I just want to ask you something.'

'Yes?' she swallowed hard. Conversation was not her strong suit; questions made her nervous. 'I've been lying here trying to work out what the trigger might be to set off the women's revolt that's rumbling out there,' I indicated the newspaper. 'I know the adage was true once: "You can take the girl out of the country but you can't take the country . . ."'

'"Out of the girl!" Not so much longer, I'd say,' she grimaced with a chipper satisfaction foreign to her usual pristine demeanour.

'Then you agree that women won't put up with second-rate citizen status much longer?'

'They certainly won't, Mrs O'Ryan, and high time they woke up to themselves too, I say. And you know why?'

'Well, I . . . no, why do you think?'

'I don't think, madam, I *knows*! They're going to get tired of having babies, that's what, knowing men will go on killing them, again and again and again. So far this century, what have men done to make women feel good about having babies? I ask you?'

I sat, shaking my head, dumbfounded. I hadn't heard Prinky speak more than two sentences in a row in the last five months, in fact, ever. Her bloodless, sunken face was positively animated, making her look almost healthy. She smoothed her tartan skirt beneath her and parked on the end of the bed. Chocolate Two opened one eye, growled, dug a deeper hole in the quilt and promptly went back to sleep.

'Wars and depressions! That's what the men of the world have put on the women this century. Wars and depressions! The little woman won't stay home to watch it happen again, mark my words, Mrs

O'Ryan!' She stood abruptly, straightening the back of her skirt again. 'I hope the tea's satisfactory, Mrs O'Ryan?' It was business as usual.

'Lovely, thank you, Prinky. Thank you so much for talking with me.' She exited hurriedly.

I picked up my diary. I'll write to you for half an hour, I promised. I would have little energy left in half an hour. Perhaps it might mean I could get some sleep.

Prinky was right. The twentieth century so far was not proving profitable for us women. And half the world are still slaughtering one another! In my short lifetime we've seen bloodbaths from Gallipoli to Bullecourt to Rabaul . . . then Mussolini's fascist troops, Hitler's goose-stepping soldiers, Hirohito's kamikaze pilots. Now Vietnam's been split in two. Where will that lead? North Korea's marching into the South. Robert Menzies is back in charge. He knows the people love a good war. We'll get into whichever one breaks first, I suppose.

We're looking good for the Davis Cup though. It's in New York this year. Bromwich, Sedgeman and McGregor look set to lead the way. It's all male, predictably. I used to enjoy tennis. Those days are over. I'll walk again though, I'm determined. Dr May Ling referred me to a specialist in Port Hedley but I was laid too low to get there. Eventually Jock insisted on paying for him to come to me. He diagnosed my complaint, after much discussion with colleagues and rechecking of test results. No wonder Ma has never had much faith in the medical profession. They're an uncertain lot.

MS, they muttered, MS for short. When I commented on the cruelty of giving a disease that could take forty or fifty years to kill you a hieroglyphic 'MS for short', they had the grace to look a little sheepish. It struck me as ironical that it had not occurred to the medical profession, any more than it ever has to the professional war mongers, that letters of the alphabet and cute desensitized words do not fool the people actually involved.

Multiple sclerosis. It's a neurological disease, of the brain and spinal cord. 'It interferes with the brain's ability to control the body, Mrs O'Ryan.' I knew that! Sometimes the electrical messages from the brain can't get through to the body muscles at all. Paralysis results. 'That's what's happening to you at the moment, Mrs O'Ryan.' Other times, the message goes to the wrong place, causing all those abnormal body reactions I've had for more than half a lifetime. Then, without warning, the brain gets it right again and I get on with a normal life.

They don't know what causes it. It may be an unidentified virus, or the body's reaction to a virus. The measles virus may be responsible in some patients. 'It could be that the body becomes allergic to itself and starts attacking its own cells in an immune response, Mrs O'Ryan.' Funny how doctors overdo your name when they're telling you bad news.

I'm not horrified by the news, really. I've known it had to be something obscure for some time. There's less than a thousand known cases in Australia at the moment, so that's a small claim to fame, isn't it? It's not the best disease in the world to have, mind you, but you can't die from it, not quickly anyway. It's a slow creep. I'm lucky because I get long remissions between attacks, though they'll shorten as time goes on. They've got me on low dosage morphine to help the pain.

I'm writing up my diary and making plans for the future. Some days are easier than others. I get a bit muddled and rather intense about things, but when it comes to sickness, it's difficult not to take it seriously at my age.

377

My first bad year unfolded, each day much like the last, except for the outside world, which filled my empty room with constant news. Chocolate Two and I lived our lives through everyone else's. She seemed to have forgotten words like *walk* and *play*, and just about had me convinced she was interested in politics and history. So many things were happening, we were rarely bored. Aboriginal stockmen now had to be paid award wages and women had to receive seventy-five per cent of male wages. Officially that is. It was a good start, but unemployment was growing again so women and blacks would likely lose their newly won rights before they'd even come in. There was talk of cutting immigration intakes too. Migrants, now called New Australians, looked destined to have their families spread across the globe, yet again.

We were in the Korean War, up to our elbows in blood, as David would have said. The year 1951 was barely underway when President Truman fired General MacArthur. We were as shocked as the Americans. The President said he took the decision in order to avert World War Three. We were intensely sceptical. Was it merely another political ploy for some devious purpose?

I took all these matters up with my regular visitors of course. Ma disagreed with me quite often, taking the final word with absolute, God-fearing surety. Just about everyone else agreed with my opinions, undoubtedly believing the best therapeutic course of action was to ensure I was not excited in any way. Extraordinary how people think when you're flat on your back that you don't need excitement! It's about the only thing anyone can really give you that means anything. Your old dreams aren't worth much after a while. Thus, I often found it better to be alone. I could escape into the world with my newspapers, radio, and books. I could reread Ruth and Amelia's letters and picture myself out in the Never Never, living off the salt of the earth. I could luxuriate in the knowledge that Ruth's Time had come. 'My dearest, dearest Billy,' her last letter had begun, somehow announcing her wonderful news from the very start.

My long journey is over! A lifetime journey, over thousands of days . . . and thousands of miles. I am with my mother, as I write you. I'll be with her until she returns to the Dreaming. In the time that we have, we're heading back to the centre. Sometime soon.

Oh Billy, what fortune has come to me, this last year or so! I just hope you're well when you receive this, or I'll feel awfully guilty to be feeling so happy, so at peace. When Amelia first arrived, I thought that reward enough – another mother of my own vintage to share the trials and tribulations of a fast-growing, thoroughly modern child of illegitimate parentage! She made it easier to leave Rosa behind too. She said: "It's our white God who's orchestrated this reunion you know, Ruth!" but that's plainly silly, and anyway, she had a twinkle in her eyes. She's settled in well, amongst the tribe. I told her I'd thank anyone's God for this!

My mother is a small, oddly dainty lady in appearance, in spite of the rough life she's lived. She says she was beautiful in her day. To my mind, she still is. She's black as the ace o' spades, with huge brown eyes that look like they've been around for ever. Truth is, they have. She's nearly seventy and has an irregular heartbeat. She asked me to call her Wirratye, which means Mother who has lost child, so neither of us can ever forget, even for a day, just what precious time we have to share.

She's finished with the bloke she came here with – he was a no-hoper. She just hadn't got round to going back. It's a big trip for a little old lady, all alone. She's good, though, don't you reckon? Taking a lover, in her late sixties! I can feel your approval, and shrieks of delight!

Gwwirra, my name for Ma, has told me about my father. (Gwwirra stands for Great and Wonderful Wirratye – there had to be a *Great* in there, or I might forget my not-so-humble life with Billy Batchelor!) My father was the station owner, where Gwwirra lived and worked until they told her to go, 'cos she was too old. It was just a couple of months after he died, and that's half a dozen years back now. His name was Jonathon Brady, an Irishman with a big temper and a soft heart, Gwwirra says. They called him Black Jack, but it was an affectionate term, although I can't help thinking maybe it was a nickname for his extracurricular activities.

She's told me how they used to grade the children to be taken to the orphanages and the homes. By degrees of skin colour. If you were light, like me, you went to a church orphanage. (She said if I'd been caught stealing or anything, I'd have had a better chance of not getting sent to an institution, first up. How lucky was I to be sent to Rosey and Nathan Batchelor!) If you were darker, you went to a Government or privately run home that wasn't as well equipped and you didn't get as many offers for adoption.

Gwwirra said she broke her heart ten times a day, the first few years. Then it got easier. She just stopped thinking about it 'cos she couldn't handle the pain any more. All she wanted to know was that I was okay. She asked Black Jack, countless times, but he always said he didn't have any idea, and no way of finding out. He was still demanding sex from her – his wife was an invalid. My mother got pregnant lots of times after my birth – can't remember how many; black women on white stations could all perform abortions by then. Can you imagine what my Gwwirra's life's been like?

I folded the letter quickly, as I always did at that point. It was just too difficult to read on, without pause, without a few tears for all the Ruths who might have been . . . I couldn't finish it again this day. I hauled myself back to the present.

Our own small plot of earth was still lying fallow, following Jock's unsuccessful attempt to make a decision about what to grow on the property. The Government offered special assistance to returned soldiers to go onto the land so we decided to lease out a part of it. We had several enquiries. I selected a young married couple, Patrick and Sylvia Silvester, who'd been on active service in Darwin. They moved into Pharaoh in the autumn, deciding to plant tobacco. We had few frosts and apparently the soil was ideal. We were one of the most efficient tobacco growing countries in the world. With only a thirty-five-hectare holding, and a small part of it already irrigated, the young Silvesters had made a wise choice; the local market was solid and the export market expanding. If they worked hard, there'd be a good living in it for them in a year or two.

The next winter was thankfully short. With the onset of spring, my brain unscrambled its messages and pushed new life and energy back into my muscles, though it took until the summer to walk confidently. The doctors said the energy and re-learning process required to make my legs move again would probably be self-defeating. What they weren't saying out loud was that while the brain was being overworked in one department, it was likely to pack up in another. They must have thought I was basically stupid. I wrote in my diary, 'Prognosis: Determination!' and set to work.

For the first few weeks, I took a lot of falls, but I'd learnt how to fall over the years. With Prinky close by, picking up my crumpled body two or three times a day, I finally got it together. Jock said the radio name they'd given me in Cairo was spot on; I had become Billy Blue. It sent my memories soaring back to days when I had a purpose, a pay packet, a worthwhile position that even afforded me a brush with fame. I missed it, missed the excitement, missed being in the centre of the action.

In one way, I remained the centre of my world, living life from a stately home atop a hill, ten miles from the place of my birth; a million miles from anywhere! Between the mountains and the sea was still between a rock and a hard place, still a godforsaken corridor in northern New South Wales. And some other things were certain too. My homesickness would have made me return, even if I hadn't become ill, just as my body sickness would ensure I remained.

Now that I was well again, what could I do? I had had a long time to think about it, but logical thinking and pain do not make a fecund partnership. I had no more direction on my feet than I'd had on my back.

Just as I was deliberating how long my memory would hold up the joys of being healthy as opposed to the anger of being useless and healthy, Prinky decided to go out to the centre and spend her last days with Amelia, Ruth and Gwwirra. She had long viewed Amelia as a surrogate daughter, and was firmly convinced she would not live past seventy, figuring Ruth's ma might be able to give her a few tips. And like everyone before her who had taken the reins of my life at one time or another, she believed she would be in the way, now that I was up and fighting. I mourned her departure far more than I could have imagined. I didn't really understand why. I barely knew her. Perhaps I was jealous?

It was just Jock and me again. We had drifted out onto a thick, slack wire during my long illness, existing for one another in the evenings, after supper when Prinky had gone to her quarters. She had escaped as soon as she possibly could since we'd turned the third and fourth bedrooms and second bathroom into a self-contained bed-sit. Some nights we chatted, though I had lost interest in his work and he knew it. It was difficult to get excited about a school house and today's kids. Perhaps I was jealous of his life too, in charge of other people's children? I didn't care to think about it too much.

We began again tentatively, with tiffs and small, unfinished arguments linking our sentences, maintaining communication of a sort. There was no doubt Jock was somewhat sorry to see the end of Prinky. While she approved of no man, and was scornful of his dedication to study and career, as the truth would out after she'd gone, she apparently got through about his general neglect and overall uselessness, without completely alienating him. He appeared to have switched off much of the time, but it soon became apparent that the old Prinky had once again left her mark.

I dispensed with Banduk and Jabaljari, telling them it would only be temporary. I intended to return to work. Jock insisted on helping me around the place, including learning how to cook. It was most annoying, but he was so placidly willing to be taught that in spite of myself, I started to enjoy showing him the ropes of running a house and kitchen. Sylvia Silvester (she got the nickname of SS when I'm sure she would have much preferred to be called Mrs Silvester), was eight months pregnant by the time I was back in full swing, so I stepped in to feed the plantation help for a few months. Each night when Jock arrived home from school, he'd get into the kitchen down at Pharaoh with me, peeling potatoes, skinning chickens and rabbits, cutting up vegetables for the soup and washing the baking pans from my afternoon cook-ups. By Christmas, our circumspect abrasiveness had ironed itself out without major eruption. We were the best of friends again.

Jock's sexual appetite returned to roughly the level it had been from the start – moderate. I was neither particularly willing nor particularly unwilling. It all seemed a bit pointless. The doctors had made it clear it would be a miracle if I ever conceived. On this point, the evidence was overwhelmingly in their favour. Conception besides, Jock's lack of experience and skill did not exactly make me look forward to the *quickies* we managed to have now and then and when I added up the years since I'd been involved in highly athletic passion with Harry Carmichael, it appeared to me I didn't have much experience to write home about any more either. It didn't really matter. I didn't blame Jock for our ordinary sex life; I had no passionate expectations in the first place. If I'd wanted it changed, I could have forced us to talk about it, I suppose. The same must surely be said for him. We still kissed and hugged a lot, in the brotherly way of the times.

What I was beginning to blame him for was my isolation and purposeless life. The years stretched unremittingly before me, years that would not all be as good as '52 had begun. I was not a do-gooder like my mother. I could not take up causes for the sake of them, rattle charity tins or make buns and bed jackets for the poor and the sick. I had to *do* something! SS had her baby boy and returned to the kitchen. I was no longer even needed to cook soup and stews for the farm hands.

'If we were in the city, I'd be able to get a job by now,' I started cornering Jock after tea. 'Lots of married women are working in Sydney and Brisbane now, even those who don't need the money.' It had become a familiar opening gambit. Jock's eyes would drop to the *Kurra Mail*, trying to pretend it wasn't happening again. We had the money to go to one of the cities and be there, on the spot, when a job came up, but that would put Jock in the situation I was currently in. We both knew it would take months to find something suitable and it was not a consideration for me to go alone. Apart from the fact that it would kill Ma and Pa, it would be unfair to put Jock through the worry, not knowing when my health might take a turn for the worse.

'I was talking with Figgy on my way home,' Jock mentioned casually one evening. The news had just finished and the ABC *Playhouse* had begun. I'd been looking forward to it all day.

'I particularly wanted to hear this, dear,' I informed him.

'Figgy was saying James is heading back to Sydney next week. They've offered him a job back at the *Bully*. It's been a long wait for him.'

'What do you mean?' I was only half listening.

'Well, he's been back from the front six years and it's the first break he's had. City papers don't forgive easily.'

He had my attention now. I'd read of it, but somehow it hadn't registered. It had simply not occurred to me that I knew a qualified man, who'd served in the war, who hadn't been given a break either. My long introspection had thrown my perspective and made me pitifully self-centred.

'What's Figgy going to do without him? He'll have to throw in the towel, won't he? He must be at least eighty! Ma said only the other day that Constance would be sixty-five if she was a day.' I looked at the newspaper I'd held in my hands for the best part of four decades, felt the tears springing to my eyes.

Kurra was dying. It had little to offer young

people in the way of work, the beach had eroded, the streets and houses were so old and tired, a barrel of paint could not save them now. Every second shop in Oodoolay Street remained closed after the war, St Matthew's Church was falling down around our ears and even St Pat's was in need of repairs. Who would be interested in coming to the district to run a local rag that hadn't made a profit in years?

'Why don't you buy it?'

I looked at him, stunned. 'Who, me? What do I know about newspapers?'

'Wouldn't take long to pick up. Imagine it! All the issues you could raise. It'd be like having your own radio programme running twenty-four hours a day!'

The idea was beginning to take hold. 'I couldn't run a business that didn't make a profit,' I said firmly. 'How could I make it run at a profit? I'll have to give it some thought . . .'

'Don't take too long, Lovely. Figgy is planning to advertise in the city dailies next weekend. He's throwing in the house rent-free to make it a bit more attractive. They're planning to visit Saucy in Charleston and expect to be away twelve months. He might just find somebody prepared to take it on, for a year's stint anyway.'

'One of the smartest things I ever did was marry you, Jock O'Ryan,' I said appreciatively, and I meant it too.

The office was unseasonally hot. I wondered whether somebody would call Sister Mac out of retirement if I turned on the fan. It was the spring of '53.

The revamped *Kurra Mail* was at last on the streets of Tarrenbonga and Port Hedley, though it wasn't a free press any more. Interestingly, the nominal charge seemed to make people value it more.

I turned on the fan. It was impossible to think in such an oppressive atmosphere. My off-sider, Betty Frieden, a newcomer to Kurra, gave me a cross-eyed look, but kept on with her typesetting. She was one of those lucky breaks, Betty. The wife of our first full-time chemist, she'd worked for the *Melbourne Age* for years, knew everything about newspapers and their advertisers; knew the urgency, the breaking of stories, the adrenaline. We had plenty of news, but what was selling papers was escapist and distant. Anything too close to home had no appeal. What would I use for the lead tomorrow?

Elizabeth II had been crowned, our young princess who drove trucks during the war. Nobody could get enough of her. We could run something every day and sell out. All the events around town, no matter how small, were opened and closed with three cheers: God Save the Queen! God Save the Queen! God Save the Queen! The Armistice was signed in Korea and the boys came home again. Nobody seemed to care much. Australia was selected by Britain as the perfect place for atomic testing. Nobody seemed to care much about that either. I started digging around trying to get a lead on what the population did care about these days. Apart from God and the Queen, we seemed to be living in a vacuum. Was this the remission, before the next assault?

I thought about Jock's challenge to me years ago. The *Mail* was the perfect vehicle to begin a campaign to make our white schools bilingual. I'd written to Ruth, asking her advice. Since Amelia had joined her, their school at the foot of the Olgas was attracting anything upwards of forty kids every week. Rosa and Christopher, Amelia's boy, were fluent in English and several Koorie dialects; Rosa was nearly old enough for school in the Alice, and Christopher Dakin-Moon, born during one of my long relapses, must be about four. With long periods between communications and both mothers intent on keeping white materialism to a minimum, birthdays come and go, unheralded. Ruth wrote back, encouraging me to try, but was unsure of the success my campaign was likely to have. By the time her letter arrived, I was no longer sure the idea would even merit serious consideration. Who needs skills to communicate with a minority race you can keep oppressed?

Betty asked me if I'd like a glass of water. I was feeling rather odd. She packed it with ice. I ran a piece across the back of my neck. I still didn't have tomorrow's lead story.

'You all right, Billy?'

'Yes, Betty, fine thanks. It's warm in here, isn't it?'

She appeared confused. 'It's probably the smoke,' she said.

What the population was hungry for was laughs; life had been too hard for too long. *The Goon Show* was all the rage with the young. The manic boyscout Bluebottle was being mimicked in every pub from Hobart to the far north of Scotland. It was all a load of gibberish to the uninitiated. I had a secret dream I shared with no one that one day Jock and I would go to England and meet the Goons, especially Peter Sellers. *The Glums* had developed a cult following too, but my favourite was Tony Hancock's *Educating Archie*. Archie was an opinionated fool, a pretentious, social-climbing snob. Everyone was ignorant, except him. There were a few Archies in Kurra. I decided to run Tony Hancock's life story as the lead and make a decision about bilingual schools later.

'Betty, we'll run with Hancock. I think I'll just go and lie down in the back room for a minute or two. I feel a bit faint.'

'You're as pale as I've ever seen you. I'll call Mackie.'

'You'll do no such thing! I'll be perfectly all right when I've had a short rest.'

She helped me onto the bed at the precise moment my brain decided to bring up lunch. It had been a lovely lunch too. 'I'm so sorry, Betty,' I lurched forward, breakfast following lunch. She began mopping up. I felt instantly better, but still couldn't breathe properly. I staggered to the back door, a north wind howling through the trees, ripping the wire door out of my hands to crash against the wall. A faint memory of another time, long long ago . . . I slipped away to meet it.

'Well, lovey, this is a fine state o'affairs!' the comforting voice greeted me. She was old now, but she had aged well.

'Hello, Sister Mac. Why do you still move so quickly when you hear I've fainted? It's absolutely silly.'

'Yeah, I know. Got into the habit, I s'pose. But ya bin asleep two hours, Billy. Not ya normal behaviour, is it? I called Dr May Ling. She's comin' in ta see ya.'

'You seem amazingly cheerful, Sister Mac. I suppose new scores for old melodies are the stuff you medicos dream on, eh? The challenge! What part of the brain has packed it in this time? "Interesting, but we have variations on vomiting today. She bought up her lunch first this time." Fascinating. "Slept for two hours after fainting today." It's riveting, Sister! I can't wait for the new diagnosis.'

Dr May Ling arrived. She did surgery twice a

week at the condemned house where I was born, though it had been renovated a couple of times since then. We could really call it an honourable bush hospital these days. She began prodding my stomach and lower abdomen.

'What on earth are you doing?' I opened my eyes with a start.

'When was your period due?' she asked lightly.

'I have no idea,' I replied. 'Haven't taken any notice for ages.'

'I see,' she said slowly. 'Shut the door, Mackie. I'm going to do an internal, Mrs O'Ryan.'

My mind had already departed for the land of bedrooms, injections, isolation and pain. I closed my eyes and tried to relax. It was an absurd instruction, like being told to behave like a big girl when you're bent over double and the teacher is about to whack you on the bottom in front of the whole class.

'You can open your eyes, Mrs O'Ryan,' the cool Dr May Ling drolled on. It must be good to have so much power. I envied her in a way, though not particularly, this day. This morning I was a professional business woman too. 'Mackie, would you ring Mr O'Ryan at the school house and get him over here, please? I'd like to speak to Mr and Mrs O'Ryan together.'

Mackie obeyed, her worn-out face beaming like a cat on heat.

'What on earth is going on, Doctor? I insist on knowing immediately. You can tell me again when Jock gets here. Pretend I'm dumb and don't grasp anything the first time. That shouldn't be difficult – you doctors think all your patients are dumb.' I sat up awkwardly and straightened my clothes. Her thin black eyebrows raised and the deep-set, Chinese eyes began to sparkle. She helped me to my feet and shook my hand.

'Congratulations, Mrs O'Ryan. I'm happy to inform you you're at least three months pregnant.'
Like any normal woman might do, I fainted.

## EIGHTEEN

# 1954

A good many people were shocked when they learnt I was having a baby, but almost everyone was appalled when they realized I intended to continue working until the birth.

Quite a few expressed predictable sentiments: 'Just what I would have expected of her!' It was difficult to know if anyone actually meant it in anything other than a derogatory sense but it made for some distraction from the hysterical world communist scare sweeping across the Pacific. I wrote Ruth that my pregnancy was fast replacing McCarthyism as the most popular topic along Oodoolay Street.

Ma and Pa had long since given up trying to influence me on major issues, but it was easy to see they were none too happy, and Sister Mac firmly believed I should spend my confinement in bed.

SS at Pharaoh decided she would be doing all the washing and ironing for the period of my confinement (though we now had a twin-tub washing machine), and Ma had taken the decision she would be moving in with us at The Brolga for the last and first few weeks, before and after the birth.

While the women busied themselves with the sewing and knitting of little clothes, the men lingered at Shaft's to discuss the O'Ryan miracle – and the risks. Jock and Pa were quick to inform about my dubious celebrity status. 'She's gonna be in 'er fortieth year, I'd reckon,' one old-timer surmised accurately.

'No!' gasped a mate, expressing the disbelief of the newer blokes.

'Gotta be! She wus the same age as Amelia Moon and the first little Frannie O'Ryan. Gotta be turnin' forty in '54, I'd swear me life on a pack o' Bibles.'

'Shit,' echoed the bar.

'She's gotta lot o' guts,' piped up Mugga, a worthy postman if ever there was one.

'Ain't 'er guts I'm worried about!' roared Michael Shaft, Pigeon's bastard son, ensuring a good laugh from the regulars. Michael didn't have the timing of his late father when it came to cracking jokes, but he enjoyed telling them enormously and usually got at least a round of chuckles from his customers.

Pa was not much of a drinker – had never been a man's man in that sense – yet the announcement of my impending motherhood had lifted him into another plane. His impending grandfather status overwhelmed him. He ambled down to the pub every other night, as fast as his walking stick would take him. Ma was quite disgusted, of course, though it was difficult to know what aspect of his behaviour was getting her down the most.

'He's come over weird all of a sudden, Rachel,' she moaned, dropping into the *Mail* one afternoon on her way home with the groceries.

'How do you mean, Ma?'

'Huh! You know men. Who knows? You'd think he was having the baby himself! I can't believe how childish he's become, drinking and all. It's positively embarrassing, that's what it is.'

I couldn't help smiling. Nobody could mix metaphors like Ma.

'Never mind, Ma. It'll be over soon.'

'Oh my dear! You're not threatening, are you?'

'No, no, Ma! Pregnancies take nine months,

remember? It'll be over soon. Do try to relax,' I pleaded pointlessly.

Dr May Ling told us we had a 50/50 chance of a happy ending. My age and the MS combination were unknown factors, so when it was all boiled down, 50/50 was utter guess work on her part. It may even be medical hyperbole, since our chances might more realistically be 40/60 or 20/80? I decided to strike a blow for motherhood and female instinct and call the odds at 90/10.

'It would be a foolish man who'd argue with you on that platform,' Jock smiled wondrously, looking upwards to the heavens.

'So you'll agree that I should continue working, as long as I'm coping and not getting too tired, dear?'

He took a deep breath, his shoulders heaved. He breathed out slowly, satisfyingly. The message he conveyed was more than an acceptance of inevitability or fait accompli; he was profoundly grateful to be able to put his trust in my faith. He finally believed that I could do anything I wanted to do, provided I wanted it badly enough. He saw no value in constructing barriers, by way of antiquated male, or medical opinion, any more than he viewed my work at the *Mail* as stressful or tiring. Since I never complained about it, how could it be?

'I'd rather see you driving a car and pushing a pen, Lovely, than doing housework and standing for hours in the kitchen preparing meals. You're close to the hospital too,' he'd added enthusiastically. Perhaps that was the point? If he didn't believe I was going to make the distance in the first place, why bother to argue the toss: 'as long as the business needs her, she'll cope with the loss more easily'. He was desperately afraid, too.

For the next three months, I cared little for the public opinion raging around me. Since I was violently ill every afternoon around three o'clock, as well as most evenings, straight after dinner, it was possible to plan my days for maximum results during the vertical hours, leaving me little time left to worry about anything. By the time the afternoon and night sickness had passed, the town had stopped criticizing me and begun suggesting names to Jock.

'I suppose we should think about a name, Lovely?' he raised one evening. 'You are getting extremely large, dear . . .' I sighed, patting my moving stomach with a degree of fondness. Half my life I'd been dreaming about this baby, yet the reality of the last few months had altered my perceptions, somewhat.

The way I've always figured it, it's hard to get the meaning of things when the fun and celebrations are at their height. The months of vomiting had helped me, earthed me, for the terrifying, wondrous tasks ahead. Most afternoons I took a long walk along the stony beach to the start of the rock flats that lead out to Bunyip Point, thinking about our baby, wondering what sort of a life he'd have.

I picked up a shell and listened to the murmur of the sea's insouciant rhythm, rolling out for another long swim to another shore, returning again, washed up on the beach, undefeated. I watched it swell once more, rejuvenated, rolling back the tide like a magic carpet. If I could steal a shell full of the sea's spirit and hold it close to my nervous heart . . . if I could keep Ruth's red soil from slipping through my fingers, I might make me a mother, a good mother. An old mother?

I had begun sending up daily prayers: 'God, let me have some beating sunshine before You send the rain?' and 'Please, God, let him be healthy, that's all I ask.'

As often happens with habitual prayer, one thing leads to another and you find you're flowing freely with the requests and ebbing rather badly in the worship and grace departments. I went from my outrageously generous offer to God to do anything He liked with me, provided the baby was healthy, to attempting to strike a bargain that I felt would be fairer to all parties concerned. The furthest thing from my mind was to question God's omnipotence over all things; all I was asking Him to do was turn a blind eye for the twinkle of a light second. 'Dear God, give me the first five years because he needs his mother on her feet for a decent start. I'll cope with whatever You throw me after that, honestly I will!'

Every afternoon I walked, the time rushed out ahead of me. Jock would drive down to the edge of the track after school, blowing the horn, always relieved to see me smiling and waving.

'Looks like we're in for a summer storm,' he said one evening in mid-February, as he helped me up the path to the car. 'Heaven knows, we need the rain. The Silvesters will be pleased. Micky could do with it too.' Even the tracks to the beach were parched and burnt, making the climb back to the road more difficult each day. 'This walk might be getting a bit beyond you, Lovely? Perhaps a walk around the property from now on, eh?' I wanted to argue of course, but he was right. It was getting down to the water's edge and back up to the road that was nearly killing me.

I looked back longingly at the vista, realizing it might be many months before I saw it again. I was nearly eight months pregnant. The sea would have to wait. I was the sea now – the sea and the earth and the sky!

The summer storm Jock predicted gathered quickly in the heavens. By nightfall, Kurra and surrounding districts were under siege. A tropical cyclone was rushing towards the south Queensland coast, packing wind speeds of 200 miles an hour. We were ten miles inland but took the warnings seriously, battening down for gale-force winds. We would escape the full force of the storm, but expected to be sideswiped.

The Pickle River was a sluggish trickle you could ride your bicycle over when we returned from Kurra that afternoon. By next morning, following twelve hours of torrential rain, it was a raging torrent. We were marooned at the top of a floating hill, the same hill that had saved the Prescotts' lives on Black Tuesday, twenty-seven years ago. Jock and Patrick Silvester struggled to tie down the pumps and irrigation system; SS and the baby and I stood on the verandah helplessly, watching our world floating by.

On the far side of the river, a family of petrified cattle hung onto life on a small mount of raised earth. The winds had eased. A news flash declared the cyclone was turning back to sea. The worst was over. Out of nowhere, a bridge swept by across the river, crashing into trees that had stood for hundreds of years, ripping them to shreds with a hungry ease. The cattle would not have known what happened. Dumped unceremoniously, the bridge and mangled trees continued on their way. The banks widened and collapsed simultaneously. Jock and Patrick were forced back up the hill. They moved the chooks, the goats and Butcher into our backyard, joining us on the verandah.

'The wind has changed,' I informed them quickly. 'The cyclone's turned out to sea again. This should be the worst of it.'

Jock nodded grimly. 'When have you ever known the weather men to be right when nature loses control? Let's telephone Ma and Pa, make sure they're all right. We'd better call Micky and Thea too.'

He picked up the phone and turned the ringer a few times. The line was dead. It wasn't long since the lines had gone through.

'Marvellous, isn't it?' Jock uttered with an attempt at bravado he did not feel. 'We create modern technology to make the difference in an emergency and when the emergency comes, it doesn't work.'

'Ma and Pa will be all right, I think.' I spoke my thoughts to add moral support. 'They can get to the Town Hall pretty quickly. I am worried about Micky and Thea and the children though. Mini Mini is always the first to flood. Micky should have filled in Billadambo years ago and dug one further out.'

'That won't make no difference, Mrs O.,' said Patrick. 'They probably like it close in case of fire anyways.' He shouldn't have said that. It made me worry more. Mini Mini had not been lucky down the years. Jock sensed my fears and put a comforting arm around me. 'God wouldn't be that cruel . . .' he murmured.

'I hope you're right,' I replied less confidently, thinking of Thea, who was pregnant again. Just then, the phone rang.

'Ah, we're alive!' Jock rushed to pick it up. 'Yes, hello . . . Micky, hello . . . You all okay? . . . Missing? She can't be missing. When did you last see her? . . . Oh my God! . . . Don't give up, don't give up. She's a fighter, she'll be there somewhere . . . Micky? Micky! Hello, hello? Damn. Lost him.' He replaced the earphone, rewound the handle and tried for another connection. There was no response. The exchange girls would be flat out coping at all.

'For heaven't sake, Jock, who's missing? Sarah? Frannie? Frannie missing? God, no . . .' We stared at one another in silence. The radio flashed another newsbreak. The cyclone was on its way again, straight for the coast. This was the one they'd been dreading; it would be the worst in eighty years before it blew itself out, they said.

I was grateful my baby lived an insulated existence in my womb, protected from all external influences. That was one thing the medical profession had been absolutely sure about since scientists had been studying the unborn. Jock nervously lit us both a cigarette.

The rain began again, swept in by a howling wind. Jock tried Micky again. The line remained dead.

'Let's have a beer,' suggested Patrick.

'Good idea,' Jock responded, moving to the refrigerator with an inexplicable sense of urgency. As we waited for him to pour, we heard the crack of a stockwhip close by. The first bottle smashed to the floor. The telephone cable had been whipped from its great tree trunk poles and was floating down the river, dragging a fence with it. The fence became a Pied Piper. The poles were bending, snapping, crashing into the mess of gathering debris, hearing the call of the fence, straightening up into smaller soldiers, marching onward to some distant war.

'I can't bear to look!' cried SS, sheltered in the hub of her husband's muscular shoulder. Thousands of tobacco leaves expired before us, drowning like tea leaves in a large, brown, swirling pot. Patrick was devastated, his usually cheerful, ruddy complexion drained of colour and hope.

The roar of the rain and the wind on our galvanized roof increased, amplifying the fear in all our hearts. The water chundered into the downpipe, cascading over the spouting and the tanks, rising around Pharaoh at a terrifying pace. Night fell early, crushing sheets of grey rain hastening its fall. We picked at our tea, then slipped into a game of cards. The radio continued in the background, the news more depressing by the hour. We tried to keep one another's spirits up, but every sentence thrust the knife in deeper. As so often happens when everyone is walking on glass to avoid worrying one another unnecessarily, the truth tends to emerge more loudly. Perhaps there was just too much tragic history of nature's wrath in our past to be safe on any subject. SS knew little of the details of the past anyway.

'If that was Birrie Bridge that floated by before, they'll be able to erect something temporary for Kurra until they can build a new one, won't they?'

'Oh yeah, easy,' replied her husband. 'They could swing a footbridge across, a hundred yards from the station, near the railway gates. Should have moved that bridge years ago anyways.'

The world began to spin for me, visions of Joey in the water tank near Birrie Bridge, with the fire all around . . . visions of Ma and Pa and Sister Mac, trapped at Rosebery, underwater, drowning . . . my best friend, Frances, caught out at Mini Mini in the Great Fire. Coming home from the funeral, Chocolate dead on the hearth. I reached down to Chocolate Two. She was at my feet, alive, chewing the mat.

Watching the water rising had mesmerized me, exhausted me, overwhelmed my large, tired body. I put my head down on the table and took some deep breaths. Jock was at my side, speaking, but I couldn't understand his words. I think he was praying. I came out of it quickly.

'I'm not going into labour, Jock, so don't even entertain the thought,' I said.

'How can you be sure?' squealed SS.

'Because I've made up my mind, that's why,' I replied stubbornly. 'I am not having this baby until I know that everyone is alive and well, and that's final. This bloody country, with its fires and droughts and floods! We are a contrary race, aren't we? We love the things that treat us badly . . .' I faded out again.

When I returned to consciousness, I was in bed and

Jock was perched on the windowsill, watching. I lay perfectly still, sorting out the confusion in my brain. I was in bed. No pain. It was light. Jock, watching. The rain? Was it raining? The wind had dropped.

'Did they find Frannie?' I asked loudly, surprised at the sound of my voice. 'I'm not dreaming, am I?'

'No, Lovely, you're awake. You look okay. How do you feel?'

'Have they found Frannie?' I asked again.

'It's only a few hours since you sent to sleep, dear. We don't have any telephone wires, remember?'

'Well, can't you take the car into town and . . .?' It came to me then. It all came back. 'Is it over? Has it passed?'

'Yes, Lovely. It's over. I think they must have blasted the river upstream somewhere to take in more water. The levels are going down quite rapidly this morning, too quickly without help.' The morning news came on. Three children had drowned. My God, three children. The army had been called in to evacuate the farming population around Maclean, twenty miles to our north. The second news bulletin reported eighteen dead, 'and mounting,' Bryce Danielson read with a tremor.

'Why didn't we invest in a bloody boat, Billy?' Jock paced the room, looking out across the moving panorama with increasing frustration. I held my tongue. When I'd suggested it last winter, he'd said he'd think about it, make a decision. Never did.

'How long will we be stranded?' I asked, hauling myself out of bed sideways. I felt bigger and older than I'd ever have believed it possible to feel.

'I don't know, Billy,' he snapped.

I went to the toilet and washed my face. SS and Patrick were awake, and playing with their baby. In my heart of hearts, I knew Jock and I were not going to be permitted a happy start with ours. It was enough that we would be thus blessed. We would have to pay dearly for the blessing. I could smell death, hovering, floating outside our huge windows, along with the rest of the junk; old tyres, oil drums, a wardrobe, one tiny slipper, half a haystack, half a car, a woman's jumper, a dead cat. The farmers' world was floating by . . . his tip, his livelihood, his life.

The humidity was unbearable. 'Thousands of homeless,' Bryce Danielson continued. 'Major roads and railway lines completely wiped out . . .'

'Jock, I'll die if we have to wait another day for news of Ma and Pa, and Than and . . . Frannie.'

'Yes, I know you will.' He wiped his brow. It was early morning and the air was already suffocating. The humidity was probably as high as the temperature.

We put our heads together and decided the horses would get through. The water was subsiding rapidly. Jock and Patrick should certainly attempt it. It was agreed. As we talked, a black snake curled its way onto the verandah. Jock got up quietly, reaching for the rifle by the front door. He stepped outside and fired one shot, accurately. 'Be careful.' I couldn't resist the age-old warning as they pulled out, a little after ten o'clock. The horses moved forward at a walk, splashing their way out of sight.

Sylvia Silvester and I had nothing in common. On this day, we shared our lives. It was the first time and would be the last. The Silvesters had not taken insurance. They would not be able to pay us next month's rent. They were bankrupt and SS was pregnant again. Patrick would have to go back to jackerooing. Their big chance to make it on their own floated past our windows. She'd go home to her parents in Bendigo and he'd go up north, cutting cane, if there was any cane left to cut. Four hundred miles of coastline had been slashed into one long, sandy quarry. He might be lucky to get a job cleaning up.

I was already convinced that Frannie was dead. I tried to psyche myself into the worst possible scenario, but couldn't. If Than was dead, I couldn't tell Ruth, not by letter. I would have to lie by letter for as long as it took, until I could fly to the centre to tell her. I had the darkest conviction in my soul that because she'd been allowed to find her Gwwirra, it would be at the cost of her son's life. But my brain could not accept that Ma and Pa were gone. It was not going to be like that – not for them.

We got through the afternoon, talking to one another, listening to ourselves. My baby kicked unmercifully, leaving me exhausted and grossly uncomfortable long before nightfall.

'Where are they? Where are they?' I began pacing.

'Sit down, Billy.' SS was stern. 'You're making me dizzy,' she added. I sat. I was making myself sick. The water had lowered sufficiently for SS to venture out to feed the goats and Butcher. The chooks were scattered; it was impossible to get to the henhouse. 'Leave it to the men, SS,' I yelled from the verandah. 'They can wait until morning.'

Chocolate Two went for an investigatory swim, returning excitedly, a large dead beast hanging from her mouth. 'Chocolate Two! What have you got? Drop it, at once!' I screamed, hanging over the back verandah railing with recalcitrant power. The poor thing dropped it in slow motion, gazing up at me with mournful eyes. It was her best find ever. A dead platypus! What spoilsports humans are. We watched it float away.

On the distant grey horizon, three riders came into view. It took a few minutes to work them out. Patrick led with Dr May Ling clinging on grimly behind him, followed by Jock, then Than. He was alive! What could his presence mean? Was it worse than I had dared imagine? 'SS!' I yelled to the storeroom below. 'The men are back!'

Than pulled up, with Patrick and Dr May Ling a little behind Jock, who leapt over the steps, bundling me into his arms.

'Ma's fine. Sister Mac's fine. The family are all okay. They found Frannie. She'd fallen asleep in a wardrobe.'

'She'd what?' I stammered.

'She'd gone to sit in the wardrobe to escape the terrible roaring noises of the wind and rain, then fallen asleep. She slept through the entire search late into the evening. Woke the whole house in the middle of the night, banging on the door, which she'd shut behind her, screaming she needed to go to the toilet!'

'I don't believe it!' I sat down heavily. The relief was overwhelming. There were still some questions that needed answers though. 'Why did Than come back with you?'

'Mini Mini's underwater. Thea's suffering terrible morning sickness and can barely cope, what with Frannie and the mess they've got out there. The girls have stayed with Micky but Thea's staying over at Rosebery tonight. It's company for your ma too. Than wanted to see you, so he'll stay over and pick up Thea in the morning. You don't mind, dear, do you?'

'Of course I don't mind,' I answered cautiously, wondering what was being kept from me. The Brolga had never been so well patronized. 'Are you sure you don't mind, Lovely?' Jock pressed.

Than bounded into the family room and gave me a hug. He was in his twenty-third year; it was hard to believe. It seemed such a short time ago that he was born. He had been blessed, or cursed, with his parents' good looks – and he knew it. His dark face was offset by huge black pupils set in pure white eyes, square jaw and unlined, shining skin. He stood six feet tall, muscular like his father from years of farming, the debonair, casual insolence developed to a finer tune than Micky had ever managed.

'Aunty Billy, you look terrific preggo, ya really do! At least you're above the waterline here. We had tea last night with our feet completely submerged. It come up right into the kitchen, Billy, you shoulda' seen it!'

'It came up, Than, not come up.' I shook my head. He was bright, but lazy. Micky had never known better to correct him, and it was far too late now, but Ruth would kill me if I didn't still try on the rare occasions I saw him. I wondered at Thea's complaisance. Though she had taken the young Than into her heart, she seemed to lose interest as her own brood multiplied. It was hard to deny the probability that she'd shown early commitment in order to secure Micky's hand.

Dr May Ling accepted a sherry gratefully. She had been on her feet twenty-four hours. I figured her visit with us was as much an excuse for a rest as it was to check on my health.

'I was absolutely sure something terrible had happened when I saw you all riding in. Just shows, women's instincts aren't always right,' I laughed, charging my glass in a broad sweep around the room. Than gave me a lingering stare. Jock looked away. I felt a cool wind blowing around my feet. 'What is it?' I demanded in a small voice.

Dr May Ling scrunched her high-set eyes until they looked like two stitched gashes across her forehead. 'At the height of the cyclone, your father had a heart attack, Mrs O'Ryan. He's very ill – in hospital. I'm afraid his condition is critical, but he is stable. Dr Marsden is with him.'

'Who's Dr Marsden?' I asked wildly, clutching my stomach as though it was about to fall out.

'He's a heart specialist. He came over with me from Tarrenbonga, as soon as we got the cyclone alert for the coast. The flying doctor couldn't have made it this far south, too busy, and in this weather . . .' She spared me a condescending statement about how fortunate we were to have such a good man on the spot.

'What are his chances?' My own heart was pounding.

'It will be twenty-four hours before we know his prognosis.'

'I must see him. Jock?'

'He's not conscious at the moment,' Dr May Ling intercepted, 'and Marsden won't allow visitors yet anyway, apart from your mother. I certainly wouldn't be allowing you to travel through the floods either. I'm afraid you'll have to sweat it out, Mrs O'Ryan.'

I was certainly sweating – badly, and breathing heavily too; my stomach rose and fell, rose and fell. Dr May Ling wanted to examine me. The baby was kicking ferociously.

'Oh Pa, don't leave yet, please don't go yet . . . I need you. God, don't take his life for my baby's. It's not fair, not fair!'

Without Pa, nothing would ever look the same again. But it would feel the same, as long as I could feel. The sensations, the colours in his eyes, the pats on the back, the gentle chastisements, the shy statements of love. I will not lose him, nothing of his stature could ever be lost. I will cry, but not in grief. I will keep him close to me, lifelong close and he will walk with me, talk with me, help me bring up my baby. And when his body is gone, he will help me love my husband more truly . . . inside my head, the conflict will go away. Losing the conflict, waiting for the peace. Waiting and pain, pain and waiting.

'There is a very strong history of twins in your family, isn't there?' Dr May Ling punctured the great mound of flesh in front of her with a cold stethoscope.

'Why, y-y-yes,' I stuttered. My water broke.

'I was a twin,' said Jock in a rasping whisper, 'and Micky and Thea have two sets of twins.'

'Jock and Than, help Mrs O'Ryan into the bedroom. Mr and Mrs Silvester, we are going to need lots of boiling water, towels, sheets.'

'Am I having twins?' I cried, the pains closing in now.

'I picked up two heartbeats, Mrs O'Ryan.'

'Jock?'

'I'm here, Lovely, I'm here.'

'She shall be saved in childbearing.' 1 Timothy 2:15 – how many times had I heard it? Saved? The Madonna and Child propaganda machine, written by all of God's men. It is wonderful to be a mother, a beautiful experience to give birth. Paul, you fool! You liar! What would you know?

Motherhood! Who needs it? Women don't need to be mothers any more than they need spaghetti. But when you're in a world where everyone is eating spaghetti, thinking they want it, need it, you start thinking so too. What has motherhood done for women? Cleaned up sex? Cleaned up women from Eve's evil transgressions? Who set it all up as Eve's fault? Men! Who planned for women to be the mothers? Men! A father and a son, no less. How much more evidence is required to prove the barbaric cruelty of the beneficiaries of woman's pain?

Romance has contaminated science. Women have childbearing equipment. To choose not to use that equipment is no more blocking what is instinctive than a man with muscle equipment choosing not to be a weightlifter. I was biting on a rag. I chewed it clean in half. Jock replaced it with a flannel. How much longer? I didn't think I could take much more. I'd never thought of myself as a coward.

'How much longer . . .?' I cried out.

Black rain, pouring down. There was no more pain, just a long tunnel, light, golden light at the end. My soul, dead and risen, floating away with two little boys, baby boys, in search of their lives. Robbed before they'd begun. Waiting to lose. I was in Egypt where no one is afraid of death. Ruth was with me, strengthening me with her laws, the impersonal force that makes it impossible to be afraid of death. Pa was there, waiting. He was afraid. Afraid of death.

'Billy, Billy, wake up, darling, wake up!' Pa was leaning over me, alive. He was alive! I was alive. I could hear screaming. Babies screaming. I looked up at him joyfully. 'You're all going to be fine, Lovely,' he said. It wasn't Pa at all. It was only Jock. My eyes filled with tears, unbeckoned. 'Don't be sad, dear. You're all going to be fine.'

'Pa?' I whispered.

'No, it's Jock. Can you see me now?' Fading in, fading out.

'Jock?'

'Yes, darling.'

'The boys?'

'The boys?' He looked furtively at Dr May Ling. She came forward, bending over me, close, coming into focus. 'Congratulations, Mrs O'Ryan. You have two beautiful daughters. About five pounds each, I'd say. You were a very good girl.'

She put them in my arms. I began to laugh. I knew it was odd behaviour, but I couldn't help it. 'I'm nearly forty years of age and I'm a good girl, no, a *very* good girl, for delivering ten pounds of baby girls into the world! Isn't that silly? Look at you, my God, look at you, little ones . . . You won't believe what you've let yourselves in for, you couldn't possibly know . . .' I laughed hysterically. Dr May Ling tried to calm me.

Jock waved her aside. 'Let's leave her for a few minutes, Doctor. I don't think we can possibly know what she's going through right now.'

# NINETEEN

# 1954...

'Hello there,' chirped Sister Mac in her scratchy, masculine voice. 'We've 'ad a bit of a crisis but ya bin 'oldin' ya own the last week or so. It was touch an' go, lovey, at first.'

'The babies?' I tried to sit up, but it was no good.

'Mathilda and Jenna are doin' wonderfully well. I'll get 'em for ya.'

'She's bin dreamin' of the birth again,' I heard her telling someone at the door. 'A lot go back to the birthin' when they're close to the end, ya know. She kept askin' 'bout Jenna. Can't say I blame 'er – we don't need 'er goin' into shock again.'

'Will she understand how it's happened?'

'Oh yes, Rosa, she'll understand all right. Ain't no flies on your Aunty Billy. Still, Jock's takin' it hard . . .'

A dark young girl entered with Sister Mac, holding a dark-skinned baby. Sister Mac held a fair one.

'Where's Jock?' I asked suddenly, unsure I wanted to be alone.

'He's at school, love. Ya bin out of it nigh on six months now.'

'Six months?'

'Your ma an' I bin lookin' after you and the babies. James took leave from the *Bully* to keep the paper goin'. Everything's okay. We bin copin'.'

The girl placed the dark baby in my right arm. 'This is Jenna,' she said.

Sister Mac sat on the edge of the bed. 'An' this 'ere's Mathilda,' she announced proudly, placing the fair one in my left.

They were beautiful. They were both beautiful.

'A throwback from Jock's father?' I whispered. They looked almost identical, except . . . they were different colours. It was quite odd. Neither of them looked like Jock or me.

'I'll explain it to ya, Billy, if ya want.'

'Yes, later. Just let me hold them.'

I was conscious, but strangely high. I wondered what they had me on. There were two drips in place and I could feel a catheter. I was grossly uncomfortable – perhaps I had bedsores? There was something in my mind I badly wanted to ask, but it wouldn't surface. I couldn't think beyond Jenna . . . Mathilda. They were so tiny. How could they be six months old?

'Ya pa's 'oldin' up, Billy. Touch an' go for 'im too, but 'e's 'angin' on. Kurra's bin prayin' like it never prayed before, love, and . . .'

'Where's Ruth?' I asked immediately. The sun was shining. My babies were asleep in a little cot under the windowsill.

'Hello. She's in the centre, Aunty Billy. With Grannie.'

'Who are you?'

'I'm Rosa.'

'Rosa? Rosataca? My little Rosa . . . oh my God! Oh Rosa,' I wept, reaching for her behind blinding tears. 'How, how did you . . .?'

'Uncle Jock rang Aunty Amelia. Do you remember, Christopher and I go to school at the Alice?'

'Does Ruth know you're here, Rosa?'

'She will by now. Christopher was going out to tell her. It's school holidays, you see. Aunty Amelia said she'd want me to be here, more than anything else in

411

the whole world. I know she would too.' Big tears streamed down her pretty black face. 'She misses you so much, Aunty Billy, but Gwwirra's getting old . . .'

'Oh darling, I miss her too. My Ruthy. Dear, sweet Rosa . . .' We rocked in each other's arms for a few moments, then she pulled her shoulders back and wiped my face with a damp towel. 'Forgive me. You mustn't be upset, Aunty. I'll get Jenna and Mathilda for you.'

She was only eight years old. So grown up. So strong. A new version of Ruth, more confident, but carefully taught, solid, built for life. Long thick black curly hair, bright, inquisitive eyes, warm, smiling heart. And long arms. Ruth didn't have long arms. The father? What was his name? Childs. Yes. Jay Childs. Whatever happened to Jay Childs . . .?

The rain was pouring down the window pane. A solitary black bird sheltered under the eaves of the verandah. Where was everyone? Where was Jock? Where were my babies? Pa? Ruth? Where are you?

'Hello, Lovely. Welcome back.' He kissed me on the forehead. The kiss was dry.

'Jock? Are you all right?'

'Hey, that's my question. How are you?'

'I'm fine. Fine.'

'The girls are beautiful, darling. You still like the names, don't you?' We'd discussed girls' names only once. I didn't like them but I supposed I would be accused of postpartum depression if I decided I wanted them changed now.

'I guess so,' I said, somewhat ungraciously. 'What happened to me? Is it the MS again? It feels different.'

'Mixture of things, dear. Your heart nearly gave out. Yours and Pa's, both together. You had heart attacks within hours of each other. So many forces, beyond our control . . .'

'Dr May Ling? Did she save my life?'

'Perhaps. You weren't ready to go. You fought almighty hard. You wanted to hold your babies. I've never seen you so strong. You and Pa. It was as though you were hanging on, together.' He shook his head, defeated by a language unequivocally wanting for descriptions of miracles.

'Ma? How is she?'

'Strong and tough, never doubted either of you for a minute!'

A little unexpected smile crept into my eyes. Ma, with her masquerades, still fooling everyone, nearly everyone. 'Forces, beyond our control . . .?'

Dr May Ling was explaining dominant and recessive genes.

'We have potentially conclusive figures on second generation rats, Mr O'Ryan. The allele for black rats are dominant over the allele for white; when a homozygous black mates with a white in the first generation, all the offspring will be heterozygous black. Mating between these offspring then results in a mixture of black and white rats. The ratio averages three to one, any white rat having inherited one recessive white allele from each of its parents. It's only ten years ago they proved that inheritable characteristics could be altered by DNA taken up from outside the cell . . . it is fascinating, Mr O'Ryan. The twins have identical DNA on the one hand, but different on the other. I'll have to write a paper on it.'

Jock looked confused, but impressed. 'All this medical terminology, Doctor! What does "potentially conclusive" actually mean?' She laughed, the soft, easy laugh I remembered from the first time I met her. The patient must be getting better.

'Good morning,' I said.

'Well, good morning, Mrs O'Ryan!'

'Good morning, Lovely.'

'What does it matter who got the recessive alleles and who got the dominant? They're healthy, aren't they?'

'Yes, darling, they're both perfect.'

'Then let me hold them!'

'Of course, Lovely, of course.' Rosa came in with the babies. 'Oh my dear girl,' I struggled up, 'are you still here?'

'I only arrived four days ago, Aunty Billy.'

'Oh.'

'You've been struggling in and out of conscious-ness for forty-eight hours,' Dr May Ling explained. 'By tomorrow, you'll be back in control.'

I hugged my babies. They seemed a lot bigger than yesterday.

I had missed many months of my daughters' lives and had no intention of missing any more. The prob-lem was, I had to learn to walk again before I could set things straight, the way they should be.

With Pa improving as rapidly as I, Ma and Sister Mac began to take it in turns to share the respective loads, the natural inclination on the part of both women being to take charge of the girls. They began removing them to Rosebery during the afternoons, on the pretext that I needed rest. Rosa was flown back to the Alice when the September holidays were over. I had barely started to get to know her and she was gone. I missed her already, my link with Ruth, and was beginning to feel very much alone.

'Why can't she stay until Christmas?' I'd asked.

'She has to go back to school.'

'I could teach her, while I'm learning to walk again.'

'She has to go back to school.'

'She could go to school at Kurra.'

'Drop it, Billy. She's going back to the Alice.'

'Have I been given six months to live, contracted polio or the plague, or what?' That was ignored. I presumed an answer, any answer, would legitimize the question.

'I'd like to feed the girls from now on, Sister Mac, thank you so much.'

'Of course, Billy, whenever we can manage to get everythin' done an' there's time, sure ya can.'

'I want to feed them *every day*, Sister Mac.'

'It ain't always possible, lovey.'

Ma took up the issue a couple of days later, but I was gathering strength. 'Let's make it possible, shall we, Ma? I am their mother, after all. It's important they learn that, don't you think?'

'Of course, dear, although it's important too that they get used to being handled by others.'

'They've been handled by everyone but their mother since they were born, Ma!'

'That's nobody's fault, Billy. We're all doing the very best we can.' Oh God, spare me the martyr treatment! 'I'm not arguing that, Ma,' I managed to say, 'I'm asking you to try and understand how I feel. It's time I took over their management. I'm walking quite well now and Banduk and Jabaljari are waiting for their old jobs back.'

'You can't possibly be considering having those black fellas in the house, Billy, what with Mathilda and all. What on earth did I teach you?'

That was the straw that did it. I held my tongue and waited until Jock and I were alone. He started in, before I could open my mouth. 'Ma and Sister Mac are rather upset, Lovely. Don't you think you're being a bit heavy-handed with the instructions?'

'You too, huh? That's about what I'd expect. I know, oh yes, I know. You've all been absolutely wonderful and I'm extremely ungrateful and behaving like a spoilt child!' My heart was bruised and as

415

much as I knew I was right to insist on taking charge of Jenna and Mathilda, I did not have preconceived expectations that Jock would know it too. 'I'm not just the sick little woman who gave birth to two girls eight months ago, Jock – I'm their mother, for God's sake! You're acting as though I'm still on my death-bed and you all own them. Let me in, Jock – let me in, or I'll damn well take them and leave the whole bloody lot of you!'

Jock's shoulders pushed back, as though a knife had been thrust into his spine. He had seen me angry before, but never like this. He was smart enough to know I would remain so until the matter was re-solved. 'What do you want me to do, Lovely?' he surrendered instantly, tired, resigned, his kind face shrouded.

'I want Ma and Sister Mac out of our house and I want them out for good. I will not have my daughters brought up the way I was brought up. I will not!'

He was visibly shaken now, a startled look jump-ing into his face. 'You're overreacting, aren't you?' he stumbled over his words, reaching for a cigarette without thinking to offer me one.

'Thanks,' I snapped.

'I'm sorry, darling, here.'

'Out, Jock, out! You have to help me get them out.'

'Do you have any ideas?' he asked pathetically.

'Do *I* have any ideas? I've been in a bloody coma for months, Jock. What were you thinking about, for heaven's sake? Ma and Sister Mac are in their sixties! Their attitudes and values belong to the last century. It's already quite obvious they favour Mathilda. By the time our daughters are school age, Mathilda will be thinking she's Christmas and Jenna will be think-ing she's a Ruth. I'm scared, Jock. I won't have it! Support me – or else! And don't try to hide behind old-world proprieties because I'm up to my neck and drowning in bloody Christian gratitude and good manners.'

'What do you mean, *or else*, Billy?' Jock's gentle nature, immersed in shock, was aggravating me greatly.

'You can't work it out for yourself, Jock? Well, I'll spell it right out for you. I am not going to drop dead in the next six or twelve months and my daughters are going to be brought up by me, or I'll take them out to the centre and join Ruth and Amelia and Prinky and you won't be able to do a damn thing about it. Don't forget, I've got the money to build a decent home in the Alice, too!' I thundered on. 'Life's improving there every day. Rosa's happy at her school; our girls would likely get a better start in a growing town than one that's still living in the dark ages! I'm also going to write a will and make my wishes very clear as to who will be in charge, should anything happen to me before my daughters are grown up. Is that clear?'

At last he grasped the seriousness of the situation. His face had turned a ghostly white. '*My* daughters, Billy? *Our* daughters, surely?'

'Then start behaving like it, or they'll be mine, mark my words.'


In the chrysalid state, following a long illness, the world is murky brown. There are no shades or variations. It's just mud, solid mud you're stuck in. When the body starts to re-emerge from this all-encasing shell, other living creatures are affronted by your life. Nature's plan: survival of the fittest. 'You should be dead!' they mocked me silently. 'We were ready for that – we are not ready for this!'

In their minds, I've already passed over. In their hearts, I am now a dead saint, and they are now living martyrs. My human response of rebirth

417

is clumsy and inappropriate. 'Hope springs eternal . . .' after the grieving is done. They had already mourned my departure. I was the devil's own personified Cassandra. Wasn't it enough that I couldn't even get the alleles right? Why couldn't I just behave like the well-bred woman I was, and quietly take my leave? 'Think of your reputation!' I could see them pointing their fingers at me, angels all of them, lining up to do God's thankless work.

'Two for you and one for you, two for you and one for you. Don't cry, Jenna. You're only a half-caste, darling. You're already getting half again what you deserve! We're being awfully kind to you. You're an ungrateful little coon, aren't you?'

'Oh no, oh dear me, no!' I screamed. Jock shook me into full consciousness. 'It's all right, Lovely, you were having another nightmare.'

'I have to break the cycle, Jock, or I'll go mad!'

'Perhaps, some professional help?'

'Yes, I'll call Dr May Ling in the morning.'

'Good. I'll get the girls.'

'No. I'm getting up. I'm going to be getting up from now on, Jock, so you can start behaving like a normal man again. Remember how to do that, dear?' He looked away.

Just as I thought. He had me buried too.

We were just getting around to having the babies christened when their first birthday suddenly loomed into view. Along with my miraculous return from the dead and Pa's relatively good recovery from his third heart attack, we expediently decided to throw a multifarious celebration for the entire town.

My private reasons for initiating such a grossly extravagant and personally unwelcome public celebration were all about Ruth. It was over six years since I had seen her. I needed her now, her strength, her wisdom. I needed her love and friendship. She could oil the wheel for me . . . keep me alive another eight years. I knew it, as surely as the beautiful brolga would be dancing across the Pickle River in the morning. I had to get her here, and the reason had to be big enough for her graciously to accept the airfares. She had no money. She wasn't paid to teach because the Education Department didn't accept her qualifications. Qualifications of life could not be written on a piece of paper.

Michael Shaft had a truck you could sling a ramp and roll a wheelchair onto so we asked him to bring Ma and Pa. I didn't like him much, but how many times had I been reminded of the prayers the whole community had sent up for me and Jenna and Mathilda? Apart from our old faithful Mugga, none of the locals had seen me for over twelve months. I figured they'd be hanging out for their full penny's worth of the doppelgänger and her little siblings; the ghostly one and the ghoulish one.

Banduk and Jabaljari worked twelve-hour days in the run-up to the big day. There was the tarpaulin to be erected, the coloured lights to thread through the natives and poplars along the driveway into The Brolga plus the party equipment – tables and chairs, glasses and kegs – to be collected and set up. Ma had a small group of church women organized to assist her with the food. The christening cake had been made for months, naturally enough.

'Anyone would think it was a crime to christen babies at twelve months old.' I ratted to Jock one night, following an accidental eavesdropping on our party line.

'To Catholics, it is,' he replied.

'O'Ryan to the end, aren't you? One of the main reasons I'm going to be around for a very long time, Jock O'Ryan, is to make sure you can't go back on your word.' As usual, he was totally shocked. It was intensely frustrating.

'Do you want to . . . talk about it?' he proffered hesitantly, fairly terrified at the thought of my response.

'About what, Jock?' I nailed him coldly.

'Nothing,' he muttered.

'Good,' I voiced sweetly.

Then, the worst of it – Ruth couldn't come. Her mother was dying. She'd found her Gwwirra, and now she was dying. Even the Dreamtime offered no guarantees. 'My dear, dear Billy,' she'd written. 'This'll be a short note and I know you'll understand. Gwwirra's real sick. I've had to bring her to the Alice, for the white man's remedies . . . I couldn't leave her now. She may not even make it through the night. I hope the party is a great success. Don't listen to the gremlins, remember you are a brolga. Dance, Billy, dance! Lots of love, Ruth. PS. Hugs and kisses to Jenna and Mathilda.'

I prayed for her mother and questioned the gross injustices of life. 'Don't listen to the gremlins. Remember you are a brolga . . .'

As usual, her advice was good. In spite of the disappointment, my spirits lifted and the party was a huge success.

'Never seen 'er lookin' so well,' the locals said.

'Motherhood agrees with her,' everyone agreed.

'Jenna's nowhere near as black as I was expectin'! Why, she's lighter than Ruth, if me memory serves me correctly.'

'Of course she is! Light brown, I'd say.'

'Olive, jist about.' Michael Shaft put his stamp on the town's revised opinion.

'Best thing you ever did, Lovely,' Jock said later. 'It's stopped the talk. They've seen Jenna and know she's just as pretty as Mathilda, and not black. Seeing her has normalized the situation, taken the edge off the gossip.' He was extremely pleased and relieved by the turn of events. I wanted to protest, tell him I didn't know him any more. I wanted to ask him why black was so ugly to him, but I already knew the answer. He would never get over the shame he felt for his father now, now that one of his daughters would always be there to remind him. Well, I was too tired to be bothered arguing. It wouldn't alter anything. He was as locked into his attitudes as Ma and Pa and Sister Mac were to theirs, as Ruth and Amelia . . . as we were to ours. I was convinced we saw the world differently because we were women for our time.

As I was trying to rationalize why Jock had not grasped the same message as I from his time in the world, away from Kurra, my baby girls started to assert their individuality upon us. Mathilda was a proper little girl, co-operative in all matters of feeding and toilet hygiene. She liked everything in its place, neat and tidy, white and pink and pretty. She didn't cry; when she was in trouble, or wanting attention, she screamed, a piercing, shrill avalanche of wailing that could waken the dead. Jock was the only one who could stop the pitiful howling once it had truly set in. She was slow to start walking. She had no need to hurry. Everyone adored her, attended her every need. And, she had picked up in the cradle one of the great complexities of human existence – that we were still there, even when she couldn't see us. The high-pitched screams demanded we continue to communicate with her, no matter where we were.

The antithesis of her sister, Jenna giggled and cried, gently, predictably. Her demands were simple and she was not interested in details. She liked games nearly as much as food and was happy to have company, but just as happy to be left to amuse herself.

She loved peekaboo too, but was totally unconcerned when we disappeared completely. She appeared to have no fear and took her first steps early. Mathilda then feared that her sister would leave her, setting up a screaming session every time Jenna took a duck's waddle out of the nursery. 'Why don't you just copy her, Mathilda? Then you can go with her?' I'd mumble to myself as much as to her. She would look at me as though I was a monster, asking her to do something that would hurt.

'It's odd, and very scary,' I wrote to Ruth. 'I wish you could throw some light on it. Mathilda got all the early attention and security and she's afraid to be on her own for a minute. Jenna got none and she has no fear at all! The continuing distinctions drawn between them because of the colour of their skins alarms and depresses me. I'm terrified of what will happen to them if anything happens to me before they're grown up.'

Ruth was back in the centre with her remarkably resilient mother in their self-supporting camp, a camp visited twice a week by the tourist buses these days. She replied promptly, a regular mail service now operating from Ularu. 'I've consulted all the elders and Gwwirra about your worries and they all say, don't worry. Just love them both, equally,' she wrote.

My ma says to remind you of the pages of history. She said white royalty and the upper classes have always had nannies and wet nurses for their babies and their children and most of them turned out okay, by white folks' standards. Most of the nannies throughout the world have been black too (though considering how you turned out, old girl, I suppose that's not a great recommendation . . .) Seriously, Billy, bet ya Rosa's paternal grandmother was somebody's nanny. And I was. But she won't be, no siree, any more than your little Jenna will be. (By the way, Rosa's gettin' real curious about her father. Any suggestions for me on how to handle it?)

Gwwirra also said to remind you that I had no upbringing at all during the early years of life. Let's face it, I was dragged up in the orphanage, a non-person, worse than that . . . we were low-grade, dirty, dumb animal-people. Yet not even knowing whether Ma was alive, I never stopped loving and believing in her, did I? Eventually found her too. And I didn't turn out all bad, Billy, did I?

Oh yes, and one more history lesson, Mrs O'Ryan . . . no, Miss Billy Batchelor! You like a fight, you've always liked a fight, but be careful you don't pick one that turns itself back on you. Remember the north wind that carried away the beautiful young girl? All spirits are not good spirits. If you blow too hard, Billy, you might finish up with somethin' mighty similar to that which you're trying so damn hard to destroy. The most important things Mathilda and Jenna need to learn's the origin of their world, the creatures they see, the natural forces of the wind and the rain and the sun, and all the stars above. The more people who caress them and love them, the better. Let out the sails, Billy! Let out the sails, old girl.

Finally, to your request, my dear, sad Billy. I promise, if you are permanently bedridden in the future, I'll come and care for you and the girls. I've discussed it with the elders and Gwwirra – everyone agrees. Amelia would stay here and look after Christopher and Rosa. Prinky would look after Gwwirra, or Gwwirra after her! They're a funny pair. So you see, Billy, there's nothing to worry about. Everything will sort itself out, you'll see.

And for a time, it did. We moved into a period of relative bliss, whipped along expeditiously by two ever fascinating, ever demanding little girls, my continued good health and Jock's new-found peace. Having finally obtained his education degree, he felt satisfied with his career and settled down to catering to our every need. He loved us so much, he would have died for us quite cheerfully if we'd asked.

While we stretched out for a spell, enjoying life in a parochial, focused sort of way, Ruth's problems were just beginning, her world expanding traumatically.

In the first instance, Than hitched a ride to Melbourne to see the Olympic Games and came back engaged to a divorcee, assumed to be nearly twice his age. Mrs Elizabeth Ruebeck returned with him and settled into Nan's old Temperance Tea House, now a modern guesthouse run by a war widow, Mrs Maudly. Nan had died of lung cancer during my long coma after the girls' birth.

Elizabeth Ruebeck insisted on the traditional rules of courtship that applied to a forthcoming virginal wedding, obviously well aware of small-town attitudes, or perhaps just the power of small-town gossip. She was a tall, fair, plain-looking woman, stylishly groomed, quietly elegant. She struck a startling contrast to Than, with his rough country ways and dark good looks. The mirror of Micky and Thea was impossible to deny.

Ma and Pa, Sister Mac, Michael Shaft and all the old-timers were mortified by the match. 'The situation would be comical, if it were not so tragic,' Ma sighed heavily, expressing the opinion of two generations. It was not long since the Queen's sister, Princess Margaret, had given up her Group-Captain Townsend because of her duty to the Commonwealth and her belief in the Church's teaching that Christian marriage is indissoluble. And she wasn't even a Catholic!

Micky and Thea were also surprisingly distraught, given they'd shown a relatively remote interest in Than's life since their own full-blood youngsters came along. They took the unprecedented step of writing to Ruth, asking her to visit and talk some sense into him. It was a brave request, if not a stupid one. It did not occur to them that Ruth would no longer hold the Christian beliefs taught her by her white enslavers, nor that her only concern would be for Than's happiness.

She too took a surprising course. She replied to Micky and Thea, advising that since she'd been in regular communication with Than since she left Kurra Kurra, she saw little point in visiting Mini Mini to 'talk some sense into him'. There was nothing she could teach him now about the desires of the heart. She would however attend his wedding, should it go ahead. 'Sour grapes,' was Thea's reaction.

'All we've done for 'im, and his own bloody mother won't even lift a finger to help. Thanks for nothin', Ruth!' was Micky's.

Simultaneously, Ruth was coping with a rebellious, ten-year-old daughter. Rosa had put an ultimatum to her mother; track down her father or she would leave home on her sixteenth birthday, travel to America and find him. She had discovered from Prinky that one of Ruth's old schoolmates was living in South Carolina. She would make Saucy Barnawarren-Keele's home her base until she found him! She had it all worked out.

How Saucy and her husband and family would view the arrival of a stranger from the past, in particular, a young black woman from the Australian outback, was not an issue to Rosa. She had been brought up in a secure atmosphere of affection and love. As one of a large family, caressed and cared for by everyone with whom she had come in contact, she was naïve of the ways of the white man. Even her schooling in the Alice was sheltered. It wasn't just because it was a pure black education. Alice Springs was still considered so racist, none of the rules applied 'outside' anyway. The teachers could be excused for protecting their young until the last possible moment before maturity. The dream of the Dreamtime would be over soon enough.

The mere thought of Rosa travelling to Charleston to live in a house, in a suburban street, in a big city, in a racist community, was a terrifying proposition to Ruth, if indeed Saucy would welcome her in the first place. Then there was the small matter of her father's reaction, if he was still alive and trackable. Would he want to know he had an Australian daughter? Of course he wouldn't, nor would his wife, no doubt. And who knows, he may have managed to find a white woman and have half-caste youngsters, living in no-man's-land, reaching for the stars white money can buy. How would Rosa cope with that?

'My children sure haven't turned out the way I planned,' Ruth wrote despairing notes, sometimes twice a week.

I thought I'd got it right the second time. We were so sheltered at Rosebery. I thought if you kept things quiet, they'd stay quiet. Even when Reverend Moon and your Ma and Pa decided to find a wife for Micky, it was never once mentioned out loud, you know, that he was Than's father. I wasn't even asked if Micky really was the father! It was assumed. Now my daughter calmly (not so calmly) tells me she wants to get to know her father and I'm the bad egg for havin' kept him and her a secret from one another. Shit, shit, shit! as Than would say.

In another letter, she asked for my opinion of Than's fiancée. I had only met Mrs Ruebeck once, briefly. 'White, and bright,' I told Ruth. Than was a wild lad, as his father had been. He got his pilot's licence at twenty, was playing Black Jack in the illegal casino in Tarrenbonga at twenty-one and was rumoured to have slept with half the married women in Kurra. That he had decided to marry a woman of quite obvious maturity and apparent intelligence seemed to me to be something of a breakthrough. I conveyed the most of it to Ruth. She replied philosophically, unwittingly helping me enormously with my own fears and frustrations.

> Just as I thought. In spite of his upbringing, he has not been severely handicapped! I've now worked out what biological mothers are for, Billy. We're just here to give them our hereditary strength, our genes and to go through the agonies of childbirth. It's our job to nurse them for minute or two, then fling them out into the world and watch them take their chances and survive, against all odds. We actually dare to believe they'd never survive without our upbringing, our guidance, our wisdom, our great hands of mother-hood! Well, Billy, it's a bloody sham! Kids can survive through just about anything, and they'll do what they want to do in the end, no matter how much you and I try to bend them our way. We did what we wanted, didn't we?

I wrote Ruth how good she was for my soul, and went on with my life. Jenna and Mathilda were 'two handsfull worth, Mummy,' as Jenna would mimic. Not to be outdone, Mathilda would scoff, 'You *are*, Jenna! I'm not! I'm a good girl.' Banduk and Jabaljari were remarkably patient with them, keeping them amused most afternoons while I had a nap. Then Jabaljari would bring them in for their naps; Mathilda liked her own bed, Jenna liked to cuddle in with me. By the time Jock arrived home from school, we were up and about, playing and preparing the evening meal. Just like a normal family.

I was doubly blessed to have Jenna and Mathilda in the fifties. For most of the decade, Australia seemed to be in a kind of aftershock. War and depression, drought and fire had all taken their toll. 'People always play it safe, coming out of a war,' Ma said. When television came in, most people just sat down for a couple of years and stared mindlessly into the box. It was a relief for folk to be unaccountable for hours, every night. The country voted Menzies in again – for the fifth time. Pa had always voted Liberal, so had I, though I hadn't always seen eye to eye with Menzies. We got used to being winners. Jock always voted Labor. It didn't seem to matter what happened, nobody changed their vote. It had been part of who we were to remain the same for such a long time, our generation simply couldn't change now.

But the younger generation were clawing their way out of the mire. They had a new name and a new music and money jangling in their pockets. The age of the teen had arrived, along with *The Blackboard Jungle*. Jock and I rarely went out but I just had to see *The Blackboard Jungle*. It had taken so long to reach Tarrenbonga. We left the girls with Ma and Pa and went to the pictures. It was the first time I had ever seen a black man in a starring role in a high-budget Hollywood movie. Sidney Poitier stole the show for me but the theme, 'Rock Around the Clock', stole it for the kids.

'We're getting left behind,' Jock mused, as we drove back to Rosebery.

'I used to think I'd mind, but I don't really, do you?'

'Not in the least. Though they'll have a lot more opportunities than we had.'

'Why did you decide to teach, Jock?'

'Security, wages and the promotions offered. When the farm couldn't support me, I had to find something that could. Employment prospects were low, as you well remember.'

'Did you have any regrets?'

'Yes, yes . . . on my first day as a pupil-teacher, confronted with thirty-five youngsters from eight grades. Yes! I was only a youngster myself. We got 19 shillings and 10 pence a week and earned every penny of it. The classrooms were pokey and dark. I once taught sixty kids in grades five and six. They were almost sitting on one another's laps – we had twenty-eight large desks. I had to delegate two children each day to sit at chairs pulled up to my work table.'

It was a long speech for Jock. I waited for him to realize it and ask me why I was asking. 'Because you'll be teaching our daughters in a couple of years,' I answered in due course.

'Ah. I will not show them any favouritism, Lovely.'

'I know that. But you'll have to show them that they are still the most special children in the world, dear.'

'They know that.'

'They may not, when you start treating them like everyone else.'

'Don't start into me about how to teach, Billy. I will continue, as I have always done.'

'Does that mean Jenna will do yard duty while you're teaching English and Geography to Mathilda and the rest of the class?'

'What are you insinuating?'

'That's what happened to Ruth. The Education Department are quite clear on the subject of blacks and half-castes, aren't they? You can't teach them. They're not as bright, smaller brains, lower IQs. Ring any bells, Jock?'

'I'm not going to be dragged into this, Billy. Please, just leave it alone.'

'How can I? You said you intend to do as you've always done and that means one of my daughters is about to be discriminated against. You may not even realize you're doing it. You've been so carefully taught!'

We had reached the front gates of Rosebery. The subject would be dropped for another time. Ma wanted to hear all about the film, her life bereft of outside entertainment since Pa's most recent heart attack. He had nodded off in his chair. The girls were sound asleep too. I looked at their sweet round faces and curly heads and wondered for the umpteenth time how we'd managed to produce such rare, re-splendent individuals. The haunting memories of Ruth's babies' faces flashed back to me as I stood and gazed at my own.

I had not done enough to help in the case of Than's engagement. He had taken his Mrs Elizabeth Ruebeck out of Kurra, cursing us all as he left. What he would do, what he could do, nobody knew. He could run a farm, of course, and there was work up north again. Perhaps he would get a job cutting cane, as Patrick Silvester had, and so many before him. It wasn't much of a future, not for all the pain his life had caused his mother, nor for the survival of the great Christian ethics so righteously upheld all those years ago.

I would not, could not let her down again. We had to get through to Rosa between now and her sixteenth birthday. There was some time, though Ruth was probably right; if she was determined to go, she would find a way.

By the time the Rome Olympics were over, 1960 was feeling quite different from the long and tedious fifties.

Princess Margaret had fallen in love again and married a commoner, restoring our faith in second chances and English justice. The charismatic John Kennedy had received the Democratic Presidential nomination and was raising our hopes for an exciting future with his plans for a New Frontier. The first woman prime minister in the world was elected in Ceylon, an irony for most of the women of Sri Lanka, an encouraging step forward to ambitious women in the West. Civil war broke out in the Congo and I thanked God Amelia was in the Alice, and the Congolese mobs were fighting one another.

At last, change was in the air. I decided to take the plunge and tell Jock of my latest idea. It made me sad to see Pharaoh going to ruin again. We needed another Silvester couple, but nobody was beating a path to our door following several advertisements in the local papers.

'Let's give Banduk and Jabaljari a year's free lease and see if they can do something with it. They've been extremely loyal to me, and very good to us and the children. I think –'

'I couldn't agree more. I think that's an excellent idea, Lovely,' he said. It was hard to make him out sometimes. Just when I thought I could peg his attitudes and reactions to a tee, he'd turn around and behave completely unpredictably. More and more, he reminded me of my father.

The year was drawing to a close. I had taken to using short names for the girls – Matty for Mathilda, because I hated Hilda almost as much as Mathilda, and Jo for Jenna, because . . . well, it just happened that way. They were growing up. My heart had pumped irregularly at the proximity of the school year and the thought of my babies leaving me for the big wide world, a world monopolized and manipulated by my husband – their father. I had tried to reason out whether I was frightened for them, or for myself, but start school they had duly done, and were none the worse for it by the end of their first year. In fact, they did it easily, far easier than I.

It was at the close of the year that Mugga arrived with a letter from America – addressed to Miss Billy Batchelor. He was curious about the mode of address, not to mention the name on the back of the envelope; fortunately, his memory did not recall it. My own curiosity rattled and paralysed me. I waited until Matty and Jo were asleep before tentatively opening the aerogramme. It was from Jay Childs. He was taking a sentimental journey to Australia for the twenty-year Coral Sea celebrations in '62 and wanted to catch up with Ruth. He was writing more than a year in advance, hoping I'd still own Cranberry Vineyard and pass on his letter to Ruth, 'who by now is sure to be outback with her own family.'

Ruth had told him that was her plan! Told him, all those years ago, before she told me? Had it always been a part of her plan, to head him off for ever? He said nothing of his own situation. My God, what was I to do? Was this kind fate, or cruel justice? Was Ruth to lose her daughter, as she had lost her son? Were the gods conspiring to refuse her any peace, just as she had found some answers for her life?

The following day, before I could make any decision about how to pass on Jay's letter, a hurried note arrived from Ruth. 'Would it be okay for Rosa and me to visit in the New Year? We've been offered a lift with a friend, departing here around 1 January. I need your help with Rosa. Things are kinda' worse than I dared imagine. Her night job at the supermarket . . . well, she is not working at the supermarket, Billy. We're in bad trouble and I just don't know where else to turn. You're the only white woman I know who's seen both sides and won't make moral judgements.'

I read it several times, then put the two letters

together and hid them in the camphor chest. There would be time to tell Jock when I had calmed down and contemplated the worst of it.

# TWENTY

# 1961...

I'd been awaiting Ruth's visit for what seemed like half a lifetime. Though I had promised myself years ago I would never again count on tomorrow, it was difficult not to plan, to dream. My Ruthy, the one true friend of my life, who loved me irrevocably, who understood the very beating of my heart – how I had missed her! How many times had I played down the emptiness, the long, slow years without her?

Yet nothing is ever as bad as it seems, I talked confidently to myself. My Ruth will be home soon. We will solve Rosa's problems together! We can do anything we want to do, as long as we want it badly enough.

Christmas had come and gone, rendered a huge success by Matty and Jo, though Pa was poorly again. What we had planned as a large celebration at The Brolga reverted to a small affair at Rosebery. It was easier that way. The girls didn't mind. Grandma allowed them to muddy the floors, stick their fingers in pudding bowls, sneak sausage rolls for breakfast and stay up late watching television. Then, just as I'd think my oldies had changed unrecognizably, they'd revert to form; Ma would lose all patience with their incessant chatter and, to keep the peace, Pa would rock them on his knee and tell them stories. He had countless droving tales, tales of the days when thousands of sheep and cattle followed the tracks of the early explorers and the telegraph, epic voyages taking months or years to complete. He told them how the men battled the wet seasons and the droughts for their livestock, surviving plagues of rats and poisonous plants and hostile blacks. His stories improved with age. I'd heard exactly the same ones for the first time at around their age, when he came home from The Great War.

Poised in the balance, the New Year held all of our lives in its hands; Ruth and Rosa were due to arrive any day, Jock had received a long-awaited promotion to Head Teacher of the primary school at Tarrenbonga, Banduk and Jabaljari would be shearing their first sheep in a few weeks. Matty could not imagine what on earth she was going to do to fill in six long weeks without school and Jo was desperate to never have to go to school again.

The most difficult adjustment of all, for everyone, was Ma and Pa's eviction from their home. A lifetime of security and comfortable habits, a lifetime of service, of the clickety-clang of the train that governed their days – was all but over. They had been living on at Rosebery through the grace of the new stationmaster who took over when Pa retired at sixty-five. Baxter was a bachelor who'd been happy to have the company, the housekeeping and Ma's cooking. But he had found a wife. The time had come.

We decided to build a granny flat at The Brolga, but in the meantime, they were to move in with us. How Ma would cope with the loss of her power and manipulation over all she surveyed did not bear thinking about. Jock said we would cope. I said that was not what concerned me. He said if she didn't cope, we'd have trouble coping, but cope we would. It was a vicious circle. He was so excited about his new career, I don't think he thought about the fact that I'd be stuck with them, all day, every day. The little voice I kept well hidden from myself most days, most years, got bigger then: 'You selfish girl, you wicked thankless child!' it whispered in the wind. But I thanked God for Ruth's impending visit. With the girls at school, and Ma trying to take over our lives, I'd be wanting to go to work again, though I supposed I'd be too old for anyone to employ me now. James looked like he'd be running the *Mail* till retirement and it did cross my mind I could write articles for him, at a pinch.

Ma and Pa moved in during the second week of January. We expected Ruth and Rosa around the third week, and school recommenced at the beginning of February. I was grateful to have my health.

'Isn't it wunnerful to have Grandma and Grandpa here, Mummy,' Matty contributed on their first night, bringing beams of joy all round. She could be trusted to say the right thing at the right time, needing people far more than Jo.

'What'll we do tomorrow, Dad?' asked Jo. She hated school, but in a way, needed it more than Matty. She spent too much time on her own, daydreaming mostly. 'I've got some papers to prepare for my new school, Jenna,' Jock replied. 'Why don't you play dolls with Mathilda?'

'Dolls are silly. I'll go down to Pharaoh and help Bandy and Jaby.'

'Couldn't you leave the school work until evening, Jock? Really, there's only a few weeks to go and I need to help Ma and Pa get settled.'

'I've got a lot more than a day or a night's work, Lovely. It'll take until school starts to get it all done. I should have started last week.'

'So that means I can expect no support from you over the next few weeks, does it? God, I wish you did a man's job!'

'What is that supposed to mean?' His face had fallen, he bit his lip. He had not intended to respond, and wished with all his heart he could retract the question. The 'school teacher is a child among men' arguments had worn very thin down the years.

I took pity on him and held my tongue. I was tired, just thinking about the energy required to get through until the girls were back at school. The double vision had returned suddenly, a few days before, but I was keeping it to myself. My legs felt like jelly beneath me, my arms and back and head ached continuously. All I had to do was hang on a bit longer. I could do it. I would see my babies back to school, on my feet, on my feet, please God, on my feet. I would be on my feet when Ruth came. I had to be.

On the morning of 20 January, Mugga drove out with a telegram from Rosebery, sent from Carrington, just a few hundred miles away. 'Dear Billy STOP Regret to tell you Gwwirra died quietly in her sleep three days ago STOP Have got a ride back to the Alice, leaving tonight STOP We'll telephone you after the ceremonies STOP Much love RUTH AND ROSA STOP.'

'Oh dear God,' I cried, an overwhelming sense of loss seizing me, a mixture of sympathy for Ruth and pity for myself. I did not realize until that moment how much I had been counting on her visit, counting on her presence, her strength, as I always had, always would; she, with her dark problems, problems I knew little of yet, and I, with my dark clouds of sickness and isolation gathering – with my memories and regrets.

Would I ever see my Ruthy again? Would I ever see those black eyes laughing again or feel the warmth of her love, the accepting, nonjudgemental friendship she gave without effort?

'God moves in mysterious ways,' Pa whispered, well-meaning. I did not want to hear it.

'God is no friend of mine today,' I wept.

'You mean of Ruth's, don't you?' Ma corrected.

'No, Ma! I mean of mine! Ruth's mother was old and tired and went quietly. They said their goodbyes before they left. Ruth wrote me about it. She will be sad, but not sorry for a merciful end.' I began to sob. 'What purpose, God? What lousy, rotten timing, God? Why? Why? Why? How much more do You want?'

Jock put his arms around me. I shook them off. I found no comfort in his comfort. He looked at me meekly, desperately, as a faithful hound whimpers when his master is down. I hated him then, hated him for his sincere affection and constancy of love. I wanted my health back, wanted the world I'd left behind, the world for ever denied me now. And I wanted my Ruthy. I did not want my husband's undying love, nor his silent respect. I did not want it! I wanted him to sweep me off my feet, take me on a honeymoon, take me to the theatre, take me dancing, take me walking, take me to our bed and tell me of my loveliness. What use calling me by the word? Rescue some life before it's too late . . .

He moved across to the television. The large furniture piece filled our family room, the sun reflecting light from the windows and the pictures on the walls into its square, silver screen. Ma pulled down the blinds. It was snowing in Washington. The forty-three-year-old President was making his inauguration speech. He was easy on the eyes; his words were easy on the ears . . . 'Let the rest of the world know that this hemisphere intends to remain master in its own house.' It was powerful rhetoric. It did nothing for my spirit. 'Ask not what your country can do for you – ask what you can do for your country.' A literary quote, but who had said it? I tried to concentrate. I had the feeling Mr Kennedy had just made it his own. Following the speech, a news

438

bulletin announced the successful trials of an oral contraceptive pill for women.

What sort of a world would Jenna and Mathilda know? If a Roman Catholic could get the top job in America, and women could plan when, if, they have babies, perhaps even racism is conquerable? There's no cure for multiple sclerosis though. It's not a fashionable disease. David said so, centuries ago. 'Not common enough to be worthy of charitable support, nor sufficiently documented to arouse research interest,' he'd said. I guessed it would be many years before its own slow creep arrested medical or public attention.

'Why don't we laugh any more?' I suddenly asked my husband and my parents. 'What's the matter with us? It's 1961 and we've many blessings to be glad of. Let's laugh! Laugh, Jock, bloody laugh, Ma!' They looked at me oddly, managing embarrassed, half-mast smiles. I could see they had slipped into their: 'Billy's about to become hysterical,' mode, but I was unstoppable, gathering a passionate, high-pitched speed. 'What a boring life we've allowed to happen here! We do nothing with our days. We go nowhere. We get up in the morning, cook and clean and work, then we eat, clean up again, watch television, go to bed and get up and do it all over. If it wasn't for the girls, we'd be morons by now! We've forgotten how to entertain, we've forgotten how to communicate, we've forgotten how to laugh! We've lost our own identities. Our lives revolve around two little girls, who have their own lives to live! We're already pinning all our hopes on our offspring, living our lives through them.

'Ma and Pa, Jock . . . we've got to lift our game. We've got to start enjoying our lives for our lives' sake . . . we can't be depending on the children to . . . For God's sake, I haven't even had a honey-

439

moon! When did you ever take me anywhere, Jock? You've had me cooped up here because of your precious ego, precious studies, precious promotion, because you've never been able to stand the thought of spending the money I inherited. Not even on a lousy holiday! Jesus!'

Ma closed her eyes in horror. Pa shook his bowed head.

'Don't be shocked, Ma. I haven't started yet . . .' I collapsed. I did not faint, nor was I weeping when I fell. I simply collapsed. Jock picked me up off the floor and carried me to the bedroom.

'I'm sorry, Lovely,' he said.

'Sorry?' I repeated. 'Easy word, isn't it?'

'Yes, sorry we didn't do more while we could. That's what this is about, isn't it?'

'I don't know. I don't know anything any more . . .'

'Yes you do. You know you're coming out of remission again.' I laughed sarcastically. 'Sounds like the good end of the stick when you say it like that, doesn't it?'

'Billy, it isn't too late for us to go out, enjoy life, take a trip maybe?'

'When? Would you allow me to take the girls out to the centre to see Ruth? Of course you wouldn't, not now, if ever? They're at school! And I'm on the way down again. I could have gone last year, or the year before. God, why didn't I? Why didn't I?'

Jock put his head in his hands. An occasional sob shattered his low, steady voice, shook his broad, thick shoulders. I had never seen him so wretched, so lost. 'You'd already lived a full life when we met again, Lovely. You'd achieved much of what you set out to achieve. You'd travelled, had success, war experiences, lovely. I had done very little. My life experience was minimal. Three weeks after we married, you inherited a small fortune.

'It became more important than ever for me to achieve something in my own right. When the girls were born, I thought that was enough. But it wasn't. I've needed this promotion, Lovely, for my identity, my sense of purpose . . . I needed to know I could support you and the girls, even though there's no literal need. I put our lives on hold because I had to get a degree, not to equal yours, but to achieve a self-respecting career for myself. Can you understand that? I've been working hard for me, but also for you, Lovely. I wanted you to be proud of me . . . I wanted to be proud of myself.'

It is a lie that suffering ennobles the spirit. It does not. It reduces it, embitters it and puts intolerable strain on faith. How can an almighty God of love condone utterly irrational waste and suffering? Thwarted souls, waiting for some goal or other to be achieved before the living starts! The suffering plunders along, ripping out the years, crippling the body and the mind. And then the heart takes a last vindictive look and packs it in, seething with indignation for all the men who made it so.

'I don't want to understand, Jock. What sense in understanding opportunities lost for ever? They're gone. Understanding won't bring them back.'

'But, Lovely, understanding the reasons why can help the present, the future?'

'The present has already gone. The future? I suppose it will come. I am too tired tonight to think of it. Will you put the girls to bed and say goodnight to Ma and Pa?'

'Of course, darling. Rest. Ruth will come soon, I promise you.'

The day before school started, Jabaljari found Chocolate Two floating in the dam. The girls were devastated.

I was confined to bed and learnt of the disaster from the tears that began down by the old vegetable patch. Running as fast as their little legs would carry them up to my bedside, they cried until they could cry no more. 'We'll make a grave in the violet bed,' Matty declared in her authoritative way. 'Can we get the minister or the priest over to say some doggy prayers, Mummy?' Jo was full of the usual philosophic questions. 'Is there a heaven 'specially for dogs, Mummy?' and without waiting for an answer, rushed on, the babble of her mind wanting to know everything at once. 'If all the dogs go to one heaven, Mummy, how does God stop them from fighting?'

'When you die, you love everyone, Joey!' Matty scorned.

'That's silly, Mathilda,' Jo replied hotly. She called Matty by her full name when she was cross, instinctively following her father and grandmother's pattern with me. 'Why would God make us love everyone when we are died?'

'When we are dead, dear, not when we are died.'

'Well, why would He?' she persisted. 'I'm gonna hate everyone when I'm died.'

I wanted to correct her, but was forced to concentrate on suppressing a giggle. Both girls burst into fresh rounds of tears, suddenly remembering the point of the conversation.

'Daddy will hold a ceremony for Chocolate Two when he gets back from town.' I straightened myself up. 'Go down and ask Bandy and Jaby to help you dig a grave for her. I think it's a lovely idea, Matty, to put her in the violet bed. Why don't you pick some flowers and make a posy for her?'

'We have to put a stone on her grave,' Matty said, as they jumped off the bed.

'We can say, *Here lies Chocolate Two, drowned in the dam,*' Jo suggested.

'That's awful, Joey. We have to say something about God.'

They disappeared, their grief temporarily forgotten with the work to be done. Ma sat down beside me. 'You'll miss Chocolate Two more than anyone, won't you, Rachel?' A couple of unwelcome tears rolled down my cheek.

'She's been good company over the years.' Especially when I've been sick, I thought. Ma was thinking it too.

'At least I'll be here this time, Rachel. You won't be so alone.'

'Yes. Yes, I'm grateful you and Pa are here. What ever happened to time, Ma? Forty years ago you nursed me when I was sick. Funny how the world circles, returns us to base. You never lose your kids, do you?'

Her eyes closed for a moment, my thoughtless comment exploding in her heart. She had lost Joey, would probably outlive me. What was it all about? I saw her then as an old woman, silver hair thinned out and wiry, framing a tired, wrinkled face. Her powerful bosoms had dropped and lay exhausted on her chest, propped up from underneath by an imponderable waist, an analogy of her life. Her dominions had all gone, defeated by her husband's illness and forced retirement. She had lost her home and with it, her potency. Ma's martyred stage, the long run over, helpers, props – all gone. In their place, impotency; an invalid husband, a bedridden daughter, a heartbroken son-in-law who arrived at the end, as he always had, just as the curtain was going down. And granddaughters, one fair, one dark, arrived at the beginning, just before the next show began. Could she rally for one more performance? Was the indomitable spirit still there, tucked away under the wounds and scars of all the wars and woes of her life?

It was her nature to take control; her life's experience. I would have to let her. The kookaburra on the tree outside my window was laughing . . . I could hear the tinkling of girlish laughter, moments before the tears returned . . . a man was laughing, slightly hysterically.

Dimly, in the hush of dusk, I could see two girls from long ago, sitting down on the edge of the bed.

'Is that you, Ruthy?' I whispered.

'Yes, Billy. I'm here. Wendy Barr's here too,' she said.

They began to sing in pure, sweet tones.

> 'Kookaburra sits on the old gum tree-ee,
> Merry merry King of the bush is he-ee.
> Laugh kookaburra, laugh kookaburra,
> Merry your life must be.'

I don't remember much of '62. Devastating bush fires again, but further south. Prince Charles was attending school at Gordonstoun. An old friend of Jock's, a master at the exclusive school, invited him to a function, but he declined. Thea was going; I wanted Jock to go, tried to talk him into it, but he never did anything except go to work, come home and help Ma, sit and read to me and the girls, sleep, start again.

Sister Mac dropped in regularly, a sprightly seventy-two-year-old, back working part time at the hospital. She retired four times before they agreed to release her to part time. Kurra hadn't kicked on since the war. It was a sleepy hollow and but for the baby boomers, few though they were, the hospital would have closed down. Ma and Sister Mac said the town just wasn't the same as it had been in the old days. I found it difficult to perceive, since everything I knew of it was exactly, precisely the same.

Marilyn Monroe was found dead in her bed. There was an empty bottle of Nembutal by her side, the same sleeping pills I took. Some days I looked at them and wondered . . but I didn't have the courage. God, I was a coward! What I would give to have the strength to feel one hour of power again, one moment to take control of my life – and death, one chance to be master of my own destiny, once more to know the feeling of independence and total self-control. Freedom, freedom! No more pulling and shoving, poking and prodding. No more waving my children off to school from the window. No more pity in my husband's eyes. No more martyrdom from Ma. No more stray tears streaming down Pa's wrinkled, shrunken face.

I took twelve one night while Jock was reading to the children. The energy required to get them down stopped me. I just couldn't continue; was violently ill. I don't think anybody ever knew. I never tried it again.

James Barnawarren visited one day, or week. He'd finally found a buyer for our *Kurra Mail* and was back writing for the *Bully*. He'd never married, and really looked like an old bachelor these days – slightly scruffy, and overweight. He drove up from Sydney for Figgy's funeral. But for the ongoing deaths, I wouldn't have had many visitors. The Barnawarrens had long retired to Tarrenbonga. Constance would probably go out to live with Saucy in Charleston. James was telling me about the Cuban crisis when I bolted upright in bed and seemed to come out of a long, dark tunnel with startling clarity. 'My God, James, Jay Childs was due here earlier this year for the Coral Sea celebrations! Rosa, Ruth? What happened? I must know, I must know at once!'

I tried to climb out of bed, predictably falling back heavily. My memory was blocked. I could not even recall sending Jay's letter on. 'There, there, Billy, hold it. I'll get Mrs Rosey and find out what happened. My, you're quite flushed. You look as beautiful as you ever did, all fired up! Are you okay?'

'Yes, yes, of course I'm okay,' I responded indignantly, as though the question were absurd.

Ma bustled into view, wiping flour from her hands onto one of my old gingham aprons. Ma had come down in the world – no lace edges in sight. 'What's this, Billy? Trying to get out of bed? Have you lost your senses?'

'No, Ma, quite the reverse! I'm just recovering them. What happened to Ruth and Rosa and Jay Childs? I can't remember a thing.'

'Well, never mind, dear. We'll discuss it tomorrow. You'll stay for tea, James, won't you?'

'Ma! Sit down right now and tell me what happened. Right now, Ma.'

'But –'

'Right now, Ma. I'm coming out of it, Ma, and don't you dare resent that as you've done in the past. Don't you dare! And don't try to stop me from walking again, because I will start tomorrow. Today, right now, I want to know what happened to Ruth and Rosa. Sit down and tell me.'

Pa heard the commotion from his usual spot on the verandah and wheeled himself inside, pulling up at my door. 'Come in, Pa. God, it's good to see you looking so fit. I'm going to look as good as you in no time at all.'

'That's my girl,' he whispered, his voice almost gone. It had only been slightly husky when we last spoke. He poked at his unlit pipe. I shot a raised eyebrow at Ma, who was looking awkwardly at James.

'Sit down, James,' I ordered.

'I think this is family business, Billy,' Ma reproached.

'This is no time to be preoccupied with the subtleties of good breeding, Ma. James is not going to tell anyone and I refuse to ask him to leave. In any case, what could possibly be so bad? Begin!' Ma was clearly flustered, looking to Pa for guidance. 'Fill in the missing pieces for me, Pa?' I pleaded, leaning over my quilt, reaching for his skeleton hands. 'Why don't I have any letters? Do I have any letters?'

'Well, yes, dear. Rosey, get the letters please?' his voice scratched painfully. Ma disappeared. He summoned James to fetch him a glass of water. My nerves were stretched to breaking point by the time Ma isolated the special letter that answered my question.

I took the blue folded pages out of an envelope numbered thirteen, sensing the ominous undertones all around. Ruth had begun with businesslike efficiency, quickly getting the details out of the way. '. . . Jay flew straight to Alice Springs from Sydney. I met him at the airport, took him to his hotel, told him about Rosataca. We all had dinner together – they got along famously! He then flew us to Sydney for the Coral Sea celebrations and we all returned to the centre. Jay decided to stay. That's it, Billy,' she concluded page one.

Ma was making great business of retying her apron and wiping her hands. 'Everyone like a cuppa now?' I ignored her.

Page two was difficult to read. 'Rosa's been drinking very heavily, Billy, and taking drugs too. I've been absolutely beside myself, more than I've said. But she hit it off with Jay, straight up, and it seems he was really in love with me all those years ago (married once, but it didn't last), talked me into letting him stay and help straighten Rosa out. We decided the only way was to get her away from the Alice, so we're going bush for a while, taking a complete break from everything. This'll be one of the last

447

letters for a while, dear, for that reason.' So many unanswered questions, but they would have to wait.

Ma returned with a tea tray, said as soon as Jock got home, we'd eat. 'I'll be joining you in the family room for tea,' I piped up firmly.

'Of course you won't, dear,' she responded sharply.

'Oh yes, I will, dear; Jock will carry me out. Where are the girls?'

'Mathilda is having her piano lesson and Jenna has detention, for the second time this week.'

It was odd, being there again, having been there all along. The twins rushed in, hugged and kissed me, as though nothing had changed. How could they know I was feeling them, seeing them, for the first time in many months? They had grown so . . . I could hardly believe my eyes. Mathilda was slimmer, leaner than Jenna, her curly hair a light, mousy brown with wonderful streaks of golden sunshine highlights. Jenna was round and plump, her shiny dark skin framed by thick, long midnight locks. They were very different at first glance, but when you looked at length, there was much in their features that remained identical.

I had so much to catch up on and found myself strangely impatient for Jock's arrival. It was difficult to focus on James, with so many new things of my old world demanding re-appraisal. He didn't seem to mind, taking a background role with gentlemanly grace. When Jock arrived, I was sitting in a lounge chair, having insisted on James' removing me there. Jock was clearly not expecting it.

'I've spoken to those lazy good-for-nothing blacks down there again and told them if they don't pay their back rent this week, they can take notice to quit,' he huffed and puffed authoritatively, unaware of my presence. Ma was scurrying around the kitchen, trying to give him warning.

'Hello, Jock,' I said cheerfully. 'Look who's come to visit.'

Jock's face dropped, then rose. 'Hello. Why, hello, Lovely! Oh, hello, James.' He walked over and kissed my forehead, 'You're up, dear? It's wonderful to see you here. James,' he turned slowly, shook his hand. 'Deeply sorry about your pa.'

'Thanks. I figured Billy would never forgive me if I didn't drop over and say hello,' he offered quickly, by way of explanation. 'It's obvious I've come on a good day.'

'It's a new day, James!' I smiled and cried all at once as Jenna edged her way into the couch beside me. I'd forgotten how good it feels to have your own little girl snuggling into your body, tickling and gig-gling, never still for a moment.

Later, when James had gone, and the girls were in bed, and Ma and Pa had retired to their quarters, I took up the matter of Pharaoh and the Cranberry Vineyard of old. Everyone always took so long to come to terms with my returns from the dead – I had no patience or time for drawn-out recoveries.

'How far behind in the rent are they?' I asked first, knowing Banduk and Jabaljari would have nowhere to go if they were forced off our land.

'Four months.' He had learnt to spare me protest. 'They've tried, I suppose, but they haven't got the wherewithal for farming. They know how to hunt, how to squat, but they're not European, dear . . . they have to go. We can't afford the upkeep of Pharaoh and the farm without regular return.'

'I would like to see the books tomorrow, Jock,' I said quietly, concealing my anger as best I could.

The next day I studied the receipts and payments journals. Jock had obviously been practising con-siderable economies in every direction, taking a hard line on spending on the girls' dresses, reducing the grocery bill in half. The gardener had been re-trenched and the usual jobs given every month or so to the boy scouts seemed not to have been done, or otherwise he had paid them out of his own pocket, a most unlikely phenomenon. I knew that my husband was a cautious, moderate man, but I had not pre-viously admitted to myself that he was mean. As I turned the pages, I realized we were in sound finan-cial state. I began to think again on all the years we'd been married, all the years we'd been stuck here, without a holiday, without so much as a trip to Port Hedley or Sydney, or even Brisbane. A hard deter-mination gripped my soul, and an anger born in part from jealousy that he had taken over the man-agement of the estate. But more than anything, I was angry because he was forcing my daughters and par-ents to live like poor country cousins. That he wanted to kick out Banduk and Jabaljari was bad, but this was intolerable!

My anger slowly subsided as the day wore on. Matty and Jo were full of high jinks and stories I had heard, yet never heard before. My heart could not remain cold and stern in the face of their laughter and the warmth of the sun shining directly on my face, where I sat with Pa on the verandah. The hills changed colour several times, midnight blue into uncertain grey, as I woke and dozed, startled and lulled into security by the newness, yet the sameness of my world.

'It is difficult to know a man, really know him,' Pa had counselled, 'with all the winds of change that blow through a marriage.' Jock was not mean of spirit, that I did know. He was a penny-pincher to a degree, having lived so long on a lowly teacher's wage. Neither was he a bullying male, with excessive need to puff up his ego by taking an uncompromising control of our lives. In fact, he had the qualities of a well-balanced gentleman of an older school, a British school ironically enough, having outgrown or out-manoeuvred the worst of his Irish Catholicism. If I handled the situation carefully, I could turn the tide however I wanted it to flow. I always had been able to, and nothing had changed. The same was true now of his daughters. They too had learnt the tricks of the female trade and could bend him to their will, just as easily.

They were not yet aware that all the important lessons of life, the very best of reputations, were already set. Still, I was grateful for the years. At last, grateful they were old enough to know right from wrong and truth from lies. I could take some chances now, must take some chances, before it was too late.

'Mummy, Grandpa wants you,' Matty called from the verandah.

'Okay, darling. I'll be there in a minute,' I called back, walking with the aid of my stick.

It had been a snail's recovery, this one. I was getting older. The body relearnt old tricks at a new pace, a slower pace. But we were going to the centre for Christmas of '63, and nothing could stop us now. Even Ma and Pa were excited, though perhaps the thought of a house without two boisterous girls for a few weeks was underpinning their exuberance for our long-awaited holiday.

Our three generations were getting on pretty well since my return to the world of the living. Everyone had adjusted into new grooves. Banduk and Jabaljari had responded to a warning and were back on target, and on time with their rent too. Even Jabaljari's 'cousin' arriving, with her tribe of youngsters, invited no more than one or two dry comments from Jock and Pa, both of whom I suspect enjoyed enormously the frustration I felt at not getting the opportunity to raise a few hackles over their presumed disapproval.

Ma was lying down; her blood pressure was up again. She did too much, particularly given the weight she was carrying, though as she said, her body had been carrying the same weight most of her life. I went out to Pa. He looked awfully pale and lonely, sitting in the rocker in the filtered light of the late afternoon. I fell heavily into a chair beside him. 'Hi, Papa, how are you feeling?' I'd slipped back into the habit of calling him Papa lately. He seemed so small and vulnerable in the big chairs that sustained him.

'Joey? Is that you, Joey?' His eyes were sparkling, though they stared out across the fields. His mind wandered some days; other days he was alert and aware of everything going on around him.

'No, Papa, it's Billy.'

'Ah Joey, sell the family silver! Sell it. Hock it, lad, don't store it for your old age. Do you hear me now?'

'Yes, Papa,' I choked back the tears that were coming rapidly now. Should I call Ma? Would this pass in a minute? He reached out for my hand. I took both of his in mine. They were cold, very cold. 'I'll get you a blanket, Papa. It's getting cool now.'

'No! No, don't leave me, Joey. I'm sorry, sorry. Religion took up too much of my time . . . no, religion was greedy, too greedy. Drained my heart, drained all the passion I should have given you and Rachel, little Rachel. Where are you, Rachel?'

'I'm here, Papa.'

'Don't cry, little girl. Nothing to cry about. Remember the poem . . . going over the range? Over the range . . .'

'Papa? Are you asleep, Papa?'

He stirred, opened his eyes briefly, then slumped forward. A kookaburra called out from the telegraph pole. Matty and Jo were squealing on their bicycles down by the dam. Bandy was on the tractor. From the house, I could hear the news coming on. The announcer said President Kennedy had been shot! How could that be? It didn't make any sense. Then there was silence.

Pa had quietly slipped away.

# TWENTY-ONE

# 1964

There was an eerie quiet around the homestead the day Ruth came. The bellbirds and the kookaburras had left The Brolga a few days before, in search of food and water. The drought would be long and hard.

She came alone, as I expected. She had always been alone when she came to Kurra Kurra. She arrived on the midday train from Sydney; Mrs Baxter, the station mistress, drove her out on our freshly tarred road, chattering away about the lost crops and livestock from the incessant, blistering sun. Ruth nodded but said nothing. She knew only too well how easy it was to speak of grim despair when you were securely employed as a stationmaster. In any case, her heart was too full to speak of the weather with a stranger.

I heard her greeting Ma on the verandah. Grappling with the iron frame, I edged my way forward as fast as I could. We fell into each other's arms at the kitchen door. I could hardly believe how good it felt. We were as one. One friendship; unthreatened, unexploited, unencumbered by anyone or anything that had been, or might be. We had crossed over into the twilight, our half-lives shining bright and full. We had come home. At long last, we were at home in the world.

'Why did we leave it so long?' she cried.

'I have asked myself that a hundred, no, a

thousand times,' I wept with her. She wiped our eyes with her strong, black hands. The tears and bubbling lips ignored my automatic attempts at ladylike control.

'Oh shit!' I splattered saliva all over her hot pink shirt.

'At last you've learnt to swear naturally, Billy. Congratulations! I can see you've become an expert at adjusting the sails, old girl.'

We sat down at the kitchen sideboard. Ma made herself scarce. I stared into the face I knew so well, had missed so much. She stared into mine. We traced the lines of laughter, and the lines of pain. Nature had been indiscriminate in her tracking of our lives. We were middle-aged, and looked it. But memories are always young and the eyes see what the mind decrees. She was beautiful, as beautiful as I remembered, more beautiful with age than I had dared to hope.

'My illness has taken its toll, Ruthy,' I offered by way of self-conscious explanation for my palsied face and crippled body.

'You could never disappoint me, Billy,' she answered fully.

'You've said that before,' I smiled.

We darted around for a while, unsure where to begin, already begun, without a beginning. 'There are gaps in my memory,' I remembered instantly. 'What's happened to Rosa, and Jay?'

'Jay has taken her to his parents' home in New Orleans.'

'Oh Ruth! Ruth. You'll go and join them once you visit with me, won't you?'

'No, Billy. No, I don't want to go. Jay never grew up, as I knew he wouldn't. I can't live with him. I sure tried. Rosa has her own life to live; I have to let her go. She may return, who knows? What can I do? We don't have them to keep them, do we?'

'I don't know, Ruthy. You and I don't, it seems, but Ma's generation did. And Gwwirra had you, for her last few years.'

'Yes, that's about all black mothers and mothers of sick daughters get.' She looked at me aghast, belatedly aware of what she'd said.

'Don't worry, little black nurse of mine! I can handle the truth quite well these days.'

'What is the truth, Billy?' Without warning, she looked old and worn, her face settling into a deep gorge of bloodied scars.

'I think love is the only truth,' I replied, with just a trace of mordacity.

'I wish I could be so certain,' she chuckled. 'I think maybe the dream of love is true. There's not always time for the real thing, not any more. Maybe never. And love is not always true anyway. But there's always time to dream, to keep on dreaming. And there's always truth in dreams. Less disappointment, too,' she sighed.

'One thing's for sure, Ruthy. A good reputation is not the truth! It stops the brain, stops the heart, stops the body. As soon as you believe in something totally, you close off your life. You plug yourself up. It's religion at its most honest, at its absolute worst. It's the great reducer, the great controller, the great fake!'

'It's the white man's idea of how to get to heaven,' she snapped.

'You've become angry, Ruth.'

'Yes? Yes.

'Does good win over evil, Billy?' she asked, without pausing for an answer. 'Your God instructs us to help and protect the widows and the orphans. But only if the widows and the orphans are white. For the blacks, food parcels appease the conscience. You can't know, Billy, even you, can't possibly know how demoralizing it is to be given handouts from your own rapist; it kills the dignity of people and —'

'Oh yes, Ruth, oh yes I can!' I came to life with a wild enthusiasm I had not known in years. 'You think I don't know? All women know, but sick people, male or female, know just as well as black people. We're dependent, Ruth, disgustingly dependent. We didn't plan it either. Your people never allowed such weakness, such pathetic reduction of pride or dignity, such elevation of prejudice. Infanticide . . . euthanasia . . . when you outlive your usefulness, the spinal cord is hammered with a rock. Instant death. I remember. Harsh decisions for harsh conditions. I remember what your people do to twins too. Practical solutions, when it comes to girls. Suffocate the weaker, can't afford to feed both. You're right, of course. Survival of the fittest.'

She put her arms around me, hugged me very tight. I responded likewise, every part of me glad to be alive. 'Standards, rules, cultures, passed down from generation to generation. Homage, for homage sake?'

'You think Aboriginal law's as locked in as English law, Billy?'

'You're still full of brawn, Ruth. You used to say I was quicker than Ned Kelly, but it was always you.'

'English? Australian? Who are you? If you've worked out who you are, you'll have a law you can grapple with.'

'Remember the stories I told you of Gomah in Cairo? He said we rise and fall, and only the children know. When they grow up, it's easier to forget.'

'I remember, Billy. So what have you managed to put out of mind, from when you were a kid?'

'I haven't had need to forget — but like the kids in Cairo, your entire childhood is riddled with memories you'd be better off without. What do my girls, 'specially Jenna, know, that one day it'll be easier to forget?' We smiled secretly at one another. We knew what we knew.

And I was lost, deliciously lost, lost in conversation. It didn't matter what she said, I said, she said; we were one. We could have died, there and then, and it would have been enough.

Jock and the girls came home from school. Matty was polite, Jo effusive.

'They have your eyes,' Ruth said fondly, 'but they're not identical, are they? And Jo's colour is gorgeous, the softest brown.'

I nodded sadly. 'My children will have a short childhood, Ruth.'

James Barnawarren rang from Sydney to welcome her home. His manners and charm never missed an important event.

'He's still in love with you, Billy, after all these years?'

'No, no, not at all. Just an old flame-friendship. Perhaps a connection with the one who got away? Hanging onto a dream that can never disappoint . . .'

The girls came to say goodnight, Matty's quick pecks, Jo's loud, wet kisses. Jock excused himself and went to his study. Ma lingered. We talked of Pa for a while, eyes smoky, voices incautiously accounting snippets of memories aloud, our hearts merged with Ma while our own private thoughts were tucked away for another time.

'Beloved old codger, that he was,' Ma concluded, brushing aside her tears self-consciously, ever mortified by her own displays of sentimentality. She made us a cup of tea. 'Don't stay up too late, please, girls. Remember, Billy, you've just had another bad turn.' Her duty done, she retired. We were alone again.

'Everyone still wants to put me in cotton wool,

Ruth. But there's no point to it. Let's go out onto the verandah.' I pulled myself up aggressively, the frame rocking precariously around me. 'I wish I could still walk unaided, Ruth. We could go down to Pharaoh, for old times' sake.'

'Well, let's do that tomorrow anyway! I can wheel you in Mr Nathan's old chair.'

I could not think about tomorrow, with the sky so big. The milky way lit our little world and we could just see the blossoms on the old fruit trees, floating slowly to the ground. 'It's their time, Ruth,' I said, as though I knew she was thinking the unthinkable too, sensing the end approaching. 'I'm not afraid, Ruth, so there's no need for you to be. I've had a fair life and my vision has improved!' We both laughed. My vision had never been good, but now it was almost gone. What I could see was blurred and multiplied. 'Sometimes the world looks better blurred, Ruth.'

'I think most times it would be better, blurred,' her voice smiled, a rich, deep-centred Ruth-smile I'd missed for half a lifetime.

'Did you bring your diary?' I asked suddenly.

'Of course! I put it by your bedside table earlier.'

'Oh Ruth, I can't wait to read it. I've nearly finished my fourth, you know. You can start reading them, any time.

'I was trying to write down, sort out, before you came, why you and I were the only women friends we ever had.'

'And?'

'Not that easy, I'm afraid. We were products of our time, of course. We shied away from adult female friendships. It was suggestive somehow – sexually inappropriate. We jealously guarded our men friends, men friends of our boyfriends and husbands too. They got our time, our care, our souls. We were so busy struggling to make our own nests and not too willing to let any other female get too close. There weren't many around for the most part either.'

Ruth leant forward and clasped my hand. 'Remember when I first took up with Micky? Even our friendship took second place while I was busy proving myself equal to his shallow ways! God, what fools we made of ourselves, all in the name of gettin' a Man!'

'We believed in romance, breathlessly, helplessly. For a while, like Santa Claus.'

'Yes.'

'Do you think women will ever grasp that life begins and ends with yourself? That all you ever have that you can trust, is you? Men know it. They've always known it. Their lives don't change much, for anyone. They just keep on, the way they want to go, when they want, how they want. We service their needs. They throw us crumbs.'

'Hey? Mathilda and Jenna? Crumbs?'

'In a way. If we give them spirit, they'll soar high and be swallowed up by their world, a world that is not our world. If we have ambition for them, we give them the capacity to betray. And when we have girls, Ruth, they search for their fathers; when they find one close enough to mould, they give up the truth their fathers know and do what I did. Make a home, have babies, get old, get sick . . . die.'

We floated with the stars and the falling blossoms for a long time. I saw our bedroom light go out. Ruth spoke, predictably. 'You must be desperately tired. Let's go to bed. We've got all the time in the world.'

'Not yet, just a little while longer?'

'Your marriage with Jock. It's been good, mainly?'

'Yes. Mainly. All the men I've ever known have been disappointments to me.'

'Me too.'

'Ma still lives by: "Blessed is the man who's found his work and one woman's love." When I start feeling guilty about how miserable I've been to Jock on occasions, I think of that.'

'Yes, you found your work, but had to give it up . . .'

'I've been dining out on you for years, Ruth – a black woman doing what she wants to do! Now, you've given up your work to come and spend time with me. When will women ever learn? Why can't we get out of our hearts' own way?'

'Well now!' The black eyes mocked me, played with me, just as they used to do. 'Would ya 'ave it differently, old girl?'

'Could I have known the greatest love of my life – our friendship – if it were not so?'

'You serious, Billy?'

'Yes, I am. You have made every happiness that's come my way greater, sustained me through every trauma, every new beginning, every questioning day. Whenever I've lost my way, I've found it again because of you. I've been blessed, Ruth. But for you, I would never have broken out of the conventions of my time. Oh, granted, I've reverted to form in appearance and reality, but my heart is ever on the outside track with you, Ruth. Why, I still believe in Wendy Barr . . .'

She threw her head back and laughed, a girlish laugh so long forgotten. 'You want to know something real, real wondrous?'

'Please?'

'When I first came to live with you, I also believed in your Wendy Barr! You thought I was so grown up, but I was just a lonely girl, like you. I needed your dreams then, as I do now. Let's start again tomorrow. I want to hold our conversation in my heart so I don't forget a word of it.'

'And I want to read your diary! You win. Goodnight, my dear, dear friend. Welcome back.'

'Not . . . welcome home, Billy?'

'No. Just . . . back.'

'I'll see you to your room.'

The next afternoon, she wheeled me down to Pharaoh. Banduk and Jabaljari came to welcome her home. Two magpies screeched, then took up the mating game. We smiled, secretly.

We reviewed each other's diaries, school kids again, questioning the author's point of view.

'So we're all bluffin', are we?' she cajoled.

'Of course we are, Ruthy. We're all half-castes, didn't you know? Half-brothers and -sisters, half understanding, halfway home but never quite getting there.'

'You've never been half of anything in your life, Billy Batchelor!'

'Ruth, Ruth, the opposite is true! I've been half a daughter, half a career woman, half a lover, half an emancipated woman, half a wife, half a mother. I've been half a fighter for justice and discrimination, half a believer in God . . . Dear Ruth, this is the stuff that makes a good reputation, half a century later!'

'You have never been half a friend to me, Billy.'

'No, no. That's for sure! Our friendship slipped through a crack in the conditioning process. You have been the great success of my life, Ruth, the most important truth of all. Make sure my little girls know, won't you? Help them learn to look under the rocks for their dreams.'

'I will, Billy, I will,' she promised, her shining face looking back up to The Brolga, where the spirits and the north wind whistled around the beautiful dancing girl.

'Let's say goodbye here? Please? Red earth, hot sun, strong hearts; love.'

'With the sails full-blown, Billy?'

'Yes! Oh yes, Ruthy, always with the sails full-blown! With the sails full-blown . . .'

I am Ruth.

The hearse slowed to a halt. We did too. Jock and Mrs Rosey and Sister Mac were right in front of us. Jenna snuggled into my side. Mathilda sat a little apart. They were hot and sticky, trying ever so hard to be still. A northerly wind whistled around the car. Otherwise, it was awful quiet. Silence, but for the winds of time.

Cigarette smoke drifted through the divider. The air seemed a bit friendlier, more commonplace than it was before.

The pallbearers were lifting out the casket. Rich dark mahogany. She would 'a' liked that. A moment of cloud passed over the sun . . . shadows on the mass o' colour tied to the lid. It was the season for violets, but the folks hadn't sent any. It was good. Depressing flowers, violets. She'd be real glad they'd chosen such beautiful colours. Not burdened her in death with purples and whites.

'What a dreadful job,' the driver said.

*Tell me about the very first evening star, Ruthy . . .*

'I s'pose it's passed from father to son?'

He nodded. 'Why else would ya do it?'

Somebody opened the door. We got out, two small hands gripping mine. *Tell me how the kangaroo got its tail, Ruthy!*

'Is Mummy with God, Ruth?'

An odd, assorted group, swaying slightly. We

walked across the green lawns and huddled in a circle round the broken mound of earth.

'It's a blessin',' some bloody fool behind me said.

'Mercy with a blunt knife,' she called from the grave.

Quiet, steady voice reading The End. The white collar was stiff but the long black gown blew recklessly in the wind, like an English professor lecturing his students. Fragments of petals . . . bouquets scattered across the lawns, swept by the wind, wind for the sails to take her home quickly.

Human effort, to stand and wait. My hands started shaking. I clasped the little ones' tight, wishin' for her strength, half as much would do. And the verses just kept on flowin': 'We could be in Galilea a thousand years ago . . .'

No. No! We're romping through the blackberries out back of Rosebery. *Tell me again how the brolga came to be, Ruthy?*

It was our Dreamtime; no present, no future, just the wind and a red land beneath a bright blue sky. Friends for life. Friend rushing away, ever further out, waiting to leave. Waiting.

Ashes to ashes. They lowered her deep into the earth, beautiful still, held frozen in time. 'Whither thou goest, Billy,' I whispered, as she took my heart with her.

'Freedom at last, old girl.'